Catherine. Catherine was in his bed.

In three heartbeats, William went from dumbstruck to breathless. She was stunning, with her fair hair spilling over his pillow like a river of moonbeams.

"You have come to me," he said, not quite believing it.

She clutched the bedclothes to her chin and nodded.

Now that she was here, he could show her she had nothing to fear in his bed. He undressed quickly, dropping his clothes on the floor and lifted the bedcovers. Ignoring her sharp intake of breath, he slid in beside her.

"Turn toward me, I want to look into your face."

He held her eyes as he ran his hand up her side to the tantalizing swell of her breast. Gritting his teeth, he reminded himself to go slow. He moved his hand back to her waist, then over the curve of her hip and down her thigh.

He was ti_____desire, he kissed her fa_____er ear, he murmured, "

Praise for KNIGHT OF DESIRE

"A lavish historical romance, evocative and emotionally rich. KNIGHT OF DESIRE will transport you."

—Sophie Jordan, *USA Today* bestselling
author of *Sins of a Wicked Duke*

Please turn this page for more praise
for KNIGHT OF DESIRE…

"KNIGHT OF DESIRE is akin to stepping into another century; Mallory has a grasp of history reminiscent of reading the great Roberta Gellis."

—Jackie Ivie,
author of *A Knight Well Spent*

"Stunning! Margaret Mallory writes with a freshness that dazzles."

—Gerri Russell, author of *Warrior's Lady*

"Medieval romance has a refreshing new voice in Margaret Mallory!"

—Paula Quinn, author of
A Highlander Never Surrenders

"Mallory spins a masterful tale, blending history and passion into a sensuous delight."

—Sue-Ellen Welfonder, *USA Today* bestselling
author of *Seducing a Scottish Bride*

"Margaret Mallory writes with intense passion and beautiful, believable emotion."

—Lucy Monroe, bestselling
author of *Annabelle's Courtship*

Knight of Desire

~

Margaret Mallory

FOREVER

NEW YORK   BOSTON

This book is a work of fiction. Names, characters, places, and incidents are the product of the author's imagination or are used fictitiously. Any resemblance to actual events, locales, or persons, living or dead, is coincidental.

Copyright © 2009 by Peggy L. Brown
Excerpt from *Knight of Pleasure* copyright © 2009 by Peggy L. Brown
All rights reserved. Except as permitted under the U.S. Copyright Act of 1976, no part of this publication may be reproduced, distributed, or transmitted in any form or by any means, or stored in a database or retrieval system, without the prior written permission of the publisher.

Book design and text composition by TexTech Inc.

Forever
Hachette Book Group
237 Park Avenue
New York, NY 10017
Visit our Web site at www.HachetteBookGroup.com.

Forever is an imprint of Grand Central Publishing. The Forever name and logo is a trademark of Hachette Book Group, Inc.

Printed in the United States of America

First Printing: July 2009

10 9 8 7 6 5 4 3 2 1

To Cathy Carter, my sister and librarian extraordinaire,
who read my first pages and told me to go for it,
and to my husband, Bob Cedarbaum, who supported me
on faith without ever reading a word.

Acknowledgments

A first book requires a lot of thank-yous. I am tremendously grateful to my agent, Kevan Lyon, for her grace, wisdom, and unflagging support. Many thanks to the folks at Grand Central for taking a chance on a new author. Alex Logan deserves a prize for guiding me through the publishing process. Both she and Amy Pierpont provided thoughtful comments that made this a much better book. Thanks also to Claire Brown for the gorgeous cover. I would not have made it to publication without the guidance and support of other romance writers. Thank you to the members of the Olympia and the Greater Seattle RWA chapters, volunteer contest judges, presenters at the Emerald City Conferences, and my critique buddies.

I am grateful to my father, who taught me all about heroes. Some men are honorable because of the example set for them. Others, like my father and the hero of this book, choose to be honorable in spite of it. Thanks also to my mother, who is probably the reason all my female characters are strong.

I appreciate all the friends and family who were amazingly supportive when I decided to change careers and take up the uncertain life of a writer. Special thanks go to Cathy, Sharon, Nancy, Laurie, and Ginny for reading manuscript drafts before I had a clue what I was doing. Most of all, I thank my husband. When I wanted to quit my job to write just as the first college tuition payments came due, he told me, "Whatever you want, honey." They don't come better than that.

Knight of Desire

Prologue

The creak of the stable door woke him.

William's hand went to the hilt of his blade as he lifted his head from the straw to listen. Soft footfalls crossed the floor. Soundlessly, he rose to his feet. No one entering the stable at this hour could have good intent.

A hooded figure carrying a candle moved along the row of horses, causing them to snort and lift their heads. William waited while the man reached up to light a lantern hanging on a post. No matter what the intruder's purpose, fire was the greater danger. The moment the man blew out his candle, William closed the distance between them in three running strides.

As he launched himself, the intruder turned.

William saw the swirl of skirts and a girl's face, her eyes wide with alarm. Reflexively, he threw his arms around her and turned in midair to cushion her fall just before they slammed to the ground.

"Please forgive me!" he said, untangling his limbs from hers and scrambling to his feet. "Have I hurt you?"

He would have offered his hand to help her up, but she sprang to her feet as fast as he, her hair falling free of the hood in a mass of bright waves. She stood with her weight forward on her feet, eyeing him warily.

William stared at her. How could he have mistaken this lovely and fragile-looking girl for a man? Judging by the fine silk gown showing at the gap in her cloak, this was a highborn lady he had assaulted. Her features were delicate, her full lips parted.

He squinted, trying to tell what color her eyes were in the dim light. Without thinking, he reached to pull a piece of straw from her hair. He drew back when he caught the gleam of the blade in her hand. He could take it from her easily enough, but it unsettled him to know he frightened her.

"Who are you, and what are you doing here?" she demanded. She was breathing hard and pointing the blade at his heart. "Answer me at once, or I will scream and bring the guard."

"I am a knight in the service of the Earl of Northumberland," he said in a calming voice. "I arrived late, and the hall was filled with guests, so I decided to bed here."

He was not about to tell her he was hiding in the stable. When he had delivered Northumberland's message in the hall tonight, he had glimpsed a certain widow he knew from court. Preferring to sleep alone, he had made a quick escape.

"Now that you know my purpose in being here, may I ask the same of you?" he said, cocking his head. "I believe it is you who should not be found out alone at this hour."

She did not answer him, but even in this poor light, he could see her cheeks flush.

"Surely you know it is dangerous for a young lady to be wandering about alone at this time of night—especially with the castle crowded with men and the wine flowing freely."

"I could not sleep," she said, her voice sharp with defiance. "So I decided to go for a ride."

"You cannot go out riding by yourself in the middle of the night!" Lowering his voice, he added, "Really, you cannot be that foolish."

Her eyes flashed as she pressed her lips together—and a disturbing explanation occurred to him.

"If it is a man you are meeting, he does not value you as he should to ask you to come out alone like this." He judged her to be about sixteen, half a dozen years younger than he was. Young enough, he supposed, to be that naive.

"Running to a man?" she said, rolling her eyes heavenward. "Now, that would be foolish."

She slid her knife into the sheath at her belt, apparently deciding he was not a threat after all. Before he could feel much relief at that, she turned and reached for the bridle hanging on the post next to her.

"I am going now," she announced, bridle in hand.

"I cannot let you," he said, wondering how he would stop her. It would cause considerable trouble for them both if he carried her to her rooms, kicking and screaming, at this time of night.

"Surely this can wait for the morning," he argued.

She stared at him with a grim intensity that made him wonder what trick she would try to get past him.

"If I tell you the reason I cannot wait," she said finally, "will you agree to let me go?"

He nodded, though he still had every intention of stopping her.

"Tomorrow I am to be married."

The surge of disappointment in his chest caught him by surprise. Although he was told the castle was crowded because of a wedding, it had not occurred to him that this achingly lovely girl could be the bride.

When he did not speak, she evidently concluded more explanation was required to convince him to let her go. "I do not expect this will be a happy marriage for me," she said, lifting her chin. "My betrothed is a man I can neither like nor admire."

"Then you must tell your father; perhaps he will change his mind." Even as he said it, William knew that with the wedding set for tomorrow, it was far too late for this.

"I am the only heir to an important castle," she said impatiently. "I could not expect my father or the king to take my wishes into account in deciding what man will have it."

"What is your objection to the man?" William had no right to ask, but he wanted to know. He wondered if this young innocent was being married off to some lecher old enough to be her grandfather. It was common enough.

"He has meanness in him, I have seen it." Her eyes were solemn and unblinking. "He is not a man to be trusted."

Her response surprised him once again. Yet, he did not doubt she gave him the truth as she saw it.

"Tomorrow I will do what my father and my king require of me and wed this man. From that time forward,

I will have to do as my husband bids and submit to him in all things."

William, of course, thought of the man taking her to bed and wondered if she truly understood all that her words implied.

"Tonight you must let me have this last hour of freedom," she said, her voice determined. "It is not so much to ask."

William could have told her she should trust the judgment of her father and her king, that surely they would not give her to a man so undeserving. But he did not believe it himself.

"I will ride with you," he said, "or you shall not go."

She narrowed her eyes, scrutinizing him for a long moment. With the lamp at his back, the girl could not see him nearly as well as he could see her. A double advantage, since he did not want to frighten her. He was well aware that, despite his youth, there was something about his strong features and serious countenance that intimidated even experienced warriors.

"You must let me do that for you," he said, holding out his hand for the bridle. He almost sighed aloud in relief when she finally nodded and dropped it in his hand.

As he saddled the horses, he tried to ignore the voice in the back of his head telling him this was madness. God's beard, the king himself had a hand in arranging this marriage. If he was caught taking her out alone at night on the eve of her wedding, the king would have him flailed alive.

"Keep your head down," he instructed as they rode across the outer bailey toward the gate. "Make certain your cloak covers your gown—and every strand of that fair hair."

The guards remembered he arrived carrying messages from Northumberland, "the "King-maker." They gave him no trouble.

William and the girl rode out into the cold, starlit night. Once they reached the path that ran along the river, she took the lead. She rode her horse hard, as if chased by the devil. When at last she reined her horse in, William pulled up beside her, his horse's sides heaving.

"Thank you for this," she said, giving him a smile that made his heart tighten in his chest.

His breath came quickly as he stared at her. She was stunning with her face aglow with happiness and her fair hair shining all about her in the moonlight. When she flung her arms out and threw her head back to laugh at the stars, he stopped breathing altogether.

Before he could gather his wits, she slipped off her horse and ran up the riverbank. He tied their horses and followed. Pushing aside thoughts of how dangerous it was for them to be here, he spread his cloak for her on the damp ground beneath the trees.

She sat beside him in silence, her gaze fixed on the swath of moonlight reflected on the moving surface of the dark river below. As she watched the river, he studied her profile and breathed in her scent. He thought she had long since forgotten his presence when she finally spoke.

"I will remember this night always," she said, giving his hand a quick squeeze. "I will hold it to my heart as a happy memory when I have need of one."

He took hold of her hand when she touched him and did not let it go.

She fell silent again, and he sensed that her thoughts, unlike his own, were far away again. Experienced as he was with women, he was surprised by his intense reaction to this girl. All of his senses were alive with the nearness of her—his skin almost vibrated with it. And yet, he felt a profound happiness just sitting here with her and gazing at the river on this chilly autumn night. He never wanted to leave.

When she shivered, he forced himself to break the spell. "You are cold, and we have been gone too long already. If someone notices you are missing..."

He did not finish. She knew as well as he the disaster that would follow if she were caught. Resigned, she let him help her to her feet.

They rode back at a slower pace, riding side by side this time, still saying little. William tried to fix it all in his memory: the moonlight, the dark river, the gentle snorting of their horses. The girl, he knew, he could not forget.

The guards at the gate wordlessly let them in. When they reached the stable, William helped her dismount. The feel of his hands on her slender waist as he set her down—closer to him than was proper—made his heart race and his head feel light.

Looking down at her, he felt a longing so intense it caught at his breath. His gaze dropped to her mouth. Only when she took a step back did he realize he had been about to kiss her. It was wrong for many reasons, but he wished with all his heart he had done it. With a sigh, he left her just inside the doorway and led the horses into the pitch-black of the stable.

When he returned, she whispered, "I am most grateful to you."

"Lady, I would save you from this marriage if I knew how."

He spoke in a rush, not expecting to say the foolish words that were in his heart. He was as good as any man with a sword, but he had no weapon to wield in this fight. Someday, he would be a man to be reckoned with, a man with lands and power. But as a landless knight, he could only put her at risk by interfering with the king's plans.

"I will do my duty and follow the wishes of my father and my king," she said in a strong voice. "But I thank you for wishing it could be otherwise."

He wished he could see her better. Impulsively, he reached out to trace the outline of her cheek with his fingers. Before he knew what he was doing, he had her face cupped in his hands. He felt her lean toward him. This time, he did not stop himself.

Very softly, he brushed his lips against hers. At the first touch, a shot of lust ran through him, hitting him so hard he felt light-headed and weak in the knees. He pressed his mouth hard against hers. Dimly, through his raging desire, he was aware of the innocence of her kiss. He willed himself to keep his hands where they were and not give in to the overpowering urge to reach for her body. If she had shown the slightest sign she had been down this path before, he would have had her down on the straw at their feet.

He broke the kiss and pulled her into his arms. Closing his eyes, he held her to him and waited for the thundering of his heart to subside. God have mercy! What happened to him? This girl, who trusted him blindly, had no notion of the danger.

Swallowing hard, he released her from his embrace. He could think of no words, could not speak at all. With deliberate care, he pulled her hood up and tucked her long hair inside it. Then he let his arms fall to his sides like heavy weights.

"I did not want his to be my first kiss," she said, as though she needed to explain why she had permitted it.

His gut twisted as he thought of the firsts the other man would have with her.

She took a quick step forward and, rising on her tiptoes, lightly touched her lips to his. In another moment, she was running across the yard, clutching her cloak about her.

———

For many years, William dreamed of that night. In his dreams, though, he held her in his arms by the river in the moonlight. In his dreams, he kissed the worry and fear from her face. In his dreams, he rescued her from her unhappy fate.

In his dreams, she was his.

Chapter One

Ross Castle
England, near the Welsh border
June 1405

£ady Mary Catherine Rayburn sat on the bench in her bedchamber and waited for news. If the prince received her latest message in time, the king's army should have caught her husband with the rebels by now.

She pulled up the loose sleeve of her tunic and examined her arm in the shaft of sunlight that fell from the narrow window. The bruises were fading; Rayburn had been gone a fortnight. She let the sleeve fall and rested her head against the stone wall behind her.

Not once in all this time did her husband suspect she had betrayed him. But he would know it now. She had been the only one in the hall, save for the men who went with him, when he disclosed the time and place of his meeting with the Welsh rebels.

She buried her face in trembling hands and prayed she had not made a mistake. What else could she do? Nothing short of discovering Rayburn with the rebels would convince the king of his treachery.

If Rayburn escaped unseen, he would return and kill her. What then would happen to Jamie? It was unthinkable that her son would be left alone in the world with that man.

The cold of the stone wall penetrated the heavy tapestry at her back, causing her to shiver. Her raging fever had only broken the night before. She'd been the last to fall to the illness that had swept through the castle.

Exhausted, she closed her eyes. How had she come to this? She thought back to the beginning, before Rayburn's betrayal of the king—and before her betrayal of Rayburn.

The king had been so certain of Rayburn's loyalty when he chose him as her husband. At sixteen, she had been quite the marriage prize. She possessed that most rare and appealing quality in a noblewoman: She was her ailing father's only heir. More, she was heir to one of the massive castles in the Welsh Marches, the strategic border area between England and Wales. That made her betrothal worthy of the king's personal attention.

At the age of ten, she was betrothed to a young man whose family, like her own, was closely aligned with King Richard. The match lost its luster the moment Henry Bolingbroke usurped the throne. Consequently, her father was pleased when, a short time later, the young man had the courtesy to fall from his horse and break his neck. When the new king "offered" to select a husband for her, her father was happy for the opportunity to demonstrate his new allegiance.

King Henry deliberated carefully, dangling her as a prize before powerful men he wanted in his debt. When her father fell gravely ill just as the Welsh revolted, however, the king acted swiftly. He could not afford to leave Ross Castle and the surrounding borderlands without a strong man to defend them. As her father lay on his deathbed, the king's soldiers escorted her to his castle at nearby Monmouth for her wedding.

She crossed her arms over her chest and rocked herself as the memories came back to her. She had known Rayburn to be a cold man. She did not expect tenderness from him. Still, her wedding night had been a shock. He managed, just, to take her virginity.

Perhaps it was the novelty that made it possible that first time. He ordered her to put out every candle and wait in silence on the bed. Only later did she understand that the sounds she heard in the dark were her new husband touching himself to prepare for the task.

There were no kisses, no caresses. It was, at least, mercifully quick. As soon as he was finished, he left her. She cried through the night, believing her life could not be worse.

How naive she had been.

He made weekly visits to her bedchamber, intent on getting her with child. She tried not to hear the foul things he said in her ear or to feel the rough hands rubbing over her thighs and buttocks. When he succeeded, she forced her mind far away as he pounded and grunted against her flesh.

Over time, it became increasingly difficult for him to do his duty. When he could not, he beat her. Sometimes the violence excited him, for just long enough. He took to drinking heavily before he came to her. The drink only made him more violent.

By a miracle, she conceived. Her pregnancy saved her life. Rayburn still lacked any redeeming qualities, but he ceased to terrorize her in the bedchamber.

Then, a few weeks ago, he decided he must have "an heir to spare."

She had no regrets about what she did to save herself this time. And to save the Crown for Harry. One day, Harry would be a great king, the one England deserved. Still, she was bone-weary from the strain of her deceit.

Her eyelids grew heavy as her mind drifted to the soothing childhood memories of playing with Harry at Monmouth. Those were happy times, before her mother died and before her friend became prince and heir to the throne. She curled up on the hard bench and let her eyes close.

"M'lady, what are you doing out of bed?" The maid-servant's voice roused Catherine from a troubled sleep.

"What is it?" she asked, sitting up.

"Men at arms approach the castle," the woman said, her voice pitched high with tension.

"What banner do they fly?" Catherine demanded.

"The king's, m'lady."

The surge of relief that flooded through her was so intense she had to grip the bench to steady herself.

"What does it mean, m'lady?" the maid asked, twisting her apron in her hands.

"I do not know," she said, trying to sound reassuring, "but we should have nothing to fear from the king's men."

If Rayburn was caught, why would the king send armed men here to Ross Castle? Perhaps Rayburn had escaped and they were looking for him? Would he come here to hide? Panic rose in her throat. She forced herself to be calm.

Nay, if Rayburn's treason was found out, he would hardly come here. Faced with the risk of execution or imprisonment, he would flee to the Continent. She was almost sure of it.

"M'lady, the king's soldiers are almost to the gate. The men are waiting for you to say what they must do."

"Since they fly the king's banner, we must open the gate to them," she said. "But tell the men to wait until I come."

"But, m'lady, you are too weak. You must not—"

Catherine silenced her maid's objections with the lift of her hand. "Help me dress. I must know what news they bring."

Holding the maid's arm for support, she got to her feet. Her head swam at first, but the feeling passed quickly enough. She nodded approval at the first gown the maid held out and let the woman dress her. Her mind was occupied with a single question: Why would the king send his men here after the battle?

"There is no time for that," she said when the maid brought out an elaborate headdress in blue brocade. "A jeweled net will have to do."

Ignoring the maid's protests, Catherine twisted her hair in a roll and shoved it into the net. As soon as the maid fixed a circlet over it to hold it in place, Catherine sent her running to the gate with her message.

She was relieved to find Jacob waiting outside her door. Gratefully, she took the arm the old man offered and smiled up into his weathered face.

"Let me give your apologies to the visitors," he said,

his brows drawn together in concern. "I'll tell them you are too ill to greet them."

"Thank you, Jacob, but I must do this," she said. "They shall not set foot inside the castle walls until I assure myself they are truly the king's men." *And until I know what it is they want.*

After so many days in the darkness of her bedchamber, the bright sun hurt her eyes when she stepped outside the keep. She felt weak, but the fresh air cleared her head as they walked across the inner and outer bailey. Half the household waited near the gate, anxious about the armed men on the other side.

As soon as her son saw her, he broke free from Alys and flung his arms around her legs. She knelt down to kiss him.

"Jamie, stay here with Alys while I go speak with these men," she told him firmly. "Do not go out the gate." She gave a meaningful look over his head to the housekeeper, who responded with a quick nod.

When she stood up again, bright sparkles crossed her vision. She'd never fainted in her life, and she could not permit herself to do so now. She would meet her duty to protect her household.

She waved the others back and went to stand alone in front of the gate. At her nod, the men dropped the drawbridge over the dry moat with a heavy thud.

Through the iron bars of the portcullis, Catherine could see the men on horseback on the moat's other side. They had a hard look to them, as though they had seen much fighting and were prepared for more.

She turned and gave the order. "Raise the portcullis, but be prepared to drop it at my signal."

The iron chains clanked and groaned as the men turned the crank and slowly raised the portcullis.

As soon as it was high enough for her to pass under it, she stepped out onto the drawbridge. She sensed the waiting men's surprise. They stared at her, but they remained where they were, just as she intended.

———

As they rode toward Ross Castle, William Neville Fitz-Alan's thoughts kept returning to the traitor's wife. The traitor's widow now. Lady Rayburn's last message to the prince led to her husband's capture and execution. Rayburn deserved his fate. But what kind of woman could share a man's bed for years and yet betray him to his enemies?

William wondered grimly if she had been unfaithful in other ways as well. It seemed more than likely. In his experience, fidelity was rare among women of his class. The knightly ideals of loyalty and honor certainly did not guide female behavior. Perhaps it was desire for another man, then, rather than loyalty to Lancaster, that led her to expose her husband's treachery.

Regardless of her motive, both he and the king had cause to be grateful. The lady, however, now presented a political problem for the king.

With his hold on the Crown precarious, King Henry needed to give a strong message that traitors *and their families* would be severely punished. The powerful families needed this message most of all. As the wife of an English Marcher lord who turned against the king, Lady Rayburn should be sent to the Tower—a place where "accidental" death was a common hazard.

On the other hand, Prince Harry insisted it was Lady

Rayburn who had sent him the anonymous messages about rebel forces. However, few of the king's men believed it, and the man who delivered the messages was nowhere to be found.

The king was keeping his own counsel as to what he believed. The truth, in any case, was irrelevant. In the midst of rebellion, the king could not leave a border castle in the hands of a woman. The Marcher lords who were supposedly loyal were nearly as worrisome as the rebels. If one of them took Ross Castle—whether by force or by marriage—the king would be hard-pressed to take it back. The king wanted it in the hands of a man of his own choosing.

William was the man the king chose. His loyalty had been proven through the severest of tests. Even more, the king understood that William's hunger for lands of his own was so deep that, once he had them, no one would ever take them from him. Ross Castle would be safe in his hands.

William led the attack that morning, catching the enemy unprepared. At the king's command, his guard executed Rayburn on the field. The traitor's head barely left his shoulders before the king declared his lands and title forfeit and granted them to William.

William rode straight out from the battlefield to secure his property, the blood of the enemy still wet on his sur-coat. But there was one last price he had to pay for it.

The king put the fate of the traitor's widow in his hands.

The choice was his. He could send the lady to London to be imprisoned in the Tower for her husband's treason. Or, he could save her—by making her his wife. The king sent the bishop along to grant special dispensation of the posting of banns in the event William chose to wed. The king knew his man.

The prince would be enraged if Lady Rayburn was imprisoned. While the king could disregard the prince's feelings, William could not. Young Harry would be his king one day. William would have wed the widow regardless. It was not in him to let harm come to a woman or a child if it was in his power to prevent it.

His thoughts were diverted from the problem of the woman when he crested the next hill. Pulling his horse up, he stopped to take in the sight of his new lands for the first time. Lush green hills gave way to fields of new crops surrounding the castle, which stood on a natural rise beside a winding river. The castle was an imposing fortification with two rings of concentric walls built around an older square keep.

Edmund Forrester, his second in command, drew up beside him. "On the river, easy to defend," Edmund said approvingly.

William nodded without taking his eyes off the castle. All his life, he'd wanted this. In his father's household, he was provided for, but he had no right, no claim. His position was always precarious, uncertain. Now, at long last, he had lands of his own and a title that declared his place in the world.

If only John could be with him on this day of all days! Four years since his brother's death, and he still felt the loss keenly. John was the only one with whom he shared a true bond. Still, he was glad to have Edmund along. They had fought long years together in the North. There were few men he trusted, but he trusted Edmund.

William spurred his horse and led his men in a gallop down the path to the castle, his heart beating fast with anticipation. Although the lookouts should have seen the king's banner as they rode up, the occupants of the castle took their blessed time opening the gates. He was fuming long before the drawbridge finally dropped.

As the portcullis was raised, a slender woman ducked under it and walked out alone onto the drawbridge.

William squinted against the sun, trying to see her better. Something about the way the young woman stood, staring them down with such self-possession, caused his men to shift uneasily in their saddles.

Her move was so daring that William smiled in appreciation. Clearly she intended to give the guards opportunity to drop the portcullis behind her, should he and his men prove to be enemies. There was one flaw in her scheme, however: The castle might be saved, but the lady most surely would not.

Chapter Two

Catherine scanned the soldiers on the other side of the dry moat as she waited for one of them to come forward. They wore armor and chain mail, and their horses looked as if they had been ridden hard. A lone churchman rode with them, his white robes bright in a sea of burnished metal.

She watched as the churchman dismounted and walked onto the drawbridge.

"Father Whitefield!" Fortunately, her father's old friend did not hear her exclamation. Recalling his quick rise in the church since Henry took the throne, she dropped to a low curtsy.

"'Tis good to see you again, child," the bishop said, holding out his hands to her.

"What is this about, m'lord Bishop?" she whispered. "Why does the king send armed men here?"

"I bring you a message from the king," the bishop said in a voice that echoed off the castle walls.

What sort of message required a bishop and armed men?

"I am sorry to tell you this, my dear," he said, patting her hand, "but your husband was killed today."

"Praise be to God!" Catherine cried out and fell to her knees. Squeezing her eyes shut, she clasped her hands before her face. "Praise be to God! Praise be to God!"

"Lady Catherine!" the bishop roared above her. "You must beg God's forgiveness for such sinfulness."

Catherine knew it was a sin to wish her husband dead. But God, in his infinite wisdom, had answered her prayers and removed Rayburn from this world.

Praise God, praise God, praise God.

"...shameful behavior...unwomanly..."

She was dimly aware the bishop was still speaking. She ignored him and continued praying.

"Mary Catherine!"

When he shouted her name, she opened her eyes.

"Get up, get up," the bishop said, jerking her up by the arm. "There is more I have to tell you."

He pulled a parchment from inside his robe, broke the seal, and unrolled it. Holding it out at arm's length, he gave her a solemn look over the top. Then, he began to read. "All lands...forfeit to the Crown...grant these same...for faithful service..."

Catherine could not take in the words. Her head spun as the bishop droned on and on.

"In plain terms," he said as he rolled up the parchment, "the king declares Rayburn's title and all his property, including Ross Castle, forfeit. He grants them to the man who defeated your traitorous husband in battle today."

The breath went out of her as if she had been punched in the stomach.

"Why would the king do this to me?" she asked in a whisper. "After all I have done for him? After the risks I took?"

The bishop leaned forward and narrowed his eyes at her. "You should have foreseen this from the moment your husband raised his hand against the king."

"But *I* did not raise my hand against the king!" she protested. "It was the king's decision, not mine, that I should marry Rayburn. You know that very well."

"Mind your tongue," the bishop warned, his face red with anger. "'Tis not wise to criticize your sovereign."

"Does the king say what I am to do?" she asked, panic welling up in her. "Where Jamie and I shall live?"

The bishop cleared his throat. "All is not lost, my dear." He paused to give significance to what he was about to say. "With the king's blessing, the new lord of Ross Castle has agreed to take you as his wife."

"The king wishes me to marry again?" Her voice was rising, but she could not help it.

The bishop's steady gaze told her she had not misunderstood him.

"Nay, he cannot!" She backed away from him, shaking her head from side to side. "He cannot ask this of me again!"

The bishop grabbed her arm and whispered ferociously in her ear, "This is the only way the king has of saving you."

She covered her face. "I will not do it! I will not!"

"Catherine!" the bishop shouted. "Stop this at once!"

"You must ask the king to spare me this," she pleaded, clutching his sleeve. "Please, Your Grace, you must ask him!"

"Come to your senses, woman," the bishop said, taking her by the shoulders. "You have no choice."

"What if I refuse?" She felt the anger rising in her chest.

"That would not be at all wise," the bishop said, his voice quavering.

"You must tell me, Your Grace," she pressed.

"The king will have you imprisoned."

The blood drained from her head as she finally understood. Why did she not see it before? Henry was fighting rebellions on both borders. His hold on the throne was weak. If he did not move quickly to put her estates into the hands of one of his own men, one of the Marcher barons would take it.

"You should be grateful this FitzAlan will have you," the bishop spat out. "The king did not require it of him."

Through clenched teeth, she said, "Perhaps the Tower would be a better choice for me."

"Think of your son. What will happen to him if you are imprisoned?"

The bishop hit his mark squarely. There was nothing she would not suffer to save her son.

"How long do I have," she asked weakly, "before I must make my choice of prisons?"

When her head was clearer, when she did not feel so ill, perhaps she could find a way out of this.

The bishop's nostrils flared. "The marriage is to take place at once."

"At once?" she asked, stunned. "Am I to go from one hell to another with no reprieve!"

Her burst of anger left her feeling drained and light-headed.

"When?" she asked, fixing her gaze on the wooden planks of the drawbridge beneath her feet. "When will he come?"

Please, God, let it be weeks and not days.

"He is here now."

She looked up to find the bishop peering over his shoulder. In her distress, she had forgotten about the others.

The soldiers at the front moved aside to allow a single rider on an enormous black warhorse to come forward. Unable to move, Catherine watched in horror as the huge animal bore down on her. Its hot breath was on her face before the man reined it in.

She swallowed and forced her gaze slowly upward to take in the man. Her eyes rested first on his hand, grasping the hilt of his sword as though he sensed danger and was prepared to meet it. She followed the line up his arm. When she reached his chest, her stomach tightened. His surcoat was streaked with blood. Blood of his enemies, blood of the vanquished.

Her eyes were drawn inextricably upward toward his face. She saw grime and blood and matted hair. Then her gaze met the raging fury in the beast's eyes, and she fainted dead away.

When the bishop greeted the bold young woman on the drawbridge, William realized this was Lady Rayburn herself. Since he knew what the bishop had to tell her, he shut out the bishop's words and lost himself in contemplation of the woman.

Of course he hoped she would be attractive, though it made no difference to his decision. Luck was with him. While she may have the soul of a snake, Lady Rayburn appeared—at least from this distance—to be young and exceedingly pretty, with a lithe, shapely form.

He was jolted to attention when she dropped to her

knees, crying out, "Praise be to God!" It took him a long moment to comprehend she was thanking God for her husband's death. How could the woman weep on her knees with joy at the news of her husband's death? Even his mother was not as heartless as that.

When he heard her liken her prospective marriage to him to a prison, his shock turned to outrage. She should be grateful to him for saving her. Instead, she was ridiculing him! Edmund grabbed his arm, but William threw him off and spurred his horse onto the drawbridge.

As he rode toward them, the bishop took several steps backward. But the woman did not move, even when his horse was snorting above her. Haltingly, she raised her eyes, as if taking in every inch of horse and man. When her gaze finally reached his face, their eyes locked.

His heart stopped.

It was her. He was almost sure of it.

Her eyes lost focus, and she swayed on her feet. With a quickness learned in battle, he swung down from his horse and bent to catch her before her head hit the ground. Her fair hair fell free of the mesh net and spread in silken waves over his arm and the rough wooden boards of the drawbridge.

Chaos swirled around him. But William saw nothing but the young woman in his arms. It was her. The girl he dreamed of.

Before he could lift her, a weight slammed onto his back. Small fists beat him as a high-pitched voice wailed in his ear, "Let go of my mother! Let go of her!"

"Get the boy off me!" William called to the nearest man.

The man pulled the boy off and held him with

outstretched arms as the boy kicked furiously at the air. He was a dark-haired boy who looked to be only three or four.

William held the boy's eyes. "I will not harm her. I promise you."

The boy nearly succeeded in kicking him in the head.

No sooner was the boy lifted away than a face as round and pink as a fat friar's was before him, shouting, "My lady has been in bed with a fever these last five days!"

William leaned back to see who was chastising him so harshly. It was an older woman, clearly a servant of some kind.

The woman put her hand to the pale cheek of the lady in his arms. "What have you done to her?" she wailed. "My poor mistress! God save us!"

William stifled a curse. Through clenched teeth, he said, "I have come to save the lady, not harm her."

The edge in his voice should have sent the woman running. It did not, but at least she ceased her yowling.

"Show me where I should take her," he said, making an effort to speak calmly. "We cannot leave her here in the middle of the drawbridge."

The woman blinked at him and then hoisted herself up with astonishing speed. She picked up her skirts and bustled past him, calling, "This way, this way!"

William got to his feet with the lady in his arms and walked through the gates of his castle. He followed the plump servant, who glanced over her shoulder every two or three steps and waved her hands about. He heard the murmurs and knew the servants dipped their heads and stepped back as he passed.

But he did not truly see any of them.

All his attention was on the warmth of her body against him, the feel of slippery silk fluttering against his hand. She weighed almost nothing. When a breeze caught her hair, the scent of wildflowers filled his nose, sending him back to a moonlit night by a river.

Before he knew it, he was climbing the steps to the keep. Just then, the boy broke free of his captor and wrapped himself around William's leg.

"Do you want him to drop your mother, you foolish boy?" Before any of his men could move, the plump servant charged back and grabbed the boy by the scruff of the neck.

"I shall see to your mother, child," she said as she thrust the squirming boy into the arms of another servant. "Be a good boy and Mary will take you to the kitchen for a sweet bun."

William signaled for his men to remain behind in the hall and followed the woman up the circular stair to the family's private rooms above.

"I am Alys, the housekeeper," the woman informed him as she puffed up the steps before him. "I've known Lady Catherine since she was a babe."

The woman in his arms stirred. Forgetting himself, he bent down to shush her and almost kissed her forehead. He gave his head a sharp shake to remind himself that this woman, who seemed so fragile in his arms, argued with bishops. And worse.

At the entrance to the solar, he paused to survey the elegantly appointed room, with its dark wood furniture, rich tapestries, and lovely window seat overlooking the river. This was his. No more having a home at the pleasure of another man. His children would grow up knowing where they belonged.

With a start, he realized the woman he carried was the one who would bear those children.

He looked down at her. Though her eyes were closed, he saw the pinch between her brows. Just how long had she been awake?

"In here, m'lord," the housekeeper called from one of the bedchambers that adjoined the solar.

He carried the lady into the chamber and carefully laid her down on the high bed. As he stepped back, he caught sight of his blood-smeared surcoat. What he must look like to her, coming straight from the battlefield. No wonder she fainted.

He took Alys by the arm. "I need to wash," he said as he walked her out of the bedchamber, "and my men need food and drink."

"I'll see to it at once, m'lord." Alys turned to leave, but he kept his hand firmly on her arm.

"I know you care for your mistress." He could tell by the spark in her eyes that she was pleased he saw this. "So you must help her understand."

Alys looked up at him, her expression serious. "Understand what, m'lord?"

"It is the king's wish that she and I marry this very day." He ignored Alys's sharp intake of breath and continued. "It will not be safe for her if we do not. That is what you must make her understand."

Alys pressed her lips into a firm line and nodded.

"I will return within the hour to tell her how it will be done," he said. "Now, where can I have my bath?"

Chapter Three

William recovered his senses as he scrubbed himself clean of battle grime. Over and over, he reminded himself of what he knew about the woman he was about to wed. She spied on her husband, delivered him to his death. Without a shred of regret or pity, she betrayed the father of her child, the man she shared a bed with for five years.

These were truths. What were dreams to these?

Either she had changed since she was that girl in the stable or he was mistaken about her then. How long were they together that night? An hour? Two? What could a man know in that time? Especially a young man driven to distraction by the nearness of a beautiful girl in the moonlight.

He learned about the nature of women at his mother's knee. The only time he forgot the lesson was with the girl in the stable.

She was as beautiful as ever, so he'd have to be cautious.

He felt ready to take charge when he returned to the solar, dressed in his finest. Thank God the bishop had insisted he retrieve his best clothes from his packhorse before they rode off. He lifted his hand to knock, then stopped himself. He needed no one's permission to enter here.

When he pushed it open, he found Lady Catherine and Alys sitting at a small table near the window. Alys toppled her stool leaping to her feet. Lady Catherine, however, watched him steadily through the steam rising from the cup she held to her lips. She did not flinch a muscle.

Without taking her gaze from his, she set the cup down and said in a clear voice, "Alys, go ask the bishop to join us."

William wondered what she was up to but figured he would find out soon enough.

Alys gave her mistress a look that said she did not think it wise to leave her alone with him. But when Lady Catherine nodded, Alys did as she was told.

Alone for the first time, he and his soon-to-be wife assessed each other for a long moment. He did not see even a flicker of recognition in those vivid blue eyes. Wisps of memory whipped through his head. He could not reconcile those brief, intense memories of the girl with what he knew of the woman before him. But then, she was so very lovely, he was finding it difficult to think at all.

Her smooth porcelain skin held a faint touch of color now. "I am glad to see you are not so pale as before," he said.

"I do not usually faint," she was quick to assure him, "but I have been ill."

"I hope you are feeling better, for we must settle matters between us now."

Something about the set of her jaw told him she had used the last hour to assess her situation and make a plan.

It made him glad for the negotiation skills he had learned in the service of Northumberland.

"It was kind of you to agree to marry me," she began.

So, her opening gambit was a blatant attempt to appease him.

"You did not seem to think so upon first hearing it." He meant to convey amusement, but a trace of anger showed in his voice.

Ignoring his remark, she continued. "I understand the king gave you a choice."

Her slight emphasis on the word *you* was not lost on him.

"In sooth, he did not," he said with a shrug. "I could not have it on my conscience that a lady might be unjustly imprisoned when I could prevent it."

"Many men in your position would not make the same choice."

Only if they had not laid eyes upon her. Any man who looked upon that face would not find the choice a difficult one. Desire burned in him, hot and demanding, at the thought that he would have her in his bed this very night. The knowledge that she betrayed her first husband and loathed the idea of marrying him did not dampen his ardor at all.

Desiring her was one thing. Trusting her, quite another.

"Will you flatter me by saying you prefer marriage to me over imprisonment, or do you yet see the two as equal?" Again, he was unable to keep the edge from his tone.

She had the grace to blush. "My objection was to another marriage and so soon," she murmured, dropping her eyes. "Not marriage to you, in particular."

"Well, it is about me, is it not?" he snapped.

His instinct for masking his feelings had been honed at an early age. Why did it fail him now? Exasperated with himself, he got up from the table and stood with his back to her, looking out the window. Hell, he would have married her, regardless of his own desires. But now he wanted her. Badly. Very badly. He hoped she had not seen it.

Her next words brought him sharply back to the conversation.

"I will agree to marry you on one condition."

He turned and raised an eyebrow at her. "You believe you are in a position to bargain?"

"I do."

The firmness in her tone told him she had seen the naked desire in his eyes and realized the power it gave her.

"Your safety, your home, your position—these are not sufficient reasons for you?" he asked.

"If you cannot also promise me this," she said, unmoved, "I will choose exile or prison, rather than wed you."

He could not believe his ears. She *preferred* prison to marrying him. "What is it, then, that you must have from me?"

She took a shaky breath, giving away how tense she was beneath her outward calm. Still, she looked directly into his eyes as she made her demand.

"I must have assurances about my son. You must promise me that you will not harm him. More, that you will protect him and his interests." She cleared her throat. "That is my price."

He told himself she did not know him, could not know how much her words affronted him. Taking a deep breath, he sat down beside her and placed his hand on top of hers on the table. She flinched but did not attempt to remove it.

"I will do these things," he said, holding her gaze, "and I would have done them without your asking."

She hesitated, then gave him a faint smile.

At that moment, the subject of their discussion burst into the room. Lady Catherine did not chastise the child for interrupting. Instead, she enveloped the boy in her arms, kissing the top of his dark curls. The love between mother and son was so palpable that William felt warmed by his nearness to it. His throat felt tight, and he knew he wanted this also for his own children.

The bishop entered the room at a slower pace.

"I asked you to come, Your Grace," Lady Catherine said, "because there are certain promises that must be included in the marriage contract."

So that was her purpose in calling for the bishop. His oral assurances made in private were not sufficient.

William was not offended. On the contrary, he admired the lady's determination—and her cleverness—in finding a means of binding him to his pledge. He hoped she would be as fierce in protecting the children they would have together as she was her firstborn.

"The contract is already drawn." The bishop touched his fingertips together and shifted his eyes to William as he spoke. "I assure you, all matters of importance are covered."

William held his hand up. "I will give your clerk the necessary changes. We've no more time to waste, so let's be done with it."

The bishop made a sour face. "As you wish."

The door banged behind him.

"Come, Jamie," Lady Catherine said, sounding exhausted now. "Mother must rest now."

Her son kissed the cheek she offered and scampered out of the room. As soon as he was gone, she slumped against the back of her chair.

"I cannot give you more time," William said, looking at her pale face and feeling guilty. "The wedding must take place today."

She gave him no response but merely turned those startlingly blue eyes on him.

"I am known as a strong fighter and commander. Once you have the protection of my name, you will be safe," he explained. "Even the king will not threaten you as he does now."

He fixed her with unwavering eyes. "And no one will dare touch you once you carry my child," he said, the words coming out hard, fierce, "for they know I would follow them to hell and back to take my vengeance."

Catherine felt clearheaded as she sat in the steaming tub of water, sipping another cup of the hot broth Mary forced upon her. Remarkably, she'd fallen into a deep sleep after FitzAlan had left her. She felt much better for it.

She carefully reviewed her meeting with FitzAlan. His short bronze hair had been damp, and he looked freshly shaved. Without the blood and grime, he was a handsome man. He had a strong face, with broad cheekbones, a wide mouth, and hard amber eyes. He was tall and well built, with a commanding presence that made him seem much older than he probably was.

Aye, he was a handsome man. A very handsome man, indeed.

He wore a tunic of rich forest green that reached to his knees, with a dark gold cotehardie underneath. A jeweled belt rode low on his hips. The fine clothing did not disguise the warrior beneath. As he said, he was a soldier and commander other men feared.

Her mind went to his bald statement that she would be safe once she was known to carry his child. She quickly pushed aside the thought. She would marry this stranger to protect her son, but she could not think now about sharing his bed.

She recalled how he looked looming above her on the drawbridge. Despite the warmth of the water that enveloped her, she shuddered. In dealing with him, she would do well to remember the raging lion splattered with blood.

Alys burst into the room, bringing a rush of cold air with her.

"Are ye not dressed yet?" Alys said, wide-eyed. "Mary, what is wrong with you? FitzAlan's pacing the hall like a caged bear."

"Two hours to prepare for a wedding," Mary grumbled as she held Catherine's robe out for her.

Two hours to prepare for a marriage. Water streamed down Catherine's legs as she stepped out of the tub.

"I laid out your best gowns on the bed," Mary said as she wrung water from Catherine's hair.

"This one is still your finest," Alys said, wistfully running her hand over the finely stitched beading of the gown Catherine had worn to her first wedding.

"There's no time to alter it," Catherine said. While she

was still slender, she had been slight to the point of frailty at sixteen. "The blue will do."

"Ah, this one is lovely on you," Mary said, picking up the gown and matching headdress made of intense blue silk with gold trim. "Your eyes look bright as bluebells in it."

The two women worked fast, braiding, pinning, lacing, and prodding. When they finished, they cooed over the gown. It fit snugly from the bodice to the decorative belt low on her hips, then fell in soft folds to the floor.

Her hair was still damp and itched under the heavy headdress. When she looked in the polished steel mirror Mary held for her, she was glad she wore the sapphire earrings and necklace. They had been her mother's favorites.

The rumble of men's voices rose to meet her as she descended the stairs. Catherine touched the necklace at her throat. She could do this. She must.

As she entered the hall, FitzAlan's men seemed to turn to her as one. The cavernous room grew quiet.

From across the room, FitzAlan's amber eyes fixed on her, freezing her in place. Her heart thundered as he strode toward her, his expression intense, determined. She felt a surge of sympathy for the men who faced him in battle. If she could have moved, she would have fled back up the stairs.

She tried to get her breath back as he bowed and took her arm.

Before she knew it, they had signed the marriage contract, said their vows, and followed the bishop across the bailey to the chapel in the East Tower. The bishop must have said the blessing and the Mass, though she heard not a word of either.

Numbly, she placed her fingers on her new husband's arm and stepped out of the chapel. She shivered at the unexpected coolness and looked up to see that the sun had sunk below the line of the castle walls.

It was done. In a single day, she'd gone from being wife to widow to wife again. Her heart seized as she realized she had not even told her son.

She was unsure what would happen next. She stole a glance at FitzAlan but could read nothing from his stern expression.

As they reentered the hall, Alys appeared at her side. "The wedding feast is ready to be served." With a roll of her eyes, she added, "Such as it is."

"And Jamie?" Catherine whispered, her throat tight.

"Don't you fret about him, m'lady. His nursemaid's taken him off to an early bed."

Thank God for that. Jamie had grown used to having free rein of the castle in Rayburn's absences. It would not be easy to keep him out of FitzAlan's way.

Catherine mustered a smile for Alys and let FitzAlan lead her to the table. Cook and the other kitchen servants had worked a minor miracle to provide them with an impromptu wedding feast. She knew they did it for her. She appreciated their kindness, but she was far too tense to eat a bite.

She took a piece of bread and looked down at the table, barren of adornment. She could not help thinking of her wedding at Monmouth Castle. Despite the servants' efforts, this one could not be more different from the first.

Monmouth was where her friend Harry—*Prince* Harry now—had spent most of his childhood, so she'd been there many times before her wedding. Still, she had never seen it so crowded with guests, all dressed in expensive silks and velvets. The Mass was long, the wedding feast elaborate, the entertainment endless.

She had been so anxious to perform her part with dignity, she scarcely gave a thought to what awaited her in the bedchamber. Perhaps it would have been different if she'd had a mother to warn her.

She thought fleetingly of the wild midnight ride she took the night before her marriage. If she had known what her life with Rayburn would be like, would she have kept riding?

She thought of the young man who accompanied her that night. 'Twas a shame she had no face to go with the memory of him. When he knocked her to the ground, she was so terrified she noticed nothing beyond the sheer size of him. Later, she saw the outline of his shoulder-length hair, but his features above the full beard were always in shadow.

In sooth, he'd seemed all hair and beard to her.

Her thoughts were so tumultuous that night, and they had been followed by her first harrowing night with Rayburn. It was surprising her recollection of the young man had not been lost altogether beneath the layers of terrible memories since.

But she did remember him. The warmth of his large hand holding hers as they sat watching the river. The tickle of his beard against her skin in that brief kiss. The unexpected comfort of his arms when he held her at the end.

What she remembered most clearly and held to her heart, though, was the young man's kindness and gallantry. When her life was at its lowest ebb, it was this memory that saved her.

William stole glances at his new wife as they ate, though she was so lovely it made him ache to look at her. When she entered the hall, he thought his heart would stop. The gown she wore hugged and flowed, showing every feminine curve and line. And how could eyes be that blue? He had no notion how long he stood gaping before he went to greet her.

She was tearing her bread to bits now. It wounded his pride to see how wretched and tense the woman was. God knew, she was not a virgin bride, with reason to fear the unknown. She had shared a man's bed for years and borne him a child. Admittedly, he was a stranger to her. He would expect her to feel some unease. Yet, her reaction was so extreme he could not help feeling it as a personal slight.

What did the woman think? That he would throw her on the floor and force himself upon her the moment the bedchamber door closed?

Lord above, he did want her enough to take her like that. He could think of little else except having her naked beneath him. Still, it was disturbing that what he looked forward to with such lust, she so obviously dreaded. Once he had her alone, he was confident he could change that. When a man has no wealth of his own and no real status, he knows why women come to his bed. And why they return.

It was not good for a man to want his wife this much. Surely, once he bedded her a few times, he would be over his obsession. Perhaps it would take a few dozen times. His palms were sweaty and his breath came fast just thinking of it.

He was a fool to be disappointed she did not recognize him from that night long ago. True, he had filled out since then, and he no longer wore a beard. He should thank his lucky stars she did not know him as the bedazzled young man who lost his judgment and gave in to her whims.

He turned to look at her again. She was gazing off at nothing, her lips curved up in a slight smile. A wave of longing came over him. God help him, but he hoped a time would come when she would think of him and smile that same dreamy smile. Aye, she already had too much power over him without reminding her of that night.

He would make sure, however, she did not forget their wedding night.

He touched her arm.

She jolted upright and turned wide eyes on him.

"Everyone is waiting," he said in a low voice. "'Tis time for us to go up to the bedchamber."

From the look of horror on her face, he might have said he was going to take her there on the table, with all the guests watching. He took her arm and helped her to her feet. The castle household clapped and shouted as they followed them across the hall toward the stairs.

God's beard, the lady was shaking! Where was the bold woman who met him at the gate a few hours ago?

They had made short shrift of many of the usual traditions with this hasty marriage, so he felt no compunction about turning the crowd back before they reached the bridal bedchamber. After barring the solar door behind them, he turned to face his bride.

She looked like a goddess, with her head held high and her chin out. But her eyes gave her away. He would have done anything to wipe away the fear he saw there.

He was at a loss as to how he should approach her. Glancing about, he was relieved to see that someone had had the foresight to leave them wine and bread and cheese. Though the refreshments were meant to revive the newlyweds after their efforts in the bedchamber, he could use the diversion now.

"Come sit with me and share some wine," he said, gesturing to the small table.

Catherine's shoulders seemed to relax just a bit. "Thank you, Lord FitzAlan."

"Now that we are husband and wife, you must call me William," he said as he watched her slide gracefully into one of the two chairs at the table. "And I shall call you Catherine."

He remained standing behind her, wanting to put his hands on her shoulders and run his thumb along the curve of her neck. He had been longing to do it all evening. She gave him a furtive look over her shoulder, uncomfortable having him where she could not keep watch on his movements.

"Why don't you pour?" he suggested.

She did as he asked, then took a long drink.

"Let me help you take off your headdress." He leaned down and whispered, "I want to see your hair, Catherine."

"My maid can do that." She reached up quickly, as though to prevent him from touching it. "I will call her."

"Don't."

She began to unfasten the headdress, but her hands were shaking so violently that William took over the task. When all the pins were out, he lifted the headdress off and set it on a nearby stool. He uncoiled the thick braid from around her head then loosened it with his fingers.

Her hair was still damp in places. He sank his fingers deep into the waves and shook her hair free, releasing the scent of wildflowers. Closing his eyes, he put his face into her hair and breathed in until he was dizzy with the smell of it.

He pushed the hair aside to kiss the delicate curve of her neck. At last. Another woman would have sighed and leaned back into him, or turned and pulled him into a deep kiss. But his new wife remained rigid.

So much for his resolve to calm her with conversation before touching her. He sighed, knowing he should not have lost himself like that. Sinking into the seat beside her, he took her hand. He was glad for some physical connection, however tenuous.

Catherine covered her eyes with her other hand. To his bewilderment, her shoulders were shaking. She was weeping! After what seemed like an eternity to him, she seemed to recover herself somewhat.

"I am sorry," she said in a tremulous voice. "I do not mean to annoy you."

What was he to do with her? He patted her hand, which seemed so small in his, and waited. He felt desperate, but he could think of nothing else to do. At last, her breathing steadied and she dropped her hand from her face. She looked at him cautiously from red-rimmed eyes and attempted a smile.

Even this small sign caused hope to spring up in his heart.

"I wish I did not frighten you," he said.

"You are not to blame." She spoke so softly he had to lean forward to hear her. "My husband...Lord Rayburn..." She cleared her throat and tried again. "He was not a kind man. I had cause to fear him."

"If you truly feared him, how could you risk betraying him as you did?" He knew he was being blunt, but he found it hard to believe her.

"I had to." From the way she pressed her lips together, he could tell this was all the answer she intended to give him.

"In what way was he unkind to you?" William asked.

"It would distress me to speak of it."

He did not want to upset her just to satisfy his curiosity. "You need not speak of it. But I would have you know, you need not be afraid of me."

He patted her hand again, since that seemed to be the only thing he could do to soothe her.

What now? It did not look too promising a wedding night, with her so pale and miserable beside him. He'd never forced a woman. He was not going to start now with his wife. In his youth, he'd seen soldiers rape peasant women. As a commander, he prohibited such vile behavior in his men. It violated everything a knight should be.

He rubbed his hands over his face and gave a long sigh. "Perhaps you are too soon from your sickbed to make a marriage bed," he said, pushing a stray strand of hair behind her ear. He paused to give her time to contradict him before giving her his final dispensation. "God willing, we have many years of married life ahead. Tonight, you must sleep."

The relief in her eyes hurt his pride.

"Thank you. I am so very tired," she said, rising from the table.

He grabbed her wrist. "Catherine, it is important that everyone believe we consummated our marriage this night. No one must think we are not fully bound."

"Yes, of course," she said, pulling away from him.

Good Lord, she looked as if she intended to run before he changed his mind. He stood and rested his hands firmly on her shoulders.

"I *will* have my rights as a husband." He held her eyes with a look that was meant to sear through her. "I want children, and I will have them only with my wife."

After a moment, she said in a soft voice, "I would like more children as well."

Her words set off such an intense surge of longing that he had to struggle to keep from pulling her hard against him. She must have sensed his weakening resolve. When she tried to step back, he tightened his grip on her shoulders.

"I want you in my bed," he said. "And I will not wait long."

He kissed her lightly, holding back the passion that threatened to overtake his will. She held herself very still, as if she knew that if she responded in the slightest, she would find him pressed against her, every inch touching, and there would be no turning back.

But she gave no quarter. He broke the kiss, his heart pounding in his chest. Without another word, he led her to her bedchamber door. She closed it swiftly behind her.

He told himself he had waited years for her; he could wait one more night. But sleep would not come easy. Not with Catherine so near and his body aching for her.

Chapter Four

Catherine paused at the entrance to survey the room. The hall was empty, save for a few of FitzAlan's men, who sat near the hearth cleaning their weapons. FitzAlan, praise God, was not among them.

The rest of the household must have broken their fast hours ago. How did she sleep so late? It was a wonder she was able to sleep at all with FitzAlan so near. She awoke feeling almost in full health again. However, after days of eating almost nothing, she was famished.

Nodding to the men, she hurried to the table to take her breakfast. She was so hungry she could think of nothing but the food in front of her for some time.

After putting away an unseemly amount of food, she looked up and caught the men exchanging amused winks and nods. Apparently, they had set aside their work to watch her eat.

Did these Northerners have no manners? She gave them a severe look. She was gratified to see them go back to cleaning their weapons, albeit with a snort or two of stifled laughter.

Alys bustled into the hall, calling, "Good morning, m'lady!"

Heavens, why was everyone full of cheer this morning? First those men acting like boys, and now Alys smiling as if she'd found a bag of gold coins.

"Where's Jamie this morning?" Catherine asked her.

"Jamie? Why, he's gone with Lord FitzAlan."

Catherine jumped to her feet. "What? He has taken Jamie?" Her throat was closing in panic. "Where, Alys? Where has he taken him?"

"Pray, do not fret, m'lady. He only took the boy to the stables to look at that huge animal of his. Jamie begged him." Touching Catherine's arm, she added, "I would have come for you if there was anything amiss."

Catherine closed her eyes and tried to calm herself. Jamie was all right. He had to be.

At the sound of a loud commotion coming from the entrance, she opened her eyes just as FitzAlan strode into the hall. Jamie was on his shoulders, grinning from ear to ear. The relief that flooded through her made her knees feel weak. She took a half-step back and put a steadying hand on the table behind her.

Jamie waved wildly at her, shouting, "Mother! Mother!"

He gave a high-pitched giggle as FitzAlan swung him down. As soon as her son's feet touched the floor, he ran to her, excitement radiating from his face. She dropped to one knee to catch him and clutched him fiercely to her chest. Praise God, he was all right. Forcing herself to release him, she leaned back and gave him what she hoped was a cheerful smile.

"He says I may ride on his horse with him," Jamie told her, his eyes dancing. "Can I, *pleeaaase*?"

"Of course." Looking up at FitzAlan, she added, "I hope I may come along when you do."

She was not about to let FitzAlan take her son outside the castle without her. Anything could happen.

"You could show me the lands near the castle, if you feel well enough to ride." FitzAlan examined her so closely she felt her face flush. With a slight lift of his eyebrow, he said, "You do look in fine health today. Very fine."

Her blush deepened; she could not mistake his meaning.

"The rest of my men just arrived, and I need to arrange an escort to travel to London with Bishop Whitefield," he said. "Can you be ready in an hour?"

———

Glancing at her son, Catherine was amazed by how at ease the boy was. He rested one small hand on FitzAlan's arm while pointing at one thing after another.

Jamie's excited chatter gave an unexpected sense of normalcy to the ride. As they rode across the green fields, she found she was almost enjoying herself. She leaned back and closed her eyes. The warm summer sun felt good on her face after so many days indoors.

"I understand from Alys and Jacob that you managed the estates for your father when he was absent."

She snapped her eyes open. So, FitzAlan already knew to go to Alys and Jacob for information rather than the useless man Rayburn had appointed steward. She must keep her wits about her. This was not a man she should underestimate.

The muscles in his jaw tightened, and then he said, "Of course, you did the same for Rayburn."

"I have been the mistress of Ross Castle since I was twelve, when my mother died," she answered him. "I only did as other women do when their lords go off to fight, though perhaps I took on the duties younger than some."

"Then you can tell me what I need to know."

He proceeded to pepper her with questions about the tenants and about what most needed his attention on the estates. At first, she believed he was merely making conversation. But when he pressed her for her opinions and listened closely to what she said, his interest seemed genuine. Never once had Rayburn—or her father—sought her advice.

"May I go?" Jamie interrupted. He was pointing toward a small group of men and boys working in a nearby field.

FitzAlan raised his eyebrows at her in a silent question. Pleased that he would defer to her, she nodded. Jamie ran off to greet the tenants as soon as FitzAlan set him on the ground.

Before she could dismount, he was at her side. He lifted her down as though she weighed nothing at all—and did not release her. With his large hands holding her waist, she felt like a trapped hare. It did not help that he was looking at her as if he'd like to gnaw her bones.

She twisted away from him and hurried after Jamie through the field. In an instant, FitzAlan was beside her. He walked so close the heat from his body seemed to pass through their clothing to her skin. Each time his arm brushed hers, it sent tingles through her body.

"Those are two of our tenants, Smith and Jennings, and some of their children. Smith is always willing to take on extra work."

Good heavens, she was blabbering, but the way his gaze swept her from head to foot made her nervous.

"Why is Smith so willing to do extra work?"

"Smith?" She looked at him blankly before she recalled what she had just said. Without stopping to think, she blurted out the truth. "His wife is such a shrew that he is glad for any excuse to be away from his cottage."

FitzAlan responded with a smile that reached his eyes. The saints be praised, the man had a sense of humor. What next?

"What of the other man, Jennings?"

"If you want something delivered far from home," she said, "Jennings is your best man."

"He is the most responsible?"

"In sooth, he is not, though he serves well enough," she admitted. "But none of the other men like to leave if Jennings stays behind. They fear if they leave their wives alone, their next child may have Jennings's green eyes."

God help her, had she truly said that?

FitzAlan's deep laugh rang out over the fields. The sound startled her; it seemed so at odds with his serious nature. He looked younger and less formidable when he laughed. And even more handsome. More trouble, that was. All the maids would be atwitter over him.

FitzAlan nodded toward a third man, working apart from the others. "Who is that?"

"Tyler. The only one to give me cause for complaint," she said as she watched the man in the field with narrowed eyes. "Tyler is not blessed with an honest nature."

When they reached the tenants, FitzAlan spoke with them about the crops and the weather. As they took their leave, Jamie begged to stay and "help" Jennings's children with their work.

"I'll look after the lad, m'lady," Jennings assured her, "and return him to the castle before supper."

She thanked the man. Too late, she realized this would leave her alone with FitzAlan.

It was a perfect day, so clear she could see the Black Mountains across the border in Wales as they rode. The warmth of the sun and the gentle breeze touching her face soothed her. As FitzAlan asked her questions about various noble families of the area, the ease she felt earlier returned.

After a time, she ventured a question of her own. "I hear you come from the North. Did you know Northumberland and his son 'Hotspur' Percy?"

"It is not possible to live in the North without knowing something of the Percys." Giving her a sharp look, he asked, "Why do you wish to know about them?"

Clearly, it was a mistake to ask about the powerful family that had twice conspired to remove the king. Why could she not be quiet?

"I am curious, that is all," she murmured. "There are so many stories about them, especially Hotspur."

"Hotspur was as brave and reckless as they say," he said in a flat tone. He paused so long she thought he meant to close the subject. Before she could think of something to say to fill the awkward silence, he spoke again.

"When Hotspur was sixteen, he was in such a rage after a skirmish with the MacDonald clan that he chased after them alone into the hills." His tone held a note of disapproval. "Northumberland and King Richard had to pay a fortune in ransom for his return. Hotspur was always rash and hotheaded; he did not change as he grew older."

Encouraged by this lengthy response, she risked asking another question, one that had long plagued her. "Why do you suppose the Percys turned against King Henry?"

It was well known that Henry Bolingbroke would not have been crowned in the first place without Northumberland's support. Catherine had never understood why the Percys later became so intent on removing him.

"The Percys resented Henry for not rewarding them more for their support," FitzAlan explained. "King Henry, on the other hand, believed they already held too much power and wealth."

He glanced at her, as if checking to be sure she was truly interested, before continuing.

"Relations went from bad to worse when they argued over who should collect the ransom for some Scots Hotspur captured in battle. The king insisted the ransom go to the Crown."

"Was that the usual custom?" she asked before realizing the awkwardness of her question.

"'Twas customary for the man who made the capture to collect the ransom, but the king had the right," he answered carefully. "I will tell you, Hotspur had strong feelings about making these particular hostages pay him. They were men from the MacDonald clan—the ones who took him hostage as a youth."

Catherine leaned forward in her saddle. "Hotspur must have waited years to make them pay for that humiliation."

He nodded. "Eventually, Hotspur joined forces with Glyndwr in open rebellion and called on his father, Northumberland, to do the same."

Fascinated, she asked more questions. He answered, though somewhat reluctantly. When she pressed for details about battles he fought in, he pulled his horse up and turned to look at her.

"*Was* it you who sent the messages to Prince Harry?"

His voice held surprise and a touch of uncertainty. "You truly did serve as the prince's spy?"

"Did you think a woman not capable of seeing what was under her nose?" she asked, narrowing her eyes at him. "Or did you think that, though seeing it, a woman would lack the courage to do what ought to be done?" She knew she should not be belligerent with him but could not seem to help herself.

"I had not made up my mind what you did." Oddly enough, he was smiling. It did nothing to dampen her temper.

An even more insulting possibility occurred to her.

"Did you believe I was a traitor?" Her voice was high-pitched, even to her own ears. When he did not deny it, she demanded, "You could marry me believing I might have supported Rayburn in his treason against the king?"

What made her dare speak with such insolence to Fitz-Alan? Rayburn would have pulled her from her horse and beat her to within an inch of her life for less.

"I should apologize for upsetting you," he said, though he did not look sorry.

Behind the laughter in his eyes, there was a fire that burned right through her and made her throat go dry. She heard his words from the night before in her head: *I will not wait long.*

She kicked her horse and rode ahead.

After a time, he eased his horse beside hers. In a mild tone, he asked, "How did you obtain your information for the prince?"

She took a deep breath. He had answered her questions; in fairness, she should do the same.

"Whenever my husband discussed rebel plans with his

men, he would send the servants away and have me wait on them."

She refrained from telling FitzAlan of her other sources of information.

"Your husband trusted you."

She shook her head. "'Twas more that he never considered I would act against him."

"How soon after your marriage did you begin spying for the prince?"

"I did not think of it as spying, not at first," she said as she guided her horse around a rabbit hole in the path. "I would tell him bits of news I happened to hear. I gave him nothing truly useful until just before the Battle of Shrewsbury."

"What was that?"

"I learned Glyndwr was leading a Welsh army in the direction of Shrewsbury, to join Hotspur's forces," she said. "So I sent an urgent message to the prince to warn him."

Hotspur, in his usual headlong fashion, had moved his army so quickly that neither his father nor the Welsh could get to Shrewsbury before the king engaged his army there. Hotspur's death in the Battle of Shrewsbury ended the first Percy conspiracy.

Thinking of that now, she asked, "Why do you think the king did not take more retribution against Northumberland after Shrewsbury?" She and Prince Harry had discussed this many times, but a Northerner might have a different perspective.

She was letting her curiosity get the better of her again. FitzAlan, however, did not chastise her.

"Northumberland was too powerful," he said. "Since

he had not taken up arms with Hotspur at Shrewsbury, the king could wait. Northumberland was growing old. Hotspur's death should have put an end to his ambitions."

It had not. Only this spring, Northumberland was involved in a second conspiracy to remove Henry from the throne. This time, he barely escaped into Scotland with his life.

"They said the messages the prince received were anonymous," FitzAlan said, turning the subject back to her.

"The prince knows my script, so I never took the risk of signing or using my seal."

"When did Rayburn cross over to the rebels?" he asked.

"'Tis difficult to say," she said, looking off at the horizon as she thought. "For a long time, he played both sides. He provided funds and information to the rebels but would not risk meeting with them."

"Until yesterday," FitzAlan said in a flat tone. "When, thanks to you, we captured him."

Just yesterday! A single day since she waited in her bedchamber for news of Rayburn. She shook her head. So much had happened since. For a time this afternoon, she'd forgotten how her life was tied to the stranger riding beside her.

She thought she could like this William FitzAlan, if she did not have to be married to him. Already, he had shown her more kindness and respect than Rayburn ever had.

She would put off her marital duty for as long as she could. For once he took her to his bed, she might not like him nearly so well.

Chapter Five

Catherine's tight-lipped expression made William want to pound his fists on the table in frustration. No matter how congenial their conversations during the day, each evening she grew withdrawn. Four days—and four long nights—he had waited to consummate this marriage.

And yet, she remained as skittish as ever.

He went riding with her each afternoon, though he had no time for it. While it was good for the tenants to see their new lord riding his lands, his first priority was the castle. He did not know when he would be called to fight again, so he was working feverishly to shore up its defenses.

Ross Castle would be safe before he left it.

He was equally determined to consummate this marriage. With luck, Catherine might conceive a child before the king sent him off chasing rebels through Wales for weeks on end.

And so he went riding. He hoped the ease that was growing between them during their afternoon sojourns would lead her to accept him as her husband at night.

So far, it had not.

At first, he brought Jamie along on their rides to please

her. To his surprise, he found he enjoyed the child's company.

A smile tugged at the corners of his mouth as he recalled how Jamie had leapt on his back and pounded at him when he first arrived. After the violence of their initial meeting, Jamie took to him quickly. In sooth, William liked the way the boy pulled at his sleeve and chattered away at him.

Aye, he and young Jamie got along just fine. If only the boy's pretty mother took to him half so well.

Busy as he was, all he could think of was bedding her. He imagined her delicate fingers running down his belly, her warm breath in his ear, her soft skin under his hands. Four days wed, and he had not even seen his wife's breasts! Lord, how he wanted to. He swallowed hard and looked at her again.

Seeing how she clutched her goblet for dear life, he had no reason to hope tonight would be different. And yet, he did.

He stood and held out his arm to her. He was not amused by the looks his men exchanged. It was early to retire, but he did not care. He was done with waiting.

As soon as they reached the solar, she fled into her bedchamber with her maid.

"Come sit with me when you have finished preparing for bed," he called after her as the door closed in his face.

His irritation rising, he stalked into his own bedchamber to undress.

"Good evening, m'lord." His manservant's voice startled him from his thoughts. It had slipped his mind that Thomas had arrived today and would be waiting to help him undress.

"I hope you did not look at your new bride like that," Thomas remarked as he knelt to remove William's boots.

William gave him a quelling look. "Just because you have served me since I was twelve does not mean you can say what you will," he said, though they both knew Thomas could speak his mind with impunity.

William pulled his tunic over his head and threw it in Thomas's direction. Unperturbed, Thomas snatched it from the air and waited for the shirt to follow. Showing his usual good sense, Thomas helped William into his robe and left the room without another word.

William washed his face and hands in the basin of water Thomas left for him. Frustrated, he ran wet fingers through his hair.

Surely Catherine must be ready by now.

The solar was empty, so he called her name outside her chamber door. Getting no reply, he eased the door open. God grant him patience. His wife was sitting on the trunk at the foot of her bed, wringing her hands as if waiting to be taken to her execution.

As he stepped into the room, she gave a startled yelp and jumped to her feet. He might have laughed if his heart did not feel so heavy. When he noticed the maid cowering in the corner, he jerked his head toward the door. It gave him some small satisfaction to see her scamper out like a frightened mouse.

"M'lady wife, I have told you I will not harm you," he said in a quiet voice. He held his hand out to her. "Come, let us sit and talk."

Hesitantly, she came to him and took it; her fingers were icy cold. He led her to the window seat in their solar. After handing her a cup of warm spiced wine, he sat beside her.

To calm her, he talked about what he accomplished that day. Then he asked her advice about the stores that would be needed to withstand a long siege.

When he felt her tension subside, he risked resting his hand on her thigh. She started, but he did not remove his hand. The warmth of her skin through the thin summer shift filled him with such lust. He wanted to lift her by her hips onto his lap and have his way with her right here.

It took all his concentration not to rub his hand up her thigh. He would force himself to go slowly, but he was determined to move things forward tonight.

"Catherine." He lifted her chin with his finger so she would have to look at him. "Surely you know this cannot go on."

He dropped his gaze to the swell of her breasts beneath the thin cloth. His throat was dry, his erection painful.

He brushed his lips against her cheek. "How can I make you forget your fears?" he breathed into her ear. "What can I do?"

He pushed her heavy hair back and moved his mouth along her jaw. "Does this help?"

As he made his journey down her neck to her delicate collarbone, he asked his questions against her skin. "What of this? And this? And this?"

He was lost in the smell of her skin, the feel of its softness against his lips. And the anticipation of having her naked beneath him. To be inside her at last. For surely it would happen this time. He ran his tongue over the swell of her breast above the edge of her tunic.

"Perhaps you could tell me something of your family?"

Her voice, high-pitched and sudden, startled him. He bolted upright.

"Catherine, when I asked what I could do, I was not asking you to suggest new topics of conversation, and you know it."

She was pressed against the wall behind her. But he would not be deterred so easily this time. He eased the shift off her shoulder with his finger and kissed the exposed skin.

"Mmm, lavender," he said, nuzzling her neck.

She remained as stiff and unyielding as ever.

Since his efforts at seduction were failing so miserably, he would try goading her.

"You are being a coward, Catherine."

Looking straight into her eyes, he put his hand again on her thigh. This time, he did rub it firmly from knee to hip. Lord in heaven, it felt good. So good, he almost could not hear her speak over the rush of blood in his ears.

"Truly, I do wish to know more about you. Do you have brothers? Sisters? What of your parents?" She spoke in an insistent, frenetic rush. "I know you come from somewhere in the North, but where precisely is your home?"

Exasperated, he cut her off. "I have no home in the North."

Perhaps if she had asked him to speak of something else, his patience would not have snapped. But he had his own secrets, and he saw no reason to share them with his wife. He pulled her roughly to her feet.

"I have waited longer than any other bridegroom would," he said, so frustrated he wanted to shake her. "You made vows to me before God. As your husband, I could order you to my bed. I could drag you there kicking and screaming. It is my right."

"I know it," she whispered, her eyes cast down.

His anger seeped from him. God in heaven, she was still frightened of him.

"I don't want to force you," he said, and heard the pleading in his voice. "I am asking that you come to me, Catherine. And that you do it soon."

He wanted her warm and willing in his arms. He wanted her clinging to him as he carried her to his bed. He wanted to see her weak and spent from their lovemaking. He wanted her to reach for him in the morning and do it all again.

He wanted, he wanted, he wanted.

She held herself rigid, waiting for him to release her. Unhappily, he let her go. He went to his bedchamber alone, hoping it would be the last night. Without bothering to remove his robe, he fell facedown across his bed.

He must have dozed, for he woke with a start to the sound of her screams. Heart pounding, he grabbed his sword from where it hung on the bedpost and ran to her bedchamber. In the darkness, he nearly collided with her maid.

"Lady Catherine is having one of her nightmares, m'lord," the maid said breathlessly. "I will fetch Alys. She knows what to do."

"Go quickly," he urged her, and went to Catherine.

She was thrashing on the bed and moaning, "No, please, no!" When he tried to quiet her by taking her in his arms, her movements became more violent. He stood back, feeling helpless.

Alys came rushing in, her voluminous night robe billowing behind her. By now, Catherine had awakened. She sat up in the bed, her hands over her face, shaking violently. And still, she could not bear to have him touch her.

The housekeeper put a steadying arm around his wife and held a small vial to her lips. She drank it down and rested her head on Alys's shoulder.

"That devil Rayburn is gone, thanks be to God," Alys murmured as she held Catherine and smoothed back her hair. "He cannot harm you now."

After a time, Alys eased Catherine onto the pillows and gingerly backed down the steps from the high bed.

"The draught will bring her a peaceful sleep, m'lord," Alys whispered as they left Catherine's bedchamber. "You've no cause to worry now."

Alys would have continued out the solar, but he put his hand on her arm to stop her.

"But I do have cause to worry." He nodded to a chair, and Alys sat down obediently. "Tell me what Rayburn did to her. All of it. Now."

Alys looked away and said, "Lord Rayburn beat her viciously. We could hear her screams." There was a note of pleading in Alys's voice. "There was nothing I could do, save tend to her after."

She grabbed a handful of her robes and wiped her nose and eyes. "May that man burn in hell for all eternity!"

"You would have protected her if you could," William said. "He was a powerful lord and her husband."

"I told Lady Catherine it would be a simple matter for me to slip poison in his soup, but she forbade it." Alys shook her head in obvious regret. "She would not have me blacken my soul by committing a mortal sin."

She stopped to blow her nose again. "The beatings stopped once she was with child."

"That was the end of it?" He hoped she would tell him it was, but he did not think so.

"That's what we thought. But then Jamie caught a fever and nearly died, poor lamb."

William was confused. "Are you saying Jamie's illness led Rayburn to mistreat her again?"

"I know it did," Alys said, nodding her head vigorously. "I heard him shouting at her about one son not being enough, that there was nothing for it, but he must get her with child again. She cried and pleaded with him, promising nothing would happen to the boy."

"I heard her screaming as he dragged her up the stairs." Alys bit her lip and sniffed. "Next morning, I took care of her, as I always did."

William did not know what to do with his rage. It pulsed through him, blurring his vision. He wished Rayburn were still alive so he could kill him. No matter how Catherine deceived Rayburn, she did not deserve such treatment. No woman did.

Could she not see he was different from Rayburn? He would never lay a hand on her. He was a man of honor; it was his duty to protect her. He renewed his determination to be patient. In time, she would see he would not harm her. She would come to him.

—

Three more days of waiting, and William's patience had worn thin to breaking. He could not sleep and was so short-tempered that his men had taken to avoiding him. Edmund—the only man who dared—finally confronted him.

"What is it with you, man?" Edmund demanded as William stomped past him in the bailey yard. "I had supposed bridegrooms to be a cheerful lot, but the men are ready to join the Welsh just to get away from you."

When William only growled at him in response, Edmund said, "What complaint can you have? You have a woman in your bed every man here would sell his soul to the devil to have."

A glint came into Edmund's eyes. "Oh no, William, tell me you did not do something foolish to upset that pretty wife of yours?" Grinning now, Edmund shook his head in mock disbelief. "Did you let her catch you with that serving maid? The one who flounces her wares at you every chance she gets?"

"Don't insult me," William said sharply. "I am wed but a week, and you think I've already committed adultery?" William turned on his heel and resumed his march across the yard.

"If married life suits you so poorly," Edmund said, catching up to him, "you can send her away."

When William ignored him, Edmund took hold of his arm, forcing William to turn and face him.

"If it is your new wife who is making you such a miserable horse's arse, 'tis an easy matter to be rid of her. All you need do is tell the king she was party to Rayburn's treachery."

"Never speak against my wife again." The deathly calm of his voice made Edmund step back. "'Tis only because of the bond we share from many years of fighting that they will not be scraping your bloody carcass from the bailey ground today."

His body vibrated with anger as he stepped close to Edmund. "It will not save you a second time."

Chapter Six

William strode toward the stables, hoping a long, hard ride would improve his mood. Before he reached them, he heard a trumpet blast.

"Who comes?" he called up to one of the men on the wall.

"They carry the king's banner, m'lord."

There was no time to change into something more suitable for greeting a royal visitor, so he headed straight for the gate. It could not be the king. Henry was in the North finishing off the last remnants of the rebellion there.

William recognized the young man who rode through the gate at the front of the men-at-arms as Prince Harry. As the prince dismounted, William dropped to his knee. At the prince's signal, he rose to receive his future king.

"FitzAlan, I am glad to find you here. The king wishes me to report—" The prince stopped midsentence, his attention caught by something behind William.

"Kate!" the prince called out, his face transformed by a boyish grin.

In another moment, Catherine was beside William

making a low curtsy. Prince Harry pulled her to her feet. After bestowing enthusiastic kisses on both her cheeks, he lifted her off the ground and spun her in his arms.

If the prince's behavior was not surprising enough, Catherine's was astonishing. She threw her head back and laughed. Then she pounded on the prince's shoulders, shouting, "Harry! Harry, put me down at once!"

The prince did as she commanded. "I am always happy to do the fair Catherine's bidding," he declared, giving her a dramatic bow.

The prince turned and gave William a grin and a wink. "Truth be told," he said in a loud whisper she was meant to hear, "your lady wife was a tyrant as a child."

The prince put his hand to his heart and gave an exaggerated sigh. "I was in love with her when I was a lad of seven. But, alas, she was an older woman of ten and would not have me."

The men crowded around them laughed. William did not.

Catherine stood too close to the prince, squeezing his hand, chatting at her ease. William would have given a good deal to have her smile at him in precisely that way. Seeing her grace another man with it hit him like a blow to the chest.

He ceased to follow the words of their conversation, seeing only the affection and delight the two found in each other. Before he knew it, the three of them were walking to the keep. Focused as he was on how tightly she held the prince's arm, he almost failed to notice that Prince Harry was speaking to him.

"If you would be so gracious as to put me and my men up for the night," the prince was saying.

"It would be an honor." William was surprised by how normal his voice sounded.

"Only one night?" Catherine asked.

"I am sorry, my dear Kate," Prince Harry said, patting her hand on his arm, "but you know my time is not my own."

My dear Kate? The prince was talking to him again, but William could barely take in the words. *My dear Kate?*

"The king wishes to know whether there have been rebel attacks in the area since your arrival at Ross Castle."

He must have mumbled something appropriate, for the prince seemed satisfied.

William narrowed his eyes at Catherine. She was looking radiant in a close-fitting, rose-colored silk gown that flowed gracefully as she walked. Had she dressed with particular care today? The prince had given no advance warning of his visit. At least not to William.

Once inside the keep, Catherine sent servants scurrying in every direction to prepare rooms and refreshments. As soon as the prince excused himself to change, William took his wife by the arm. He marched her into a passage just outside the hall, where he could speak with her in private.

"You appear to know the prince quite well," he said in a harsh whisper.

"We have known each other all our lives," Catherine said, surprise in her voice. "You must know he spent his early years close by, at Monmouth Castle. Our mothers were close friends."

"Yes, of course," he said, feeling foolish.

"William, I must speak with the cook now," she said, clearly anxious to get back to her duties.

He could think of nothing else to say, so he let her go. At least she had called him "William" for once.

At supper, the prince chose to sit between William and his wife. And William chose to refrain from pushing his royal arse onto the floor. It annoyed him further to see what the kitchen, under his wife's direction, had produced on such short notice for their royal guest.

William was heaping pheasant onto his trencher when he became aware that the eyes of everyone at the table were on him.

"What is your opinion?" the prince asked, leaning forward and looking at him expectantly. "Will they come this summer?"

Fortunately, it was easy to guess what the prince was asking. The question was on everyone's lips: Would the French send an army to support the Welsh?

"I cannot say," William said, shrugging a shoulder, "but we must be prepared for it."

"Aye, we must!" Without pausing, the prince began to speculate as to where the French might land their forces. Then he launched into a discussion of how the English could then drive them out of Wales.

William should be glad for the opportunity to discuss military strategy with Prince Harry. After all, the prince was in command of all English forces fighting the Welsh. The young man showed such remarkable talent for military command that Parliament had given him the responsibility two years ago, at the age of sixteen.

Tonight, however, William did not care about a French invasion. To hell with the damned French.

As soon as the nursemaid took Jamie up to bed, William began to calculate how many hours before he could follow with Catherine. When the prince rose to his feet, he felt hopeful.

"May I take your wife for a walk in the garden?" The prince was already holding his arm out to Catherine as he asked the question.

William could not very well tell the heir to the throne he would rather have a dagger twisted in his gut. If he gave his consent without much grace, the prince did not seem to notice.

———

Catherine took great solace in having even a short visit with her friend. Though Harry had an air of authority about him now, she could still see in him the boy who pulled her hair and slipped beetles down her back. Despite his annoying pranks, they had always been close.

She was glad Harry had those early years running wild at Monmouth, before his father usurped the throne. Being heir to the throne, especially in such troubled times, was a heavy burden.

"You make a fine prince, dear Harry," she said, squeezing his arm as they left the hall. "One day, you will make an even finer king."

"God grant my father many years," Harry murmured.

They sat on a bench in the garden to talk.

"You should not have taken the risks you did," he said, shaking his head.

They had had this argument many times before.

"It is over now, and I am safe," she reminded him with a smile.

"It was a close thing. My father—" Harry stopped and seemed to struggle to rephrase his words. "The king was so angry with Rayburn that he was inclined to send you to the Tower, despite my arguments."

The tension between the king and his heir was no secret. After criticizing Harry for being too weak when he was young, the king now appeared at times to consider him a threat. The king resented all the praise of Harry's military successes and his popularity among the common folk. For Harry's part, his innate sense of honor was violated time and again by actions his father took to retain power.

"'Tis a good thing FitzAlan chose to wed you." Harry looked off into the distance, his face grave. "If the king had imprisoned you or permitted an 'accident' to befall you..." He sighed and squeezed her hand. "I have forgiven my father many things, but I could not have forgiven him that."

They sat in silence for a time.

"FitzAlan seems to be a good man," Harry said in a soft voice. "Can you be happy with him, Kate?"

"Happy?" she said, surprised at the question. She paused to consider it. "You would not want to stand in William's way. But, beneath his fierceness, there is kindness in him."

In sooth, there was much to like and respect about her new husband. She felt more at ease with him each day. Soon, she would trust him enough to go to his bedchamber, as he asked.

Luckily, William could follow the men's conversation at the table with only half an ear. They talked, as they always did, of the Welsh rebels and their leader, Owain Glyndwr.

For the hundredth time, he heard them complain of the rebels' uncanny ability to strike and disappear into the woods. They made the usual uneasy jests about the claim that Merlyn, Arthur's mythical magician, had returned to aid Glyndwr. William had heard it all before.

He flicked his eyes to the doorway again. Catherine and the prince had been gone for the better part of an hour.

At the sound of a woman's laughter, he leapt to his feet. Prince Harry and Catherine entered the room, arm in arm and smiling into each other's eyes. Someone tugged at William's arm. Without taking his eyes off the pair, he shrugged the man off.

"William!"

"What is it?" he hissed, turning to find Edmund beside him.

"Do you want to find yourself in chains in your own dungeon, man?" Edmund said out the side of his mouth.

William turned his attention back to the couple. His blood pounded through his veins as it did on the verge of battle. Feeling a hard jab in his ribs, he turned and glared at Edmund.

"You are looking at the Prince of Wales with murder in your eyes," Edmund persisted in a low, urgent voice. "Some of his men have taken notice."

This time, William took heed of the warning. Glancing about, he saw the two knights watching him, their hands touching the hilts of their swords. He relaxed his stance and smoothed his features, and the two knights did likewise.

He did not slip again. He maintained an easy, bored

expression—even when Prince Harry drew his wife to a small table against the far wall for a game of chess.

From the corner of his eye, he watched the two laughing and talking. Just when he was sure he could not feel more wretched, their laughter died. They leaned across the table and spoke in low voices, their game forgotten.

Frustrated that he could not hear their words, he moved closer. His heart missed several beats as Catherine reached out to touch the scar under the prince's eye, where he had taken an arrow at the Battle of Shrewsbury. Despite the wound, he led the attack on Hotspur's flank.

The prince made a face and leaned back from her touch. "Please, Kate, I know it is hideous to look at."

"Nay, it is not. That mark is a sign you are special to God, that he protects you," Catherine said earnestly. "If it were otherwise, that arrow surely would have killed you."

Their exchange ended when William took position behind his wife and put a possessive hand on her shoulder. Feeling her body tense at his touch, he clenched his jaw so tightly it began to ache.

The prince showed no sign of discomfort at being caught in the midst of an intimate conversation with another man's wife.

"Becoming a prince must have made me a better chess player," he said in a voice heavy with irony. "Lady Catherine is the only one who has retained the ability to beat me."

William had not bothered to observe the chess pieces before. Dropping his gaze to the table now, he saw that the prince's king was caught in the cross paths of Catherine's bishop and queen.

"You win this time." With a flick of his finger, the prince knocked his king on its side. Then he stretched his arms and added, "But once is luck."

"'Twas much too easy," Catherine said, looking off to the side as though exceedingly bored. "Soon I shall find it too dull to play with you at all."

William was startled to hear her openly insult the prince. Before he could gather himself to say something to soften her words, the prince guffawed and slapped the table.

"You shall regret those words, sweet Catherine," Prince Harry said, his eyes gleaming. He began putting the pieces back into place for another game. "This time, I shall humiliate you. Nay, I shall make you weep with remorse!"

The prince's loud challenge drew the other men, and wagers were made. Observing the game, William could see that the two players were well matched. Catherine fought hard, but this time it was her king that was toppled.

William pulled out his leather purse and paid coins all around. None, save him, had dared bet against the prince.

Catherine excused herself then, and the men settled into talk of war and rebels again. Without the distraction of his wife, William's usual interest in military matters returned. As they talked into the wee hours, he found he could not help liking Prince Harry. He was so young and earnest. Yet, there was power in him, too. He was a man other men would follow.

William chastised himself for overreacting. Harry was

an honorable man. He and Catherine were friends. William was slow to see it, since he never had a woman friend. Even his lovers were not friends. Especially his lovers.

These finer thoughts left him as he came into the hall the next morning. Prince Harry and Catherine were already at table, engrossed in conversation. When Catherine saw him, she murmured a greeting and went silent.

The prince, however, enthusiastically resumed their conversation of the night before.

"The Welsh rebels have only succeeded in taking control of most of Wales, because English forces have been divided," the prince said. "Now that the rebellion in the North is crushed, we shall turn all our attention to Wales."

Prince Harry expounded at length upon his strategy for laying siege to the castles the rebels had taken in Wales. All William wished to know, however, was what the prince and his wife had been talking about before he sat down.

It was not, he was certain, strategies for laying siege.

To his surprise—and growing annoyance—the prince did not take his leave after breakfast. He stayed for the midday meal, which had even more courses than last night's supper. Then, he suggested taking a ride around the lands surrounding Ross Castle.

God's blood, would the man never leave?

William's mood darkened further when Prince Harry dropped back to ride beside Catherine. He could hear their light chatter and Catherine's occasional laughter behind him. When he could take no more, he turned his horse and led the way back to the castle.

He made a point of riding just in front of the pair. "Such a wicked girl you were," he heard the prince say. "You were older and bigger, yet you never once let me win."

"It was skill, not size, that decided it," she replied.

What on earth are they talking about? William pulled his horse up and turned around to look at them.

"Then let us have a race now," the prince said.

"Harry, I cannot!" Catherine protested. "I am a grown woman. You know I cannot."

They were even with William now. Prince Harry turned away from Catherine to address him. "She—"

The moment the prince's back was turned, Catherine spurred her horse and took off.

William could not believe it. Too stunned to move, he watched her ride so recklessly that he feared she would fall. She was several lengths ahead when the prince took off after her. Soon, he streaked past her.

When William caught up to them at the gate, Catherine was shouting at her opponent. "If I did not have to ride in this cumbersome gown, I would have won!" It was an outrageous lie, and the gleam in her eyes made it clear she knew it.

Prince Harry called out to William, "You are a fortunate man to have such a wife!"

Before William could get to Catherine, the prince had his hands on her and was lifting her to the ground. William came up behind them in time to hear Prince Harry say in a low voice, "Will I ever find a woman like you, dear Kate?"

The good-byes were tedious. William was anxious for them to be done. At long last, the prince was mounted and headed out the gate. And still, the man turned one last time to wave at Catherine. William ground his teeth as he watched her wave back. When she wiped away a tear, he turned on his heel and strode off with no destination other than to be away from her.

A true knight did not murder his wife.

———

Catherine felt William's eyes burning holes into her as she waved good-bye to Harry. When she turned, he was stomping off as if headed for a fight. She had sensed his anger building since the chess games the night before. Fearful of aggravating him further, she did her best to speak to him as little as possible.

What happened to the kindness she thought she saw in him? Just when she began to trust in it, the man turned back into the furious warrior on the drawbridge.

To think she'd nearly convinced herself to go to his bed!

Chapter Seven

*A*pparently, his lady wife was too despondent over the prince's departure to show her face at supper. She sent word down that she was not well and would not join them in the hall. The surreptitious looks his men exchanged when they thought he was not looking only confirmed his fears.

William began to drink in earnest.

Irritated by the sight of the empty seat beside him, he grabbed a full pitcher of wine from the table and stomped out of the hall. He was well into his cups when Edmund found him on the outer curtain wall, perched on the lower ledge of the crenellated parapet.

He gazed out at the countryside in the fading light of the summer evening. "I have my own land now, Edmund," he said, swinging his arm in a wide arc. "And by God, isn't it fair!"

Edmund grabbed William's other arm. "This may not be the best choice of seats for serious drinking."

"'Tis a fine spot," William countered. "I've never seen better." He tilted his head back and took another long drink from the pitcher, ignoring how it spilt down his chin and neck.

Edmund leaned against the parapet. "Are you sharing?"

William turned the empty pitcher upside down. "We shall have to get more. I, for one, have not drunk nearly enough."

Edmund let out a long sigh and shook his head. "William, William, William. You are not looking at how the situation is to your advantage. If you consider it properly, you will see you have much to gain here."

Even drunk as he was, William understood the direction of Edmund's remarks.

Edmund held up his hands. "Do not get angry with me. I am just looking out for your interests."

He should stop Edmund now. Instead, he waited to hear Edmund confirm the ugly suspicions that had been playing in his head since the prince's arrival.

"Young Harry is not the first royal to find himself desperate to have another man's wife in his bed," Edmund said. "Kings have been known to provide titles and riches to a husband who will turn his head and forgo his rights for a time."

Edmund took his lack of response as permission to go on.

"From the hungry way he looks at her, I don't believe he's had her yet," Edmund said in a thoughtful tone. "The arrangement will be worth a good deal more to you when he is king. Rumor has it the king is ill, and Harry may be on the throne before the year is out. It would be best to make him wait, if she can manage it, but I would not count on it."

He should encourage his wife to manage the prince's "interest" to his own advantage? The rage that roared through him was so great he could not speak. He feared he might lose his reason and murder Edmund on the spot.

"You cannot expect the prince's interest to last long once he has had her, especially with all the great families thrusting their daughters under his nose," Edmund continued, oblivious to the danger he was in. "When he is done with her, you can take her back...or not."

Blithely, he gave William his final word of advice. "If you want to be sure your heir is your own blood, you'd better get her with child now, before the prince takes her to his bed."

In one motion, William surged up, lifted Edmund off his feet by the front of his tunic, and threw him hard against the parapet. The man was lucky William did not toss him over it. Without looking back, he stormed down the walkway and took the steps down the side of the wall two at a time.

He would see this wife of his, and he would see her now.

She played her first husband false. Why did he think she would not do the same with him? What had made him so ready to believe the tale of Rayburn's violence against her? She had played him for a fool, all the while saving herself for her lover.

She acted like a frightened, untouched virgin with him. But she'd shown no fear with Harry. Even through the haze of drink, he knew what bothered him most was her obvious affection for the prince. He thought of how she stood so close to the prince, smiled at him, touched his face. It tore him apart.

He would show her what a man could give her, and she would never want that boy again.

As he made his way up the stairs to their rooms, the steps seemed to shift under him several times. He found the solar dark and empty, but there was a dim light under her bedchamber door. When he pushed it open, it made a very satisfying bang against the stone wall.

Catherine and her maid sat up straight in their beds,

staring at him. With the single word "Out!" he sent the maid scurrying from her pallet. He barred the door behind her.

When he turned to face his wife again, she was standing beside the bed. Her hair fell in a tumble of golden waves over her shoulders. With the candlelight behind her, he could see the outline of her body through the thin night shift.

God, but she was beautiful. And she was his.

———

Catherine jumped from the bed but got no farther. The drunken madman towered over her, huge and menacing. She struggled to breathe against the rising hysteria closing her throat. Covering her face with her arms, she turned and cowered against the bed.

Suddenly, he was behind her, his heavy weight pinning her against the bed. The hot breath on her neck, the smell of sour wine, sent memories of Rayburn flashing through her head. She closed her ears to the man's drunken mutterings so she would not hear the vile things he said.

His hands were everywhere, rubbing up and down her sides and moving over her breasts. When he lifted her shift and moved his hands over her bare buttocks and thighs, panic nearly paralyzed her. Desperation gave her the strength to pull herself along the side of the bed to reach for the blade under her pillow. When she moved, he fell against the bed. Then he slowly slid to the floor.

She stood over him, breathing hard and holding her knife in front of her. When he started to push himself up, she made ready to stab him. His attempt was a feeble one, though, and he collapsed back onto the floor. Except for making occasional piglike snorts, he lay still after that.

Her only thought was to get away before he awoke.

She found her maid hovering outside the solar door. "Go fetch Alys and Jacob at once," she said, shaking the woman's arm. "And take care not to wake anyone else."

She stepped cautiously around the large form sprawled on the floor. She stayed in her chamber only long enough to slip a gown over her head and grab her riding boots and cloak.

Alys and Jacob were waiting for her on the stairs.

"Fetch Jamie and meet me at the stables," she whispered to Jacob.

As soon as Jacob had gone, she turned her back to Alys and held her hair up.

"What has happened, m'lady?" Alys whispered as she fastened the gown. "Where are you going?"

"Come, I must hurry." Catherine took Alys by the hand and pulled her down the stairs.

She did not speak again until they were crossing the bailey in the pitch dark. "I am going to the abbey. I will ask Abbess Talcott to let me take vows and remain there."

"But you cannot, m'lady," Alys protested. "You have a husband."

"I will seek an annulment."

Jacob arrived at the stables just behind them with the sleepy boy in his arms.

"Let me take Jamie on my horse, m'lady," Jacob said. "I can manage him better, if it's a fast gallop you have in mind."

Fortunately, the guards at the gate tonight were men who had long been in her family's service. They asked only if she wanted more men for protection. When she refused, they followed her order to open the gate.

William lay very still, eyes closed, knowing any movement would worsen his already throbbing head. The carpet beneath his face was uncomfortably damp from his drooling. His mouth was gaping like a fish, so he closed it. It was as dry as dust. Still, he would have resisted the driving need to quench his thirst a while longer if he did not need to piss so badly.

He eased himself to his hands and knees, intent on making his way to the garderobe.

Looking around the room from his position on the floor, he tried to place where he was. In front of him was an open chest with gowns hanging over the sides in a jumble. He stared at the bed and the tapestry on the wall.

Catherine's bedchamber. He was in Catherine's bedchamber.

Bits of memory from the previous night came to him. He sat back on his heels and tried to recall the whole of it. He remembered drinking on the wall. And Edmund talking. A surge of anger made his head pound as he recalled Edmund advising him to turn a blind eye while the prince bedded his wife.

The anger was replaced by mortification as he recalled the sound of the chamber door banging against the wall and the sight of the two women cowering in their beds. Had he really come to her so drunk he could barely walk?

A feeling of longing swept over him as he remembered the feel of Catherine's soft skin, warm from her bed. Then he recalled how roughly he had handled her. When she was finally ready, he had meant to be gentle with her. Instead, he had rubbed his hands over her as if she were a whore, unceremoniously pulled up her shift, and pushed her against the bed, ready to take her standing then and there.

He covered his face. God help him, he could not have behaved worse if he set his mind to it.

When he stumbled into his own chamber, he found Thomas had thoughtfully left a large cup of ale and bread slathered in salty pork grease. He poured water into the basin and washed the grime from his face and neck. He took his time, trying to think how to make his apology. No matter what she had done, it did not excuse his behavior. And, in the clear light of day, he had to admit she may not have done anything inappropriate with Prince Harry.

He looked down at himself. Well, at least he could attempt to look like a lord rather than a disheveled drunkard. Clairvoyant as usual, his manservant appeared at his door at that moment. Thomas, however, refused to meet his eye. Damnation, he did not need his manservant condemning him as well.

Without a word, Thomas brought him a rich dark brown cotehardie and matching hose to wear. He then helped William into a rust-colored houppelande that fell to the knee. Its wide sleeves were slit from below the elbow to the shoulder to show the cotehardie beneath.

"Is this not a bit dull, Thomas?" Noblemen were typically outfitted in more colorful attire.

"I thought dullness might be an advantage today, m'lord."

"Thomas—" he began to shout, but winced when it gave him a blinding flash of pain.

"You want to give the *appearance* of quiet dignity." Thomas pursed his lips and nodded. "Aye, the penitent look of a pilgrim would be best."

"Enough, Thomas."

He did not think Thomas would show such disapproval over mere drunkenness, but he could not fathom how the man could know of his other behavior. Then he remembered the maid he had sent scurrying from Catherine's bedchamber.

He raised his arms as Thomas fastened the rich jeweled belt Northumberland had given him low on his hips. So, he was to have a touch of finery after all.

"Where is she?" It hurt his dignity to ask Thomas, but the sooner he found Catherine and tried to make amends, the better.

"Who, m'lord?"

"You know very well who." William ground his teeth, which only aggravated his pounding headache. "My lady wife. Where is she?"

"I do not know, sir," Thomas replied with annoying calm. "She certainly would not have informed me."

"Get my boots so I may go find her," William said, wanting to throttle the man.

"You will need these," Thomas said, bringing him his tall leather riding boots.

"What? She has left the castle?" William asked. "I thought you did not know where she was."

"I don't," Thomas replied as he helped William into the tight boots. "But I did hear she left on horseback late in the night."

"What?" William shouted. "When was this?"

"I understand she left not long after you went to bed, m'lord." Thomas's voice was rich with unstated meaning.

William pulled the man up by his tunic until they were nose to nose. "Where has she gone?"

Thomas remained unruffled. "I suggest you ask the housekeeper." As though it was an afterthought, he added, "I heard old Jacob accompanied your lady."

"What other escort did she take?" William asked.

"None but Jamie."

God help him, she rode out into the night with only an old man as escort. It was madness.

He stormed down the stairs to find Alys. Was it his obscene behavior that drove Catherine to go, or had she planned to sneak away to join her lover all along?

He would find her and bring her back, prince or no prince.

He found Alys in the kitchen, consulting with the cook. "Now," he ordered, pointing toward the open door.

After exchanging glances with the cook, Alys followed him out.

"Alys, if you value your life, you will tell me where she was meeting Prince Harry."

"Prince Harry?" Alys pinched her brows together. "What are you asking, m'lord?"

"I know she has gone to meet him." He was so angry he could have shaken the woman, if it would have done any good. "Where are they?"

"She would not trouble the prince, what with the rebellion and all." She made it sound as if he was accusing Catherine of rudeness rather than adultery. "Nay, she sought refuge elsewhere."

Refuge.

He threatened and cajoled. It was only when he gave Alys his solemn promise he would not harm Catherine that she finally told him where his wife had gone. When he heard it, the blood drained from his head.

Good God, he had driven his wife to a nunnery.

Chapter Eight

When they pounded on the abbey gates in the middle of the night, Abbess Talcott asked no questions and calmly ordered a guest room to be made ready. This morning, she sat patiently while the three ate their breakfast. As soon as they finished, however, she sent Jamie off with a young novice to feed the animals. One look from the abbess and Jacob made his own exit.

Catherine sat across from the abbess now in her personal parlor. It was clear the older woman would be put off no longer. The abbess poured sweetened wine and let the silence between them grow as she waited for Catherine's explanation.

Abbess Talcott had been a close friend of Catherine's mother. Like her mother, the abbess had come from one wealthy family and married into another. When her husband died leaving her with no children, she announced her intention to take vows and lead the quiet life of a nun. She backed up her intention with the gift of a substantial portion of her lands to the church. That gift was how she came to be the head of this fine abbey straddling the Welsh-English border.

After recounting the events of the past two weeks, Catherine told her of FitzAlan's drunken attack on her the night before.

"So you see," Catherine finished, tilting her chin up, "I had no choice but to flee."

If she expected words of sympathy from the abbess, she was to be disappointed.

"Let me review what you've told me, Mary Catherine," the abbess said, fixing Catherine with direct eyes. "This FitzAlan agreed to marry you to save you from imprisonment—or worse. He did this knowing little about you, except that you spied on your first husband and helped bring about his death."

The abbess pursed her lips and tapped a forefinger against her cheek. "He is either a brave man or a foolish one.

"The king granted your lands to FitzAlan, whether or not he married you," the abbess continued. "As I see it, the man gained nothing from this marriage, save for the honor of rescuing an innocent woman—or rather, a possibly innocent woman—from the Tower."

The abbess took a sip of her wine. "A chivalrous gesture, I must say. And all he expected from you was that you share his bed and provide him an heir—what any wife is expected to give her husband."

As the abbess put it, her behavior did not seem as justified as she knew it to be.

"But, m'lady Abbess—" she began, but stopped when Abbess Talcott put her hand up, commanding silence.

"You entered into the marriage contract and yet you have refused the man your bed. You are not an underage girl, my dear. When you did not willingly submit, he would have been within his rights to force you. Instead, he was kind and patient with you, beyond all reasonable expectation."

This time, Catherine could not help interrupting to defend herself. "But he was senseless with drink when he came to me last night!"

The abbess arched one eyebrow. "Few new husbands would wait so long without turning to drink."

Catherine looked down at her hands, twisted in the skirt of her gown. "When he came to me like that, I could only think of Rayburn."

She stilled her hands and lifted her head to meet the abbess's eyes. "I cannot live like that again. I will not. I've come to ask your permission to take vows and remain here at the abbey."

The abbess patted Catherine's knee. In a kinder tone, she asked, "Did FitzAlan harm you, my dear?"

Catherine shook her head. "But I feared he would."

The abbess sighed. "Mary Catherine, you cannot punish FitzAlan for the sins of your first husband." Under her breath, she added, "May God punish him throughout eternity.

"Do you understand what FitzAlan has done for you?" the abbess pressed. "What would happen to your son if you went to the Tower?"

"Must you remind me?" Catherine asked.

"Jamie would be taken from you. As you have no close male relative, he would be placed under the guardianship of someone unknown to him—someone likely to feel burdened by the care of a traitor's son."

Catherine did not want to hear this.

"FitzAlan could have sent your son away. Instead, you

say he is kind and affectionate to the boy." The abbess's
tone had a sharp edge of exasperation now. "You are foolish if you do not recognize this for the great gift it is.

"You know what you must do," the abbess concluded.
It was not a question. "Return to your husband, ask his
forgiveness, and fulfill the vows you made before God."

The abbess poured them both more wine and gave
Catherine time to mull over what she had said. When
the chapel bell rang to call the nuns for Terce, Catherine
expected to be dismissed. But the abbess was not finished
with her yet.

"Since your good mother is not here to advise you..."
The abbess hesitated, as if unsure how to put her thoughts
into words. "I will tell you, most men are not like Rayburn."

The abbess cleared her throat and began again. "It may
be hard for you to believe now, but many women find happiness in the marriage bed. It can be...joyful." Her eyes
were moist as she patted Catherine's hand. "You must let
yourself be open to it."

The quiet of the abbey was suddenly broken by the clatter of horses' hooves and the discordant sound of men's
voices. The two women rushed to the window overlooking the courtyard to see what was causing the commotion
below.

Catherine drew in a sharp breath. "It is Lord FitzAlan."

A half-dozen men on horses accompanied FitzAlan,
but Catherine could look at none but him. The courtyard
seemed to reverberate with his presence as he circled, his
horse prancing and tossing its head. He was hatless. The
late morning sun showed the hard planes of his face and
glinted on the sun-lightened streaks of his bronze hair.

William must have sensed them watching, for he looked up then with an expression so fierce Catherine gripped the abbess's arm for support. He kept his eyes fixed on her as he dismounted, threw his reins at one of his men, and strode purposefully toward the entry below.

A high-pitched sound came from the back of her throat. Frantically, she looked about the room for a means of escape.

"This way." The abbess stepped briskly to the opposite wall and opened a narrow door hidden by the paneling. "Wait in the chapel until I send for you," she said, motioning for Catherine to hurry. "Pray that God grants you the strength to do your duty—and the wisdom to be thankful for his blessings."

As soon as Catherine had made her escape, FitzAlan burst in through the other door. He looked sharply around the room before bringing his gaze to rest on the abbess.

A nun stepped around him, giving him wide berth. "My Lady Abbess, I tried to stop him and ask his business here, but—"

"It is all right, Sister Matilde," the abbess said, staring down the tall, well-muscled man filling her doorway. "If this is Lord FitzAlan, I have been expecting his visit."

Belatedly recalling his manners, FitzAlan made a low bow. "M'lady Abbess, I am Lord William Neville Fitz-Alan. I hope you will forgive me for interrupting you."

Ignoring him for the moment, the abbess sent a second trembling nun for honey cakes and more sweet wine. Since propriety did not permit her to be left alone with a man, she directed Sister Matilde to take a seat at the far end of the room, where the nun could not easily overhear their conversation.

Only then did she gesture to FitzAlan to sit in one of the ornately carved chairs she had brought to the abbey from her home. She permitted herself some minor comforts here in her private parlor, where she received guests from the outside world.

The abbess took more than a little satisfaction in knowing that her black robes intimidated even the most powerful men. FitzAlan was no exception. He looked distinctly uncomfortable—and not just because the chair was far too small for his frame.

She suppressed a smile. Now that he had blustered his way in, it was apparent FitzAlan had no notion what to do next. He kept clasping his hands, as if about to speak. The gesture was familiar to her. Her husband had also been a man who found action easier than words.

She let him suffer, enjoying it to a degree that would require penance later. When a servant arrived with the wine and honey cakes, she took her time pouring.

"You've had a hard ride this morning," she said at last, her voice dripping with false sympathy. She offered him the plate of honey cakes. "I thought perhaps you did not take time for breakfast."

He rubbed his neck in growing discomfort. She was pleased to see he understood she was chastising him for stampeding through her gates and breaking the peace of the abbey.

"The cakes are warm," she said, encouraging him to eat. She watched him choke down two, from either politeness or extreme hunger, and wash them down with the wine. She really must assign the baking to someone other than Sister Katrina.

Seeing no reason to delay any longer, she asked, "Did

you know your wife came here asking to take vows and remain with us permanently?"

"The housekeeper said as much," FitzAlan conceded.

His face colored in a most appealing way. She found herself beginning to like the man. Of course, she had noticed how handsome he was as soon as she laid eyes on him. Taking vows did not affect her eyesight.

"That an annulment could even be considered now suggests"—she paused deliberately—"relations are not as they should be between you."

The young man choked and appeared to be trying to speak, but she held up her hand. "Of course, Catherine's coming here in the middle of the night with only an elderly man as escort was quite sufficient to tell me that."

FitzAlan looked mortified, another hopeful sign. By now, he probably realized his wife had related more of his behavior the night before than he would wish.

"I know I frightened her," he confessed readily enough. "But I swear to you, I would never harm her."

"I do not speak plainly to embarrass you, Lord Fitz-Alan." It was only a partial falsehood. As it was in service of a worthy purpose, God would forgive her. "I have known Lady Catherine since she was a babe. Perhaps I can help you understand her."

"I would be most appreciative, Lady Abbess," Fitz-Alan said with a touch of desperation in his eyes.

"I understand you have been patient with Catherine." Giving him a pointed look, she added, "For the most part." It would not be wise to be too soft on the young man.

"I am not sure how much you know of her marriage to Rayburn." She could barely say that horrid man's name without spitting. "If Catherine's mother had been alive, she would have been able to guide Catherine's father and the king in choosing a better man to serve their purposes. Without her good influence, they chose a perfectly loathsome man who mistreated Catherine horribly.

"I, for one, was not surprised when Rayburn turned against the king." The abbess hoped she did not sound as if she thought the king deserved to suffer for his bad choice, though she did.

"Catherine got her loveliness from her mother." She sighed. "Before Rayburn, she had something more—a radiance about her, a light in her eyes. He took that from her."

She was frustrated at not being able to describe it more clearly, but FitzAlan nodded as though he understood.

"I counsel more patience. Give her time to trust you, and she will be a good wife to you."

"I want her to be content with me," FitzAlan said, "for the sake of our children, as much as for me."

Abbess Talcott sensed from the way he said this that he wanted something for his children he had not had himself. Aye, she was pleased with him. Very pleased, indeed.

"If you can bring that spark back into her eyes, I promise she will bring you joy—and many children." She hoped she had not winked at him, but old habits die hard.

"My wife's coming here could have caused difficulties for you and the abbey," FitzAlan said. "I apologize for that."

The abbess nodded. "I could not have allowed her to remain here. In her haste, Catherine forgot the king gave her but two choices—and one of them was not joining a nunnery."

The abbess signaled to Sister Matilde, who rose immediately and went to speak to someone just outside the door.

A few moments later, they heard light footsteps coming up the stairs. FitzAlan got to his feet, but the abbess signaled for him to wait where he was. She stepped outside the open door and met Catherine at the top of the stairs.

"Tell me," she asked in a low voice as she took Catherine's hands, "have you decided to comply with your marriage vows and go with your husband?"

Catherine nodded, her eyes cast down.

"Surely, it is God's will that you do."

Though FitzAlan was only a few yards away, Catherine did not even glance in his direction.

"Your new husband seems to be an honorable man who cares for your happiness. A woman cannot ask for more." His fine looks were certainly an added blessing, but the abbess did not say this aloud.

She embraced Catherine and took the opportunity to whisper in her ear. "I will soon learn what message the emissaries from the French court have brought to Owain Glyndwr."

"You will send me news when you have it?" Catherine whispered back.

"Aye." The abbess released her and said, "God bless you both."

She turned and went down the stairs with Sister Matilde, leaving Catherine alone to face her husband.

Catherine clasped her hands together to control their shaking and entered the parlor. Unable to look into her husband's face, she fixed her eyes on his boots and walked across the room to him. She'd practiced her apology in the chapel. But when she opened her mouth to give it, her throat closed.

William's face was suddenly in her line of vision. The saints have mercy, he'd dropped to his knee before her. She could not read the deep emotion in his amber eyes, but she could not look away if she tried.

"I apologize for frightening you last night," he said, enfolding her clasped hands in his. "I should not have come to you drunk...and...in that manner."

The apology was so unexpected that she could think of no reply.

"But you did not need to leave," he said more forcefully. "You had only to speak to make me stop." A look of unease flitted across his face. "In sooth, you might have had to shout, but I did not intend to hurt you."

Unsure what he expected of her, she murmured, "Thank you."

"I have come to take you back, but I will give you my promise." He spoke his next words slowly and deliberately, his eyes never leaving her face. "I swear to you, Mary Catherine FitzAlan, I will never harm you."

His apology and promise made, he rose to his feet and said, "That is not to say I think you are without fault in this."

Catherine felt her face color, thinking of her refusal to come willingly to the marriage bed. "I am most sorry for my failures, m'lord husband," she stammered. "I intended to ask your forgiveness as soon as I came in."

"You broke your word to me." He loomed over her, his fists clenched, his voice sharp with anger. "You agreed to tell no one our marriage was not consummated. Now

I find you've told Abbess Talcott as well as the house-keeper."

"I am sorry," she said, surprised to learn this was what he was most angry about. "In my fright, I forgot my promise."

"You may as well have announced it in the hall," he said, raising his voice and spreading his arms wide. "Everyone you did not tell outright will know it when they hear you came here seeking *an annulment*!"

After a few moments of silence, he took a deep breath and ran his hands through his hair.

"We shall return at once," he said, his voice deadly calm now. "You will not leave Ross Castle without my permission again."

She nodded her agreement. Obediently, she took his proffered hand, but he made no move toward the door.

"You will keep your word to me in the future," he said, fixing her with a look that was as hard as granite. His words were both a demand and a warning. "I cannot abide deceit."

———

Catherine averted her eyes as William marched her past the half-dozen men waiting with their horses in the court-yard. He headed straight for Jacob, who stood alone a few yards away from the others.

"You should not have been party to this foolishness," William said, tapping a menacing forefinger on Jacob's chest. "You took a great chance with my wife and Jamie, traveling alone at night as you did. You and I shall come to an understanding, or you shall not remain in my ser-vice. The men at the gate who let you pass shall answer to me as well."

Catherine appreciated that William gave the reprimand out of the other men's hearing. She understood, too, why he said it in front of her. It had been reckless of her to travel with only the old man for protection. Old Jacob would do anything she asked, and she had taken advantage of that.

Hearing Jamie's shout, she turned around to see him break loose from the novice's hand and run across the courtyard toward them. Instead of coming to her, he barreled into William. He shrieked with pleasure as William caught him. Reminded of Abbess Talcott's reproof to be grateful for William's kindness toward her son, she felt ashamed.

William put the boy on Jacob's horse, gruffly telling the old man to take care with him. It was a sign Jacob would be forgiven. Catherine made herself turn to acknowledge the other men. None would meet her eyes. Forgiveness would not come so easily for her.

The ride back to Ross Castle was long and silent, broken only by Jamie's occasional question and Jacob's murmured reply. After a time, even Jamie picked up the somber mood and grew quiet. Finally, Ross Castle came into sight. The ordeal was almost over.

As soon as they were within the protective watch of the sentries on the walls, William sent the others ahead.

"There is something I must ask you," he said to her.

William lifted her down from her horse. He took her elbow and began walking with her, slowly and without direction. The ground was rough, and she had to watch her step.

Suddenly, he stopped and pulled her around to face him. "I want to know the nature of your relationship with the prince."

She raised her eyebrows in surprise. "What is it you wish to know?"

"I can think of no other way to say it, except bluntly." William looked off in the distance and then back at her, as if expecting her to discern his question without his asking it.

When she continued to look at him blankly, he said in a strained voice, "I must know if you have lain with him yet."

She did not immediately respond, because she simply *could not*.

"If you have," he said in a gruff voice, "it must stop."

Her hand went to her mouth, and she stepped back from him. "You would say such a thing to me!" she said, torn between shock and outrage. It was unthinkable. She turned on her heel to walk away from him, but he grabbed her arm.

"You betrayed your first husband while you shared his bed—a favor you have yet to grant me." His voice was caustic. "Why should I believe you would not betray me as well?"

Before now, the intensity of his desire for her had so overwhelmed her that she had failed to perceive the depth of his distrust of her. Why had he chosen to marry her?

"I see what you think of my character, husband," she said, spitting out the word *husband*. "But how could you believe it of Harry? He is selfless and righteous and honorable." She was ranting now, and she did not care whether her defense of Harry was helping her case or not. "How could you think he would be a guest in your home and bed your wife?"

She jerked her arm from his grasp but remained facing him, defiant and angry.

"If you have not yet acted upon what is between you," he said, his eyes spitting fire, "then I am telling you now that you shall not."

She slapped him so hard that the stinging of her hand brought tears to her eyes. Seeing her handprint on his face brought visions of the marks Rayburn had left on her.

She covered her face and crumpled to the ground. She was both startled by her own uncontrolled rage and humiliated by William's accusations.

The future seemed very bleak, indeed.

Eventually her raging emotions receded, leaving a heavy tiredness that weighed down every bone and muscle. William knelt beside her, but she did not look at him. Staring, unseeing, into the distance, she made one last attempt to make him understand the impossibility of what he was suggesting.

"Harry does not think of me that way," she said. "He is like a younger brother to me and I an older sister to him."

William put his hands on either side of her face, forcing her to look at him. "My mother gave herself to whomever she pleased, regardless of the consequences to anyone else. I will not tolerate such behavior in my wife.

"We must have this understood between us." His eyes held hers with a burning intensity. "I will not share my wife with another man, whether he be prince or king or commoner. I keep what is mine."

As they remounted their horses and rode in silence to the gate, Catherine was grateful he had not asked the one question she could not answer honestly. She had one secret she would keep from him, no matter what his threats or her promises.

One secret she would never tell.

Chapter Nine

The tension was thick at the table. News of her flight had spread through the castle—and likely to everyone in the village below as well. William's men were restless. The servants gave her worried looks as they carried in jugs of wine and heaping trays of food. Beside her, William was as silent as the grave.

As soon as the interminable meal ended, Catherine made her escape.

"Jamie, come with me," she said, taking his hand. "I will tell you tales of King Arthur before you sleep." They were his favorites, so she knew he would not argue.

She sat beside Jamie on his bed and recited every Camelot story she knew. When she could no longer justify keeping him awake, she made him say his prayers and kissed him. With a nod to the nursemaid, she slipped out.

Jamie had slept in her bedchamber until Rayburn came home unexpectedly one night. That was the only time Jamie saw Rayburn hit her, but he was so upset by it she did not risk it again. The next day, she settled him into his own chamber on the floor above.

Her feet dragged as she went down the stairs. Knowing what she must do did not make doing it any easier. When did she become such a coward? William was not like Rayburn. As furious as he was with her today, he did not strike her. He might punish her by keeping her under lock and key, but his sense of honor would not permit him to physically harm her.

Perhaps sharing his bed would be no worse than unpleasant. Women all over England submitted to their husbands; most seemed none the worse for it. Aye, she would hope for the best.

Her maid was waiting for her in her bedchamber. "You may go now, Mary," she said after the woman had helped her out of her gown and into her night shift. "I shall not need you until morning."

Mary smiled and raised an eyebrow. "Of course, m'lady."

There were few secrets one could keep from one's maid.

"Tell Thomas he will not be needed either." Covering her embarrassment as best she could, she said, "I shall help my husband prepare for bed tonight."

The look of approval on Mary's face did not make Catherine feel any better.

Once she was alone, she went into William's bedchamber. She stood uncertainly before the bed. Remembering William liked her hair down, she loosened it from the braid the maid had just made and climbed up the step to the bed.

———

William sighed as he made his way up the stairs. Catherine had been as nervous as a cat at supper. Then she left in such haste, he could have no hope she would come to him tonight. Though he forced her to return, she did seem to accept she must fulfill her marriage vows to him.

If he had any reason to believe it would be tonight, he would be running up these stairs.

Making her so angry had not helped, of course. He was now inclined to believe her relationship with the prince was yet innocent. Still, he was glad he made it clear to her he would not tolerate infidelity. He knew from experience how lightly many noblewomen took their marriage vows.

He was not ready to face his empty bed, so he continued up the stairs to the upper floor. When he stepped into Jamie's chamber, he nodded to the startled nursemaid who sat in the corner stitching.

He watched the boy's face in the lamplight. Jamie, who was always in motion when awake, had the face of a cherub in the peace of sleep. The sweetness of his expression made William think of his brother John at that age. William had not been allowed to visit his mother's home often. But when he came, it was to see John.

"God protect you," he said, touching the top of the boy's head.

Having no more excuse for delay, he trudged down the stairs to his and Catherine's rooms. He gave yet another heavy sigh when he saw no light under her door. For the hundredth time that day, he reminded himself of the abbess's advice. He must give Catherine time to trust him.

Where was Thomas? God's beard, the man did not even light a lamp for him. Further punishment for his sins—as if he needed to be chastised by his manservant.

He felt his way in the dark to the table and lit the lamp.

He yawned and stretched his arms wide as he turned toward the bed.

Catherine. Catherine was in his bed.

In three heartbeats, he went from dumbstruck to breathless. She was stunning, with her fair hair spilling over his pillow like a river of moonbeams. It was a long moment before he thought to drop his arms.

"You have come to me," he said, not quite believing it.

She clutched the bedclothes to her chin and nodded.

Now that she was here, he could show her she had nothing to fear in his bed. He uncurled her hand from the coverlet and pressed it to his lips.

"It pleases me very much that you are here." He squeezed her icy fingers to reassure her and kissed her cheek. "I will give you no cause to regret it."

He undressed quickly, dropping his clothes on the floor before lifting the bedclothes. Ignoring her sharp intake of breath, he slid in beside her.

She was wearing her tunic, but that meant he would have the pleasure of taking it off. He tentatively placed his hand on the flat of her stomach. Imagining the feel of the smooth skin beneath the cloth, he closed his eyes. He was determined to go slowly and not frighten her. But he wanted her so badly that would not be easy.

He had wanted her for such a long, long time.

"Turn toward me. I want to look into your face."

As she turned, his hand slid from her stomach to the dip of her waist. He smiled at her. He hoped his eyes did not have a predatory gleam. But he thought they might.

He held her eyes as he ran his hand up her side to the tantalizing swell of the side of her breast. Gritting his teeth, he reminded himself to go slow. He moved his hand back to her waist, then over the curve of her hip and down her thigh.

He was as tight as a bowstring.

His only thought now was that he had to touch her skin. He tugged at her tunic, but it was caught beneath her.

"Help me." He heard the desperate, pleading note to his voice, but he didn't care.

She rolled onto her back and lifted her hips, the saints be praised. Without touching her, he drew the shift up to her waist. His heart pounded in his ears. She lifted her shoulders and raised her arms as he eased it up and over her head. His hand shook as he reached to touch her. Then he shut his eyes, his whole being focused on the silky softness of her skin.

Repeating his earlier journey, he slid his hand along her side with exquisite slowness. When he brushed the still softer skin of the side of her breast, his breath caught. How long he had waited to touch her. No other woman felt this good.

In a daze of desire, he kissed her face, her hair, her neck. Against her ear, he murmured, "I have dreamed of this."

He pulled back to look at her again. Good Lord, she had her eyes squeezed shut and her arms clenched in front of her breasts. He pried one hand free and held it.

"What is it?" he asked as he looked at her across the pillow.

She did not speak or move. He pressed her hand against his cheek and turned to kiss her palm.

When she opened her eyes, he asked again, "What is wrong?"

Her eyes were wide, her lips parted. She seemed to

have trouble finding her voice. "I did not know what to expect. Since you were ready at once, I...I thought it would be over quickly."

William guffawed. So, she had taken a good look at him as he climbed naked into bed.

Grinning, he pulled her into his arms and buried his face in her neck. "You have good cause to fear I will be much too quick this first time."

Her naked body felt glorious against him. As he moved his mouth down the curve of her neck, he whispered, "I promise I shall do better the second time. And still better the third."

He was lost in the feel of her. Her breasts against his chest, her legs against his thighs. And, oh yes, her stomach against the length of his erection.

"I have longed for this," he murmured, breathing in the scent of her skin. How could a woman smell this good?

It was no longer enough to feel her breasts against his chest; he had to touch them. The sensation of her breasts filling his hands was heaven itself. He trailed kisses down her throat to her breastbone. He turned his head to feel the softness of her skin against his cheek. The wild beating of her heart matched his own.

He kept one breast cupped in his hand as he dragged his tongue across to the other. When he reached her nipple and flicked it with his tongue, she squeaked. He smiled.

Intent on claiming every inch of her, he eased himself down her body. He ran his tongue along the undersides of her breasts and planted slow wet kisses across her flat belly. He fought the temptation to move farther down and taste her. Though the thought made his cock throb, he did not want to shock her. All things in good time.

Still he toyed with the temptation. He grazed the silky skin of her inner thigh with his fingertips as he kissed the inside of her knee. So close. Before he knew what he was doing, his hand was gripping her buttock and his mouth was where his fingers had been and was moving upward.

All he wanted in this life was to taste her and then drive into her until her screams rang in his ears.

He got up on his hands and knees and shook his head.

He looked down at her breasts and sighed. How long he'd waited to see them. To touch them. He gave each nipple a light kiss, then wanted more. When he took the tip of one in his mouth and sucked, he was rewarded by her sharp intake of breath. He slid down to feel her body beneath him. She felt so good against his chest, his thighs, his shaft. All the while, he sucked her breast harder, losing himself in the sensation.

The urge to enter her was almost more than he could bear. Perhaps if she'd not kept him on edge every minute of the last week, he would not be so close to losing all control. He lifted his head and, breathing hard, tried to calm himself.

Dragging his gaze up from her breasts, he saw her perfect mouth. How had he missed kissing it? He desperately needed her kisses—deep, deep kisses—before he entered her. As he slid up her body to take her mouth, the sensation of skin rubbing against skin set his every nerve tingling.

She opened her legs as he moved, and he gasped as he unexpectedly found himself at the threshold. With all his being, he wanted to keep moving until he was deep inside her. One strong thrust. The urge almost overpowered him. And yet, he held back. He wanted her mouth on his first.

"Kate," he moaned as he lowered his mouth to hers.

He anticipated a warm joining of mouths and tongues as a prelude to the joining of their bodies. But she kept her lips firmly together. Something was wrong, terribly wrong. But he was sliding into her now. It was too late. He could not stop. The urge overwhelmed him, taking over his body. His mind was one with his body, set on the same goal.

He had to have her. He had to have her now.

At last. At last. At last.

He came in an explosion of pent-up lust and longing, hunger and desire. She was his. She was his.

When he was able to move, he rolled to his side, taking her with him. He had not performed with such speed since his youth. Happy, but a little embarrassed, he held her close and kissed her face and hair.

"Sorry, Kate," he whispered, and kissed the tip of her nose. "I shall go slower next time."

"Slower?" she asked in a startled voice. She did not sound grateful for his good intentions.

He leaned up on one elbow to see her better, but he could not read her expression in the dim lamplight. Gently, he smoothed back her hair.

He hated to ask, but he had to know. "Did I hurt you?"

She shook her head and said in a soft voice, "It did not hurt at all this time."

"It hurt you before? With Rayburn?" He did not want to remember that she had belonged to another man and disliked even more having to mention the man's name here in his own bed.

Catherine tried to turn her head away, but he would not let her.

He rested his forehead lightly against hers and asked, "Did he never give you pleasure in bed?"

She drew her brows together.

This was worse than he had thought. He sighed and lay back down beside her. Perhaps he should have expected this. But he had not. In his vanity, he had never doubted that once he had her in bed, she would enjoy it.

He had heard, of course, of wives who considered going to their husbands' beds a duty to be suffered, an obligation necessary to meet their husbands' vulgar needs and produce heirs. All of his own experience, however, was with women who came to his bed for pleasure. They sought him out and returned for more.

His wife's voice brought him back abruptly to the present.

"May I go to my chamber now?"

"You are welcome to sleep here." He hoped she would.

"I am sure I could not sleep," she said, her brows going up in surprise. "And Jamie would not know where to find me. He has bad dreams sometimes."

"If you do not wish to stay tonight, I will not insist upon it," he said, still hoping she would change her mind.

Her foot was on the step beside the bed almost before the words left his mouth.

"Catherine," he said, grabbing her arm to delay her escape, "you have a husband now who wants you in his bed. You must tell Jamie he can find you here when you are not in your own bed."

As she raced out the door, he called after her, "But teach the boy to knock."

———

The succeeding nights were no better.

He told himself he would not take her if she did not

also want him. But each night he did. As he moved inside her, he would close his eyes and think of the other Catherine. The girl who threw her head back laughing and reached for the stars.

She came to him each night without his asking. She told him she prayed daily for another child. Though he knew he did not take her against her will, he felt shamed by what he did. Each encounter left him feeling emptier than before.

Though she denied him nothing, she rejected him wholly. When she left his bed, as she always did, he told himself he hoped she would not return the next night.

But in his heart, he knew if Catherine did not come to him, he would go to her. He knew better than to want something from a woman she could not give. And yet he could not stop himself from wanting more from Catherine.

Other men kept mistresses. There were plenty of women who would gladly fill that role for him. Beautiful women. Eager women.

But he wanted no woman but Catherine.

Chapter Ten

Catherine could let her guard down, knowing she would not run into William as she went about her tasks. Early this morning, he received a report of raiders crossing the border and took a group of men to flush them out.

He seemed grateful for a reason to be away.

She met with Alys as usual. She approved the housekeeper's plan to send the household servants to do a thorough cleaning of the gatehouse while most of the men were out of the way. Next, she spoke with the cook. She wanted a hearty supper prepared for the men when they returned this evening.

At midmorning, she sent Jamie off with his nursemaid and settled herself gratefully into the quiet solitude of the solar with her embroidery. She felt confused and on edge. William's behavior bewildered her. When he looked at her with that weary sadness, she found herself wishing for the burning looks he used to give her.

She perceived she was somehow the source of his wretchedness. But how had she failed him? She had every reason to hope he would get her with child soon. She went to his bed every night. It was not nearly as bad as she had expected. In sooth, she'd grown to like the way he kissed her face and hair... and some of the other things he did as well. Most of it was so unsettling, though, that she found it difficult to sleep afterward.

If only she had another woman to talk to! Her mother had said little about what went on between man and wife in the bedchamber beyond vague allusions to duty and perseverance. She had no sisters, no close female cousins. The only person she might have such a conversation with—though she blushed at the thought—was Abbess Talcott.

'Twas unlikely, however, that William would approve of a visit to the abbey any time soon.

She was startled from her thoughts by the crash of the solar door against the wall. Looking up, she was astonished to see Edmund Forrester filling her doorway.

"There you are!" He said it as though he'd caught her someplace she should not be. "I've been looking for you."

She could smell the strong wine on him from across the room.

"The servants know where I am," she said with a calmness she did not feel. "Any one of them could have brought a message to me."

He did not respond to her subtle reprimand for entering the family's private living quarters without invitation. Instead, he stared at her in a way that made her glad for the heavy table between them.

"What is it that you need, sir?"

With the household servants all working at the gatehouse, no one would hear her if she screamed. She chided herself for letting her imagination get away with her. She'd never felt easy with Edmund, but she had no reason to fear him.

She set down the embroidery frame she was clutching to her chest and posed her question again. "What is it that I may do for you?"

He turned and shut the door. She jumped at the sound of the bolt sliding home. Before she could gather her wits to look for something to use as a weapon, he pulled up a stool and sat across the table from her.

"There are any number of things you could do for me," he said with a broad smile. "But as you are my best friend's wife, I will not suggest them."

She fought the urge to wipe her damp palms on her skirts. She would not give him the satisfaction of seeing how frightened she was.

"I presume I have permission to use your given name?" he asked with false politeness.

She glared at him. "You do not."

"*Catherine.*" He drilled his fingers on the table, quite aware, she was sure, of the effect on her taut nerves. "You made a fool of William, claiming you could have an annulment a full week after your wedding night."

"How dare you speak to me of this?" she said, gripping the sides of her chair. "Leave my rooms at once."

"Everyone thought William unable to perform his husbandly duty." Edmund leaned forward and gave her a long, penetrating look. "But we know better, don't we, Catherine?"

Catherine folded her arms and fumed in silence, waiting for him to have his say and leave.

"You should have seen the ladies at court!" he said, leaning back and slapping the table. "I swear, the widows gave him no peace. Poor William developed the skills of a diplomat trying to keep the women with living husbands out of his bed."

Edmund dropped his smile and tapped his finger on the table. "If an annulment was yet possible, the defect was not William's."

Despite herself, her face flushed hot.

"At first, I did not believe it possible he had not taken his rights as a husband," Edmund said, rubbing his chin. "And yet, it explained much. He'd been on edge and foul-tempered ever since the wedding."

He narrowed his eyes at her. "How did you convince him not to touch you? Did you claim disease?"

Catherine stood, so angry now she was shaking. Putting her hands on the table for support, she leaned across it to make her own threat. "I shall tell my husband how you have spoken to me. I suggest you take yourself some distance from the castle when I do."

Edmund grabbed her wrist and held it. "Who do you think William will believe?" With his other hand, he slowly ran his finger up the length of her forearm. "A woman who deceived her first husband and sent him to his death? Or his best friend?"

When her gaze wavered, he said, "You may as well sit, for we are not yet done with our talk."

"If you leave marks on me," she said, looking pointedly at where he held her wrist, "William just may believe me."

When he released his grip, she hugged her arms to herself and sank back into her chair.

"I know he beds you now."

Her face grew hot again as she imagined the servants whispering each night she sent her maid away. It would be easy for Edmund to learn of it, if he had a mind to.

"Even William, tolerant as he seems to be of your

antics, would not risk having all the Marches laughing at him a second time."

She tried not to listen, tried to keep from hearing the offensive things he was saying to her. Surely he could not go on much longer.

"How is it, then," he said, his tone shifting from mocking amusement to accusation, "that William is even more miserable than before?"

She was stunned. How could Edmund be asking her the very question that troubled her?

She met his eyes without flinching and pointed to the door. "I will tolerate your insolence no longer. Get out."

Once again, he acted as though she had not spoken.

"Your husband was happy for an excuse to leave today," he said, raising his eyebrows. "Rumor of a few ragged men crossing the border was not sufficient cause for William to lead the party himself—unless he wanted badly to be gone."

The words stung and Edmund saw it.

"I have my suspicions as to the reason for William's misery," he said, watching her closely. "I wager you are as cold as stone in bed."

Cold?

"God's beard, that is it!" he said, slapping the table. He shook his head and gave a short laugh. "'Tis not enough for William to have a wife so beautiful that all the men lust after her. Nay, our William must have her warm and willing, too."

Edmund leaned forward, his humor gone. "You will never make him happy," he said, his eyes burning into her. "Leave before it is too late, before he gets you with child. You need a better plan this time. I can help you."

Catherine was stunned again. Edmund was sincere. In

his own way, he was trying to protect his friend. But from what? From her?

"William wants me to stay," she stammered. "I promised him I would not leave again."

"As if a promise matters to you!" he said, pounding the table. "William is not the first fool to trust you. Is destroying one husband not enough for you?"

His words were so harsh she felt as if he'd slapped her. It was useless to argue Rayburn deserved neither honesty nor loyalty.

"I'll not sit by while you bring William down," he said, shaking a finger at her. "Know I have my eye on you. Be warned, I will discover your secrets."

"I have no secrets." *At least none you will ever find out.*

Edmund barked a laugh and leaned back in his chair, his mood changing once again. "Perhaps another woman will divert him in time. If William wants a woman who takes pleasure in bed, there are many to oblige him."

She looked up, unable to hide the question in her eyes.

"Not yet, but he is bound to," he said with a grim smile. "If he gets another woman with child now that he is wed to you, he will hate himself. And he'll not forgive you for driving him to it. William wants no bastards."

In her mind's eye, she saw William as he was on that first night, his eyes burning with ferocious intensity. *I want children, and I will have them only with my wife.*

She lifted her chin. "No man hopes for children outside of marriage."

A look of surprise crossed his face, then shifted to smug satisfaction. He stood and leaned over the table.

"You do not know, do you, Catherine?" he said, a mocking smile on his face.

She glared up at him, refusing to ask what he meant.

"William has not told you who his father is, has he?"

" 'Tis FitzAlan," she blurted out, "is it not?"

"If William has not told you who his true father is, then he has told you nothing that matters." He shook his head. "I feared lust had blinded his good judgment, but I was wrong. He trusts you not at all."

Edmund went to the door, then turned to give her his parting words. " 'Tis an open secret who his father is," he said. "You must be the only one in the realm who does not know it."

———

Hours later, Catherine was still angry and upset about the encounter with Edmund as she sat in the kitchen garden watching Jamie. He was following a kitchen maid from plant to plant, asking questions as the girl gathered herbs.

How dare Edmund corner her and speak to her like that! She tried not to think about what he actually said. The hateful man. But she could not help it. Who was William's father? If all of England and Scotland knew, why would he keep it secret from her?

Jamie grew bored with the herbs and hopped around pretending to be a bunny. When he tired of that, he came over and tugged at her arm.

"Can we go up?" he said, pointing to the top of the wall. "Please?"

He wanted her to take him up to the walkway that ran along the top of the wall. Her spirits lifted at the suggestion. The weather was glorious, and the view of the Wye River curving through the lush green hills was breathtaking from up there.

"You must promise not to let go of my hand this time," she told him sternly. "Otherwise, I shall not take you."

As soon as they were up on the walkway, she felt herself relax. The light breeze and the late afternoon sun felt good on her skin. She could not remember a lovelier day.

She undid the circlet and net that held her hair and carefully set them on a low square of the crenellated wall. A married woman was required to keep her hair covered, but there was no one to see her. The men patrolling the wall were on the far side of the castle, near the gatehouse. William and the other men were not expected before dark.

It had been years since she felt the wind blow her hair. The sense of freedom it gave her made her want to sing with joy.

"Your hair looks pretty," Jamie said, beaming up at her.

She lifted him up and kissed him soundly.

They walked first along the south wall, facing the river. They took their time, stopping to look at birds and watch the peasants toiling in the fields. When they reached the west wall, the sun was low on the horizon over the hills. It cast a warm glow on the stone walls and the fields below.

She lifted Jamie onto a low part of the wall for a better look.

"There they are!" Jamie shouted.

She squinted against the sun and saw the line of men riding toward the castle. She could pick out William, riding at the front. As she watched, the riders veered from the path and rode across the field toward them.

Jamie waved and several of the men waved back.

What could be drawing them to this spot? As the men pulled their horses up below her, she leaned over the wall as far as she dared. She brushed away the hair blowing across her face. Then her eyes locked with William's. The burn of his gaze seared through her.

Her hair! She jumped back. Without a headdress, she felt exposed, half naked. She grabbed Jamie and ran to the closest set of steps down the wall. If she hurried, she could be inside the keep before the men rode through the gates.

~

A quarter hour after William saw her on the wall, Catherine arrived in the hall to greet him. Her color was high, and she was breathless from running.

The eyes of every man were on her as she swept across the room toward him. William was too spellbound himself to chastise his men for staring at her. As one, he and his men tried and failed to keep from staring at the rise and fall of her chest in the close-fitting gown.

The elaborate azure headdress made her eyes look a startling blue and emphasized her long, graceful neck. Though not a lock of hair showed, the image of her above him on the wall was seared into his mind. With her long tresses blowing about her, she'd looked like a fairy queen sent to enchant them. He suspected every man with him imagined the pale gold waves falling over naked shoulders and breasts.

But he was the only man who would see her like that.

"I am glad to see you home safe, husband," she said, dipping her head in greeting.

A slow smile spread across his face as he lifted her hand to his lips. "And I am glad to be home."

Chapter Eleven

After sending hot water up to William's chamber, Catherine went to the kitchen to make certain all was in order. The cook had everything well in hand, of course, but Catherine needed to keep busy.

She touched her headdress to be sure it was in place as she returned to the hall for supper. At least William did not chastise her in front of his men, as Rayburn would have. She smiled to herself, recalling the warmth in William's eyes when he kissed her hand. Perhaps he was not too angry with her.

At supper, she listened with half an ear to the men's talk of their fruitless search for rebels. Edmund's harsh words plagued her. What if he was right? Was it possible William was unhappy with what took place between them in the bedchamber?

What could be wrong? She had every reason to hope he would get her with child soon. William was able to perform each time. And he wanted to do it. Over and over.

He did seem to dawdle. Perhaps that was a sign of trouble. It made it harder and harder for her to keep her mind on something else. She sighed, at a loss.

The platters were not yet cleared from the table when William stood and announced he was tired and would retire. The men exchanged glances, and one or two smothered a laugh. They stopped when she looked at them sharply, trying to discern the source of their amusement.

When her gaze met Edmund's, he tapped his finger next to his eye as if to remind her he was watching her. Hateful, hateful man. Then he dropped his gaze to her chest and lifted his eyebrow, just to annoy her. She put her hand over her chest and glared at him.

"Catherine?" William was holding his hand out to her.

She took it, glad to leave. She'd rather be lectured about having her hair uncovered than remain in the same room with Edmund.

She had trouble keeping up with William's pace. He was not as tired as he claimed. As soon as they reached their rooms, he shouted at the maid to leave and pulled her into his bedchamber.

Belatedly, she realized he did not bring her upstairs to lecture her about headdresses.

He barred the door, which made her feel anxious and trapped. Though he made no move to touch her, her heart was racing.

"You looked so beautiful up on the wall, with your hair flying in the wind," he said in a wistful voice. "It was just like when—"

He stopped himself and did not finish the thought aloud. After a moment, he said, "'Twas nice to have a wife to greet me when I came home. It is new to me."

His kind words and soft voice calmed her a bit. He stepped closer but still did not touch her. She had the disconcerting feeling that he was waiting for her, that he wanted her to do something.

"I want to be a good wife to you," she stammered. "I beg your pardon. I should not have been outside with my hair down like a young girl."

He put his hands on her shoulders. His breath was warm on her ear as he leaned down to whisper, "Take it down for me now."

She swallowed. "Unless you want me to call my maid, you will have to help me with the pins in the back."

He spun her around. With a deftness that showed experience she did not want to think about, he had the headdress off in no time. He shook her hair loose with his fingers; it felt good to have it down again. As he massaged her scalp, she closed her eyes. A small sigh escaped her.

She was helpless to unfasten the long row of buttons at the back of her close-fitting gown, so he did that, too. Though she assured him she could manage the rest alone, he continued to help her undress. When the last garment came off, she sidestepped out of his reach and slipped under the bedclothes.

She watched surreptitiously as he removed his own clothes. Except for his arousal—which she tried not to look at—he was quite beautiful. She liked the strong planes of his face; the long lines of his lean, muscled body; his large, capable hands. In the lamplight, the hair on his head and chest glinted gold and red.

As he slid into bed, she wondered if it was possible to ever get used to the feel of a naked man beside her, the tingly feeling of skin touching skin from head to foot. He pulled her into his arms and let her rest there, her head against his chest. She loved this part. She could lie with him like this forever.

She sighed—and immediately wished she had not. William took it as a sign he should begin what they were here for.

Damn that Edmund. It was so confusing! She let William touch her in all the ways he wanted. She refused him nothing. Yet, tonight she felt a tension, an expectation. William wanted something from her, but she did not know what it was.

William rolled on top of her, his weight on his elbows, and began kissing her face and neck. The warmth of his mouth and breath felt good on her skin. Should she tell him? But she remembered Rayburn slapping her so hard she saw stars when she had interrupted his efforts. And so she kept quiet.

"I cannot do it!" William said, pounding his fists against the mattress. Abruptly, he rolled off her.

Her shock was so great that at first she could do nothing. After a few moments of tense silence, she raised herself onto her elbow to look at him. He lay with his arms crossed over his face, as if warding off an attacker.

"William?" She touched his arm with her fingertip.

He rolled away from her and pounded his fist against the mattress again.

God help her, what could she have done to cause him to behave like this?

Sitting up, she gripped his shoulder and shook him. "William, what is it? What have I done?"

When he still did not answer, she used all her weight to pull him onto his back to face her.

"You must tell me, please," she pleaded, but he kept his

arms over his face, unable or unwilling to speak to her. "Whatever it is, I am sorry with all my heart."

She ran her fingers over the side of his face, but he rolled away from her again. Pressing herself against his back, she rubbed her hands up and down his sides and kissed his neck and shoulders, attempting to comfort him. Still, he made no response. Desperate, she crawled over him and wriggled under his arm until she was burrowed against his chest.

She put her arm around his waist and patted his back. "It is all right. I am here," she murmured, just as she would with Jamie.

He took a long shuddering breath. She felt the tension of his muscles ease beneath her hands.

"I do not know why I displease you so much," she said against his chest. "You must tell me what I can do to remedy it."

William put his hand to her cheek and gave her a small smile that eased her heart. "I have wanted you to put your arms around me, and it feels as good as I imagined."

She blinked at him. "Is that all you require?"

"Nay, 'tis not all, but it is a start." His smile was slightly wider now.

"What else?"

"I want you to kiss me."

This, too, seemed a fairly simple task. She touched her lips to his, then looked at him expectantly.

"That is nice, but not quite what I want. Will you let me teach you how lovers kiss?" His smile had reached his eyes and was positively wicked now.

Her confidence faltered. She felt out of her depth, but she nodded. She wanted to please him.

His lips were soft and warm, and he kept them on hers for a long time. When she thought he was finally finished, he ran his tongue across her bottom lip. It was hard to breathe, and she opened her mouth. When he slipped his tongue inside, she gasped.

The next time, she knew what to expect and opened her mouth to him. She had trouble thinking of anything except the kiss this time, though it went on even longer.

He pulled back to look into her eyes. "I don't want you to leave me this time."

She swallowed back the surge of hurt rising from her chest. Why would he bring that up now? She dropped her gaze to his chest and said, "I promised you I would not run away again."

"That is not what I mean." With a sigh, he pushed a strand of hair from her forehead. "When I take you to bed, you let me have your body, but your mind and spirit are elsewhere."

He lifted her chin with his finger. "I do not want to have you like that anymore, Kate. I want you with me. All of you."

Her breath caught as she finally understood what he wanted. She was not at all sure she could do what he asked.

"I had to, with Rayburn," she protested. "I had to. There would have been nothing left of me." A tear slipped from the corner of her eye, and he rubbed it away with his thumb.

"I know," he said, kissing her forehead. "But you have no need to protect yourself from me. You can trust me."

He believed he told her the truth. Resolving to believe it, too, she nodded.

He looked at her thoughtfully. Then, suddenly, he rolled onto his back. Was he giving up on her so soon?

"Sit up, sweetheart."

Feeling uneasy, she did as he asked. She felt embarrassed and exposed—until she saw that his eyes were closed.

"Give me your hand," he said, waving his arm blindly.

Curiosity vied with uncertainty as she gave him her hand. She felt his hot breath on her palm as he pressed it to his lips. Then he took her wrist and laid the flat of her hand on his chest.

"I want you to touch me."

He guided her hand in a slow circular motion over his chest. The feel of the rough hair under her palm sent an unexpected sensation up her arm, right to her stomach. He released his hold and let his arm fall to his side. With his eyes still closed, he lay still, waiting.

Hesitantly, she skimmed her fingertips over his chest. The corners of his mouth turned up. Encouraged, she shifted her weight so that she could use both hands. His breathing grew shallow as she ran her fingers in increasingly wider circles. She explored the textures of his skin, sliding her fingers over the dip below his collarbone, the coarse hair of his chest, the smooth skin at his sides.

Because he relinquished control to her, the urge to escape did not overtake her. In fact, she was surprised to discover she liked touching him. He seemed all golden muscle beneath her hands.

After assuring herself his eyes were still closed, she allowed herself a good look at his member. It was, after all, sticking out right in front of her. She kept her eyes on it as she drew her fingernails from his sides to the center of his belly. His sharp intake of breath startled her, and she looked up at his face.

"Feels good," he said on a long breath.

Feeling more confident, she trailed her fingers over his hip bones, on either side of his shaft. She smiled when he shivered, enjoying the power of her touch.

Leaning over him, she rubbed firm hands up over his chest and shoulders and sent featherlight strokes down his arms. His whispered, "God in heaven," told her what she needed to know.

She kissed his shoulder and was rewarded with a sigh. Pleased, she trailed kisses along his throat and rubbed her cheek against his chest. This time, it was she who sighed. Letting her hair drag over him, she inched her way down toward the flat of his stomach, dropping kisses along the way.

She felt William's hand rest lightly on her head, touching her for the first time since the start. As he ran his fingers through her hair, she rested her head against his hip, enjoying the sensation. Tentatively, she slid her finger over his shaft. He jolted half upright, jostling her head.

She sat up straight and stared at him.

"Sorry," he said, touching her cheek. "I was not expecting it."

Her face hot with embarrassment, she averted her eyes.

"Catherine, please," he said, taking her gently by the shoulders. "I would not have you feel shamed about what we do in bed, not ever. And certainly not for something that felt so good."

He gathered her into his arms and pulled her down to lay beside him. His breath was hot against her skin as he kissed her forehead, the side of her face, her hair. When he sucked on her earlobe and breathed in her ear, she pressed closer against him.

"Here, touch me again," he said, taking her hand.

Before she could pull away, her hand was on his shaft again. Gingerly, she explored the surprisingly silky skin over the firmness underneath. His breathing changed as she ran her hand up and down its length. Breathing a little hard herself, she did it again. And again.

He groaned and pressed his mouth to her neck, sucking against her skin. Her head fell back. Of its own accord, her body moved against his in rhythm with the movement of her hand.

He grabbed her wrist. "No more. I cannot—" He broke off, apparently unable to form more words.

She understood it was not displeasure that made him ask her to stop. If she had had any doubt, the deep kiss he gave her next removed it. She felt herself merging into him as she focused with every part of her being on that kiss, on his tongue sliding in and out of her mouth.

She held on to him as he rolled her on top of him. When she lifted her head to smile at him, her hair fell in a curtain around his face. He kissed the tip of her nose. The feel of his chest against her breasts and the hardness of his shaft against her belly made it difficult to breathe.

She closed her eyes as he stroked his hands up and down her back. When he moved them along the sides of her breasts, she felt it all the way to her center. She let him draw her into another long kiss before she forced herself to pull away.

Rising to her hands and knees above him, she said with mock severity, "I thought I was to do the touching."

Obligingly, he dropped his hands. "Do what you will with me."

She leaned down to run her tongue along his collar-bone and gasped when the tips of her breasts rubbed against his chest. It felt so good she did it again. Slowly this time.

She forgot to reprimand him when large, warm hands covered her breasts. When he rubbed his thumbs over her nipples, the sensation that gripped her was so strong she had to rest her forehead on his chest.

She moaned in complaint when he stopped to lift her higher on the bed. Forgiveness came quickly as she felt the wetness of his tongue circle her nipple. At the same time, he took the other nipple between his thumb and forefin-ger. Her hips swayed as she was drawn into a swirl of sen-sation. When he took her breast in his mouth and sucked, she squeezed her eyes shut against the jolt it sent through her. Nothing, nothing, nothing felt as good as this.

Just when she thought nothing could divert her from the feeling of his mouth on her breast, she felt his fingers sliding up the inside of her thigh. He dragged his fingers up and down, each time coming closer to her center. The rampant sensations racing through her now were more than she could bear.

Her body tensed with anticipation. Closer, closer. When his hand brushed the hair between her legs, a shiver went through her. All her concentration was on willing him to touch her again. When he barely brushed her a sec-ond time, she wanted to pound her fist against the bed in frustration.

Finally, finally, he pressed his fingers to the aching spot. It was as if he had known all along exactly where she needed to be touched and how. Her body began to move against his hand.

He took hold of her hips. Every part of her skin that touched him tingled as he pulled her along his body. He eased her down until the sensitive place he had been rubbing with his hand touched the tip of his shaft.

She stiffened.

"You have trusted me this far," he said, his voice tight, strained. "Trust me for the rest."

Putting his hands on either side of her face, he pulled her into a kiss. Their tongues danced together in a rhythm her body knew. The kiss was wet and hot and not enough. This time when the tip of his shaft touched her, she pressed against it. She wanted to be touched there, to feel him hard against her.

"Do not leave me, Kate," he rasped in her ear. "Do not leave me."

As he slid inside her, she inhaled at the unexpected rush of pleasure. They lay nearly motionless, breathing hard. Her body was tight, tense, aware of every inch of him inside her. He kissed her face and hair. She resisted when he pushed her up by her shoulders, regretting any distance between them.

"You are so beautiful." The strength of the desire in his voice wiped away any awkwardness she felt at finding herself sitting astride him. And the pressure inside her felt so good.

He grasped her hips again. As he showed her how to move, the heat in his eyes almost burned her skin. Soon, her body found its own rhythm, and she was moving helplessly against him.

She leaned over him, needing to kiss him now. The tips

of her breasts brushed against his chest as their mouths joined. She pressed her hips against him as he pushed up against her. Finally, she had to break away to breathe. She leaned back, losing herself wholly to the movement, aware of nothing but the powerful sensations emanating from where their bodies were joined.

"Slower, Kate," he begged. "Slower, please."

But she ignored his plea. The sensations pulsed through her, nearly blinding her. As they overtook her, she fell forward and grabbed on to his shoulders. From a distance, she heard screaming as spasms of pleasure shook her.

"God have mercy!" she said as she collapsed over him.

He folded his arms around her and held her tightly against his chest. When she gasped, "I cannot breathe," he eased his hold and ran his fingers lightly over her back. Her skin was so sensitive that she shivered. Her body spasmed as she realized she could still feel the full length of him deep inside her.

As she listened to his rapid heartbeat against her ear, she tried to piece together what had just happened to her. A wave of embarrassment hit her.

"Was that me screaming?" she asked in a whisper.

With an inarticulate groan, he gripped her shoulders and pressed himself deeper inside her. His answer came in huffs as he thrust against her. "Aye. Aye. Aye."

She pushed herself up to lean against him, arms extended, and moved with him. The ache inside her grew. His need, his urgency became hers. Faster and harder, he slammed against her. She felt it coming again and wanted to beg him not to stop. And then she felt him surge inside her and heard him cry her name. Triumphant, she went over the edge with him.

Catherine felt light-headed from lack of sleep as she lay awake, watching the sleeping form of her husband in the gray light of early dawn. She sighed in contentment. It had been a long and wondrous night.

William taught her the joy that is possible between a man and a woman, the miraculous giving and receiving of pleasure. But she also learned something he did not intend to teach her. Something, she was certain, he did not yet know himself.

"Do not leave me, do not leave me," he whispered each time he was deep inside her.

She sensed the core loneliness in him. She understood his words meant more than that he wanted her fully with him in bed.

This physical pleasure, astonishing as it was, was only the beginning of what he needed from her.

Chapter Twelve

*F*or the first time in his life, William dreaded going to war. He did not want to be away from Catherine for a single night.

For now, King Henry and the prince were busy sweeping up the last remnants of the rebellion in the North. The Welsh had been quiet since their losses at Grosmont and Pwll Melyn in the spring. The lull in the fighting, however, would not last.

Soon, he would be off fighting the Welsh. Perhaps the French as well. Once the fighting began again, he might be gone for weeks. He tried not to think of it.

Still, he worked his men hard to keep their skills sharp so they would be prepared. He had only to catch a glimpse of Catherine, though, to be distracted. If she walked into the hall while he was talking with his men or crossed the bailey yard while they practiced with their weapons, he would stop in place and watch her until she passed from sight.

His men were amused by the change in him. They had always respected him as a sure and talented commander, a skilled fighter, a man who kept his word. But they had never been at ease with him before. Now he laughed at jokes they would never have told him before. They even teased him about the cause of the new lightness in his step.

To a man, they were green with envy when Catherine left the hall on his arm each night. Truth be told, he suspected they were all a little in love with her. Even so, they were all pleased for him.

All, that is, save for Edmund Forrester.

Edmund warned him to watch for the betrayal he was sure would come.

The next weeks passed in a blur of happiness for Catherine. She and William could not wait for night to come. As often as he could, he slipped away for an hour or two in the middle of the day to whisk her off to their rooms.

Jamie adored William and followed him around like a puppy. Every time she heard Jamie squeal with delight as William swung the boy onto his shoulders, she thanked God for her blessings. She would not have dared hope for so much only a few weeks before.

There was just one mar on her happiness: Her husband still did not trust her. Edmund's goading bothered her even more now that she bared her own soul to William every night.

"William, you have never told me about your family or your home in the North," she said as they lay in bed.

They had come to bed early, as had become their habit, and spent themselves making love. The summer evening sky was still light enough for her to see the outline of his strong features.

She decided that if he trusted her enough to share his secret with her, she would tell him about Edmund's behavior. She could be sure then that he would believe her.

She propped herself up on one elbow and rested her hand on his bare chest. "I want to know everything."

"Everything?" He waggled his eyebrows, trying to make a joke of it. "All the women as well?"

She narrowed her eyes at him. "Just the ugly ones."

He laughed and kissed her.

"Stop it!" she said between kisses. "You are trying to divert me."

He rolled her onto her back and pressed his erection against her hip. "Tell me I am succeeding."

He trailed kisses down her neck. When she gave in, she did so wholeheartedly.

She did not, however, forget her question. The next morning, she grabbed his arm as he was slipping out of bed.

"Why will you not tell me?"

"Tell you what?" he said, pretending not to understand.

"About your family."

"Must you badger me about this, woman?"

Hurt, she released his arm and said nothing more.

William began to dress. The silence was strained, but she was not going to be the one to break it. William picked up his boots and sat down to put them on.

"All right, Catherine." He expelled a deep breath, making no effort to hide his exasperation.

He jerked on one boot. "Like most boys, I was sent off for my training at an early age." He jerked on the other boot. "Perhaps I was a bit younger than most."

He stood and took his belt from the back of the chair. "I was never close to any of my family. Except for John."

She noticed how his voice changed when he mentioned John.

"He was my half brother, younger by three years," he said as he strapped on his sword. In a tone meant to convey the subject was closed, he said, "John is dead. Without him, there is nothing and no one for me in the North."

"What of your mother and father? Are they still living?"

William picked up his leather riding gloves from the chest where Thomas had set them out the evening before. "Will these be your parting words to me, Catherine? My men await me."

"Oh, you go to Hereford!" she cried, putting her hand to her mouth. "I had forgotten."

He was meeting with the other Marcher lords in Hereford and would be gone at least four days. She leapt out of the bed and into his arms. His clothes felt rough against her bare skin.

"I wish I could go with you," she said.

"That would be far too dangerous." He smiled and winked at her. "These Marcher lords are a conniving lot, so I must have my wits about me."

"But I know the whole conniving lot and could advise you," she said. "Watch out for Lord Grey. He has the land north of here and wants to add some of ours to his."

"The risk is too great to take you, since I travel with only a half-dozen men." He kissed her forehead. "I am leaving most of the men here to keep watch on this part of the border."

She leaned against him, knowing the argument was lost.

"You and Jamie will be safe here," he said, rubbing his hand up and down her back. "I am leaving Edmund in command."

"Not Edmund!" She said it before she knew it.

"He is the best man I have," William said. "I trust him to keep Ross Castle—and you—safe until I return."

She put her hand on her hip and pressed her lips together.

"That is more important to me than whether you like the man, Catherine. I do not know what you find so objectionable about him. Edmund is a good man."

She did not want to argue with William as he was leaving. Instead, she wound her arms around her husband's neck and gave him a kiss she hoped he would remember all the way to Hereford.

———

Catherine went out to the garden with Jamie, hoping the sunshine would lift the melancholy that settled over her after William's departure. She watched Jamie try to catch a grasshopper. Each time he brought his cupped hands over it, it leapt away just in time. It got away for good when William's manservant came into the garden and interrupted Jamie's concentration.

"What is it, Thomas?"

"M'lady, there are men at the gate. They've come from the North to see Lord FitzAlan." He hesitated, then added, "One of them is FitzAlan's brother."

"His brother?" She must have misheard Thomas. William just told her this morning that his brother was dead.

"He is only a youth, m'lady. A boy."

"But we were not expecting anyone," she said, unable to hide her surprise.

"I happened to be near the gate when they arrived." Thomas cleared his throat, looking uncomfortable. "One of the men escorting him recognized me and told me the boy's mother sent him."

She thought she heard Thomas say under his breath, "Saints preserve us."

"Thank you, Thomas. I will come at once." Trying to sound pleased, she said, "Come, Jamie, we have guests!"

She felt uneasy. 'Twas odd that they received no prior word of this visit. And why had William not seen fit to mention this younger—*living*—brother to her?

She hurried across the bailey with Thomas and Jamie in tow. On the way, she stopped a passing servant to give instructions.

"Jane, tell Cook we have guests and need refreshments brought to the hall at once. Tell Alys to have rooms prepared."

She did not recognize the livery of the dozen men waiting on the other side of the portcullis, but they had the look of Northerners. Perhaps it was all the ginger hair and beards, or the way they stood as though they owned the world and were almost hoping for a fight.

She signaled for the guards to open the gate and waited as the men rode in. A well-dressed youth of perhaps twelve or thirteen dismounted and stepped forward, fidgeting with his hat. He was a good-looking boy with auburn hair, warm brown eyes, and a smattering of freckles across his cheeks and the bridge of his nose. He looked not one whit like William.

The lad looked over her shoulder, as though expecting someone else. Realizing his rudeness, he colored.

Catherine had to stifle a smile as he gave her a beautiful, if rather dramatic, bow.

"I am Stephen Neville Carleton." His voice broke with nervousness as he said it. "I thought to find my brother, Lord William Neville FitzAlan, here. If you would kindly tell him I am here, m'lady, I would be most grateful."

"I'm afraid Lord FitzAlan has been called away," she told him. "I do not know if you received news of your brother's marriage, but I am Lady Catherine, your new sister-in-law."

She gave him a warm smile. Though she did not know it, from that moment, young Stephen was hers.

"Welcome to Ross Castle," she said to the men who accompanied Stephen. "I am sure Lord FitzAlan will be as grateful to you as I am for bringing his brother to us safely."

The men took turns bowing and introducing themselves.

"The servants will take care of your horses," she said, bidding them to follow her. "We have refreshments for you in the hall."

She took Stephen's arm and walked with him toward the keep. They were of a height so that her face was close to his as she asked him about his journey. He had an appealing, almost pretty face, with large dark eyes, a straight nose, and full rosy lips. As he got older and his looks turned more masculine, he would have the ladies sighing.

As they passed through the second gate to the inner bailey, Edmund came running down the steps of the keep two at a time. He shouted greetings at a couple of the Northerners who came with Stephen.

"So this is young Stephen," Edmund said, thumping him on the back. "I would not have known you. You were crawling on all fours and smelling of piss when last I saw you."

Stephen scrunched his shoulders and made a face, but Edmund did not appear to notice.

"This will be quite a surprise for William," Edmund said.

It sounded like a warning; from the wary look on Stephen's face, the lad took it as such.

As soon as she had the visitors settled at table with wine and ale, Edmund appeared at her side.

"Pardon us a moment," he said to the others. His smile was polite, but his grip on her arm was unyielding. "The lady and I have an urgent matter to discuss."

He marched her into the corridor outside the hall.

"Why was I not called?" he demanded. "William made me responsible for the safety of this castle. You should not have ordered the gate open without my permission!"

"I do not need your permission to admit guests here," she said between clenched teeth. "I admitted no dangerous men, only my lord's young brother and his escort."

"God's beard, how could you be sure it was his brother? And a man's brother may also be his enemy. William can tell you that, if you do not know it."

"But you know these men," she argued, "and that boy is surely no threat."

"My God, woman, we are in the midst of rebellion," he said, raising his hands in the air. "You shall not act so foolishly again while I am in charge."

Catherine was too angry to concede anything. "You hear me well, Edmund Forrester," she said, shaking a finger in his face. "I have been the mistress of this castle since I was twelve years old. You may order the men about, but you shall not give orders to me."

She jerked her arm from his hold and left him there, wishing she had a door to slam.

———

Thomas watched Edmund take Lady Catherine from the hall. He did not like it. Not at all. Hearing their raised voices, he grew more concerned. He drummed his fingers as he thought of an excuse to interrupt them.

The door was flung open, and Lady Catherine entered, eyes blazing and silk skirts flowing out behind her. The men in the hall stopped, their cups midair, to watch her.

She looked for all the world like a beautiful avenging angel. Thomas shook his head in wonder. Surely, God had found the perfect woman for William. A woman strong enough to break through his barriers, to demand his heart, to heal his wounds.

Chapter Thirteen

William ended his business in Hereford early and set a fast pace for home. Home. It struck him that Ross Castle was the first place he had ever thought of as his home.

His mother's house was never that. His very existence had been a source of strain. As soon as his mother could convince Northumberland to take him into his household, she sent him. William's status on Northumberland's vast estates was complex and uncertain. No one knew whether to treat him as a poor relation of Northumberland's first wife, which he was, or as the great man's son.

William's true relationship to Northumberland was an open secret. God's truth, it would have been difficult to deny he was a Percy. He looked like a younger version of Hotspur.

Although Northumberland never claimed him, he assumed William's fealty. Likely he thought William should be grateful just for being brought into his service to train for knighthood.

In time, Northumberland let him lead a few men in the frequent skirmishes along the Scottish border. William proved able and rose in the ranks. After a few years,

Northumberland gave him command of a portion of his army. Remnants of that force still served under William.

This past spring, Northumberland sent him to fight against the Welsh rebels. The great man saw no need to tell William he was sent as a diversion, a false show of Percy loyalty. While William fought with the king, his father was in York hatching another conspiracy.

When Northumberland made his move against the king, he ordered William to return to the North with all possible speed. William ignored the call. He'd sworn his oath to King Henry. All he had of value was his honor—and his fighting skills. While his father took up arms against the king in the North, William fought rebels in Wales.

William pushed aside his memories of that difficult time. At the next rise in the road, Ross Castle appeared on the horizon, and his thoughts returned to Catherine. She was the reason he left Hereford in such a hurry.

But Edmund's words of warning came back to him.

"What man would not want such a woman in his bed? But for God's sake, do not trust her," Edmund harped at him. "Have a care, or one day you'll find she's opened the gates to rebels—or made false accusations about you to the prince."

Trust came hard to a man who grew up having uncertain ties and no true place in the world. While William did not truly believe Catherine would betray him, he kept his guard up.

He tried to, anyway. His resolve was slipping day by day.

His anticipation grew as he approached the gate. He looked up at the ramparts, half expecting to see her there watching for him. 'Twas foolish to be disappointed. She did not expect him for another day.

Who would have thought three days could seem so long? All he wanted was to get her alone in their bed-chamber, to feel her naked against his skin.

He threw his reins to a stable boy and left his men without a word. Ignoring their ribald remarks, he ran ahead to the keep. He looked up at the sun. Almost noon. He would find her with the rest of the household at dinner in the hall.

He burst through the doors, and she was there, just where he expected to find her. She stood and called his name, pleasure radiating from her face. His heart leapt in his chest as he strode across the room to her, intent on sweeping her into his arms and kissing her senseless.

He did hold her tantalizingly close before she put a firm hand against his chest and offered her cheek.

"William, we have guests," she whispered in his ear.

Damn, damn, damn. Grudgingly, he released her and turned to see what fool had the poor sense to visit today.

He looked around the table, taking in each man. With a sinking feeling, he recognized the livery of Carleton, his mother's latest husband. He supposed he should stop thinking of Carleton as her "latest," since she'd been married to him for a dozen years or more.

It never ceased to amaze him how his conniving mother managed to end up with men who had a knack for choosing the losing side of every major political intrigue. Carleton had sided with Northumberland in this latest debacle. The man lost most of his lands—but was lucky to keep his head.

William nodded at the men he recognized as his

gaze moved from man to man along the table. When he came to the boy sitting next to Catherine, he started. The resemblance to his mother was striking. This boy had to be Eleanor's youngest son.

The boy stood and gave him a bow. Looking at William with their mother's bold brown eyes, he said, "Greetings, sir. I am Stephen Neville Carleton."

"Aye, I can see that is who you are." William neither smiled nor moved to greet the boy. "How is it that you find yourself here at Ross Castle?"

"William!" He heard Catherine's whispered reproach but ignored it.

The boy blushed, but he held William's gaze. "Our mother insisted on sending me."

"There is no thwarting her," William said, shaking his head. "Sit down, Stephen."

He could hardly send the boy away in the middle of his dinner. While William washed his hands in the basin a servant brought to him, Catherine filled his trencher. It had been hours since he rode out of Hereford, and he was ravenous.

"Where is Jamie?" he asked Catherine as he stabbed a hunk of roasted pork.

"He was worn out from trying to keep up with Stephen. His nursemaid took him up for a rest as soon as he finished eating."

After William ate enough to take the edge off his hunger, he leaned forward to address Stephen, who sat on the other side of Catherine.

"So, how old are you, Stephen Carleton?"

"Twelve, sir."

"Tell me, what is Lady Eleanor's intent in sending you

here?" He pointed his eating knife at the boy. "I want to hear both what she told you and what you believe is her true purpose."

The boy raised his eyebrows in a manner so reminiscent of their mother that William could not keep the sarcastic edge from his voice. "You cannot have lived with her for twelve years and not know the two are different."

Stephen paused as if considering his answer, then said, "Mother said it was past time we knew each other." After a quick sideways glance at Catherine, he added, "And she wants me to tell her of your new wife."

Catherine gave the boy a reassuring smile and patted his arm.

"I believe she spoke the truth," Stephen said. "But those were not her only reasons."

"What else does she want?" William asked.

"Although she said this was a visit, I believe she intends for you to take me into your household." Stephen shrugged his shoulder. "You are the only one of us in the king's good graces."

That rang true. But William sensed the boy was holding something back. "Tell me. Out with it now."

" 'Tis possible she wants you to arrange a marriage for me," the boy said, blushing furiously. "Not that she would wish me to marry now, but she wants a betrothal."

Stephen looked pained. "She gave me a letter for you. I expect she instructs—ah, asks—you to use your influence to get me betrothed to a wealthy heiress."

William could not help but feel some sympathy for the boy. With both him and John beyond her reach, their mother's ambition would all fall on her youngest. The woman could be relentless.

"I appreciate your candor," William said. "You are not as much like our mother as you look."

William took a drink of wine, then asked, "So tell me, Stephen Carleton, is wealth all you want in a wife?"

"Not all," the boy mumbled, giving Catherine a furtive glance. He colored again and fixed his eyes on the table.

William rubbed his hands over his face. He had not seen this young brother since Stephen had been a babe— and not for long then. Truth be told, he'd forgotten all about him. Now that the lad was here, what was he going to do with him? Should he send him back? Leave him at the mercy of their mother?

He would have to think on it long and hard.

"You can stay until I decide what to do with you," he said, and stood up. "Now I must speak with my wife."

"I have matters to report to you, things you must hear," Edmund said, also rising.

"All seems safe and sound, Edmund. I will find you later," William said, keeping his eyes on Catherine. "Come, m'lady wife," he said, offering her his hand.

As soon as they were out the doorway, he pulled her around the corner. He kissed her long and hard, not caring if a passing servant saw them.

When he moved his hand to her breast, she said, "Not here, William!"

He took her by the wrist and led her up the stairs to the solar. As soon as he closed the door, he had her up against it.

"It seems like three months, not three days," he said amidst a frenzy of kisses.

He wanted to touch her everywhere at once. With a hunger of her own, she met him kiss for kiss and touch for touch. Her little moans of pleasure increased the urgency of his desire. Unfastening the endless line of buttons was beyond him. He sucked on her breast through the bodice of her gown until he felt her nipple harden through the layers of cloth.

His cock was so hard it pained him. He would die if he didn't have her soon.

He worked her skirts up until, at last, he felt bare thighs above her stockings. Groaning with pleasure, he slid his hands along her warm skin. She caught his face in her hands and locked her mouth on his, hot and wet and urgent. When she sucked his tongue, he felt it to his toes. He thought he would explode.

He cupped her bare buttocks, lifting her off the ground, and ground against her. His need was mindless, pulsing.

Afraid of frightening her with the violence of his passion, he leaned over her shoulder to rest his forehead against the door. He closed his eyes and tried to slow his breathing. His effort at control was severely challenged when she wrapped her legs around him.

"Catherine, if you want me to stop, you must drop your legs," he said in a ragged voice. He did not ease his pressure holding her against the door. "If you leave them around me like this, I cannot be sure I will hear you if you tell me later."

Her breath in his ear was as hard and fast as his own.

"I want you inside me. Now."

The saints preserve him! With one hand, he loosed the ties that held his leggings as he kissed her fiercely. Then, in one strong thrust, he was deep inside her. The only place he wanted to be. Sweet Jesus! He hoped she would forgive him, but he could not go slowly. Not this time. As he pumped into her, her high gasping breaths sent him to the very edge. She screamed in his ear, and he went over with her.

Afterward, his legs were so weak he was afraid he would topple to the floor with her. He leaned one arm against the door until he could get his balance. With her legs still wrapped around him, he managed to carry her into the bedchamber and collapse with her on the bed.

Good God! He was light-headed and out of breath. Never in his life had he wanted a woman that badly.

They lay side by side, barely touching, staring at the ceiling. When she still said nothing, he thought uneasily of the night he caused her to flee to the abbey. Though he was not drunk this time, his behavior was no less aggressive, no less coarse. Nay, he was worse this time.

God's beard. He had taken her against the wall, faster than lightning, without so much as a greeting.

What had he been thinking? The truth, of course, was that he had not been thinking at all.

"I did not intend to misuse you," he said. "I just wanted you so much."

She took his hand and squeezed it. "And I you."

Hearing no censure in her voice, he sighed with relief. "So you will not be packing off to join a nunnery the moment I close my eyes?" He was only half joking.

She laughed. "'Tis much too late for that!"

"Aye," he agreed, smiling back at her. "No one who has seen us these past weeks would believe this marriage was not consummated."

His heart turned in his chest as he looked into her face. The spark was back in Catherine's eyes, as the abbess said. He meant to keep it there.

"Do you think I could be with child already?"

He heard the hopefulness in her voice and felt an unfamiliar joy rise in him. She would be the mother of his children. He had no words to tell her what this meant to him. Hoping to show her how grateful he was, he pulled her into his arms and gave her a long, gentle kiss.

One kiss led to another. This time, he took her with a slowness that nearly drove them both mad. When they finished, he lay sprawled across the bed. He felt suffused with well-being and peace.

He was jarred from this pleasant state when Catherine sat up and burst into convulsive weeping.

"What is it?" he asked, jolting upright. "What could be wrong?"

He had half expected something like this earlier, after he'd taken her against the door. But, God in heaven, why was she upset now? The second time, he'd been slow and gentle. She had certainly seemed to appreciate his efforts.

"I do not mean to weep," she said, wiping her tears away with her hands.

Her shoulders shook again, and she tried to turn away from him, but he put his arms around her and held her.

"Kate," he said into her hair. "Tell me."

She took a shaky breath. "It is just that I feel so close to you when we are like this."

He kissed her fingers and looked into her wet eyes, waiting for her to make sense of this for him.

"But I know it is an illusion." She wiped her hand under her nose. "'Tis all false."

He had never felt so close to a woman before, but he was not sure how to tell her that. Or whether he should. Instead, he asked, "Why do you think it false?"

"Because you do not trust me at all."

There was a long silence between them. When he did not take the opportunity she gave him to confess, she laid out her complaint in full.

"You have told me nothing. Nothing. Nothing of your family, your life. Imagine my surprise at finding a boy at our gate claiming to be your brother, when the only brother you mentioned to me is dead."

Once she started, she was going to say it all.

"I have to learn from a twelve-year-old boy that Northumberland is your father! That Hotspur was your brother!" She was sputtering now, her anger gaining ground. "I am your wife, and everyone knows this but me.

"You distrusted me because I fought my husband's treachery. Yet, I did not go against my own blood as you did." She gestured wildly as she spoke, pressing her hand to her chest each time she referred to herself.

"You fought on the king's side when it was your own father and brother who led the Northern rebels." She shook her finger at him. "Do not tell me your brother and father did not expect you to join them or that they did not feel betrayed when you did not."

William let her talk until she ran out of words. His reasons for not telling her no longer seemed important. He had hurt her, and he did not want to do that anymore.

"Where would you like me to start?"

———

Catherine listened as William told her his story.

"My mother played a high-stakes game and lost," he began. "Northumberland took his time looking for a second wife after the death of his first wife, Margaret Neville

Percy. He had three sons by Margaret, so he could bide his time.

"My mother was Margaret's niece and visited often." In an indifferent tone, he added, "She is quite beautiful.

"She was married to an elderly man named FitzAlan. She might have looked forward to life as a wealthy widow if FitzAlan had not crossed King Richard. When most of FitzAlan's lands were seized, she anticipated the need for a second husband. She set her sights high.

"She toyed with Northumberland, putting him off until FitzAlan was on his deathbed," he continued. "When she found herself with child a few weeks after the funeral, she expected Northumberland to marry her.

"What my mother could not anticipate was that Robert Umfraville, Earl of Angus, would die at just that time, leaving his titles and vast wealth to his widow, Maud. Maud was a widow but two weeks before Northumberland wed her. My mother was left to make the pretense that FitzAlan miraculously conceived a child on his deathbed. That is how I came to bear his name.

"Northumberland arranged for her to be married to one of his knights. Everyone knew I was the result of Northumberland's dalliance with my mother—most especially her new husband."

Catherine understood from this that, even as a very young child, William was aware of his stepfather's resentment.

"She sent me to live in Northumberland's household when I was six."

He spoke with little emotion, but Catherine sensed the great bitterness he harbored against his mother.

She ventured to ask, "How old was your mother when she had her affair with Northumberland?"

He shrugged. "She was married to FitzAlan at fifteen, so I suppose she was about sixteen."

"And yet you believe it was she who seduced him?" she asked. "Northumberland must have been, what, forty? And he was a very powerful man. It may have been difficult for her to refuse him."

When he did not respond, she said in a soft voice, "I cannot help thinking you judge her harshly."

William folded his arms. "You do not know her."

"You as much as called her deceitful and manipulative at table today," she said as gently as she could. "You should consider the effect of your words on Stephen. He is just a boy."

"Stephen seems to have her measure." After a moment, he took a deep breath and said, "Perhaps I should take more care with him. He looks so much like her that it is difficult for me to remember he is an innocent."

Their conversation was interrupted by a furious knocking at the door.

"Who is it?" William demanded in a booming voice.

The words were indistinguishable, but the high-pitched voice on the other side of the door was Jamie's.

She and William scrambled to the floor for their clothes. Catherine slipped her gown over her head and jumped back into the bed just as William reached the door.

"Jamie!" William called out in greeting. Scooping Jamie up with one arm, he brought him over to the bed.

"Did Mother make you take a rest, too?" Jamie asked, rubbing his eye with his fist.

William nodded. "I suspect she will make me go to bed early tonight as well."

"'Tis best to just do what she wants," Jamie said, his blue eyes wide and knowing.

William could not keep back his smile. "I will do everything she asks." He caught Catherine's eye over the boy's head. "And then I will do it all again, just to be sure I've got it right."

Chapter Fourteen

The next morning, Catherine suggested they take Stephen riding to show him some of the nearby area. It was another lovely summer day, and it felt good to be outside the confines of the castle walls. She maneuvered her horse so that she and William rode behind the others.

"Stephen is a charming lad," she said.

"Charming?" William said in a sour tone. "What good is that?"

She laughed. "Stephen will need it! Something about him tells me he has a talent for getting into trouble. He's already gone into the village without telling anyone."

"That seems harmless."

"The illness we had at the castle earlier in the summer spread to the village," she explained. "I thought it had run its course, but two villagers died of it just this week."

"Stephen seems healthy enough."

She nodded and went back to what she had been saying before. "Stephen may have more charm than is good for him, but he has a good heart. He has been very kind to Jamie." She turned to smile at William. "Just as you are."

Unable to help herself, she added, "Truly, your mother cannot be as bad as you say to have raised two such sons."

"If either of us has a soft heart toward children," he said, staring straight ahead, "do not credit it to her."

Mentioning his mother was a mistake. She regretted letting herself get diverted from her purpose.

"So, William, what are your plans for your brother?"

"I have not yet decided, but I take it you have an opinion, m'lady wife?" Before she could answer, he asked, "Tell me, do you think most wives offer their opinions on all manner of things to their husbands?"

"Aye, most certainly, to both questions," she replied so quickly that William laughed.

"All right," he said, in full good humor now. "Tell me what you've been planning to say from the start."

"Stephen should stay with us," she said without hesitation. "There is no one better to train him for knighthood than you." 'Twas blatant flattery but true nonetheless. "And Stephen will need a steady man like you to fish him out of trouble from time to time."

"I was happy to settle here in the Marches precisely because it is far away from the Percys, my mother, and all the rest. I don't want to renew those ties. Besides, if I give in to my mother on this, she will ask for more."

"If she is so horrid," Catherine countered, "how can you leave Stephen in her hands?"

⁓

"Send that boy home to his mother," Edmund warned, "before the king catches wind of his being here."

"The king knows my loyalty," William replied evenly.

"And you know the king," Edmund said. "Carleton's support for the Northern rebels makes any connection with his son too risky for you."

"There is some risk," William agreed. With rebellions on both borders, Henry tended to see threats everywhere he looked.

"The king fears that the next time Northumberland calls for you, you may come," Edmund said in a low voice. "It would take little to raise his suspicions."

"Then ask the king's permission to keep Stephen here."

Both men whirled around at the sound of Catherine's voice.

"What are you doing sneaking up behind us!" Edmund shouted, his face red with anger.

"Perhaps you need to improve your skills," Catherine replied with equal anger, "if a woman can surprise you in broad daylight in the middle of the bailey yard."

"Catherine—" William began, but stopped when she turned her glare to him.

"Stephen is twelve years old. The king will not hold him accountable for his father's treachery." She arched an eyebrow at William. "He has been known to separate a father's guilt from his son."

With that, she turned on her heel and left them staring after her.

"You must do something about that woman," Edmund said in a taut voice. "She interferes in men's affairs. She does as she pleases, and she will take you down."

"I know you mean well." The cold anger in William's voice got Edmund's full attention. "But she is my wife, and you will not speak to her as you did."

"Fine, just tell me you'll not start taking her advice,"

Edmund said. "For God's sake, remember what she did to her first husband and watch your back."

"Rayburn deserved what he got," William bit out.

"Aye, but at his wife's hands?" Edmund said. "How long did she deceive him? Five years?"

"The past is past."

"You are thinking with what's between your legs, man. Can't you see she has blinded you?"

"Then I'm a happy blind man." William grabbed Edmund by the front of his tunic and looked him hard in the eye. "Find a way to get along with her. If I must choose between you, have no doubt I will choose her."

William was tired of this conflict between the two of them. He left Edmund and marched to the keep, intent on having words with Catherine as well. When he reached the hall, one of the servants informed him that Lady Fitz-Alan was in Stephen's chamber on the third floor.

Puzzled more than angry now, he went up the stairs to one of the previously unoccupied chambers next to Jamie's. He found Stephen in bed and Catherine hovering over him, wiping his face with a damp cloth.

She looked up and saw him in the doorway. "He has the fever. That is what I came to the bailey to tell you."

———

"Let one of the servants sit with Stephen tonight," William urged Catherine when she came to bid him good night. "You must get some rest. You are exhausted."

For the last three days and nights, Catherine had shared the watch with Alys. Even when it was Alys's turn, William would wake to find Catherine had left their bed to check on him.

The lad was ill, indeed. When William looked in on him earlier, Stephen's skin was so pale that the blue veins showed through it. He'd looked unbearably young lying on the bed.

"The fever should peak tonight, so it is the most dangerous time." She gave him a tired smile. "Once the fever breaks, I will rest, and gladly."

"I'll come with you," William said, throwing the bedclothes back.

"You will only be in the way," she said, putting her hand out to stop him. Although her tone was teasing, he knew she meant it. She kissed him distractedly and left.

Hours later, he awoke to find her side of the bed still empty. He dressed quickly in the faint first light of dawn. The keep was eerily quiet as he made his way up the stairs to Stephen's chamber.

The door was slightly ajar. He eased it open.

A surge of relief swamped him when he saw Stephen. The lad lay on the bed, wan but awake, with a slight smile on his face.

Lying beside him, fully dressed on top of the bedclothes, was Catherine. She was fast asleep and holding Stephen's hand.

William walked softly to the side of the bed and put his hand on Stephen's forehead.

"I see your fever has broken," he said in a hushed voice.

Stephen nodded.

With a wry smile, William said, "Then perhaps I can have my wife back."

They were quiet for a few moments; then Stephen said, "I can tell you what I want now."

William raised his eyebrows. What was the boy talking about?

"In a bride. If you arrange a betrothal for me."

William nodded, recalling the conversation.

Stephen cast a sideways look at Catherine sleeping soundly next to him on the bed.

"I want one like her—like your lady wife."

Stephen's grin was sheepish, but the sparkle in his eyes was anything but. And the boy was only twelve! William drew in a deep breath and shook his head. His wife was right. Stephen was the sort to get himself into trouble.

He made his decision.

"There is not another woman like Catherine, but I will do my best for you," he promised. "I'll send a message to your mother telling her you shall remain here at Ross Castle."

Stephen's smile grew wide at the news. William did not return the smile. It was time for the lessons to begin.

"Let this be the last time," he said, tapping his finger against Stephen's chest, "I find you in bed with another man's wife."

Chapter Fifteen

Stephen recovered his health quickly. He was a good-humored lad, and William enjoyed his company.

Truth be told, he felt more content with his new life with each passing day. He felt he had a family, with Catherine, Jamie, and Stephen. He was not sure how it happened, but he'd come to trust his wife.

He had even told her about Hotspur's death at the Battle of Shrewsbury and what happened after. King Henry had had the grace—or perhaps the wisdom—not to ask William to fight against Hotspur that day. Instead, William was sent off to keep watch for the approach of Glyndwr's forces. He returned in time to see Hotspur fighting his way through the melee. Hotspur killed two decoys dressed to look like the king and nearly reached the king himself before he was cut down.

Hotspur died a true warrior's death.

William accepted that Hotspur should lose his life for taking up arms against the king. But he could not reconcile himself to what the king did after.

When the people refused to believe the famous warrior was dead, the king had Hotspur's body dug up and drawn and quartered. On fast horses, the four parts were taken to be displayed in the four corners of the kingdom. The bloody head was delivered to Hotspur's poor wife.

William did not change his allegiance, but he lost a large measure of respect for his king that day.

Hotspur never once spoke to him with warmth, never once acknowledged their blood tie. Yet, William had been plagued by guilt ever since Shrewsbury. Only after he spoke of the events with Catherine did those feelings ease. She seemed to understand both why he sided with the king and what the choice had cost him.

—

Catherine paced the solar, debating with herself. Now that she had badgered William into telling her all, she felt guilty for the one secret she kept from him. His fierce words to her at the abbey came back to her again and again.

I cannot abide deceit.

Though she had told him no lie, neither had she been fully honest with him. Was she wrong not to have faith in him? Not to believe he would understand? She rubbed her temples. She had a blazing headache.

She did not like to admit it, but there was another reason to tell William. Although she dismissed it at first, Edmund's threat to discover her secrets nagged at her. What if someone had seen her that day? She did not think so, but it was possible one of the servants had been there in the hall. None of them would speak against her. But Edmund had already shown he could wheedle information out of them.

She jumped when the door opened.

"What are you doing here?" she snapped.

William's eyes twinkled in amusement. "I like to visit my lady wife in the middle of the afternoon. I come often enough; I did not think to give you such a start."

Catherine let out her breath and attempted to return his smile. "I am sorry. I was lost in my thoughts."

"Then I hope your thoughts were the same as mine."

He pulled her into his arms. It felt so good that she was sorely tempted to put off telling him once again. Her conscience got the better of her.

"William, I have something to tell you."

His light mood was gone in an instant.

"All right," he said, releasing her and stepping back.

She took his hand and led him to the window seat. Sensing his tension, she feared their new bond was too fragile for this revelation. She took a moment to get her courage up.

"Come, Catherine, it cannot be as bad as that," he said, and patted her hand. "Tell me what worries you."

The anxiety in his dark honey eyes belied his soft tone. Keeping him waiting would only cause him to think of darker and darker possibilities.

"You know Rayburn hurt me." She fixed her eyes on William's hand over hers as she began her tale; it still was not easy for her to talk about how Rayburn mistreated her. "He wanted an heir, but he had difficulty...performing the task." She cleared her throat. "Sometimes he did manage it, but I did not conceive. He was becoming more and more violent.

"I was young and very frightened." She gave William a furtive glance, hoping he understood how dire her situation was. "I thought it would not be long before he killed me."

She ran her tongue over her dry lips. "There was a young man," she said, barely above a whisper. "He saved me."

"Saved you?" William said, a note of suspicion creeping into his voice. "Just how did he save you?"

"He took care of me when I was injured."

She closed her eyes and remembered that day, more than four years ago. Prince Harry had stopped overnight. Rayburn was leaving with him the next day to fight the rebels. Since Rayburn might be gone for weeks, he came to her that night for another attempt. He hurt her badly that time.

The next morning, she waited to go down to the hall until Rayburn and the other men were gone. She forgot about the young knight Harry left behind to carry a message to the king. The moment she entered the hall, the young man rushed to her side. When she refused to let him call anyone to help her, he carried her upstairs and took care of her injuries himself.

"He was very kind and courteous," she said aloud.

She remembered how the young man's face and even his ears turned red when he eased the hem of her gown up to wrap the linen strips around her injured ankle. His fingers were unexpectedly gentle.

"He wrapped my ankle for me," she murmured. "He told me he learned his skills from the monks at a monastery near his home. He said he once hoped to join their order."

William made an indecipherable sound. Still, she did not look at him.

"When he helped me to my bed, my sleeve fell back. He saw the bruises on my arm."

After his careful treatment, she was startled when he held her wrist and pushed her sleeve up to her shoulder. She remembered how the dark purple and blue of the new bruises stood out against the fading yellow ones. The young man's eyes were full of compassion when he looked into her face again.

"He saw that my injuries were not from a fall, as I had told him—and that this was not the first time," she said. "He pressed me to tell him who was hurting me and why."

It was the memory of the young knight who took her riding before her wedding that led her to trust in the kindness in this young man's eyes. And that was what saved her.

"I told him everything. That there was no hope for me. That my husband could not get me with child and that he would not stop hurting me until I conceived."

The young man put his arms around her and made shushing noises into her hair. She remembered leaning into the comfort of his embrace and weeping until she fell into an exhausted sleep. By the time she awoke, he had worked out a solution to her problem.

"He said that to save my life, I must let another man get me with child." Her voice was so low that William leaned forward to hear her. "He said letting Rayburn murder me would be a greater sin than adultery."

Catherine let the silence stretch. Nothing could have made her look at William now. She could feel him next to her, fairly vibrating with violent emotion.

Finally, she made herself say it: "I asked him to do that favor for me."

"You what!"

"He refused at first," she said. William was gripping her hand so hard now that it hurt. "He was offended that I might think he carried me upstairs with the intent of seducing me."

"That is precisely what he intended!"

"He did not," she protested, looking up. "It was not like that."

"Just how was it, Catherine?" William's amber eyes were hard and narrowed, and she saw the warning in them.

"In sooth, it was not easy to persuade him." Her voice dropped to a whisper. "But there was no one else to ask, no one else I could trust."

She felt herself blush, remembering how she pulled her gown off before she could lose her courage. The young man's eyes traveled slowly down her naked body. In a breathy voice, he asked, "Are you very, very sure?"

She knew then she had won.

"Do not tell me how you convinced him," William spat out, as if reading her thoughts. "I thought you never enjoyed having a man in your bed before me."

"It was not like it is with us," she said, surprised he might think so. "He did not hurt me, but it was nothing like what happens between us."

The memory came back to her slowly. With a gentleness she could not have imagined, the young man kissed her cheek, her forehead, her throat. He caressed her with the softest touches, all the while murmuring soothing words to her. A great calmness settled over her.

She sensed a power held back to protect her, and she was grateful. Weak, barely able to move, she gave herself over to him. He seemed to understand she was hurt in spirit even more than in body and expected nothing from her.

The young knight gave her a glimpse that day of what her life could have been like with a different man, a kind man. It had been almost more than she could bear.

———

A jagged knife ripped through William's heart as he watched her thinking of her lover.

He always hated thinking of her with Rayburn, but the man had been her husband. It helped to know she had felt neither lust nor affection for the man. But Catherine taking a lover was something altogether different.

A terrible coldness swept over him. He stood up. He had to get out of this room, to get away. He could not be here.

But there were things he had to know before he could allow himself to escape.

"This knight is Jamie's father?"

She nodded.

"How long was he your lover?"

When Catherine's answer was too slow, he demanded, "Is he your lover still?"

Her eyes went wide. "He is not! He could not be! One time was all—I swear it."

"One time?" His voice was heavy with skepticism. "Quite the miracle."

She had the nerve to say, "I've always thought so."

He ground his teeth, trying to control the rage pounding through him. "Where is your lover now?"

He would track the man down and kill him.

"I learned he died of a fever," she said, and the sadness in her voice wrenched him. "It was not long after…"

She had the sense not to say after *what,* but the vision of her writhing under the man burned across his mind.

"I can see you think I was wrong to do it," she said, standing up and clenching her fists. "But I cannot regret it. I cannot! Rayburn would have killed me if I did not conceive. And you cannot ask me to wish Jamie had not been born."

William had watched her face soften as she spoke of her lover. The man she had "persuaded" to take her to bed. He knew all he needed to know; he could stand no more.

"What I regret, William FitzAlan, is that I was foolish enough to tell you!" She was shouting at him now, tears streaking down her face. "I trusted that you would understand, that you would not think these hateful thoughts of me."

He barely heard her.

The last thing he saw before he slammed the door was Catherine standing in the middle of the room with her hands over her face, weeping. Weeping for her dead lover.

What a fool he had been to trust her.

———

Edmund and Stephen jumped back as William stormed past them down the steps of the keep. William was in such a fury that he did not even seem to see them. But Stephen, who missed nothing, saw the slow smile on Edmund's face. And he wondered why.

Chapter Sixteen

Catherine was too upset after her disastrous conversation with William to venture from their rooms. An hour before supper, Alys came to find her.

"M'lady," Alys said, giving her a quick curtsy, "there is a group of minstrels at the gate. The guards want to know if they may let them in. As Lord FitzAlan has gone hunting, I told them I would ask you."

"Do we know these troubadours?"

"Aye, we do! We've enjoyed their music many a time." Alys frowned and tilted her head. "I believe the last time was not long before Lord FitzAlan came to us."

Aye, Catherine knew them. One of them she knew very well, indeed.

"Do say yes, m'lady. It will help make up for not having musicians at your wedding feast." With barely suppressed excitement, Alys added, "And they always bring news, traveling as they do."

"That they do," Catherine agreed. "I shall tell the guards to open the gates myself."

As she and Alys crossed the bailey toward the main gate, she heard Stephen call her name. She turned to see him running headlong down the steps from the castle's outer wall.

"There are traveling musicians at the gate!" he said as he fell into step beside her.

"I swear, Stephen, you hear news faster than anyone in Ross Castle," she said, shaking her head. "No secret could be kept from you for long."

She looked at him sideways without slackening her pace. "How do you do it?"

She meant it as a rhetorical question, but Stephen answered.

"I make friends with the servants, fetch drinks for the guards." He paused, then added, "And I listen."

"Behind doors?"

Stephen would not lie to her, but he opened his eyes wide with feigned innocence.

"Have a care," she scolded. "One day you may hear something you should not, and it could cost you dearly."

When they reached the gate, she recognized the faces and colorful clothing of the band of troubadours. For longer than she could remember, this troupe had come to Ross Castle and received warm welcome here. She recalled how her mother loved the ballads, especially the "chansons d'amour."

She signaled to the guards to raise the portcullis and stepped forward, calling, "Welcome! Welcome!" She greeted each man with a smile as they bowed to her in turn.

Robert Fass kissed her hand and gave her a rakish grin. The devil looked as handsome as ever with his sea-green eyes and unfashionably long blond hair.

Robert joined the troupe three years before. No one

knew where he came from, nor would he say, but he could mimic any accent and spoke French, English, and Welsh equally well. And he had a voice to make the angels cry.

The female angels, at least.

She'd seen serving women trip over sleeping dogs, because they could not take their eyes off him. She sighed and shook her head. They would fight for his favors, and the hard feelings would cause her trouble for weeks to come.

From hints Robert gave, highborn ladies took him into their beds as often as the maids did. She suspected that was how he got his best information.

She was anxious to have a private word with him. With Stephen's sharp ears close by, it was not possible to talk now. She would have to wait and seek him out later.

——

Catherine could feel William's anger as he sat stiffly beside her at supper. He barely spoke, and not a word to her.

Fine. She was angry, too. Her disappointment in him dragged her spirits down as much as his hostility.

Thank heaven the musicians were here to provide a diversion. She sincerely regretted her decision to delay the surprise until the end of supper.

She waited until the last course of stewed fruits, sugared nuts, tarts, and cakes was brought to the table. At her nod, two servants posted at the entrance swung open the massive doors. The troubadours swept into the hall in a burst of song to the music harp and flute.

The hall erupted in cheers and clapping.

As she hoped, the musicians provided the household

a welcome respite from the tedium of waiting for the next major confrontation with the rebels. Even William seemed to put aside his ill humor and enjoy the music for a time.

That was short-lived, however.

Robert stood to give the final ballad and waited until the room fell into a hushed silence.

"I sing this song for the fairest lady of the Marches." Robert bowed low in her direction and gave her that wicked smile of his.

She could have throttled him.

He settled back onto his stool and took up his harp. The moment he began to sing, she forgot her annoyance with him.

From the first note to the last, no one made a sound to interrupt the soaring voice that filled the room. They hung on every word as he sang. It was a well-known ballad, a sad tale of a young man's undying love for a beautiful maid. As she listened to the familiar words, Catherine closed her eyes and let the music take her into the story.

Her eyes flew open as the words of the final verse came to her. In horror, she listened to Robert sing of the maid being forced to wed another. His voice filled the hall with the young man's lament: He must meet his love in secret, and his child will have another man's name.

William clenched his fist around his eating knife so tightly his knuckles were white. She did not dare steal a glance at his face. His rage was so palpable that it made her skin prickle.

The sudden, jubilant applause brought her attention abruptly back to the musicians. As Robert took his bow, he caught her eye and gave her another devilish grin.

Could the fool not see William was ready to take him by the throat?

She left the table before the applause died. In the corridor just outside the hall, she found the musicians chatting and putting away their instruments.

"A wonderful performance!" she said. "Cook has supper waiting for you in the kitchens."

She grabbed Robert's arm as he attempted to file out behind the others. When he put his hand over hers, she snatched it back.

"Must you embarrass me?" she said in a harsh whisper.

Robert threw his head back and laughed. "Most women are flattered when I sing a love song to them. It's your annoyance that makes it so irresistible."

"You had best find a way to resist, or my new husband may murder you! How is it that no husband has killed you yet?"

"I usually take care not to look at the married women when I sing love songs—if their husbands are present." He winked at her. "But tonight I could not help myself."

"I tire of your jokes, Robert." Chastising him was useless, and she wanted to talk of other matters. She leaned close and lowered her voice. "Tell me, what news have you?"

All humor left his face. "A French army is expected to land on the southwest coast of Wales, at Milford Haven, within the week."

"What!" The French had taken so long in meeting their promise to Glyndwr that she had ceased to believe they would come at all. "How many men do they bring?"

"I cannot say for certain, but it is a large force. Perhaps as many as twenty-five hundred men."

Catherine was so dismayed that Robert put his hand on her shoulder to soothe her. "From what I hear of FitzAlan, you can trust him to defend Ross Castle. Praise God, you no longer have that worthless scum Rayburn for a husband."

"I am forever grateful to you for taking my messages to the prince." With less warmth, she added, "You know the extent of my gratitude, for you take great advantage of it."

"I mean no harm." His smile was gentle this time.

"I know," she said, touching his hand where it rested on her shoulder. She knew that beneath his flirting and joking, he felt a genuine friendship for her.

"There is more," he said, lowering his voice again. "The French do not come just to help Glyndwr take the castles in South Wales. They intend to march into England itself."

"No." Catherine put her hand to her chest. "They would not dare!"

"We shall see," Robert said, giving his characteristic shrug. "I have only heard a whisper of it."

A whisper in bed, no doubt.

Robert's gaze shifted from her face to fix on something behind her. She whirled around, alarmed that someone may have overheard their conversation.

She was relieved to see it was only William. When she turned back to Robert to make the introductions, Robert was several paces away and heading for the door.

"I shall find that supper now, Lady FitzAlan," he called out just before the door banged closed.

Robert had experience with hasty exits.

William was almost blind with rage. He let the troubadour go. For now. Fists clenched at his sides, he stepped
forward to confront his wife. He stopped just inches from
her, not daring to touch her for fear of what he might do.

"Is he Jamie's father?" he demanded. "The man you
would have me believe is dead?"

She looked up at him with eyes as blue and innocent as
periwinkles. He was torn between wanting to shake her
until her teeth rattled and howling out in pain.

"What?" she said, as if she had not heard him. "Jamie's
father? I did not even know Robert then."

Her response did nothing to calm him.

"So Jamie's father was not your only lover?" He
thought his head would explode from the pressure. Enunciating each word distinctly, he said, "How many have
there been, Catherine? I want their names."

He could see she was frightened now, but she stood her
ground.

"I took no lover, save for the one I told you about," she
said, looking him in the eye. "And only the one time."

The thought nagged at him that she would not have
been so inexperienced if the two had been lovers. He sincerely doubted there would be much left to teach a woman
after she'd been with the troubadour.

"Swear to God," he demanded. "Swear to God you
have not lain with him."

She became calmer, as if she saw a means of escape.

She grasped the cross at her neck and said in an unwavering voice, "I swear before God and all that is holy, I have
not lain with him."

He did not know what to believe. While the bard had
been singing, William pictured the two of them together,

naked and entwined. Any doubts he had were swept away when he saw them, touching and whispering, alone in the dark corridor.

But, she swore before God. Either Catherine was telling the truth or she did not fear even God's wrath.

"If you speak the truth," he said, "then what reason could you have for whispering in secret with him?"

"I—"

"Now that you know a man can give you pleasure, you want to try another. Is that it? Confess, you were planning a tryst with him!"

"I would not! Robert behaves that way to tease me, truly. 'Tis a game to him."

"A game to seduce my wife?" he shouted. "I swear, I shall tear him limb from limb."

He brushed past her, charging for the door, but she grabbed his arm and clung to him.

"Do not touch him, William," she pleaded. "He is innocent."

"Innocent, you say?" he said, incredulous. "There is not a man alive who would believe that troubadour is innocent."

In a quieter voice, he asked, "But what of you, wife? Am I to believe you are innocent? What explanation can you give for what I saw here?"

"That is what I must tell you, if you will but listen," she said. "Robert gave me news of the French. We must send word to the king at once."

"You would have me believe your tête-à-tête was of politics?"

He pushed her away in disgust, and she dropped to the floor.

Standing over her, he said in a low growl, "I will get the truth from this troubadour of yours. I will put him on the rack if I have to."

She rose to her knees and grabbed his leg. "Please, William, do not hurt him!"

He watched her groveling on the floor, begging for her lover, and felt a crushing pain in his chest.

"Did what passed between us mean nothing to you?" he asked. He heard the plaintive note in his voice and hated himself for his weakness.

He turned his back on her and went out the door. The rush of cold night air could not cool his burning skin. Not since his mother sent him away as a child of six had he felt such an aching, overpowering sense of desolation. For the second time in his life, his world crashed down around him.

He loved her. Only now did he realize it. The girl he met in the stables years before touched his imagination and filled his dreams. But it was the woman, his most reluctant wife, who stole his heart. And she did it without his even knowing it.

He was used to deciding what he wanted and setting a course to get it. But he could not begin to think what he should do about Catherine and his feelings for her.

Tonight, however, he would find this too-handsome troubadour and send him packing.

———

Catherine sent her maid away and barred the door. Not that it would keep William out if he was determined to come in. She paced the floor, waiting for him to pound on her door and demand to know where Robert was hiding.

Thank God she had shown Robert the secret tunnel and hidden boat long ago. With luck, he would be well down the river by now.

William did not come. Exhausted from the ordeal, she pushed the heavy chest in front of the door and went to bed. She slept fitfully and awoke in the morning feeling bone-tired.

"The men have left the hall, m'lady," her maid called through the door. "Shall I help you dress now?"

Catherine heaved the trunk aside and let Mary in.

"I shall rest a while longer," she said, sitting down on the trunk. "My stomach is a touch uneasy."

"I shall bring you sop, m'lady," Mary said. "There is nothing like bread soaked in warm milk and a touch of honey for belly trouble."

Though Catherine felt well again before the midday meal, she sent word down that she was ill and would take her dinner in her rooms. She was not ready to see William. Also, she needed time to figure out how to get the news of the French invasion to Harry. Clearly, William would not do it for her.

Could she be sure enough of Robert's information to risk sending word to Harry? She did not like sending him a message of such import until she heard it from two sources. She was always cautious; it would hurt the prince's standing with the king and his council if the information later proved false.

Prince Harry and the king were on the Northern border. With the royal armies so distant from Wales, it was all the more urgent to get news to them of the imminent arrival of the French. If only she could be sure! Even if she could confirm it, how would she get a message to Harry?

She heard a light knock, and an auburn head popped around the door. In spite of her troubles, Catherine gave Stephen a warm smile.

"How do you fare?" the boy asked, drawing his dark brows together. "I heard you were not well."

"I am better, thank you," she replied, feeling guilty her deception had caused him concern.

"A message arrived for you from the abbey," he said, handing her a sealed parchment.

Leaving Stephen to fidget behind her, she stepped inside the doorway of her bedchamber. With her back to the open door, she broke the seal. She found two letters, one rolled inside the other. She read the hidden one quickly, with a rising sense of urgency.

The abbess, too, had received word of the imminent arrival of a French army.

God was with her. No sooner had she slipped the secret missive through the slit in her gown and into the small pouch she wore underneath than William burst into the solar.

She held the other letter in her hand as she went to join him. It gave her a good deal of satisfaction to see he did not look as if he'd slept any better than she had.

"Edmund told me you received a message," he said without greeting her. He held out his hand for it.

"'Tis from Abbess Talcott," she said coolly, and dropped it into his hand.

If he was surprised to see it was, indeed, from the abbess, he did not show it.

"As you can see, m'lord husband, the abbess hopes I may come see her soon. It has been some time since…" She faltered for just a moment. "Since I visited."

"Perhaps you would benefit from spending time on

your knees with holy women," William said in a hard voice. He narrowed his eyes and jabbed his finger against her chest. "But you shall not go outside these castle walls without me or Edmund Forrester. I will not have my wife sneaking off for some tryst."

Before she knew it, Stephen was between them.

"You shall not say such vile things to her!" Stephen shouted.

William's harsh words hurt and humiliated her, but it was Stephen's futile gallantry that pushed her to the edge of tears.

"Stephen, I am sending your escort home today," William said in a cold voice. "Go or stay, as you will."

With that, he turned and stomped out of the room.

Stephen's fair skin had gone blotchy, and his deep brown eyes showed confusion and hurt.

"William does want you here," Catherine said, touching his arm. "He is just angry now."

Stephen shrugged and hung his head.

She took his face in her hands and looked him in the eyes. "You have a home at Ross Castle as long as I am here," she said. "I want you here, and so does Jamie."

"I would rather face William's wrath than my mother's disappointment," Stephen said, attempting a smile. "She is not a woman to cross."

Catherine smiled back. "Whatever the reason, I am glad you will stay."

"Edmund told me why William is so vexed with you," he said, looking away and blushing faintly. "My brother is a fool, and I shall tell him so."

It should not surprise her that Stephen knew more than he should.

"So you would slay dragons for me, Sir Stephen?" she said, touched by the boy's blind faith in her. "You are good to offer, but I don't think you can help me with your brother."

"Surely there is something I can do for you? I would do anything you asked."

She narrowed her eyes, considering.

"Aye, Stephen, there is something."

———

An hour later, the men of Stephen's escort rode out of the castle, headed for the North. Unbeknownst to William, they carried a message from Catherine to the prince. When Prince Harry brought it to the king, the king snatched the parchment from his hands and tore it to bits in his face.

"You expect me to move my armies across the length of England," he fumed, "based on a woman's gossip?"

Within days, the king would sorely regret that he had not.

Chapter Seventeen

Catherine did not show her face at table for three days. William knew their rift was the talk of the castle. From the looks the servants gave him when they thought he was not looking, it was evident they thought him the vilest of criminals. His men, on the other hand, were embarrassed for him. Even Edmund would not meet his eyes.

Stephen was firmly in the servants' camp and vocal in his recriminations. How could William fault the lad for being a fool for Catherine? Even after discovering her cavorting in the dark with the troubadour, William's desire for her was unabated. He lay awake at night, wanting her past bearing. He swore he could almost hear her breathing.

Even in the daytime, he caught himself imagining her trailing kisses down his body or remembering how her breath caught when he entered her. He would soon go mad with frustration.

He told himself he would be justified in taking her to bed again. She was his wife. He had a right. A duty. A man needed an heir. And a godly man must avoid the sin of adultery. Unless he wanted a life of celibacy, he must bed his wife.

If he was honest with himself, it was not only bedding her that he missed. He felt her absence beside him at table and longed to hear her laugh at Jamie's antics or Stephen's jokes. Sadness settled over him when he thought of the long rides they used to take.

He missed it all.

In the end, it was pure desire that drove him to stand beside her bed in the middle of the night. Though she lay perfectly still, he knew damned well she was awake.

"You can refuse me," he said, his voice hard and clear in the darkness. The tension hummed through his naked body, every muscle drawn taut, as he waited for her response. Her silence was answer enough for him.

When he lifted the bedclothes to crawl in beside her, she did not cry out in protest. He felt her move on the bed, then heard the soft swoosh of her tunic hitting the floor. He turned toward her and, at long last, felt her naked body next to his.

In an instant, he had her in his arms, every part of her pressed against him. His hands moved over her as he kissed her hair, her face, her throat. Rolling her onto her back, he buried his face between her breasts and breathed in her scent. He sucked her breasts, first one and then the other, until her breath came in sharp gasps.

He tried to fill the yawning emptiness inside him with his passion, the feel of her smooth skin, the smell of her hair, the sensation of her body responding to his. Driven to possess her in every way, he lowered himself until his head was between her legs.

If this was sin, he was long past caring. He tasted her as he wanted to. As he'd wanted to from the first time. When she gasped in surprise, he tightened his hold around her thighs. She would have to make her protest loud and certain if she wanted him to stop. No other woman tasted like this, smelled like this. He licked and sucked and slid his finger inside her.

She writhed and moaned, but he would not be satisfied until he made her cry out. When she did, he surged up on his knees and pulled her hips against him, thrusting, fast and hard, fast and hard, until they cried out together.

He collapsed forward, panting, his weight on his outstretched arms, his forehead resting on her chest.

Neither had spoken a single word.

He lifted himself up and dropped beside her, spent.

Surely that frenzied coupling had satisfied the aching hunger inside him. But when her fingers brushed his cheek, he knew it had not. He wanted far more from her than he could trust her to give.

He lay on his back, staring into the darkness. Her fear in the first days of their marriage had been real. He was almost sure of that. But had she feigned the tenderness in the weeks that followed? Had she?

He was about to get up to return to his own bed when she moved beside him. The breath went out of him as her hand came to rest on the flat of his stomach. Then she leaned over him, her hair sliding over his skin.

And he was lost again.

———

She did not come to his bed as she used to. But each night he went to hers, and they made love. Silent, frantic, all need and want and anger. Afterward, he would leave her, unable to bear the intimacy of sleeping with her.

Though she let him into her bed each night, she

avoided him during the daylight hours. Against his will, he watched for her all day. He caught only glimpses of her—leaving a room, walking on the ramparts with Stephen, running across the bailey yard with Jamie.

He knew it could not go on like this.

When she once again did not come to the hall to take her breakfast, he decided enough was enough. He took the stairs two at a time and entered the solar.

He stood outside the closed door to her bedchamber, asking himself why he was there. He did not know whether he could trust her. Whether her feelings were true. The hard truth was, none of that changed what he wanted. He wanted their relationship to be as it had been before.

Through the door, he heard her retching. He pushed the door open to find her vomiting into a basin. As she wiped her mouth on a cloth, she looked up. The apprehension that came into her eyes when she saw him took him aback.

"Are you ill?" he asked from the doorway.

"'Tis nothing. Just an uneasy stomach."

His anger drained out of him. She looked so frail and vulnerable in her night shift, with her slim ankles and delicate feet showing below. Despite everything, a feeling of tenderness swept over him.

He took the basin and towel from her and set them aside. Taking her hand, he said, "Catherine, I want us—"

Before he could say more, there was a loud banging at the solar door. *Damnation.*

"What is it?" he shouted as he stomped into the solar.

To his surprise, it was not a servant waiting outside the door but one of his men.

"Lord FitzAlan," the man said, "we have reports the French have landed a force." He was breathless from running.

"What else do you know? Where are they?"

"They landed at Milford Haven," the man said. "'Tis a disaster, m'lord. The castles at Haverfordwest, Cardigan, Tenby, and Carmarthen have all been taken. The French are now sweeping across the south of Wales to Cardiff."

"God in heaven," William swore, "the king and his army are in the North."

"I was told messengers are on their way to both London and the king."

"We must make haste to be ready when the king calls."

William followed the man out. What he had to say to Catherine would have to wait.

The castle bustled with activity as the men prepared to leave for war. There would be a major battle when the two armies met, so William would take most of the men with him. Luckily, Ross Castle could be defended with a small number of men. The most serious threat was siege. William had worked hard, however, to ensure the castle's stores were adequate.

As soon as the news reached the king, he would race his army south. He would send word to the Marcher lords, telling them where to join him for the confrontation.

The call would come soon. As soon as tomorrow.

At supper, he asked Catherine to wait up for him. He did not know if a full reconciliation was possible, but he wanted to come to some understanding with her before

he left. He still had much to do, so it was late before he
finally made his way up to their rooms.

He found her asleep on the window seat in the solar.
The candle on the table was nearly gone. He pulled up a
stool, glad for the opportunity to watch her unobserved.

Starting with her shining hair and the delicate features
of her face, he let his gaze travel over her. His throat tightened as he took in the curves of her breasts, her waist, her
hips, and then the long line of her legs. When he reached
her feet, so small and graceful, he felt an unexpected sting
at the back of his eyes.

What was he to do with her? He could not say, but he
did not want to leave things as they were. He picked up
her hand and rubbed his thumb over it. Its very smallness
made him feel protective.

Her eyes fluttered open.

"You were smiling in your sleep," he said. "What were
you dreaming?"

Still only half awake, she said, "A dream I often have
about something that happened long ago."

"Tell me about it."

She sat up and ran her fingers through her hair. Awake
now, she gave him a wary look and shook her head. "It
will only make you angry."

"Please, I want to hear."

After more prodding and assurances, she gave in.

His heart turned in his chest as she began to tell of the
ride they took the night before her wedding to Rayburn.

"A young man was sleeping in the stable, and he went
with me." She cast a nervous glance at William and
added, "He was an honorable young man who wished to
protect me."

William nodded, which seemed to reassure her. He kept quiet and let her tell the tale.

At the end, she said in a wistful voice, "That night I felt safe and happy and free all at once."

He swallowed hard, regretting that he'd never made her feel that way again.

"I've dreamed of that night often," she said, looking off into the distance. "The dream seems to come to me when I am worried or unhappy."

He felt worse, knowing he was the cause of her unhappiness tonight.

"Is your dream always the same?" he asked. "Do you dream it just as it happened that night?"

She looked down at her hands and took her time in answering. "It has always been so, until tonight. This time, the young man became you in the dream."

William felt as if a fist gripped his heart. Taking both her hands, he asked, "Do you remember in whose service this young knight was?"

She jerked her hands away. "You are not going to chase him down and threaten his life, are you?"

"I swear, I will not."

She seemed to take him at his word, for she put her hand to her chin and paused to think. "I am certain he did tell me.... He was on an errand for someone important...."

Her eyes widened. "It was Northumberland."

"Aye, it was."

She stared at him a long while, a question forming in her eyes.

"My hair was long then, and I wore a beard," he said in a quiet voice. "At that age, my pride at being able to grow one was greater than my annoyance at how much it made me look like Hotspur."

Her jaw dropped.

"It was you?"

He nodded.

She scrutinized him through narrowed eyes. "'Tis true, between the beard and the darkness I could see little of the man's face," she said slowly. "But the difference is in more than your appearance."

"I am changed?" he asked, though he was not sure he wanted to hear.

"You are used to command now, and it shows," she said in a tentative voice. "Back then, you were...you were...more trusting."

"What do you mean?"

She bit her lip, hesitant.

"You can tell me," he pressed.

"You did not know me, yet you took every word I said on faith."

He saw the hurt in her eyes. And the accusation.

"I thought you had forgotten that night," he said, his heart in his hand. "I dream of it as well. But in my dreams, I always rescue you." It made him feel vulnerable to tell her, but he made himself continue. "I chastised myself for not finding a way to help you that night. I think that is one reason the dreams would not leave me."

"You could not know how Rayburn would mistreat me," she said without a hint of hesitation. "And there was nothing you could do. Rayburn was the king's choice."

He shrugged. Practical considerations did not release a man from what honor required.

"How long have you known I was that girl?" she asked,

an edge to her voice now. "Did you know even before you came to take Ross Castle?"

"I did not know until I saw you on the drawbridge." He closed his eyes as he recalled how he had ridden his horse up to her in a fit of rage. "It was when you fainted."

They were silent for a time, each lost in their own thoughts.

"Guilt was not the only reason I dreamed of you." He wanted to tell her all of it now, before he left for battle. "There have been other women. But from the night I rode with you in the moonlight, it was always you I wanted."

The confession was hard to make. He expected it to please her. Instead, her expression grew melancholy.

"At times in these last weeks, I believed you cared for me." She sighed and shook her head. "But it was never me you cared for. You were in love with a girl in a dream."

He came to her tonight hoping to bridge the rift between them. Even though he had doubts about her, still he came. He confessed he had wanted her—*dreamed* of her—for years.

And yet, she dismissed all this as nothing.

"You have hurt me more than Rayburn ever did," she said.

There was nothing she could have said that would have surprised or offended him more.

"I've never taken my hand to you," he snapped.

"Rayburn battered my body, but he could not touch my heart. He was predictably cruel, never once to be trusted." She looked hard at him as she spoke, her eyes revealing both hurt and anger. "But you, William, you are so kind to me that I trust you—and then you rage at me.

"You made me ache with your tenderness," she continued, her voice beginning to quaver. "And then you come to me in lust only, taking me and then leaving me more alone than I have ever been before."

"You could have refused me," he said in a choked whisper. "I told you that you could." It was his only defense.

"I missed your touch," she said, her smile bittersweet. "Each time, I hoped what we did would bring you close to me again. That it would be as it was before between us."

William covered his face with his hands, overwhelmed with emotion. When he heard her rise, he dropped them and looked up at her.

"It is you I need rescuing from now, William, for you are breaking my heart," she said, her eyes wet with unshed tears. "You bring me misery of a kind Rayburn never could."

He grabbed her wrist to stop her from leaving.

"I am sorry with all my heart for hurting you," he said, pleading. "I am sorry for it all."

"You did not even believe me when I tried to warn you of the French landing," she flung at him, her voice bitter.

He did not care if she chastised him so long as she stayed.

"I should have listened to you." The fact that the troubadour brought her news of war did not mean the man was not also trying to seduce her, but William did not say that.

"Please, Catherine, I do not want to leave with this unhappiness between us."

She knew the risk that he might not return from battle without him having to say it. It was unfair to play on her sympathy in this way, but he was too desperate to care.

All he wanted was to have that closeness between them

again. The joy. She was not like other women, not like his mother. If he could make Catherine happy, she would not leave him.

He pressed her open hand against his cheek. "I know I cannot mend it all tonight," he said, looking up at her. "But could you pretend to forgive me for this one night? We cannot know when we will have another."

When he kissed her palm, she closed her eyes as if bracing herself. He put his arms around her waist and rested his head against her.

"I promise I will be a better husband to you when I return." He meant it with all his heart.

She ran her fingers through his hair, then kissed the top of his head. The miracle of her kindness washed over him.

He knew he must not fail her again.

He rose to his feet and lifted her in his arms. He looked into her face, waiting for her answer. After a long, long moment, she nodded. He carried her to his bedchamber before she could change her mind.

Tonight he would take her with a tenderness he hoped might begin to heal her heart.

He set her on the edge of the bed and lit a single candle. When he came to sit beside her, she moved away so that they did not touch. He had a long way to go to earn her trust back.

He turned her away from him and began massaging her neck and shoulders. Her muscles were tense under his hands; he worked them until he felt her relax.

He kissed her along the curve of her neck. When he reached her ear, he whispered, "Lie down for me, Kate."

She let him ease her down onto her belly.

He undid her braid and ran his fingers through the long, silky strands. As always, he was mesmerized by the hundred shades of gold reflected in the candlelight. Sweeping her hair to one side, he leaned over and pressed his lips to her cheek.

He rubbed her scalp and temples with his fingertips until she closed her eyes. Then he moved down to her shoulders and back, massaging through the thin night shift. By the time he worked his way to her fingers, her hands were limp.

"Are you cold?" he asked, and smiled at her muffled grunt in response.

He turned his attention to her feet, rubbing first the soles and then each toe in turn. The curve of her lips told him she was enjoying his ministrations. He bent her leg so that her foot rested against his chest while he massaged her calf. He stopped to kiss her foot, her toes, to run his tongue along the sole of her foot.

He laid her foot on the bed and kissed the back of her knee. As he kissed it, he eased her night shift up her thighs.

The room was warm.

Sweat broke out on his forehead as he massaged her thighs. Slowly but steadily, he worked his way upward. When he got to the juncture between leg and buttock, he traced the delectable curve with his tongue. When she shivered in response, he gently bit her with his teeth. Once, twice, three times.

He lifted his head and gave it a shake, reminding himself that this was for her. He tried to slow his breathing.

He returned to his work with renewed resolve. As he pulled her shift up, she lifted her hips and then her chest and head. He had her naked at last.

God have mercy, his wife was beautiful.

His wife.

He straddled her to rub her back. With slow delibera-
tion, he worked his way over every inch. Then he ran his
fingers in light circles over her back. He felt himself grow
harder and harder with anticipation as he swept his hands
closer and closer, until at last his fingers touched the soft,
full curve of the sides of her breasts.

Feeling her stir at the touch, he clenched his jaw until
it ached. He wanted to feel her breasts in his hands, her
nipples hard beneath his palms.

He took a deep breath.

Hoping he could keep himself in check, he leaned on
his forearms to kiss her neck. His chest brushed against
her back, sending a jolt of hot lust through him. He
squeezed his eyes shut against the urge to rub his throbbing cock against her backside. If he did, he would never
last.

For a long moment, he remained poised over her, his
breath coming hard and fast. All he could think of was
lifting her hips and entering her from behind.

He opened his eyes as she rolled over to face him. Her
amused smile told him she knew exactly what he'd been
thinking. Eyes twinkling, she shook her head at him. He
was pleased to see a hint of the playfulness she used to
show him in bed.

"Aye, 'tis much too soon," he agreed. Sighing dramati-
cally, he fell beside her and took her in his arms.

"It is good to be here with you like this," he said, and
kissed the tip of her nose.

"Mmmm," she murmured, squeezing closer.

She gave him an openmouthed kiss that made him

forget his name. As they kissed, he slid his hands between her legs. It took the breath out of him when he felt how hot and wet she was. She would kill him for certain. She pressed against him as if wanting to melt into him.

Keeping his hand on her, he eased himself down on the bed until he could take her breast in his mouth. When he did, he heard her sharp intake of breath. He loved to hear the sounds she made. He slowly slid his finger in and out of her as he flicked his tongue over her nipple, listening to the change in her breathing.

His heart pounded in his ears as he sucked harder, and she moaned and moved against his hand. At first, he ignored her insistent pull on his shoulders. He was set on bringing her to release the first time before he entered her. But when she persisted, he obeyed.

Hovering over her, he gave her a long wet kiss. When she wrapped her legs around him, the battle was lost. He slid deep inside her in one forceful stroke.

Good God! The rush that went through him blinded him and left him shuddering. It was all he could do to stop himself from spilling his seed at once. He found her mouth. Their tongues slid together as he moved back and forth against her as slowly as he could bear.

When she increased the rhythm, he could not find his voice to tell her she must stop. She was relentless and he loved it. She arched her back, letting her head fall over the side of the bed. Her breath came in short gasps as he felt her tighten around his shaft.

And then she called his name. She was his. She was his.

With her cries ringing in his ears, urging him on, he pounded into her, again and again, until sight and sound were obliterated in an explosion that was near death.

He could barely keep from collapsing with his full weight on top of her. Breathing hard and dripping with sweat, he let his forehead rest on the bed beside her head.

"God in heaven, what have you done to me, Catherine?"

When he heard her low chuckle, a wave of tenderness swept over him. How long since he had made her laugh? He pulled her into his arms as he sank down beside her.

He lay with his face buried in her hair.

"I wish I did not have to leave you so soon," he whispered.

He needed more time. Time to heal her, to heal himself, to be with her like this. With a sense of desperation, he turned to her again and again in the night. In the heat of passion, Catherine told him she loved him.

But William—though he tried to show her with his every touch—could not yet confess his love aloud.

Chapter Eighteen

The men of Ross Castle were gathered near the gate, their armor shining bright in the August sun. Shielding her eyes with her hand, Catherine took in each man and prayed for his safe return.

The news came an hour ago. The French-Welsh army was nearing the English border, marching toward Worcester. Glyndwr's move was both unexpected and brilliant. Taking an English town for even a short time would be a devastating blow to English pride. A blow that King Henry, already hanging on to the throne by his fingernails, could ill afford.

Caught by surprise, the king was racing his army headlong across the length of England to save Worcester. William and the other Marcher lords were commanded to await him there with their men-at-arms. If Henry could reach Worcester in time, the major battle between the two armies would be there.

Catherine swallowed hard to keep back the tears. One night was not enough to recover the closeness they had before. She could not forget so soon how much he'd hurt her. Nor did she believe he'd overcome his mistrust of her.

Still, it was a magical night, and she was hopeful. Very hopeful.

She caught sight of Edmund, talking with several of the men.

"Why is Edmund not in armor?" she asked William, tightening her grip on his arm.

"Edmund is staying here with a few of the men," William said. "Glyndwr has his army moving fast, hoping to take Worcester before the king can reach it. There is almost no danger of an attack on the castle; still, I cannot leave it completely undefended."

"I have been left in charge of this castle many times," Catherine said. "I neither need nor want Edmund Forrester here."

William ran a hand through his hair, looking uncomfortable. "I am sure you managed well enough on your own, but Edmund has years of fighting experience."

She was unmoved by his argument and did not hide it.

"I warned Edmund that if he does anything to offend you, I'll not keep him in my service." He held her face in his hands and kissed her forehead. "Please, Catherine, I do not want to argue with you as I leave. I need to know my best man is protecting you if I'm to keep my mind on what is before me."

She ceased to argue. It was dangerous for a man to be distracted when he fought. For this same reason, she was waiting to tell him about her pregnancy until he returned.

Stephen appeared beside them with Jamie in tow.

"You were fighting Scots at my age," Stephen said to William, his eyes bright with anger. "You treat me like a child!"

Catherine grabbed Stephen's arm and hauled him a few feet away where William would not overhear her.

"With William gone, I need you here," she told him in a low, fierce voice. "Do not abandon me." She held his eyes until she was sure he understood she meant it.

When she rejoined William, he whispered in her ear, "What did you do, promise to marry the lad if I do not return? He's puffed up like a peacock!" He squeezed her hand. "Whatever it was, I thank you."

The men were mounting their horses, so William threw Jamie into the air one more time and ruffled the boy's hair.

Next, he turned to say farewell to Stephen. With a nod toward Catherine and Jamie, he said, "Keep them safe, brother."

Finally, he gathered Catherine in his arms and kissed her hard on the mouth in front of everyone.

He mounted his horse. "You will be safe here," he said, looking down at her. "I promise you."

"Promise only that you will come back to us."

"You need not worry for me," he said, flashing her a wide smile. "I will always come back for you, Kate. Always."

—⁓—

Those left behind at Ross Castle waited for news. They heard, first, that King Henry reached Worcester faster than anyone thought possible—and not an hour too soon. Since his arrival, however, the two great armies had been in a standoff.

While the commanders decided what to do, individual knights met in single combat on the field between the armies. This served no purpose, except to relieve the boredom. The stakes were too high to be decided by knightly challenges.

Catherine's tension over the coming battle grew as the days of waiting continued. Having Edmund unclothe her with his eyes every time she crossed his path did not help. He was, however, careful to speak politely and show her every other courtesy.

The memory of how he cornered her in the solar still rankled. While he would not dare harm her, neither did she want to be caught alone with him again. With Stephen here, there was little chance of that.

Stephen took William's admonition to keep her safe to heart. The first night, she found him sleeping in front of her chamber door. Her promises to have her maid sleep with her and bar her door were not enough to dissuade him. Only when she showed him the blade under her pillow did he finally agree to return to his own chamber.

"I would like to visit Abbess Talcott today," she announced at the midday meal, pushing her food away.

"I will be your escort," Stephen said.

Edmund shook his head. "I doubt that is what your brother had in mind when he told me to provide a proper escort for his lady wife." To Catherine, he said, "I will take you myself, since that is what William would wish. I have an errand in the village today, but I'll gladly take you tomorrow."

"Thank you," she said, thinking William must have lectured Edmund to accommodate her.

"I'll come, too," Stephen said.

Edmund took one look at the stubborn set of Stephen's jaw and shrugged. "I cannot spare another man to go with us, but there isn't much danger with the whole of the rebel army at Worcester. You are both fine riders, so we should be able to outrun any other kind of trouble."

Edmund took a piece of roasted pork with his eating knife. "All the same," he said, pointing his knife at her as he chewed, "I would not take your son along."

Much as Catherine hated to admit it, Edmund was right. It was safer to leave Jamie at the castle. He would be fine with his nursemaid for the day.

"Did you get your business done in the village yesterday?" Catherine asked Edmund. Now that they were on their way, she could afford to be friendly.

"Aye." Edmund's reply was curt.

She had to admit Edmund took his responsibility to protect her seriously. Riding in front of her, he kept a sharp watch, constantly moving his head from side to side. She turned in her saddle and found Stephen doing the same behind her. In the North, boys learned to watch for raiders from a young age.

Catherine blinked as they rode into a copse of wood, and her eyes adjusted from bright sun to dappled light. The green canopy overhead was lovely. She was leaning back to look for birds when she heard the sound of hoofbeats. In another moment, a half-dozen men on horses burst into view around the bend ahead.

Edmund turned and shouted, "Ride hard back to the castle! I will hold them as long as I can."

Catherine was unable to tear her eyes from the men galloping toward them. She watched Edmund spur his horse forward to meet them, his broadsword ready in his hand.

"Now, Catherine!" Stephen shouted. He grabbed her horse's bridle, turned her around, and slapped her horse's hindquarters. It took off with a jerk.

Over her shoulder, she saw Edmund fighting off two of the men. As she watched, four other riders rode past the swinging swords without breaking their speed. The four charged toward her and Stephen.

Too late, she spurred her horse. As she left the copse for the open field, two horses came thundering beside her, pinning her between them. One of the riders leaned down and snatched up her reins.

As the man pulled her horse to a jarring halt, she tried to keep her eyes on Stephen. He was sweeping across the field ahead of his two pursuers. Praise God, he was going to outrun them. But then Stephen looked back and saw her.

"No, Stephen, no!" she shouted as he turned his horse in a wide arc to evade the two men and head back toward her. To her horror, he was brandishing his sword as if he meant to take them all on to rescue her.

She turned to the dark, fierce-looking man holding her horse's reins. "Please, sir, do not hurt him!"

The man squinted against the sun and watched Stephen's progress without giving any sign he heard her.

Frantic, she turned to the man on her other side. "Please, he is only a boy!"

The man flashed her a smile. "If you can convince the lad to put down his sword, I can promise his safety."

Stephen came thundering down on them, and the man who had just spoken was forced to fend off his attack. Though Stephen was skilled with a sword for his age, the man easily parried his thrusts. The silent man who held her horse watched them, looking unconcerned.

"M'lady?" the man fighting Stephen called out. "I need your help."

"Stephen, put down your sword!"

Her shout caused Stephen to glance toward her. The man took advantage of Stephen's momentary distraction to take his sword.

"Listen to the lady," he said, "and you shall not be harmed."

Stephen reached for the dagger at his belt, but the man anticipated the move. Holding Stephen's forearm, he reached across Stephen's body and took the dagger.

Without taking his hands off Stephen, he said to the other man, "Rhys, do you think that is all?"

The man called Rhys flicked his eyes to Stephen's foot. At this silent signal, the first man checked both of Stephen's boots. When he had removed the hidden blade, he glanced again at Rhys. Rhys nodded, apparently satisfied Stephen was disarmed.

Ignoring the men, Stephen said to Catherine, "I am sorry I failed you."

"You could not have done more." Even in the midst of their danger, it hurt her to see Stephen look so defeated. "I do not believe these men mean to harm me," she added, and regretted the note of uncertainty that crept into her voice.

"Most assuredly we do not, dear lady," the handsome man who disarmed Stephen spoke up.

The two riders who chased Stephen had joined them by now. Catherine examined their four captors closely. They looked as though they had been traveling rough, but their clothes were finely made. She guessed they were Welsh noblemen. If she was right, their intent was likely ransom, not rape and murder.

"You are Welsh rebels?" she asked.

"Aye, that we are, Lady FitzAlan," the handsome one answered.

They knew her name. That meant they did not just happen upon her, notice her fine clothes and horse, and take advantage of a chance opportunity.

"My name is Maredudd ap Tudor," the man said, bowing his head. "These two"—he pointed to the two young men who had chased Stephen—"are my brothers, Owen and Maddog."

Both young men nodded politely. She could see the family resemblance, though neither was quite as good-looking as their dashing older brother.

Tudors? She had heard the name. She knew she had. Were they not close kinsmen of Owain Glyndwr, the rebel leader?

And then it came to her.

"Are you the same Tudors who violated holy Good Friday to take Conwy Castle?"

"That would be our elder brothers," Maredudd said, and all three Tudor men grinned.

God have mercy, she was a captive of the wily Tudors!

"The church decree to shed no blood on the holy day was not violated," one of the younger Tudors put in. With a wink, he added, "The castle guards were strangled."

The story of the unexpected attack was told up and down England. The rebels took the castle easily, since the entire garrison was at Mass in the nearby village.

"And the man holding your horse," Maredudd ap Tudor continued, "is Rhys Gethin."

Upon hearing the name, Catherine gasped aloud and brought a hand to her chest.

"I see you have heard of him," Maredudd said with an amused smile. "Then you will know why we call him 'Gethin.' It means 'the Fierce' in Welsh."

Rhys Gethin had led the Welsh forces in their great bloody victory at Bryn Glas three years before. Against overwhelming odds, the Welsh killed nearly eleven hundred Englishmen. It was said that at the end of the battle, the field was knee-deep in English blood.

"I am surprised men of such importance have come on such a lowly errand," she said, trying to keep the quaver out of her voice. She risked a glance at Stephen, hoping he would not contradict her. "You go to much trouble for little, I fear. It is unlikely my husband will pay much for my ransom."

Maredudd Tudor threw his head back and laughed. "Faith, m'lady, a man would pay a good deal for the return of so fair a woman. The rumors of your beauty hardly—"

"Enough!" Rhys Gethin's deep voice cut Maredudd off. "We delay too long. Glyndwr needs us at Worcester."

With that, he tossed her horse's reins to Maredudd and spurred his own horse forward. Maredudd tied her horse to his and fell into line behind him. The two younger Tudors followed with Stephen between them.

Catherine looked over her shoulder at the copse of wood, hoping Edmund got away.

———

They rode for hours, stopping only once to allow her to stretch her legs and relieve herself. Toward evening, small groups of men appeared out of the woods and joined them. Now she understood why English soldiers claimed the Welsh came and disappeared like fairies, with the help of magic.

At nightfall, they stopped in a heavy wood to make camp. Her legs were so weak that Maredudd had to catch her to keep her from falling when she dismounted. He led her to sit on a fallen log, holding her a bit more tightly than necessary.

"Lady FitzAlan, I would have your promise you will not try to escape," he said as he sat down next to her on the log. "You would only get lost, and I am too tired to go chasing about the woods for you tonight."

There was no point in trying. The woods were unfamiliar, and in the dark, she had no idea in which direction to go.

"If you make an attempt, I will catch you. And then you will sleep tied to me." His face broke into a wide smile. Giving her a wink, he said, "Perhaps you should try after all."

"With such charm, sir, how is it that some maid has not yet captured you?"

"Ah, but one has," he replied genially. "I am married to a remarkable woman named Marged."

"She is remarkably trusting to let you out of her sight." She surprised them both by speaking the thought aloud.

"I do enjoy your company," Maredudd said, slapping his thigh. "Marged knows I am devoted to her. Fortunately, she has the wisdom not to expect the impossible from me. In sooth," he added with a twinkle in his eye, "she is quite content with me."

Catherine wanted to roll her eyes at the man's vanity, though she suspected he spoke the truth. Maredudd Tudor was charming and devilishly handsome. Despite the circumstances, she also trusted him to protect her in this camp of armed men.

"May I speak with my young friend now?" She was anxious to talk with Stephen.

"We know the lad is Stephen Carleton, FitzAlan's half-brother," Maredudd said.

They could have guessed who she was. They found her near Ross Castle, and her family was well known in the Marches. But how did they know Stephen?

"Do not fret over the lad. He'll be returned safe and sound," Maredudd said. "If it had not been plain the boy would follow us, we would have left him where we found him."

At the sound of a scuffle, she peered through the growing darkness. A moment later, the younger Tudor brothers appeared with Stephen kicking and twisting furiously between them.

"God's beard, can you not see the lady is well?" one of them shouted at Stephen.

"We Welshmen are not the savages Englishmen are," the other complained. "Besides, no man here will dare touch her while she is under the protection of a Tudor."

Stephen saw her and ceased to struggle. The men dropped him to the ground.

"He does not believe you will be safe, m'lady," one of the brothers explained, "unless he is the one who guards you."

She saw the flash of Maredudd's white teeth in the rapidly falling darkness. "It is encouraging to find chivalry still lives in at least one young Englishman," he said. "Stephen, you can make your bed next to the fair lady. That will make it easier to keep watch over the two of you."

Leaving them in the care of his brothers, Maredudd left to talk with some of the other men. Catherine and Stephen sat huddled together while the younger Tudors cooked a supper of small game over the fire. The two men were too near, however, for them to speak freely.

They waited until after they had eaten and lay down on the blankets spread for them close to the fire.

"The Welsh commanders fear their army is too strung out," Stephen whispered. "Gethin and the Tudors back-tracked from Worcester to make sure the king did not send part of his army behind them, to cut them off from their base."

Catherine was not surprised Stephen had managed to overhear so much.

"They did not come for you," Stephen continued. "But when they caught wind you would be outside the castle this morning, you were too great a prize to miss."

This made much more sense than that the Tudors and Rhys Gethin would leave Worcester to take a single captive for ransom.

"Did you hear them say how they knew I would be outside the castle walls today?" She still could not understand this part.

"Nay, but it must mean we have a traitor at the castle," he whispered. "Who do you think it is?"

Who, indeed.

Chapter Nineteen

Catherine awoke with the prickling sensation that someone was watching her. She opened her eyes to find Maredudd standing over her.

"Good morning," he said, and nodded toward Stephen. "I see your gallant protector gave up the fight and took his rest."

Embarrassed to be talking with Maredudd while lying down, she sat up. Shivering, she pulled her blanket tightly around her shoulders. The early morning air held a chill.

"We are near Worcester, a few minutes' ride from where Glyndwr is encamped," Maredudd told her. "I sent word last night that I would bring you to him as soon as we break our fast."

She had not expected to be taken to Glyndwr himself. Unconsciously, she reached up to touch her hair. With no maid—or even a comb—she did not know how she could make herself presentable to the man the Welsh called their prince.

"Glyndwr understands rough travel. He'll not think it amiss that you did not have a maid to dress your hair,"

Maredudd said with a smile. "'Tis a sin that custom requires such lovely hair be hidden."

He squatted down and shook Stephen's shoulder. "Come, lad. Prince Glyndwr has much on his mind, and I do not wish to keep him waiting."

Catherine picked up the ornate headdress she wore yesterday. Stephen had helped her remove it last night, but there was no hope of getting it back on today.

She heaved a sigh. There was nothing for it but to make do as best she could. After painstakingly detaching the gold mesh and circlet from the headdress, she combed her hair with her fingers and plaited it into a single braid down her back. Then she put the mesh over her hair and fixed the circlet across her forehead to hold it in place. The makeshift covering left too much hair exposed, but that was that.

She looked down at the dismal state of her gown. Working methodically, she began brushing the dirt from it, top to bottom. She was so absorbed in her task that she was startled when she looked up to find Stephen and all three Tudors staring at her, slack-jawed.

She narrowed her eyes at them. "How long have you been watching me?"

There was a general shrugging of shoulders.

"Do you men have nothing better to do?" she asked, her irritation evident in her tone.

Stephen had the grace to look away. The three Tudors, however, just shook their heads and smiled.

The other men were breaking camp when Catherine and Stephen rode off with the Tudors. Praise God her captors brought her here, rather than into Wales. William was in Worcester. She could be ransomed and delivered to him this very day.

"Can you see the old Celtic fort at the top of that hill?" Maredudd said, pointing ahead. "That is where we and the French are encamped."

Catherine dragged her thoughts from her reunion with William to prepare herself to meet the rebel leader. Quickly, she reviewed what she knew of Owain Glyndwr. He was a Welsh nobleman, close kinsman to the Tudors. Before the rebellion, his home was known as a center of Welsh culture, where troubadours and musicians were always welcome.

A man who liked music, she told herself, could not be completely heartless. The common folk claimed he used magic to call up terrible storms. There were other stories she could not dismiss so easily. She had ridden out after rebel raids. She had seen the smoldering villages and heard the women weeping.

Before she knew it, they were riding through the gates of the old fort. The bailey was teeming with soldiers. They rode through the chaos of men and horses and carts to the main building. After helping her from her horse, Maredudd led her up the steps with Stephen and the two brothers following on their heels.

The guards inside the entry nodded to the Tudors and opened the second set of heavy doors. Once her eyes adjusted, Catherine saw they were in a dark, cavernous hall. There was a huge hearth against one of the long walls and trestle tables set up along the other. A number of men were in the room, talking in groups or cleaning weapons.

Only one man drew her attention, however. He was watching her from the far end of the hall.

With his hand firmly on her arm, Maredudd walked her across the room to him. Catherine dropped into the low curtsy reserved for monarchs and kept her head down until a deep voice told her to rise.

When she did, she got her first good look at the famous rebel whose name had been on everyone's lips for the past five years. Owain Glyndwr looked to be in his late forties. His sternly handsome face was lined, and the dark hair that fell to his shoulders was streaked iron gray. Catherine had the impression of long limbs and a powerful body beneath his robes. The riveting black eyes held hers.

"Lady FitzAlan, you have done great harm to me and my people." Glyndwr's words carried through the hall and reverberated off the walls.

Taken aback, Catherine could make no reply. What did he think she had done?

"I wondered for a long time who passed the information that led to my son and his men being caught unawares at Pwll Melyn," Glyndwr said. "In the end, I decided it could only be you."

How had he known? King Henry did not believe she was the one, even when the prince had told him.

"I am sorry, Your Grace," she stammered. "It was my duty."

"Prince Harry took three hundred Welshmen prisoner at Pwll Melyn," he said. "He executed them all, save one."

Involuntarily, she put her hand to her mouth. She had heard something of this before but had not believed it.

"At least young Harry does not kill for sport or revenge.

He kills ruthlessly in pursuit of his aims, as a great commander must." Glyndwr's face looked suddenly weary as he turned to gaze into the hearth fire. "The difference, however, matters not to the widows and orphans.

"He executed them all, save for my son Gruffydd, who was taken to London in chains." Glyndwr paused and pressed his lips together. "He is tortured, I am told. After he was caught attempting to escape, the king had his eyes put out."

Catherine felt the sting of tears at the back of her eyes. The truth of Glyndwr's words was etched in the pain on his face. She did not want to believe her king capable of such barbarism. Yet, in her heart, she knew he was. For the first time, she wondered if what she had done was right. Should she have told Harry he could catch the Welsh unprepared that day? Would she have, if she could have foreseen the consequences?

"I hear you have a son, Lady FitzAlan," Glyndwr said, jolting her attention back to the present. "So you will understand that I will do what I can to get my son out of my enemy's hands."

Catherine held her breath, waiting for Glyndwr to reveal his purpose in telling her this.

"You shall be my son's deliverance. His life is the ransom I will claim for your return."

Dismay and confusion warred within her. "I fear you mistake my importance, Your Grace," she said, clutching her hands together. "The king would never trade your son for me. He is not . . . a sentimental man."

She gave up trying to find a diplomatic way to explain it and said, "The king would sacrifice me without a second thought."

She felt disloyal for her frankness, but she saw what looked like appreciation in Glyndwr's eyes.

"Rayburn was a fool not to realize he had such a perceptive wife. You are right, of course. Henry would not, on his own, make a sacrifice for you."

"My husband will not be able to persuade him otherwise," she said. "I believe Lord FitzAlan would, however, be willing to pay a handsome ransom for me." She no longer cared how much William had to pay, just that he pay it quickly.

"I will not make my demand to FitzAlan," Glyndwr said, "but to the king's son."

Catherine was stunned. "To Harry?"

"I have heard troubadours sing of your beauty, Lady FitzAlan." Glyndwr smiled at her for the first time. "'Tis no wonder you have a prince besotted with you."

Catherine opened her mouth to speak, but no words came out.

"I will send a message informing Prince Harry I will take no payment but my son in exchange for his lover."

"But I am not the prince's lover!" Catherine said, finally finding her voice.

When Glyndwr looked at her skeptically, she attempted to explain. "We were childhood friends. We are friends yet. Besides, I am a married woman." Her face flushing hot with embarrassment, she said, "He would never...he would not..."

"Surely you do not believe your wedded state would stop a man from wanting you," Glyndwr said, raising an eyebrow. "And an English prince would never think such rules applied to him."

Glyndwr looked past her and nodded. Maredudd, whose presence she had forgotten, came to her side.

"Let us hope you are as precious to the prince as I've heard," Glyndwr said, dismissing her. "For you will not see your home again unless he persuades the king to release my son."

Maredudd touched her elbow and whispered, "Make your curtsy."

She did so numbly and let him lead her out to where Stephen and the other Tudors waited.

When the doors to the hall shut behind them, she broke down into sobs. "I fear I shall never see my son or my home again!"

"You shall," Maredudd said, putting his hands on her shoulders. "All will be well in the end, you will see."

"Your prince misunderstands everything!" She clenched her fists and cried out in frustration, "This ransom demand to Prince Harry will make my husband believe I have been unfaithful."

"Nay, he will not," Maredudd said, squeezing her shoulders. "He will just be happy to have you back."

She shook her head. "You know *nothing* of my husband."

⌒

Maredudd escorted her up crumbling stairs to a room crowded with chests—probably pillaged from the town. Through the open window, she saw soldiers gathering in the yard below.

"Will the battle be today?" she asked anxiously.

"I don't know," Maredudd said as he came to stand

beside her at the window. "We've been at a standstill for a week. I cannot see it lasting much longer."

"What do you think will happen?"

"We have a slight advantage in numbers, though both armies are large," he said matter-of-factly. "And the English are tired, coming from weeks of hard fighting in the North. Still, anything can happen. All I can say for certain is that there will be a great many deaths on both sides."

He excused himself to join the men below.

She watched the soldiers ride out the gate, looking magnificent in their full armor. As she watched, she thought of the three hundred Welshmen whose capture and execution Glyndwr blamed on her, and she wept for them.

And what of the fate of the English soldiers today? Of William? And Harry?

"Please, God, protect them," she prayed over and over.

For hours, she paced between the trunks of the cramped room. At long last, the gates were thrown open and the men rode back in, looking none the worse. There was no blood on their armor, no wounded comrades slung over their saddles.

She collapsed onto one of the trunks and put her head in her hands. There was still time. Before long, she heard a knock and Maredudd poked his head through the door.

She waved him in, impatient for news. "There was no battle today?"

He shook his head and sank wearily onto a trunk by the window. "God's beard, this waiting is tedious."

"Maredudd, you must ask for an audience with Prince Glyndwr for me," she said. "There is something I must tell him."

"God in heaven, what can it be? He is busy consulting with his commanders."

Seeing her recalcitrant look, he sighed. "Perhaps I can tell him whatever it is you want him to know."

"I must speak with him myself."

Stifling another oath, Maredudd put his hands on his knees and hoisted himself up. "Your servant," he said, sweeping her a low bow.

An hour later, a woman came to her room carrying a basin of water and a cloth.

"One of the Tudor men sent me. He says to tell you Prince Glyndwr will see you in an hour."

The woman was no ladies' maid. From her rouged lips and revealing bodice, Catherine suspected her usual duties involved providing service of quite a different sort.

The woman put her hands on her hips and looked Catherine up and down. "You're a bit worse for wear, you are. Perhaps we can find you a clean gown in one of these trunks."

Catherine glanced down at her bedraggled gown.

"Aye, let us take a look."

The two women opened trunks and pawed through tunics, leggings, and shirts until they were both hot and red-faced. Near the bottom of one, they found an elegant silk gown of robin's-egg blue with delicate silver trim.

The woman helped Catherine into it. Though it was a bit tight through the bodice, it fit well enough. The woman stuck her head back in the trunk and popped back out, proudly holding up a matching headdress and slippers.

When Catherine was dressed and ready, her helper beamed at her, proud as a peacock. She gave Catherine a broad wink and said, "You look like a princess."

Regal might be just what she needed for this performance, Catherine thought grimly as she started down the stairs. Maredudd was waiting for her at the bottom, just outside the entrance to the hall. When he caught sight of her, he ran his eyes over her from head to toe.

"I see conquering one prince is not enough," he said in a low voice as she took his arm, "but you must set your sights on ensnaring a second."

"I don't know what you mean," she snapped.

"I warn you, our prince is no boy to do your bidding like young Harry," he said, his tone serious. "Do not attempt to play games with him. Glyndwr will know if you tell him lies."

The guards opened the doors, and she saw that the men inside were gathered around a large map rolled out on a trestle table. They turned to stare at her as she entered.

Glyndwr moved away from the others and motioned for her and Maredudd to join him by the hearth.

"What is it you wish to tell me, Lady FitzAlan?" Glyndwr asked at once. He was not a man with time to waste on pleasantries.

It seemed best to start with the truth.

"I have thought hard on what you said about the three hundred men who died because of what I did." Her hands were sweating, but she kept them still. "I regret their deaths."

Glyndwr waited, his gaze unrelenting.

"I fear many more men will die in this battle," she said. "So I prayed to God, asking if it would be a sin to tell you what I know when it might prevent more bloodshed."

"And God answered you?" Glyndwr did not sound as though he thought it likely.

"Not clearly, no." The distress in her voice was genuine.

"So you decided to tell me without the benefit of divine guidance. What is it, Lady FitzAlan? My time is short."

Now for her lie.

"Part of the English army waits near Monmouth Castle." She looked straight into his eyes and made herself believe it as she said it. "They plan to attack you from behind and cut your army off from Wales."

After a pause, Glyndwr asked, "Who leads these men?"

"Prince Harry." She knew from what he said in their first meeting that he respected Harry's military skills.

"But the prince is here at Worcester," Glyndwr said with a smile. "He is easy to pick out on the field."

"Remember Shrewsbury?" she said, her tone challenging.

Anger flashed in his eyes. There were rumors Glyndwr arrived late at Shrewsbury and watched from the woods as the Northern rebel army folded.

"At Shrewsbury, the king employed decoys—knights dressed in the king's armor and mounted on horses like his own," she said. "Hotspur killed two of them before he was cut down."

Catherine kept her eyes steady on Glyndwr as she told her next lie. "The prince uses the same device to fool you now. It was a false prince you saw today. The true one waits to cut off your retreat and attack you from behind."

"Why should I believe you?" he said, his black eyes searching for the truth in her soul. "Why would you come to the rebel cause now, after what you did before?"

"I do not take the rebel side," she said, on the firm

ground of truth again. "But I do not want to have more blood on my hands, English or Welsh."

"So you regret betraying your husband to his death?"

"No!" She blurted her answer without stopping to think.

He nodded, and she saw that the frankness of her response lent credibility to her story.

For a reason she could not explain, she wanted to give Glyndwr the truth about Rayburn, at least.

"Rayburn gave you no true allegiance, Prince Glyndwr," she said in a quiet voice. "He would have sold you to the devil to save himself."

"You tell me nothing I did not know." With a bittersweet smile, he added, "In sooth, his lady wife would have been the better ally."

He stepped closer to her. The penetrating look he gave her sent a shiver through her, but she could not look away from the intense dark eyes. There was a magnetism about this man. She understood Maredudd's warning now. A woman might risk a great deal to be near a man who emanated such power, in the hope he might direct some of that dark passion toward her. She would have to be a brave woman, though.

"Please, let me go home," she said. "I want to see my son."

Glyndwr's eyes went flat, and he looked away from her. "As do I, Lady FitzAlan. As do I."

Guilt stabbed her for reminding him of his pain.

But she had told her lies well. She could only pray she had been right to tell them.

Chapter Twenty

The English commanders awoke to find the Welsh-French army had disappeared during the night. None could explain the unexpected withdrawal. William, for one, was glad to save his men to fight another day. No good could have come from the battle for the English. Even if they prevailed, the field would have been awash with English blood. The loss of men would have made them more vulnerable to the French, their real enemy.

However, it was hard to understand why the other army had withdrawn. A French-Welsh victory on English soil might well have forced King Henry to sacrifice his claim on Wales.

William bid the king farewell and headed for home. Prince Harry rode with him as far as Monmouth. Until it was certain the French were retreating all the way to their ships, the prince would remain in the Welsh Marches.

William had come to like Prince Harry well enough, but he was glad when they parted ways. He was tired of talking of military matters. Riding in blessed silence, he tried to resolve the mystery that was his wife.

Would he always find her in hallways, sharing secrets with princes and troubadours? Good Lord, she even admitted to passing her lover's child off as her husband's. Yet, this same woman welcomed William's young brother into her household with an open heart. She forgave William his harsh words, his lack of trust, and accepted on faith his promise to do better.

And she said she loved him.

Though he did not fully understand her, he knew for certain he could never be content without her.

A sense of well-being came over him when he saw Ross Castle in the distance. Even now, the lookouts would be reporting his arrival to the household. He looked forward to seeing Jamie and Stephen as well. He had grown attached to the boys.

He shook his head. Odd how life could change so quickly. Two months ago, he came here with no real ties. Now, for the first time in his life, he felt as if he had something to lose.

He remembered Catherine's uneasy stomach the day before he left and felt anxious. He spurred his horse ahead of his men and rode through the open gate.

Most of the men he had left at the castle were waiting for him in the bailey. Catherine was not. Scanning the group, he saw that Stephen was missing, too. And where the devil was Edmund?

As he dismounted, a small figure shot out from between the men. He tossed his reins to a waiting stable boy and lifted Jamie into the air.

"Where's your mother, big boy?"

"Didn't you find her?"

Fear ran like ice through his veins.

"Lord FitzAlan." He turned to see Hugh Stratton, one of the men he left with Edmund.

"What has happened?" William said, his heart beating wildly in his chest. "Where is my wife?"

"Lady FitzAlan wished to go to the abbey," Hugh said. "Edmund and Stephen escorted her."

William sagged with relief. His relief dissolved a moment later when Hugh could not meet his eyes.

"What is it? Out with it, man!"

"They were attacked."

God, no!

"When they did not return when expected, we went out looking for them. We found Edmund, but he's in bad shape."

"What of Catherine and Stephen?" Would the fool not tell him if they were alive or dead?

"They must have been taken captive. Except where Edmund was, we found no blood, no piece of torn clothing..."

God have mercy. "When was this?"

"Two days ago. I had the men out searching for them all of yesterday and today," Hugh said. "Edmund can speak now, if you wish to see him. Alys put a bed up for him in the keep."

William was so intent on questioning Hugh that he forgot the boy in his arms until Jamie yelled, "I want my mother!"

Jamie looked at him with eyes big and wet with tears. "I want Stephen, too."

"I shall bring them home," William promised. *And if either one is harmed, I will track the villains down and kill every one of them.*

Jamie leaned heavily against his chest as William carried him to the keep. After handing the boy off to his nursemaid, William went with Hugh to see Edmund.

William paused at the door. He'd seen more than his share of wounded men. But, God's blood, Edmund looked as if he'd been trampled by horses. Everywhere he wasn't bandaged, he was black and blue.

When William knelt beside the cot, Edmund opened one eye. The other was swollen shut.

"I did my best, but there were six of them," Edmund croaked. "I killed one before another caught me from behind."

"What sort of men were they?"

"Welshmen, highborn," Edmund said, and closed his eye.

Praise God they were not rabble! Noblemen were as violent as any men, but rarely so with women of their own class. If Catherine's captors were indeed noblemen, it was likely they took her for ransom and would treat her reasonably well.

He turned and asked Hugh, "Has a ransom message come?"

Hugh shook his head.

When William started to get up, Edmund tried to speak again. William put his hand on Edmund's arm and leaned over to hear him better.

"They were expecting us," Edmund said in a hoarse whisper. "I heard them say her name."

William left Edmund and took his men out to search for Catherine and Stephen. Though the kidnappers would have them deep in Wales by now, he ordered his men to search every wood and hut. They found no sign of

Catherine, Stephen, or the men who took them. He continued searching alone long after dark.

When he returned, he was too dispirited to face his empty bed. Instead, he went up to Jamie's bedchamber where he startled the poor nursemaid from her pallet. As soon as she scurried into the adjoining room, he slumped into the chair by the bed. Somehow, it soothed his troubled soul to watch the boy's face, relaxed and peaceful in sleep.

He awoke at dawn, stiff from sleeping in the chair.

Chapter Twenty-one

Stephen felt the lookouts' eyes tracking him as he rode across the empty fields toward Monmouth Castle in the bright moonlight. As soon as the gate was opened, he was surrounded by a dozen armed men.

"I have a message for the prince's eyes only," Stephen said to each man who questioned him as he was passed up the chain of command. "The prince will want to see it tonight."

It was well past midnight when Stephen was finally delivered to the prince's private rooms. To his relief, Prince Harry did not look as if he had been roused from bed. Stephen bowed low, as his mother had taught him.

"So, young Carleton, what brings you to travel alone at this late hour to see me?"

"Lady Catherine and I were taken captive by Welsh rebels, Your Highness," Stephen said.

"Lady Catherine?" The prince gripped the arms of his chair. "They've taken Catherine?"

"Aye, they have. They released me to bring you this message." Stephen pulled it from his belt and handed it over. "I was told to put it in no one's hands but yours."

The prince broke the seal and scanned it quickly. With an impatient wave, he sent his manservant from the room. He did not speak until the door was shut again.

"You've had a rough journey and must be hungry." The prince gestured to a platter piled high with bread, cheese, and fruit on the table next to him. "Come, sit and eat."

Stephen took the chair on the other side of the small table and accepted the cup of mulled wine the prince poured from an ornate silver decanter.

"They treated you well?"

Stephen nodded and took a long drink from the cup.

"I must consult FitzAlan on this matter," the prince said. "Lady Catherine is, after all, his wife."

Stephen's mouth was full, so he nodded vigorously. "I'll go with you," he said as soon as he swallowed. "'Tis best you don't go alone to speak with my brother."

The prince raised an eyebrow. "You know the content of the message?"

Stephen nodded again.

"These rebels are bold," the prince said. "Can you tell me why they sent a ransom demand to me, rather than FitzAlan?"

Stephen fidgeted in his chair and looked toward the door.

"Out with it," the prince commanded. "I shall not blame the messenger."

Stephen shifted his gaze back to the prince and tried to discern if he meant what he said.

"Owain Glyndwr has heard you are fond of Lady Catherine." Stephen really did not want to say this, but he saw no way around it. "More than fond."

When the prince did not react, Stephen began to

wonder if he was a little slow in the head. He judged the distance to the door again, then decided to get it over with.

"Glyndwr believes Catherine is your mistress."

He watched the prince, waiting for a violent reaction.

Prince Harry rested his chin on his clasped hands. "This is unfortunate," he said quite calmly. "Glyndwr is mistaken if he thinks the king would release her for my sake, no matter what she is to me."

The prince appeared to be lost in thought for a moment.

"There must be talk about Lady Catherine and me for Glyndwr to have heard this." He looked at Stephen and lifted an eyebrow. "Tell me, Stephen Carleton, what do you believe?"

"Lady Catherine is an honorable lady," Stephen said at once. "She would never do it."

The prince smiled. "I am glad to hear you share my high opinion of her."

Forgetting his earlier caution, Stephen added, "But I did hear talk among the men at Ross Castle. It is well known the two of you are close."

"Damnation," the prince muttered.

After that, the prince made Stephen recount every detail of their capture and the events since. By the time Prince Harry dismissed him, Stephen was dizzy with fatigue.

Stephen paused at the door. "If we both tell William it is not true—about you and Lady Catherine—perhaps he will believe us."

The prince smiled. "You are a brave man, Stephen. I shall be glad to have you at my back."

———

Why did the men who took Catherine and Stephen not send a message yet? William was nearly mad with worry and frustrated past bearing.

Edmund was more alert today. Though he was not out of danger, he seemed likely to survive. William pressed him about why he thought their attackers did not just happen upon them.

"Why would a half-dozen well-armed men on good horses be on that quiet path to the abbey at just that time?" Edmund asked.

Men of that ilk should have been at Worcester, whether they be Welsh or English.

"I tell you, William, they knew her name."

"But I've questioned every man, woman, and child in the castle," William said, pacing the sickroom in frustration. "If we have a traitor in the castle who passed the word you were taking her to the abbey, someone should have heard or seen something."

After a long pause, Edmund said in a low voice, "She's run from you before."

William stopped his pacing. *She's run from you before.* The words were like a knife in his belly.

He turned slowly to face Edmund, clenching and unclenching his fists. "Are you suggesting Catherine arranged this herself?"

"All I'm saying, 'tis peculiar," Edmund said.

He remembered what she said the night before he left for Worcester. *It is you I need rescuing from now, William. You bring me misery of a kind Rayburn never could.*

"She wouldn't leave Jamie," William said.

"She meant to take the boy, but I told her no."

"You've been against her from the start!" he shouted. "I tell you, she wouldn't do it."

"You would not let her leave the castle on her own," Edmund persisted, "so she might have used the kidnap as a ruse to get away."

If Edmund wasn't bandaged from head to foot, he'd pick him up and slam him against the wall.

"There is another explanation," he ground out through clenched teeth. "There has to be."

She promised she would not leave again. She gave her word.

"She deceived her last husband for years," Edmund said. "You've known her, what, three months?"

Less than that. But he knew her. He loved her. And she loved him. Didn't she?

He looked at the crusted blood on the bandage around Edmund's head and the seeping wound on his neck. "If you think so little of her, why would you nearly get yourself killed trying to protect her?"

"Out of loyalty to you, of course," Edmund said in his croaking voice. "You entrusted her to my protection, and I have an inkling of what she means to you."

Edmund could have no notion of what she meant to him.

"I will pay whatever ransom they ask," he said more to himself than to Edmund. "There is nothing I will not do to get her back. Nothing."

"Women are fickle. Perhaps she'll change her mind and return," Edmund said. "Or the men she trusted to take her away will play her false and hold her for ransom."

"Enough of your poison tongue!" William said, shaking with anger. "I swear to you, Edmund, injured or not, I will throw you out if you speak another word against her."

"What do I know about women?" Edmund's breathing was labored now, and his words were punctuated by long pauses. "I'm sorry...I won't say it again...No one will be happier than I...to be proved wrong about her. I..."

William couldn't berate an unconscious man, so he left.

He tried to push what Edmund said out of his head. But the damage was done. Against his will, the doubts and questions came. They raced through his mind, around and around. Was Jamie's father not dead after all? Did she go to him? Was he one of the rebels? Or that damn troubadour?

Nay, it could not be true. Surely she would not have taken Stephen with her?

William was in a poor state by the time the prince and Stephen arrived. The moment Stephen slid down from his horse, William took hold of him. It was the first time he had embraced this young brother of his.

"Your lady wife is well," Stephen said.

"Who has her? Where is she?" William demanded.

"The Tudors will take good care of her," Stephen said in a rush. "They are good men, for rebels."

"Sweet lamb of God!" William thundered. "The Tudors! Are you saying the Tudors have her?"

The prince stepped forward and put a hand on William's arm.

"Let us go inside," he said, and cast his eyes meaningfully toward the men and servants gathered around them.

"We will tell you all we know, but it is a tale too long for the bailey yard."

William escorted Prince Harry and Stephen into the keep and upstairs to the family's private rooms. As soon as they were seated in the solar with the door closed, William looked at them expectantly.

"Tell FitzAlan what happened when you and Lady Catherine were captured," Prince Harry directed Stephen. "Give him the shortened version now. Later, he will want to hear it with all the detail you can remember."

Stephen's abbreviated recounting of events relieved William's worst fears. In his darkest moments, he had imagined his wife lying raped and murdered in a wood somewhere.

He had so many questions, he did not know where to start. "Why did they take you to Monmouth?"

Stephen looked uneasily at the prince.

"I was as surprised as you," Prince Harry said, pulling a letter from a pouch at his belt and handing it to William. "This is the message they sent with Stephen."

He noticed the prince and Stephen exchange glances before he began to read. As he read the message, signed by Owain Glyndwr himself, the blood drained from his head.

"Can you please tell me," he addressed Prince Harry in a coldly polite tone, "why my wife's captors would present a demand to you, rather than seek ransom from me, her husband?"

Prince Harry met William's eyes with a hard look of his own. "I am your prince, FitzAlan. I answer to no man, save the king. Still, I will tell you what you want to know. But listen well, for I'll not speak of it again.

"I care too deeply for your lady wife to dishonor her by making her my mistress," the prince said, enunciating every word clearly. "And Catherine would never consent to it. She respects me as her future king, but she loves me as a brother. A *younger* brother."

"And you, sire?" William asked in a tight voice. "May I ask the nature of your feelings for my wife?"

"I will not tell you I've never felt desire for her," Prince Harry said, meeting his eyes with a steady gaze. "But I have known since I was twelve I could not marry her. While a woman as astute as Catherine would be an asset, I must make a marriage that is an alliance for England.

"Since I could not make Catherine my queen, and I would not make her my mistress," the prince said, "I remain her friend. And happily so."

With his speech finished, Prince Harry considered the question settled and the subject closed. He moved at once to the problem before them.

"'Tis useless to ask the king to trade Gruffydd for her," the prince said, rubbing his chin. "I am not certain my father would give up Glyndwr's son even if it were me the rebels held."

William did not disagree.

"So we must think of another means to gain her safe return," the prince said. "Stephen says she remained with Glyndwr's army, traveling west, when the Tudors split off to deliver him to Monmouth."

In the end, they agreed Prince Harry would send a message to the rebel leader advising him that the king could not be persuaded to release Gruffydd. The prince would enclose a letter from William offering a monetary ransom.

"In the meantime, we must discover where Catherine is being held," William said. "Glyndwr may refuse to ransom her. I cannot rescue her if I do not know where she is."

Prince Harry made the astonishing suggestion that William talk with Abbess Talcott.

"You never know," Prince Harry said with a smile, "what news might come to the good abbess."

———

Like most Northerners, William was related to half the nobility—and knew the rest—on both sides of the Scots-English border. Hostage-taking was so common in that region that it was almost a sport. If his wife had been kidnapped there, he could have found out where she was being held in half a day.

But he was at a loss as to how to find her in Wales. The language was different, the people hostile. Hostages taken deep into that country were not found until their ransoms were paid.

He did not know how a nun in an isolated abbey could help him discover where Catherine was, but he had no other notion what to do. He and Stephen set off for the abbey as soon as the prince was out the gates.

As they made the short ride, William could not help thinking of the last time he had ridden this path: the day he retrieved his bride from the abbey. Had he driven her to run from him again?

"Please, God, keep her safe," he prayed. "Whether she went willingly or not, bring her back."

This time, he entered the abbey grounds quietly and waited in the courtyard for one of the nuns to escort him and Stephen up to the abbess's private rooms. When he reached the doorway to her parlor, he was too surprised to speak.

It could not be! There, chatting amiably with the abbess, his long legs stretched out before him, sat Catherine's troubadour.

"Good afternoon, Lord FitzAlan," the abbess greeted him.

William stared at the troubadour as Abbess Talcott exchanged greetings with Stephen.

Gesturing toward the troubadour, she said, "May I present Robert Fass?"

"We have met," William bit out.

"After a fashion," Robert said, an amused smile lifting the corners of his mouth. The man evidently was counting on William's forbearance while on abbey grounds.

Abbess Talcott invited them to sit and passed around a tray of honey cakes. To William, she said in a low voice, "I've assigned another sister the task of baking."

All the same, William waited until Stephen devoured two with no obvious ill effects before taking one himself.

When the abbess made no move to send the troubadour away so they could speak privately, he stated his business. "My wife has been taken hostage by the rebels. She was captured while on her way to visit you here, at the abbey."

The abbess's face showed deep concern but not surprise. "I only just heard the news from Robert."

"In God's name, how did he know of it?"

"Remember where you are," the abbess reprimanded him. "It hardly matters how Robert learned of it."

"Do you know where she is?" William asked the troubadour. He was willing to overlook the man's transgressions if only he would tell him where to find her.

"Not yet," the abbess answered for him. She patted the troubadour's arm and said, "But my friend Robert is our best hope of finding out."

Holding back the oath that had been on his lips, William asked, "How would you learn of my wife's whereabouts?"

"Despite the rebellion, my troupe travels freely in both Wales and the Marches," Robert said. "I can take my troupe into Wales and look for her without being suspected."

"And why would you go to such trouble for my wife?"

Robert's eyes danced with amusement. "We are great friends. Did she not tell you?"

"Don't be foolish," the abbess chided. "Lord FitzAlan, tell us what you can about what happened."

Stephen and William told them all they knew. Robert asked a number of questions. He had the good sense, however, not to remark on the unusual nature of the ransom demand.

"The possibilities are not good," Robert said, shaking his head. "Let us hope Glyndwr doesn't send her to the Continent with the French forces for safekeeping. It would be as bad, though, if he takes her to Aberystwyth or Harlech castles."

God help him if Glyndwr held her at either of those castles. They were on the west coast of Wales, far from English soil. Both castles were considered impregnable, or very nearly so.

"I will follow Glyndwr's trail until I hear news of her," Robert said. "I will be discreet, of course."

Spying appeared to come easily to this itinerant bard. He hid a fine mind behind that handsome face and glib demeanor.

William looked back and forth between Robert and the abbess and raised an eyebrow. "The two of you helped Catherine with her spying?"

They smiled with the look of well-fed cats.

"Rayburn did not have a chance," William said.

"That devil's spawn did not deserve one," Robert said, showing a flash of anger for the first time.

William wondered who this singer of ballads truly was. The man was not raised by a peasant or tradesman, to be sure. He showed too much ease conversing with an abbess and a lord. Whoever he was, William was profoundly grateful for his help.

"The part we occasionally play in the conflict must remain a secret," the abbess advised William. "Robert can be of no help if his collaboration is suspected."

"We will tell no one," William promised. He gave Stephen a severe look to be sure his brother understood.

"Not even Edmund," Stephen said.

Chapter Twenty-two

Catherine felt very much alone traveling in the midst of a Welsh-French army of thousands. Even the Tudor brothers would have been a welcome sight to her now.

She certainly would have felt safer under their protection.

She braved a glance at Rhys Gethin, whose heavily muscled thigh was uncomfortably close to hers as he rode at her side. He'd taken Maredudd's place as her primary keeper. "The Fierce One," as she had come to think of him, had neither the fine looks nor the courtly manners of the Tudors.

Everything about the man was rough, from the well-worn tunic that reeked of sweat and horses to the long hair that fell to his shoulders in matted knots. He was built like an ox, with a broad chest and thick neck. Though he rarely spoke, the other Welshmen paid heed when he did.

He turned and fixed his intense gaze on her. With eyes as black as his soul, he was the most frightening man she had ever met.

"What is it, sir?" she asked sharply, though it was she who had stared at him first.

He nodded ahead to where the path narrowed and grunted something she took to mean he wanted her to ride in front. She spurred her horse, grateful to put a little distance between them. A shiver crept up her spine. When she looked over her shoulder, his eyes were on her like hot burning coals.

At least she was free of The Fierce One at night. Rhys Gethin camped out with the army, while Catherine was taken into Welsh homes as Glyndwr's guest. The homes were humble, but at least she had a roof over her head.

When they reached Milford Haven, the French soldiers and horses were loaded onto the ships waiting in the harbor. After the ships disembarked, Glyndwr disbursed most of his army. The fighting season was over. Only a core contingent of men rode north with them along the west coast.

Catherine's breath caught at the sight of Aberystwyth, a magnificent castle with concentric walls built in the shape of a diamond on the very edge of the roiling sea. It was one of the iron ring of fortresses Edward I built around the perimeter of Wales to demonstrate English power over the subjugated Welsh.

After little more than a hundred years, Aberystwyth was crumbling under the assault of pounding sea, wind, and rain. Catherine looked around as they rode into the castle's huge outer bailey. The main gate and drawbridge were falling down, but its rings of thick walls still made it formidable. Glyndwr had been able to take it only because King Henry diverted men to fight the Scots and left the castle inadequately defended.

From the moment they turned north, Catherine had feared Glyndwr would bring her here—or worse, to Harlech Castle. Her chances of escape or rescue from either were dismal. Still, they were better here at crumbling Aberystwyth than at Harlech.

When Rhys lifted her from her saddle, she held her breath against the smell of him. She tried not to show how much it distressed her to have him touch her.

She slept that night in a chamber high in a tower overlooking the sea. The guards outside her door seemed an unnecessary precaution. Tense and uneasy, she barred her door and fell asleep to the sound of waves crashing on the shore.

In the morning, a maid came to help her dress and to tell her she would ride with Prince Glyndwr today. Aberystwyth, then, was not their final destination.

When Gethin helped her mount her horse, she noticed he did not smell quite so bad and that someone had made an attempt to brush his clothes. Silent as usual, he escorted her to where Glyndwr waited.

"I was going to send you to France," Glyndwr said as they rode out the gate heading north.

Catherine nearly gasped aloud. England's conflict with France was unending. If she was taken there, she might be held for years and years.

"I want to go home," she said, "but I prefer the wild beauty of Wales to France."

"Then you can thank Rhys Gethin, for he was adamant I keep you here. He mistrusts our French allies."

"So, where are you taking me?"

"To Harlech Castle, where I live with my family."

Her heart plummeted.

"Your King Edward—may he rot in hell—did not make the mistake he made at Aberystwyth by building Harlech too near the sea." There was pride in his voice as he added, "There was never a castle better built for defense."

Prince Harry said the same of Harlech.

"There will be gowns and the other things you need at Harlech. I am sorry I neglected to provide better for you, but I did not foresee I would have a lady traveling with my army."

Gowns were the least of her concerns.

"You managed the rough travel well," he said with an approving glance. "Gethin says you are made of tougher stock than your first husband. But then, he thought even less of Rayburn than he does of our French allies. He dislikes men who betray their own."

He signaled to the nearest men to ride farther back.

"Rhys Gethin has made a request of me," he said. "If King Henry refuses to release my son, he wants me to give you to him to be his wife."

Catherine could not have been more stunned.

Of all the objections she could make, what she said was, "But the man dislikes me!"

"Nay, he is captivated." Glyndwr smiled with rare amusement. "He surprises us both."

"Does he not have a wife?"

"She died many years ago," Glyndwr said. "He did not seem to mind the lack of one until now."

No doubt he terrorizes the serving girls, Catherine thought to herself.

"But, Your Grace, I am already married."

"If King Henry will not yield what I ask, I may relieve you of your husband."

Catherine looked at him in horror. "If you think to make me a widow, you underestimate my husband. He is a skilled fighter."

"You are right to praise FitzAlan's skills," Glyndwr said, unperturbed. "I was disappointed when Northumberland could not persuade him to join our cause. But I was not speaking of FitzAlan's death—only of an annulment of your marriage."

"That is not possible," she said, feeling herself color. "Our marriage was consummated."

Glyndwr dismissed this difficulty with a wave of his hand.

They rode in silence for a time. Then, with seeming indifference, he asked, "Are you with child?"

She sensed it was to ask this single question that Glyndwr chose to ride with her today. Without pausing a heartbeat to consider her response, she looked directly into his eyes and said, "Sadly, I am not."

She was getting better at lying all the time.

"Good, then an annulment is possible," he said, but Catherine did not think he was pleased by her answer.

―――――

Harlech Castle served as both Glyndwr's court and his base of military operations. With the fighting season over and the autumn rains setting in, the castle was crawling with soldiers with little to do. Catherine was not left unguarded for a moment.

Guarding her must be a singularly tedious assignment. She spent most of her time alone in her chamber or praying in the chapel. Since she could not bear to feel The Fierce One's eyes on her while she ate, she rarely took her meals in the great hall. Besides, observing Glyndwr's happy family life only served to make her feel more despondent.

She had been at Harlech a week when she was summoned to the great hall for an audience with Glyndwr. Here in his court, Glyndwr maintained the outward trappings of his princely status. She bowed low before a severe-looking Glyndwr dressed in ermine-trimmed robes and sitting on a gilded throne.

"Lady FitzAlan, I have received Prince Harry's reply to my ransom demand," he announced. "He advises me that the king will not release my son in exchange for your safe return."

Since Glyndwr's son was blind and could not fight, Catherine thought the king was only keeping him for spite.

"It is as I expected, Your Grace," she said in a low voice. "I am sorry he will not return your son."

"I believe you are," Glyndwr said, his eyes softening.

He came down from the dais and led her to sit with him before the roaring fire in the hearth.

"I served with King Henry in Scotland twenty years ago," Glyndwr remarked. "He was just 'Bolingbroke' then."

"I believe he has changed a good deal since then—since he gained the throne," she said, throwing caution to the wind.

Glyndwr raised an eyebrow and nodded for her to continue.

"These rebellions have made our king mistrustful." She ventured a sideways glance at him. "And unforgiving. He will not show mercy, even when it costs him nothing."

Was it wise to speak of her king like this to Glyndwr? Was it treason? She did not know, but she wanted to give Glyndwr the truth with regard to his son, if nothing else.

"If you wish to have your son back, you must give the king something he holds very dear." She gave him the only suggestion she had. "He would exchange Gruffydd for Harlech."

Glyndwr shook his head. "You know I cannot put my son above the interests of my people."

"Then your best hope is to arrange for Gruffydd to escape," she said. "It has been done before. Perhaps you could bribe a guard?"

"My son was blinded for his first attempt to escape," Glyndwr said. "I would not have him risk so much again."

Catherine looked away from the pain she saw on the great man's face.

"When Harry takes his father's place," she said in a quiet voice, "I am certain he will pardon your son and release him." It was a paltry offering.

"I fear Gruffydd will not survive long in the Tower."

They sat in silence, staring at the fire.

After a few moments, he said, "Prince Harry enclosed a letter from your husband with his message."

She sat up straight. "A letter from William? What does he say?"

Glyndwr leaned forward and tapped his forefingers against his pursed lips before answering. "FitzAlan offers a large monetary ransom."

Catherine closed her eyes. God be praised! After the utter bleakness she had felt since arriving at Harlech, she was afraid of the hope that sprang inside her.

Her voice quavered as she put the question to Glyndwr. "Will you take the ransom my husband offers?"

Glyndwr's expression was hard now. He was no longer father, but prince.

"I will send another message, reiterating my price," he said, his voice stern. "If Prince Harry still does not comply, I have a commander who would benefit from having a wife with the political skills he lacks."

Glyndwr was no fool, so she wondered how he believed he could have her marriage annulled.

"I am considering recognizing the French pope in Avignon."

His words struck her like a thunderbolt. God chose Saint Peter's successor on Earth. A ruler who supported the alternative pope risked damnation not only for himself, but also for all his people. Even in her shock, Catherine was awed by Glyndwr's boldness.

"I will demand concessions in return, of course," he said, more to himself than to her. "Independence for the Welsh church. A guarantee that only men who speak Welsh will be appointed bishops and priests. The end of payments to English monasteries and colleges.

"It would be a small matter to add a request for the annulment of one marriage." He turned and focused his eyes on her again. "Particularly when that marriage was made without proper banns and on the very day of the first husband's murder."

Cold fear gripped her heart. As a last resort, she could reveal her pregnancy. Surely even the French pope would not grant an annulment if he knew she was with child.

⁓

Catherine paced her chamber, as she often did since her conversation with Glyndwr. If she could only have something to give her hope!

She jumped at the knock on her door. Opening the

door a crack, she saw that one of her guards wanted to speak to her.

"Prince Glyndwr requests your presence in the hall this evening," the young man said. "He wants you to enjoy the music of the traveling musicians who've just arrived."

"Thank you, I will come." She closed the door and leaned against it. *God, please, let it be Robert.*

That evening, she sat at the table, every muscle taut, waiting for the musicians. Even having Rhys Gethin sit beside her—and, God help her, share a trencher with her—could not divert her. When the musicians finally came into the hall, she nearly burst into tears.

Robert had come. With his dazzling good looks and striking blond hair, he stood out like a white crane in the midst of crows.

Robert did not let his gaze fall on her directly, but she knew he saw her, too. She wanted desperately to talk with him, to hear news of home. But how could they find a way to meet with guards dogging her every step?

She listened through the long evening for a message or a signal of some kind. It finally came in his last ballad, a familiar song about secret lovers. As Robert sang the final refrain in which the man asks his beloved where she will meet him, he put his hands together as if in prayer and glanced in her direction.

Catherine put her hands together and nodded, hoping she understood his meaning.

Her guards had spent many hours standing in the doorway of the chapel while she prayed. They were not surprised, then, when she told them she wished to go there before retiring to her chamber. She caught the annoyed look that passed between them, but they could hardly complain that their prisoner prayed too much.

She was on her knees on the cold stone floor for an hour before someone in priest's robes entered. She glanced over her shoulder to be sure her guards' soft snores were not feigned.

Robert sank to his knees beside her.

"Before you ask," he whispered close to her ear, "William, Jamie, and Stephen are all well, though they miss you."

"Praise God," she said, crossing herself. "You cannot know how glad I am to see you! How did you find me?"

"There is no time to tell you now. We must be brief. Do you know if Glyndwr plans to keep you here at Harlech? Will he accept William's ransom?"

"Glyndwr yet holds a thread of hope that Harry will secure his son's release." She reached for Robert's hand. "When he loses that hope, it will be still worse for me."

Robert held a finger to his lips, and she realized her voice had risen in her distress.

"Glyndwr says he will have my marriage to William annulled," she whispered. "He talks of marrying me to one of his men—to Rhys Gethin! Robert, I cannot bear it!"

Robert contemplated this in silence for a moment. "Aye, we must get you out. But annulments are never quick, so we have time to make a plan."

"I cannot wait much longer—"

"I must go," he whispered. "I will look for you here tomorrow night at the same time."

"If something happens and we do not meet again," she said, gripping his hand, "tell my family I love them and miss them with all my heart."

"We shall meet tomorrow," he said, giving her hand one last squeeze.

She waited until Robert was safely out of the chapel. After saying one more prayer, she rose on stiff legs to wake her guards. They escorted her to her chamber, where she bid them good night and barred the door.

Her mind was still on her conversation with Robert as she turned from the door. A shriek caught in her throat. In the moonlight from the narrow window, she could see the outline of a man sprawled on the chair beside her bed.

"Did you enjoy the music?" Maredudd Tudor asked.

Chapter Twenty-three

Catherine was so tired of riding that she was sure she would never be able to walk normally again. She lost her headdress days ago. Her hair hung in a tangled mess. Her gown was so filthy that if they did not reach their destination soon, she just might rip it off and ride naked.

Maredudd said he was taking her to his home on the island of Anglesey on the northwest coast. After establishing a false trail to the south, he took her inland and headed north, across countless streams and through endless forests. He apologized for the rough travel, explaining that Glyndwr ordered him to take every precaution. Even his own people must not learn where she went or with whom she traveled.

Catherine longed with all her heart to wash, to sleep in fresh sheets, and to eat a meal prepared by anyone other than Maredudd Tudor. The only benefit to her physical misery was that it diverted her from dwelling on how much she missed William, Jamie, and Stephen.

They crossed the isthmus onto Anglesey at low tide. A few miles farther, they reached Plas Penmynydd, the large fortified manor that was the Tudor home. When Maredudd lifted her from her horse before the entrance to the house, he had to hold on to her to keep her from falling.

Still clutching his arm, Catherine looked up into the hostile gray eyes of a pretty dark-haired woman. She was well rounded, almost plump, and a few years older than Catherine.

What caught Catherine's attention, however, was the lady's apricot silk gown. All her life, Catherine had taken her fine gowns for granted, but at this moment, she coveted this one with a piercing envy. It was so very *clean*.

"Marged, come greet me properly, love, and meet our guest," Maredudd called out.

So, this angry woman in apricot was Maredudd's wife. Catherine suddenly felt aware of her own disheveled appearance.

In that moment, a boy of about five ran out of the house and barreled into Maredudd. He lifted the boy up, laughing, and settled him on his hip. When the boy turned his head to look at her, Catherine was taken aback by the sheer beauty of the child.

"Who is the lady, Father?" the boy asked.

"This is Lady Catherine FitzAlan. She will be our guest for a time," he said, ruffling the boy's hair. "Lady Catherine, meet my lovely wife, Marged, and my son Owain, lead troublemaker of Plas Penmynydd."

Catherine nodded politely at Marged, then turned back to the boy. "To be lead troublemaker among the Tudor men," she said with a smile, "is quite a feat."

⁓

Catherine remembered almost nothing of her first evening at Penmynydd. She was taken to a bedchamber, stripped of her filthy gown, and soaked in a tub of steaming water until her skin puckered. She was asleep on her feet as the maid dried her and helped her into a plain shift for bed.

The smells from a waiting tray roused her long enough to eat. The food was so delicious she nearly cried with pleasure.

The sun was high when she awoke the next day. Sadness weighed upon her heart like a stone. How would William ever find her here in Anglesey? Would she ever see her home again? And what of the child she carried? Tears fell down the sides of her face and into her hair, but she was too bone-weary to lift her arms and wipe them away.

Sometime later, a maid peeked through her door. "I'm to help you dress, m'lady."

Catherine was about to object that she had nothing to wear, when the maid held out a lovely, pale green gown.

She decided that with God's help and a clean gown, she could face what came.

A few minutes later, she followed the maid down the stairs to the main floor of the house. The hall was empty, save for Marged Tudor and a couple of servants.

"Good afternoon, Lady FitzAlan," Marged greeted her. "I understand you had a hard journey."

The woman smiled kindly at her, all the hostility of yesterday gone.

"I do not like this business of taking a woman from her home and family," Marged said, shaking her head. "Until you can be returned to your own home, I want you to be comfortable in ours."

"I appreciate your kindness," Catherine said. "And thank you for the use of this gown."

"I am afraid yours could not be saved," Marged said. "I gave it to one of the servants to cut for rags."

"Good. I never want to see it again."

"You must call me Marged. We must not be formal, since you may be our guest for some weeks."

"Weeks?" Catherine sank onto the bench beside Marged.

Marged patted her arm. "If it were up to my Maredudd, this would be resolved quickly. But Glyndwr...well, you know what he thinks. These foolish men! Just looking at you, I can see you are not the kind of woman to commit adultery."

Catherine wondered how but did not ask.

"Still, I will admit," Marged said, "when I first laid eyes on you yesterday, you gave me quite a fright."

Catherine could not help but laugh. "You should have made me wash in the yard!"

"That is not what I meant," Marged protested. "You looked like a wood nymph with your hair all wild about you and that lovely face of yours. I thought my husband had the gall to bring home a mistress!"

Catherine looked at her, startled.

"But Maredudd let me know last night how much he missed me," Marged said, her eyes twinkling. "I should have known, but a woman needs to be shown some-times."

Marged paused to wave a servant over with a platter of food for Catherine. "Maredudd was worried bringing you on such a hard journey, but he was afraid to leave you at Harlech."

Catherine raised her eyebrows. "He thinks Glydnwr would harm me?"

"Of course not," Marged said. "But he says that if Prince Glyndwr discovers you are with child, he will never agree to release you."

"Maredudd knows I am with child?"

Marged laughed. "You were sick in the morning. 'Twas the same with me when I carried Owain."

"Why would Glyndwr not let me go if he knew?" The answer came to Catherine even before Marged spoke.

"To hold the prince's lover as hostage is one thing; to hold the prince's son is quite another," Marged said. "In exchange for the only child of the heir to the English throne, Glyndwr might ask anything—even an independent Wales."

"But this is not Harry's child!" Catherine closed her eyes and put her head on the table.

"Glyndwr would want to believe it was," Marged said, resting her hand on Catherine's back. "And that is what matters."

Chapter Twenty-four

Catherine, where are you?

William stared across the distance, as if he could find her if only he looked hard enough. From the top of this hill, he could see across the border into Wales. He rode out here when he needed to be alone.

As the weeks passed, he began to fear he might never get her back. He was a man of action. The frustration of waiting wore his nerves raw. There were days when foolish action seemed better than none, and he rode out blindly into Wales.

Other days, he lost himself in regret and self-recrimination. He made promises to God. If God would return his wife to him, he would protect her always. If God would grant this one request, he would do whatever it took to make her want to stay.

Things remained cool between him and Edmund. Although Edmund seemed to sincerely regret all he'd said about Catherine, the sight of him reminded William of how quickly he himself had questioned her loyalty. In sooth, Edmund had done little more than express the same doubts he had. All the same, William spent more of his time with Stephen and Jamie these days. He liked to keep the boys close.

He took Stephen with him whenever he went to the abbey to hear the cryptic messages Robert sent to the abbess through the hands of monks, musicians, and itinerant workers. The messages relayed Robert's journey as he trailed Catherine along the south coast of Wales, then north to Aberystwyth. Their hopes soared when, at long last, he sent word he had found her—then fell again when they read she disappeared again.

It was almost December. There had been no word from Robert for weeks.

At the sound of a horse crashing through the trees behind, William turned and pulled his sword. He sheathed it when he saw who the rider was.

"How the devil did you know where to find me?" he called out to Stephen.

"The abbess sent word she has news!" Stephen said as he drew his horse up.

"Praise God!"

They galloped all the way to the abbey. When they burst into the abbess's private parlor, they found it was not a message waiting for them this time. It was the troubadour himself.

"Heaven above," William said, clapping Robert on the back, "who would have thought I would be so glad to see you!"

When Robert laughed, William noticed the lines of fatigue etched on his handsome face.

"I have found where she is," Robert said. "It will not be easy, but there is hope we can get her out."

"God bless you, Robert," William said as he squeezed Stephen's shoulder. "I am forever in your debt."

"I was able to speak with her briefly at Harlech," Robert said. "She was well and sent her love."

William ran his hands through his hair, overcome with emotion.

"The next day she was gone," Robert said. "No one—except Glyndwr himself—knew where she went or who took her.

"Eventually, I heard a whisper that someone had seen Maredudd Tudor in the castle the night she went missing," Robert continued. "Glyndwr loves music, so it was another week before I could leave Harlech without raising suspicion.

"I followed Maredudd's trail to the south, until it disappeared. On a hunch, I went north again. I did not catch wind of an English lady again until I was all the way to Beaumaris Castle."

"Beaumaris is a fortress on the coast of Anglesey," William explained to Stephen. "It is still in English hands."

"I sought news among the Welsh servants at Beaumaris," Robert said, picking up his tale again. "I found a maid whose sister works for the Tudors at their manor house, Plas Penmynydd. From her, I learned a beautiful Englishwoman is living with the Tudors."

Robert leaned forward. "William, the house is but *five miles from Beaumaris.*"

"You know this for certain?"

"I do." Robert stretched out his long legs and folded his hands on his stomach. "Believe me, I had to work hard to get the information. That Welsh maid is homely, but energetic."

"Robert!" the abbess said, but her lips twitched with amusement.

"As I see it, there are two ways to do this," William said. "I can surprise the Tudors and take her by force. Or, I can approach this Maredudd Tudor and see if he is willing to give her up for a price."

"If you parlay with him first," Stephen interjected, "you lose the advantage of surprise."

William nodded and turned to Robert. "Do you think it worth the risk?"

Robert would understand, as he did, that there was a greater chance of Catherine coming to harm in an attack.

"I will go to Plas Penmynydd and find out," Robert said.

When William started to object, the abbess put her hand on his arm. "Robert can gain entry to the household without alerting them to your plans."

"You can take your men and wait at Beaumaris," Robert said. "Catherine has been in the household for weeks and can tell me whether Maredudd Tudor will negotiate. If she says nay, I can forewarn her to be ready for the attack."

Chapter Twenty-five

Marged frowned as she came into the solar and saw Owain asleep on Catherine's lap.

"Owain is too big for that," she said, resting her hand on Catherine's shoulder.

"Please, Marged, it comforts me to hold him," Catherine said. "I miss my own son so very much."

The two women watched the sleeping child in silence for a time.

"One thinks of beauty as an advantage in finding a good match for a daughter," Catherine said, teasing her friend, "but I swear this boy of yours will marry up. Some wealthy widow will decide she must have him."

Marged laughed. "He has his father's charm as well as his looks, so God help the woman he sets his sights on. I only hope it is an heiress and not a milkmaid."

Marged pulled a stool next to Catherine's and pushed a loose strand of hair from her face. "Perhaps we will have good news soon. It's been a fortnight since Maredudd wrote to Prince Glyndwr urging him to take your husband's ransom."

"What if Glyndwr tells Maredudd to take me back to Harlech?"

"Maredudd will find a way out before then," Marged said in a soothing voice.

Catherine did not argue, but she did not expect Maredudd to defy his prince. Though Maredudd was fond of her, he would put his family first. She could not fault him that.

She rubbed her cheek against Owain's head. "Do you think Jamie has forgotten me?"

"I am sure your husband speaks of you often," Marged said. "The boy will not forget."

Catherine did not share the other worry that plagued her. Had she been gone so long that William had stopped caring for her? Did he ever, truly, care?

"William wanted a child so very much, and he does not even know." She shifted Owain on her lap so she could rest a hand on her belly. "I want to birth this child at home."

"You're not far along," Marged said. "There's plenty of time yet."

"Are you coddling that boy again?" Maredudd called from the doorway. He was grinning from ear to ear. "Just as well he's having a rest, for it will be a late night for all of us."

He came over and shook Owain's shoulder. "Owain! A troupe of musicians is here!"

Owain awoke wide-eyed and wiggled off Catherine's lap.

"They've just come through the gate." As Owain scampered off to look, Maredudd stooped to kiss his wife. "This should cheer up my beautiful ladies."

"'Tis a long time since a troupe has come this far," Marged said, smiling up at him.

"The musicians say they've traveled across the whole of Wales this autumn, so they should carry much news."

Catherine closed her eyes to make a silent prayer. A moment later, the players entered the hall. Her prayer was answered. It took all the self-control she possessed not to run to Robert and throw her arms around him. His eyes held no surprise; Robert expected to find her here.

With her thoughts spinning wildly in her head, she did not hear Marged speak to her at first. She blinked at her friend, having no notion what she had asked.

Marged laughed and took her hand. "Come with me to talk with the cook. I want a special meal prepared for this evening."

As Catherine got to her feet, Robert gave what was meant to be a casual glance in her direction. As good as he was, he stared a moment too long at her belly.

The Welsh loved music, and the Tudor household was no exception. They kept the musicians playing late into the night. Catherine sat through it as long as she could. When she could bear the strain no longer, she put her hand on her belly and whispered to Marged that she must go to bed.

In her bedchamber, she paced the floor. At long last, the music died and she heard the sounds of feet on the stairs and doors closing. The house finally settled into silence.

She never doubted Robert would learn which room was hers. When she heard the faint tapping she was waiting for, she unbarred her door and Robert slipped in.

"I was almost without hope," she said into his shoulder as he held her. Leaning back, she asked, "Are they all well? William and the boys?"

"They are," he said, and kissed her forehead.

"Where is William? Has he not come for me?"

"The devil could not keep him away," Robert said. "He is waiting nearby, at Beaumaris Castle."

"It's been so long that I feared he did not seek my return," she confessed. Only now did she admit to herself how deep her doubts had grown.

"You will be happy to know your husband looks quite ill with worry," Robert said, lifting her chin with his finger. "I doubt he's had a full night's sleep since you were taken."

It was wrong to feel so pleased that William suffered, too. Of course, Robert could be lying.

"I see you have news for him," Robert said, letting his eyes drop to the slight swell of her gown.

She smiled. "Aye, the babe should come after Easter."

Robert turned to the business at hand. "We have two possible plans for getting you released."

When she heard them, her response was adamant. "He must talk with Maredudd. I will not have harm come to—"

She stopped at the sound of the door creaking. With growing horror, she realized that she had failed to bar the door behind Robert. She watched helplessly as it eased open.

Marged's head peeked through the opening. Her eyes bulged almost comically, then she leapt into the room and closed the door behind her.

She fixed her gaze on Catherine and began speaking in a rush. "I beg you, do not do it! I know you fear you shall never see your husband again, but I promise you shall. And when you do, you will regret what you are about to do."

Marged stopped her lecture long enough to cast a good

long look at Robert. "I can see the temptation." It was evident she could, from the way she flushed. "Truly, I can."

Marged could not seem to drag her eyes away from Robert. Her color deepened when Robert brazenly winked at her.

"'Tis true, in your condition you need not worry about bringing another man's babe home to your husband, but…." Marged's will to argue her point seemed to fade the longer she stared at Robert.

"Marged!" Catherine said sharply. "This man has not come to bed me! How could you think it?"

Catherine turned to Robert. "You must see we cannot wait. We have to tell her and Maredudd now."

Robert said in a low voice, "Are you sure this is wise, Catherine?"

She took Marged's arm. "Robert is a friend who has brought a message from my husband," she explained as she walked Marged to the door. "Go wake Maredudd and bring him here so we may talk in private while the servants sleep."

Once Catherine finally convinced Marged to fetch her husband, she turned and found Robert leaning out the window.

"Unless you are certain this Tudor is willing to come to terms with your husband," he said over his shoulder, "we should make our escape now, before the lady wakes him."

Though Maredudd's easy manner might fool some into believing he was not a careful man, Catherine knew better. Robert may not see the guards outside, but they were there.

"What I am certain of," she said, "is that we would not make the gate."

Chapter Twenty-six

𝒜 harsh wind blew the rain against William's face in icy pellets. He'd been keeping watch on the ramparts of the outer curtain wall of Beaumaris Castle since dawn, and he was chilled to the bone. He paced back and forth to keep warm. At each turn, he stopped to squint through the driving rain toward the west.

He looked again. In the dull gray light of the dismal morning, he picked out a lone figure riding toward the castle.

The troubadour was back.

A quarter hour later, he and Robert were conferring in his room in one of the sixteen towers along the outer wall.

"She has been treated well," Robert assured him again.

William narrowed his eyes at Robert. There was something he was not telling him.

"In sooth, she has grown quite fond of her captors," Robert said. "She made it clear she wants none of them harmed."

"She thinks it worth the risk, then, of approaching Maredudd Tudor?"

"I would say so, since she has already done it."

"She what!" William sighed and shook his head. "She has not changed, I see. Catherine would step right into it, once she decided that was the thing to do."

"I was shaking in my boots for fear she misjudged the man," Robert admitted with a grin.

"Since you returned alive, I take it this Tudor is willing to make a deal?"

"So he says, and your lady wife believes him," Robert replied with a shrug. "He will meet you in a wood along the road between here and Plas Penmynydd to give you his terms. He says he will come alone, and you must do the same. He wants to keep this quiet so Glyndwr does not catch wind of it."

Robert paused, then said, "You know this could be a trap."

"Aye, but I have no choice," William said. "When are we to meet?"

"On the morrow, an hour past dawn."

It was still cold when William set out the next morning, but the rain had lessened to a light drizzle. As directed, he traveled alone and put his fate in the hands of God. And Maredudd Tudor. He thought of Jamie and Stephen and prayed he could bring Catherine home to them soon.

As he came to the copse beside the dip in the road that Robert described as the meeting place, a hooded rider crested the hill before him.

"FitzAlan?" the rider called out.

William started. The voice was a woman's. As she pulled her horse up, he saw that the voice belonged to a pretty dark-haired woman.

"I am FitzAlan. Are you here for Maredudd Tudor?"

"I am his wife, Marged," she said.

What sort of man was this Tudor to send his wife out alone on such an errand?

"Maredudd went with the men who are taking Catherine to Harlech."

"What!" he exploded. "The devil's spawn is taking her to Harlech?"

"There is little time, so listen," she snapped. "A dozen men rode up to our gate this morning with orders from Glyndwr to take Catherine."

William told himself he had plenty of time to catch up to them. The ride to Harlech was long.

"What route did they travel? How far ahead are they?"

"They left not more than half an hour ago, but they are taking her by sea! Their ship is to the west, eight or nine miles from here."

Beaumaris was in the opposite direction. There was no time to ride back for his men. Even if he rode straight to the ship, he might not catch them.

"Maredudd will try to stall them, but you'd best ride hard." She quickly gave him directions.

"Are you safe riding back to Plas Penmynydd alone?"

She smiled. "Aye, these are Tudor lands."

"God bless you, dear lady."

He spurred his horse and rode like the wind. He had to get to the ship before it set sail. His heart seemed to beat in time with the pounding of his horse's hooves. Faster, faster, faster.

After what seemed like hours, he reached the coast. A half mile north, he found the manor house where Marged Tudor said Glyndwr's men had borrowed horses. He spotted the ship offshore, just visible in the morning fog.

He turned his horse off the road and pulled up in the low trees to count the figures on the beach. One man in the water, guiding a rowboat to shore. Two in the rowboat. Eight on the shore. He narrowed his eyes, searching for Catherine.

Two more men emerged from the wood dragging a woman between them. She struggled against them as they hauled her toward the rowboat.

Catherine. He'd found his wife.

The frustrating weeks of waiting were behind him. Patience, negotiation, money offers—none of it had brought her back. Now he could do what he was born to do, what he'd been trained to do, what he did best.

Percy blood ran through his veins. He was son of Northumberland the King-maker, brother to the legendary fighter Hotspur. None could touch him. It would not matter if there were ten men or twenty or sixty between him and Catherine. He would get to her.

"AAARRRRRRHHHHH!" He shouted his battle cry as he burst through the brush.

He rode to the edge of the sea where his horse could get better purchase and galloped along the shoreline. Brandishing his broadsword, he rode straight at the men on the beach, striking fear into every heart.

An unearthly cry in the distance sent a shiver up Catherine's spine. She turned toward the sound and heard hoofbeats pounding up the shore. Everyone on the beach stopped in place to peer through the fog in the direction of the sound.

As they watched, a horse and rider emerged through

the fog charging toward them at a full gallop. Horse and rider lifted and then sailed over a log as if the horse had wings. The men scattered as the rider bore down on them, sword swinging and screaming his battle cry.

William had come to save her.

She had heard stories of his feats in battle. She'd watched him practice countless times. None of it prepared her for seeing him like this. He fought with a grace and power that was both terrible and utterly magnificent.

The first two men were dead before they could draw their swords. The sword of a third went flying through the air. The man ran for the woods as William turned his horse to take another pass. At least two more fell. Then William dropped from his horse onto one man and came up swinging his sword into another. He whirled to face the remaining men, broadswords in both hands now.

"Your husband, I presume," Maredudd said in her ear. "Let us get off the beach before one of these men thinks to grab you and hold a knife to your throat."

She and Maredudd watched the rest of the fight from behind the low bushes that grew back from the shore. It was over soon. Two men were in the water, swimming toward the ship. Others had run from the beach and disappeared into the trees.

"Catherine! Catherine!" William's voice echoed as he looked up and down the shore shouting her name.

———

William looked up and down the beach, frantic.

Then he saw her standing alone in the tall grass at the edge of the beach. Catherine. An angel come to earth.

He stood for a long moment, frozen in place, not

breathing. Then he slid his sword into its scabbard and ran to her. His hands shook as he cupped her beloved face. Never had she looked more beautiful. He kissed each cheek, pink with the cold.

"I praise God you are safe!" he said, closing his eyes and letting his forehead touch hers.

He had promised himself that this time he would give her the choice. This time, she would come to him willingly, or she would not come.

"I failed in my duty to protect you. If you cannot forgive me, if you do not wish to live with me again," he said, his heart pounding in his chest, "I will make other arrangements for you."

He waited for her to speak, to rail at him for failing her. But she was silent. She would hear him out.

"I hope with all my heart you will choose to live with me. If you will, I promise I shall do all I can to protect you and be a good husband to you."

Catherine rested her palms against his chest and looked up at him with vivid blue eyes that saw the truth in his heart.

"Thank you for coming for me." She leaned her head against his chest. "Take me home, William. Take me home."

He wrapped his arms around her. "How I have missed you!"

God be praised, she was his again.

"Greetings, FitzAlan."

William pushed Catherine behind him and pulled his sword as the man who spoke stepped out from behind the bushes.

"'Tis all right," Catherine said, grabbing his sword

arm. "This is Maredudd Tudor. He has been very good to me."

"Not good enough to send you home," William said, staring hard into the man's sharp hazel eyes.

"If not for Maredudd, I might still be at Harlech," she said. "He did his best to protect me."

Maredudd Tudor gave him a broad smile full of humor. William would not trust the man farther than he could throw him. Still, he felt he owed some debt to him.

"What were you going to ask in exchange for my wife, before Glyndwr's men changed your plan today?" William asked.

Maredudd Tudor went still. "I sought a promise for a later time."

William nodded for him to continue.

"Under Glyndwr's leadership, we have succeeded in taking control of all of Wales, save for a handful of castles. Still, I fear we will not be able to maintain our hold."

"You won't," William said. "You cannot prevail against us without the help of the French. The French will promise, but they'll not send their army again."

Maredudd Tudor nodded. "Even without the French, we might outlast King Henry. His enemies are many and they divert him. But Prince Harry is another matter. He will defeat us in the end."

William sensed what this admission cost the proud rebel. He waited for the man to make his request.

"Before the rebellion, we Tudors held high offices in the service of English kings. When this is over, I want my son Owain to be able to make his way in the English world. What I intended to ask was your pledge to assist him when the time comes."

William respected the man for seeking a means to protect his son in an uncertain world. He gave his promise.

"When you call on me, I will help your son."

"I am grateful," Maredudd Tudor said with a stiff nod. Then he said, "This is yet Welsh rebel country, so you'd best be gone before the men you chased off raise the alarm."

William turned to Catherine. "He's right. We must make haste."

"Thank you," Catherine said, throwing herself at Maredudd. "You were the best of wardens, Maredudd Tudor."

Both of them were laughing as she stepped back.

"Give my love to Marged and Owain," she said.

"We shall miss you, Catherine. Go with God."

It began to drizzle again soon after they set off for Beaumaris. The last few miles, it turned into a cold rain.

When they reached Beaumaris, Robert was waiting for them at the gatehouse. William was anxious to get Catherine out of the rain and hustled her through the side door Robert held open.

"Sweet Lamb of God, what took you so long?" Robert said. "I expected you hours ago."

"We'll tell you the story later," William said, stepping in front of Robert, who was about to greet Catherine with a kiss. "I must get her before a fire."

He was grateful for all Robert had done, but the man did try his patience.

"You'll take the horses, Robert?"

Without waiting for Robert's answer, he took Catherine's icy hand, grabbed a torch, and led her into the dark corridor that connected the towers and gatehouse through the castle wall.

Chapter Twenty-seven

As soon as they reached his chamber, William sat her on a bench before the dwindling fire and began to add kindling to it.

Catherine was content to watch the firelight play across the planes of his face and spark gold in his hair as he built the fire. How she had missed the sight of him! She smiled at him each time he glanced over his shoulder. She understood his need to reassure himself she was truly here, for she felt the same.

Once the roaring blaze drove the dank chill from the room, she stood to remove her damp cloak. William looked up as she turned and slipped it off. He stared open-mouthed at her belly. Though she was not very big yet, anyone looking that closely could see she was with child.

She saw searing pain distort his face before he masked it. It hit her like a blow. How could she have been so mistaken? She had feared William might not be glad to see her. But the child? She never doubted for a moment he would be pleased about the child.

He came to her and took her hands. "You must not worry for the child. I will claim him and raise him as my own," he said in a gentle voice. "I place no blame on you. You had every reason to fear I would never obtain your release."

She was so shocked she could not speak.

"Did you love the man?" he asked in a choked voice. He swallowed, and then added, "Do you love him still?"

She did not know whether to slap him or weep.

"This child was conceived in summer, before I was taken," she said in a voice as cold as ice.

"The child is mine?" William said, breaking into a grin.

"Of course the child is yours," she snapped. "And I pray to God he does not become a horse's ass like his father!"

"Then we must hope it is a girl," he said, scooping her up off the bench. Holding her across his chest, he twirled in a circle, laughing.

He stopped and covered her face with kisses. Gently then, he set her on her feet and took her hands.

"My happiness this day makes up for all the days of sadness since you were taken from me," he said, his eyes shining. "God punished me for my pigheadedness. But now I am doubly blessed."

Unable to hang on to her anger in the face of his joy, she wrapped her arms around him. She would not let the mistake he made in that moment of surprise ruin this reunion. After all, he had accepted her at her word as soon as she told him.

"I love you to the depths of my soul," he said into her hair. "I do not know how I lived these months without you."

She pulled his head down to press her lips to his. In an instant, his kiss turned hungry, demanding. His hands were all over her, rubbing up and down her back, over her buttocks, pressing her against him.

Abruptly, he pulled away. "Are we hurting the babe?"

Feeling dazed from his kisses, she blinked at him for a moment before she understood.

"The babe is fine," she said, smiling. "Marged tells me that if a woman is healthy, she can share her husband's bed almost until the child is born."

She rose on her tiptoes and put her mouth to his ear. "I am exceedingly healthy, William."

He needed no further encouragement. They were on the bed pulling each other's clothes off without knowing how they got there.

Once he had her naked, he leaned back to run his eyes over her. In a ragged voice, he said, "You are even more beautiful than I remembered."

"With this belly?" she said, putting her hand on it as she smiled up at him.

"You are more rounded now, love. Not just your belly, but also"—he gave her a wicked smile—"your breasts."

As if unable to resist, he leaned down and nuzzled his face between them.

"I hope you do not prefer me like this," she protested, "for I will not always be with child."

He lifted his head and said, "You are my Kate and beautiful to me in all ways."

Her pulse quickened at the desire she saw in his eyes.

"How I have longed for you," he murmured as he pressed his face into the curve of her neck. "Night after night, and day after day."

"I, too," she whispered back as he trailed slow wet kisses up and down her throat.

"I lay awake nights thinking of doing this," he said, then circled her nipple with his tongue with tantalizing slowness. "And this," he murmured, and took it into his mouth.

At last. She closed her eyes.

After a time, he worked his way down to her belly. She watched as he pressed tender kisses over it.

With his eyes on hers, he ran his hand up the inside of her thigh. "Shall I show you the other things I longed to do?"

She swallowed and nodded.

He trailed kisses all the way down her leg to her toes. Then ever so slowly, he worked his way back up again. Her heart raced and her breath came fast in anticipation. His hand moved ahead of his mouth, up the inside of her thigh. Finally, his fingers reached the spot where she was aching for him to touch her.

Even as her body responded to the circling motion of his hand between her legs, she was aware of his lips and tongue inching up the inside of her leg. She forgot to breathe as he moved closer and closer to her center.

When his mouth replaced his hand, new sensations rocked through her. It felt so good. *Oh God, oh God, oh God.* Had she said that aloud? Fleetingly, she hoped she would not be struck by lightning for her blasphemy. Then that thought, along with all others, left her. All she knew was his tongue moving over her. And then he was sliding his finger in and out of her and sucking.

As the tension grew inside her, she tossed her head from side to side. She wanted to tell him, "Don't stop, don't stop, don't stop," but she could not form the words. Every muscle was taut; every part of her was focused on his tongue, his mouth. The tension grew and grew until she wanted to scream in frustration.

Then her body convulsed in waves of pleasure so intense she thought she might never recover. After, she lay limp, her limbs boneless.

When he came to lie beside her, she rolled weakly to her side. He enveloped her in his arms from behind. She heard his harsh breathing in her ear.

"I love you," he said, and pressed a kiss to her shoulder.

He ran his fingers lightly over her skin, sending tingles through her. He kissed her neck, her cheek, her hair. When he reached around to cup her breast, she felt his erection against her bottom, and she moved closer. He pressed more insistently against her, and she wanted to feel him inside her again.

His hand was between her legs, his breath hot in her ear.

"You are the only one, Kate. The only one I want. The only one I'll ever want."

When he entered her, she was engulfed in his warmth, his desire. She could no longer tell where he ended and she began. They moved as one; they were one. When he cried out, his cry was her cry, too, and she was swept away with him.

She dozed with his arms wrapped around her, happy and at peace. He wanted her back. He loved her.

When she awoke, she turned in his arms to look at him. In the firelight, he was all sharp angles, golden skin, and long sinewy muscles. How she missed seeing him like this. He was so beautiful he took her breath away.

He cupped her cheek with his hand. His dark honey eyes were intense, serious, as they gazed deep into hers.

"It almost killed me to lose you," he whispered. "I could not bear it again."

She put her arms around him and buried her head in his neck, wanting to comfort and reassure him.

Soon they were kissing. Warm, long, wet kisses. Melding, merging, deep, deep kisses. Then he was inside her again, and they were moving together. This time, the intensity of emotion between them was almost overwhelming. Catherine let down every barrier. She gave herself up to him utterly, absolutely, holding nothing back. She let his passion and love surround her, complete her, and make her whole.

She awoke hours later to a gush of cold air. She stretched and sat up as William came through the door with a heaping platter of food and a heavy pitcher. She smiled at him as she pulled the bedclothes up around her shoulders.

"The weather has turned bad," he said, draping his wet cloak over a chair by the fire. "I was told Robert left yesterday to beat the storm."

The smell of warm bread and roasted meat set her stomach rumbling as she joined him at the small table. Judging by the way he fell to his breakfast, William was as ravenous as she. They ate in silence for some minutes before he spoke again.

"I know you are anxious to be home and see Jamie," he said, "but we shall have to wait another day for this storm to pass."

She pressed her lips together and nodded.

"Will you be angry if I confess I am glad to have my wife to myself for another day?" He leaned across the table to give her a slow, lingering kiss. "Tomorrow is soon enough for putting on clothes and traveling with the men."

William had not wanted to ask questions—or hear answers—that might spoil the complete happiness between them while they were ensconced in their bed-chamber at Beaumaris. Lost in their passion, they spoke little there beyond love talk.

So it was not until they started on the long ride home to Ross Castle that they began to share details of their time apart. William gave her the mundane news of Ross Castle first. Gradually, he turned the conversation to her weeks of captivity.

He asked first about her time with the Tudors, since he knew she had not suffered unduly there. For a time, she entertained him with stories of the antics of little Owain. Then her face grew serious.

"If you had come a day later, I would be back at Har-lech." She clutched her cloak tightly about her as she rode and stared off at the horizon. "It was a close thing."

He asked about Glyndwr. From the way she spoke of him, it was clear she admired the rebel leader.

"Maredudd told me Glyndwr can always tell a false-hood, but I managed it." She gave a light laugh, and he heard the pride in her voice. "I got better each time. When I told him I was not with child, I looked straight into his eyes—and this man has eyes that see right into your soul.

"Of course," she said, her face turning grave again, "if I had returned to Harlech, he would have seen I am with child and never believed me again."

It was midday, so William called his men to halt so they

could eat and let their horses drink in the nearby stream. He took Catherine's hand and drew her away from the others. They found a flat boulder to sit on in a sheltered spot at the stream's edge to have their meal. The sun was out, but it was still cold. Huddling close to him, she took the cup of mead he poured for them to share.

"Glyndwr would have thought you carried the prince's child?" he asked as he laid out dried meat, bread, and cheese on a cloth. The question was an awkward one, so perhaps he should not have asked it.

"Glyndwr began to doubt what he'd been told about the prince and me," she replied thoughtfully. "However, on the chance he held the only child of the heir to the English throne, he would have kept me and the child under lock and key."

If that had happened, William might not have gotten her back until this miserable rebellion was crushed.

"William, you are hurting my hand."

Startled, he eased his grip. He kissed her fingers, saying, "Sorry, love."

"Edmund was badly injured when they took you," he said.

Her eyes went wide. "He was?"

"'Twas a long recovery," he said. "But he has his strength back now, except in one leg."

They sat in silence while William got up his courage to ask the question that had tormented him for months. He heard the rustle and clatter of his men packing up their things, but he ignored their restlessness. He needed to ask this question face-to-face; he could not wait and ask it as they rode.

"Edmund and Stephen both say that the Welshmen

who took you that morning…" He paused, struggling to find a way to ask what he wanted to know without sounding as though he were accusing or blaming her. "Well, they thought the men knew they would find you riding to the abbey then."

"'Tis true! I have given it much thought," she said, putting her hand on his arm and leaning forward. "We must have a traitor at Ross Castle—or in the village."

Unbidden, the image came to him of his wife laughing as she told him how well she lied to Glyndwr.

"I asked Maredudd how they knew," she said. "He said he did not meet our traitor but that Rhys Gethin did."

William was not sure what she had done, or if she had done anything at all. But he wanted her to know she did not need to lie to him. Not about this or anything, ever.

"I want honesty between us now," he said, resting his hand on her knee. "You told me I hurt you even more than Rayburn had. So perhaps you wanted to leave, to get away from me, and later changed your mind. If that is how it was, I would understand. Nay, I would be grateful you changed your mind."

He took one look at the shock and fury on her face and started backtracking as fast as he could. "I am not saying that is what happened," he said, holding up his hands. "What I mean to say is that I do not care how it happened or what you did, so long as you will stay with me now. Nothing else matters."

Catherine threw the full cup of mead in his face and jumped to her feet. "That is *not* all that matters!" Her eyes were narrowed to slits, and her voice was low and threatening.

He had seen her angry before, but never like this.

Fleetingly he thought of the blade she usually carried and hoped her Welsh captors had disarmed her.

"Honesty! You ask for honesty between us?" Her voice was seething. "You bed me for two days, all the while thinking I arranged my own kidnapping? What, did you think I went willingly, and only came to regret it when Glyndwr threatened to marry me off to the Fierce One?"

"He did what?" William said, rising to his feet.

He would have been impressed by the string of oaths Catherine rained on him if he was not quite so intent on getting an answer to his question. When she turned on her heel and stomped off, he ran after her and caught her arm.

"Who is this man you call 'The Fierce One'?"

She turned and shoved his chest hard with both her hands. "You insult me with these horrid accusations, and all you can say to me is, 'Who is the Fierce One?'"

Belatedly, he realized that if she had played no part in her kidnapping, he had committed a very grave error by asking if she had. Why could he never think clearly when it came to this woman? He would never have committed such a blunder with anyone else.

"I am so very, very sorry, Catherine," he stumbled. "I...I just could not find another explanation. And I wanted you to know that I love you, no matter what."

"I don't want you to love me *in spite of* who I am and what I've done," she ranted at him. "I want you to love me *because* of it. If you think I am someone who commits treason and breaks promises to those I care about—or, worst of all, abandons her child—then you do not know me at all.

"I do not know who you think you are in love with, William FitzAlan," she finished, "but it surely is not me."

———

Beneath her anger, Catherine's heart was breaking with hurt and bitter, bitter disappointment. While she had pined for William over those long months apart, he was thinking unspeakably low thoughts of her.

She marched over to the man holding her horse and grabbed the reins from him. Waving off his attempt to help her up, she mounted and set off down the road at a gallop.

Let them catch up to her if they could. She had dallied long enough. Her son was waiting for her.

Chapter Twenty-eight

William was beside her almost before she reached the road. Soon after, she heard the other horses following at a safe distance behind. William's men were brave soldiers, but they would let him face this kind of trouble alone.

He tried to speak to her, but she fixed her eyes on the road before her and ignored him. Eventually, he ceased to try.

At some point during the long ride, she resolved not to let her anger and resentment toward William spoil her homecoming. She had waited too long for this. When Ross Castle came into sight at long last, she thought her heart would burst. She leaned forward and spurred her horse into a full gallop.

"Is it wise to ride so hard in your condition?" William called out as he raced beside her.

She did not spare him a glance. She would be damned if she would walk her horse the last mile home. A figure on the wall next to the gatehouse jumped up and down, waving. It had to be Stephen. She waved back.

A surge of emotion had her weeping as she rode through the open gate. All the household was running across the bailey to meet her. Stephen flew down the stairs from the wall and reached her first.

She pulled her horse up and almost fell into his arms.

"I missed you so much!" She stepped back to look at him. "Why, you've grown half a foot! And you are even more handsome than before."

Stephen's face turned crimson in embarrassed pleasure.

"Where is Jamie—"

"Mother!"

She turned to see Jamie running toward her and dropped to one knee to catch him in her arms. The force of his greeting nearly toppled her. When he buried his face in her neck and clung to her, she knew Marged was right. Her son had not forgotten her.

All evening, they fussed over her. Alys insisted she sit close to the hearth and wrapped a blanket around her shoulders. Thomas put a stool under her feet. Others brought her cakes and hot spiced wine. Tears stung Catherine's eyes; she was so grateful to be home and among her own household.

While the servants ministered to her, William stood close by, silent and watchful. After a time, he signaled for them to leave, saying, "Lady Catherine is tired from her journey."

At his words, she felt the weight of her exhaustion. She held her arms out to Jamie. He crawled into her lap and soon was fast asleep against her chest.

He felt so good against her. As she watched his sweet face, slack with sleep, she saw it had lost some of its plumpness in her absence. His hair was longer and darker, too. She brushed it back and sighed for all she had missed.

Still, she had her son in her arms now. She was home.

She must have dozed, for she awoke with a start when William touched her arm.

"The two of you should be in bed," he said, lifting the sleeping boy from her lap.

A rush of cool air replaced the warm weight, and she felt the loss acutely. Looking up, she saw that William had Jamie on one shoulder. He was holding his other hand out to her. She took it and let him help her up.

As they climbed the stairs, he squeezed her hand and said, "When you were gone, I would carry Jamie up to bed and imagine you were with us, just like this."

He was trying to make up to her, but she was not yet ready. They continued up the stairs in silence, past their own rooms, to Jamie's. After William laid Jamie on his bed, she pulled the bedclothes up and kissed her son good night.

"Father," Jamie called in a sleepy voice as he stretched out his arms to William.

William embraced the boy and kissed his cheek. Jamie was asleep before they slipped outside his chamber door.

"Jamie started calling me that some weeks ago," William said, sounding defensive. "I saw no reason he should not."

"I would never criticize you for that."

In truth, the warm bond between Jamie and William made her wish she could forgive William his other transgressions. Her anger had dulled, but she was a long way from forgetting. The disappointment of learning he thought so little of her left her with an ache in her chest.

"I'll sleep here with Jamie tonight," she said.

She would not meet his eyes. She did not want to see

the hurt she knew was there. What he offered her was good. It just was not all she hoped for. She understood she needed to accept it and be grateful. But she was not ready to make that compromise tonight, not when the hurt was so fresh.

He did not argue but leaned down to kiss her cheek. When she felt the warmth of his breath and smelled the wood smoke in his hair, she was tempted to lean into him. But her heart was too bruised to give in. In time, she would be strong enough to be with him and still protect that true part of herself she valued most. The part he could not see.

But not tonight.

When Jamie's nursemaid appeared, Catherine asked her to help her undress and then sent her away for the night.

She crawled into bed next to her son and breathed in his scent: damp earth, dogs, and the barest hint of his baby smell. For the hundredth time that day, she prayed her thanks to God for bringing her home and keeping her son safe.

She lay awake thinking of the changes in her household. Not only was the bond between William and Jamie stronger, but there was also an easy closeness between him and Stephen that was not there before.

The servants' attitude toward William had changed as well. Alys, in particular, seemed to have developed a strong affection for him. She complained repeatedly how he had lost weight.

The problem was not that Catherine did not recognize and appreciate her husband's many good qualities—but that he did not recognize hers. She sighed and rested her cheek against Jamie's hair. Unbidden, the abbess's words from last summer came back to her. She should be grateful her husband was an honorable man who treated her son well. That should be enough. It must.

Hours later, she felt William slide into bed behind her, fully clothed. She was too drowsy to complain. Instead, she let herself sink into the comfort of her cocoon. With her husband's arms wrapped around her and her own wrapped around Jamie, she fell into deep sleep.

When she awoke in the morning, William was gone. She rubbed her hand over the indentation where he had slept, but there was no trace of his warmth. With a sigh, she dropped a kiss on her sleeping son's head and then climbed out of bed.

She slipped her robe over her shift and headed down the stairs to dress for the day.

She was one step from the landing before she saw Edmund outside the solar door. Instinctively, she put one foot back on the step behind her, ready to retreat. But Edmund had already seen her.

She meant to ask about his health, to tell him she was sorry for his injuries. But his gaze moved down her body with deliberate rudeness, making her conscious that her hair was loose and her robe hung open. She jerked the robe around her and glared at him.

She noticed his limp as Edmund walked toward her. He did not stop until his feet touched the step on which she stood. She did not back away, though he was so close she could smell him and feel his breath on her face.

"It is curious," he said, his eyes level with hers, "that after such a long time apart, you do not sleep with your husband."

"Get out of my way."

"Is it because you carry another man's child that William will not have you?" he asked in a harsh whisper. "Or is it you who turns your husband away? Perhaps you cannot appreciate a good man after whoring with Welshmen."

He caught her arm as she swung to slap him. They stood glaring at each other, neither one backing down.

"Which is it, Edmund? One time you say I must be as cold as ice, another you call me whore." She narrowed her eyes at him and hissed, "But we both know the true reason you resent me."

"And what, pray tell, is that?"

"'Tis because you will never have me," she said. "Do you suppose I don't know you've lusted after me from the first?"

From the way Edmund's eyelids twitched, she knew she hit her mark dead-on. She let the satisfaction show in her eyes.

"If my husband knew how you look at me, he would rip your eyes out." Thrusting her shoulder against his chest, she shoved past him.

"Then why do you not tell him?" Edmund called out behind her. "He would not believe you, would he?"

Yesterday, before the ride home, she would have told William. But now? William believed she deceived him in things more important than this.

The solar door opened. Her husband's dark amber eyes swept over her, taking in her crimson face, loose hair, nightclothes, and bare feet. Then they shifted past her to Edmund.

"You have embarrassed my wife, catching her before

she is dressed for the day," William said. "Next time, wait for me in the hall."

William gave her a nod and headed down the stairs. Before Edmund followed, he ran his eyes up and down her. She wanted to throw something after him. Slamming the solar door was not nearly enough to satisfy her.

Pulsing with anger, she paced the room. She could no longer pretend Edmund was merely an annoyance. Though she was not certain he was truly dangerous, he was her enemy. One way or another, she intended to get him out of her home.

———

The abbess must have left the abbey as soon as she received William's message telling her of Catherine's return. She arrived just as they were sitting down to the midday meal.

"You are with child!" Abbess Talcott said as Catherine rose from the table to embrace her. "What a happy surprise. William did not tell me you were blessed."

"He did not know of it," Catherine said. "I discovered I was with child after my capture."

William caught the unease in Catherine's voice and wondered if she spoke the truth. Had she known she carried his child before she left and not told him?

The abbess sat next to Catherine and squeezed her hand. "It was a charity William did not know. The poor man would have only suffered more."

"I see William has won you over as well," Catherine teased. "Even Alys adores him now. I swear, the woman goes on about poor William turning away his favorite foods. Forget that I was in the wilds of Wales, sleeping on the hard ground and growing a babe on food prepared by a rebel who could not cook!"

Catherine meant to make a joke of it, but the abbess gripped Catherine's hand and asked, "Was it as bad as that? We were so very worried about you."

"Nay, 'twas not," Catherine assured her friend. "The travel was a bit hard, for we covered long distances over rough roads. So long as I was with Glyndwr, though, I always slept in houses. It was only later, when I traveled alone with Maredudd Tudor, that we slept outside—and I had to eat his dreadful cooking!"

William listened intently; this was the first he had heard in detail of the rough travel his wife had endured. Her attempt to make light of it did not deceive him.

"Maredudd dragged me all over western Wales before taking me to his home," she said with a slight smile and shook her head. "When we finally headed toward Anglesey, we traveled on back trails through the Snowdon Mountains."

"Oh, dear," the abbess said, patting her arm, "that must have been terrible."

"Though I would have bargained with the devil for a bath and a clean gown," Catherine said, her voice losing its light tone, "I never felt afraid with Maredudd."

The pulse at William's temples throbbed as the darkness of his guilt engulfed him. Somehow, he had never let himself think of her as being truly in fear of her captors.

Catherine had gone white. Belatedly, the abbess saw that her questions were causing Catherine distress and changed the subject.

"Now that you are safely back," she said, "perhaps we can devote our attention to the question of Stephen's betrothal."

One look at Stephen's scarlet face, and Catherine was on her feet. "Shall we go to the solar, Lady Abbess? It is pleasant there when the sun is out, as it is today."

As the ladies left the room, the abbess's voice carried back to the men at the table. "I've made a list of all the heiresses of an appropriate age in the Marches. I assume you do want him nearby...."

Stephen sent William a terrified look.

"Don't worry, little brother," William said with more confidence than he felt. "I will have the final say."

———

William was on edge. In spite of having every reason to be happy, things between him and Catherine had gone horribly wrong. Their time at Beaumaris had been everything he had hoped for. And more. Somehow, he lost it all with a single question.

Catherine did not even want to sleep with him on her first night at home. At least she did not kick him out when he slipped in beside her during the night. He wanted to believe it was a sign she was warming to him, but he suspected she had been just too tired to argue.

He hoped to talk with her after the abbess left, but there seemed no opportunity. The servants hung about, waiting on her hand and foot, and he could hardly send Stephen and Jamie away. He understood too well that they needed the reassurance of having her near.

Even if he got Catherine alone, what would he say to her?

As he went into supper that evening, Stephen sidled up to him. "What have you done?" Stephen hissed in his ear.

"Now that you are all of thirteen," William said, "you believe you can counsel me?"

"No one has thrown a cup of mead in my face."

If this young brother of his did not learn to watch his tongue, it would be the death of him.

"How did you hear of that?" he demanded.

Stephen shrugged. The boy seemed to hear everything, but he never revealed his sources.

"I would hate to have Lady Catherine cross with me," Stephen said. "If I were you, I would do whatever she wants to make amends."

"So, you advise complete capitulation in dealing with women?"

"'Tis what Mother taught me," Stephen replied with a grin. "But Lady Catherine is so much nicer, I would think you would want to make her happy."

"It is all I want," William said, his eyes on Catherine, who was entering the hall. "All I want in this world."

After supper, Catherine turned to him and said in a low voice, "I cannot bear having the servants smother me again tonight. I am taking Jamie up to the solar."

She did not invite him, but neither did she ask him not to come. He followed her up, with Stephen on his heels. No doubt Stephen was coming along to whisper more helpful guidance in his ear, should he need it.

The four of them spent a pleasant hour together, and William began to relax. Then Catherine announced she was going upstairs with the boys to put Jamie to bed.

Would she return, or would she sleep in Jamie's bed again?

His shoulders sagged with relief when he heard her light steps coming down the stairs. Watching her hesitate at the doorway, he knew the decision to return had not been easy for her.

He hurried across the room to her, intent on making sure she did not regret her decision, and took her hand.

"Thank you," he said as he raised it to his lips.

Keeping his eyes on hers, he turned her hand and kissed her palm. When she did not pull back, he told himself it was going to be all right.

With his tongue, he lightly circled her palm. He felt the pulse at her wrist quicken. In bed, at least, he could make her happy. From the way she was looking at him, he suspected she was going to let him take her there.

She did. He was so intoxicated by the feel of her skin against his, the way her body responded to his every touch, the sound of her crying his name as he moved inside her, that he did not notice. Or did not let himself notice.

But after it was over, he knew. He felt so suffused with love for her that he fought against the dawning recognition. But as he clasped her to him, both of them still breathing hard, he knew. Something had changed since the last time they made love. Something was different.

Missing.

For those two days at Beaumaris, she gave herself to him wholly, holding nothing back. He felt as if he held her heart in his hands. As she held his. If not for Beaumaris, he might not know she withheld a part of herself from him now.

In the nights that followed, he made love to her again and again, trying to break down her barriers. Unable to find words that might bring her back to him, he used the strength of his love and desire to draw her. But no matter how deep their passion, there was a part of her he could not reach. A wall he could not climb. A place she guarded from him.

He satisfied her body, even pleased her. He knew he did. But when he told her he loved her, she became upset. So upset, he stopped saying it.

Except sometimes, when he was deep inside her, he could not hold back the words. *I love you, I love you, I love you.*

She did not say them back.

Chapter Twenty-nine

Catherine, you must help me understand the rebel leaders so that I can end this rebellion more quickly," Prince Harry said. "This conflict with our Welsh brothers only weakens us for the war we must inevitably wage with France."

At William's request, the prince had given Catherine a week to recover before coming to Ross Castle to question her.

"Glyndwr is a good man," Catherine told him. "He wants what is best for his people."

"What he has brought them is razed villages and ruined crops!" the prince said with irritation. "That is all this rebellion will ever bring them. They cannot prevail, so their suffering is for naught."

"Glyndwr believes God supports him, just as you do," she said in a reasonable voice. "He will not give up easily."

William listened as Prince Harry pressed Catherine for every bit of information she had gleaned during her capture. He asked her everything from the character of the rebel leaders to Glyndwr's intentions regarding the

French pope to the number of armed men defending Aberystwyth and Harlech. The two discussed the Tudors at length.

Observing their interaction, William was struck by the prince's obvious faith in the accuracy of her reports. It was easy to believe he had drawn up battle plans based on information she provided.

"What can you tell me about Rhys Gethin?" Prince Harry asked.

William sat forward and watched his wife closely. He'd been afraid to ask about this rebel—or any of her experiences with the rebels—since their disastrous conversation on the way home from Beaumaris.

"I know Rhys Gethin is a fearless and skilled commander," the prince continued, "but what is he like as a man?"

For the first time, Catherine seemed reluctant to answer.

"Gethin is a rougher man than Glyndwr or the Tudors," she finally said, looking away from the prince as she spoke. She paused, then said, "I thought him the most dangerous of all."

Keeping her eyes focused on some distant point, she said, "Glyndwr threatened to have my marriage annulled by the false pope so he could wed me to Rhys Gethin."

So Gethin was "The Fierce One." The blood pounded in William's head at the thought of her being treated like chattel and traded for favors.

"Glyndwr let Maredudd Tudor take me from Harlech to remove me from Gethin's sight," she said. "He feared Gethin might carry me off to be 'married' by a village priest with a knife pricking his back."

"So Glyndwr wanted to protect you from Gethin?" the prince asked.

"It was more that Glyndwr would not permit Gethin to force his hand," she said with a rueful smile. "You see, Glyndwr had not yet decided what to do with me."

A chill went up William's spine as he thought of how close he had come to losing her. Catherine's pale, pinched face told him the discussion of Rhys Gethin had distressed her as well.

"My wife is tired," he said before Prince Harry could press her with more questions.

"Forgive me, Kate," the prince said, hopping to his feet. He dropped his gaze to her belly for the briefest moment and blushed faintly. "I did not realize how long I droned on."

The prince was a leader of armies, a battle-hardened commander. It was easy to forget he was also a young man of eighteen, inexperienced in other ways.

Catherine touched his arm and smiled up at him. "I am not ill, Harry, only with child."

"You feel well, then?" he asked in an uncertain tone.

"In sooth, I feel extremely well these days," she said, her smile broadening. "So much better than the first weeks, when I was nauseous and bone-tired."

From the look on the prince's face, this was more than he wanted to hear. He bid Catherine a quick good night and excused himself to speak to his men.

William's stomach clenched as he thought of Catherine, ill with her pregnancy, traveling hundreds of miles over rough roads. Sleeping out of doors in the rain and mud, for God's sake. As long as he lived, he would never forgive himself.

Stifling an urge to carry her, he helped her to her feet and escorted her up the stairs. Once he had her in their bedchamber, he resolutely ignored her protests and tucked her into bed.

He sat on the edge of the bed and rubbed his knuckles against her cheek. "I am sorry I was not there to protect you or ease your discomfort."

"I do not blame you," she assured him, but he could not accept her absolution for his gross failure.

"I also apologize for suggesting you could have helped bring about your capture."

She narrowed her eyes at him, weighing the sincerity of his words. After a long moment, she said, "I want to know who gave me up, William. Someone did. Someone told the rebels I was going to the abbey that day."

She could not absolve him, but perhaps she had given him a means to partially redeem himself.

"I will do my best to find the man who betrayed you." *And make him pay dearly for her suffering.* "I'll question everyone in the castle and the village again."

"Ask about the tenant Tyler," she said. "I always suspected he carried messages to the rebels for Rayburn."

If Tyler had a hand in this, he will not see another sunset.

William kissed her forehead and left her to rest.

Back in the hall, he and Prince Harry talked by the hearth until late, going over the information Catherine had shared.

"What a woman!" the prince said, shaking his head and grinning.

"Aye," William agreed quietly.

"No prince ever had a more perfect spy," Harry gloated. "She is courageous and daring—and her loyalty is boundless.

"Boundless, I tell you," he repeated, swinging his arms wide. "By the saints, she can lie through her teeth to an enemy, make him believe every word. Yet, she could not lie to me or to you to save her life!"

William winced. Though Harry did not intend to chastise him, the young man's absolute faith in Catherine made William feel like a worm for doubting her.

"As you know, the king is keeping his Christmas court at Eltham Castle this year," the prince said. "Come to Monmouth and we'll ride there together."

The prince was reminding him that he was expected to make an appearance. With Northumberland still spouting rebellion from Scotland, the king required reassurance of William's loyalty. Reluctantly, he agreed to meet the prince at Monmouth in two days' time.

"Tyler was the man."

Catherine looked up to find William in the solar doorway.

He came to sit beside her and took her hand. "After the prince left this morning, I went to the village. I heard from several folk that Tyler bought a cow a few weeks ago. No one knew where he found the money."

"That is suspicious."

"Aye. And now he's disappeared, which only confirms it. No one has seen him since the day you returned. Likely he feared you may have learned of his role from your captors."

"Or else he knew I would suspect he was involved."

"I've sent men out looking for him," William said. "Eventually they'll find him and bring him back."

She had expected this news to set her mind to rest more than it did. William, too, still seemed uneasy.

"What is it?" she asked.

"I intend to take Stephen with me to Eltham."

"I am so pleased," she said. "It will be good to have the king and others see him as William FitzAlan's brother and not just as Carleton's son."

Her smile faded when she noticed William was not meeting her eyes.

"As always, I'll be leaving Edmund in charge of the castle's defense while I am gone."

She put her hand on her hip and glared at him. "You did not want to tell me, because you knew full well I would not like it."

"He is my second in command," he said. "I leave him in charge because I have confidence in him. It would be a grave insult to him if I did not."

The patience in his voice grated on her nerves.

"I do not trust him," she said, making no effort to hide her irritation. "I do not wish to be in his care."

"How can you say that when he nearly died trying to protect you?" William said. "He would do it again without hesitation. He takes the trust I put in him seriously."

"What of the other men? Surely you can put one of them in charge and take Edmund with you."

He reached to brush back a strand of hair that had escaped from her headdress. She slapped his hand away.

"I have other good men, but Edmund is by far the best fighter among them." He softened his voice and said,

"He's sworn to try to make amends with you. Why do you object to him so much?"

"I told you already I do not trust him." She gave him a sideways glance and saw that was not enough for her stubborn husband. Against her better judgment, she said, "I do not like the way he looks at me."

He gave a deep sigh and spread his arms out. "Catherine, I cannot send men away for looking at you, or I will have none left. All the men look at you. They cannot help it."

Anger surging in her veins, she got to her feet so she could glare down at him. "You misunderstand me, and I begin to wonder if it is deliberate." She shook a finger in his face. "I tell you, husband, if you saw how Edmund looks at me, you would not like it either."

His nostrils flared and an icy coldness came into his eyes. In a quiet, dangerous voice, he asked, "Has he touched you?"

Edmund had not touched her, except for that one time months ago. Even then, all he truly did was slide his finger down her forearm. She was not prepared to see him dead for these offenses—yet. Grudgingly, she pressed her lips together and shook her head.

William's expression relaxed. "I will warn Edmund not to do or say anything that might offend you."

"But you will still leave him here?" She could barely keep herself from stamping her foot like a child.

"When I cannot be here, I must leave my best man in my stead. I do it to keep my promise to protect you."

"You failed to keep that promise once already." She blurted the words out in anger before she knew what she said. They burned hot in the air between them.

"I did not mean that." Although she regretted her hurtful words, she was still so angry her hands shook. "But it distresses me beyond bearing that you dismiss my opinion on a matter so important to me."

"The king trusts me in matters of military defense," he said, a note of pleading in his voice. "Why can you not?"

"Perhaps you should trust me more than you do Edmund," she snapped. "But then, you've never trusted me, have you?"

With that, she marched into her bedchamber and slammed the door behind her.

———

William tapped at her door. When she did not answer, he called out, "I will send Edmund away."

She opened the door a crack. "When?"

"He'll be gone today."

She opened the door no farther. "If you think I don't know why you are doing this, you are sorely mistaken."

"I'm showing I respect your wishes."

"You are doing this so I will not be too angry to come to your bed tonight."

Should he admit that was part of it? Probably not.

"If it makes you unhappy to have Edmund here, I want him gone."

The door banged shut. Apparently, he'd given the wrong answer. God help him! He hovered outside her door, trying to think of what else he could say, but he could think of nothing.

With a long sigh, he went down to write a message and have his talk with Edmund.

"You've upset my wife," he told Edmund a short time later.

"Pregnant women are known to get strange notions," Edmund said with a shrug. "Who knows why?"

"I am recommending you for service with the king's brother, Thomas Beaufort. He's a good man and close to both the king and Prince Harry."

"After all our years together, all we've been through, you will throw me out for her!"

"I warned you that if I had to choose between you, I would choose her," William said. "And I'm not throwing you out; I'm finding you a better position. 'Tis an honor to serve Thomas Beaufort."

"She's ruined you. Can't you see it? She's a lying who—"

He grabbed Edmund by the throat. "Don't say it if you want to live."

The blood was pounding in William's ears he was so angry. If Edmund ever spoke to Catherine like this, why had she not told him?

Edmund put his hands up, croaking, "All right, all right!"

William waited a long moment before he released him.

Edmund rubbed his throat as he tried to get his breath back. "You are right," he said when he could speak again. "I did not mean to offend her, but you must put your wife first. Your offer to find me a place with Thomas Beaufort is generous."

"I want you gone today." William slapped the sealed parchment he'd written for Beaufort into Edmund's hand. "You'll find Beaufort attending Christmas court at Eltham."

"I hope we can part as friends," Edmund said.

"Mind what you say about my wife in the future, or I'll see that Beaufort dismisses you," William said. "If I don't kill you first."

The business with Edmund left him in a sour mood. It was followed by a miserable night alone in his bedchamber. With only the solar between them, Catherine seemed as far away as when she was held at Harlech Castle.

He was still in a foul mood when he arrived at Monmouth the next morning.

Chapter Thirty

Catherine was relieved that Edmund was gone—and she felt guilty at the same time. Perhaps she was too hard on William. The wound from what he said to her on the way home from Beaumaris was still raw. That he dismissed her judgment regarding Edmund only added salt to the wound. He gave in to keep the peace with her, not because he trusted her opinion.

What was keeping Jamie? Jacob took him to see a litter of new kittens in the stable, but they should have been back by now. It was almost time for supper.

She paused in her sewing and cocked her head. What was that noise? She heard a crash and a bloodcurdling scream, followed by more screams and shouts. She sprang to her feet. Before she reached the door, it opened.

Edmund filled the doorway. Panic closed her throat. She backed up slowly. With the door open, the shouts and clatter coming from below were louder.

Edmund closed the door and leaned against it. "Thought you were rid of me, did you?" he said with a wide smile.

Her breath came in short, shallow gasps, making her feel light-headed.

Edmund went to the table and poured wine from his flask into an empty cup he found there.

"Come, Catherine, drink to my success," he said, waving her toward one of the two chairs.

When she took the seat he indicated, he pushed the cup toward her and raised his flask. She touched the cup to her lips as he took a long pull from the flask.

She forced herself to take several slow, deep breaths before speaking. "May I ask what we are celebrating?"

She did not know what his game was, but she must play along to give herself time to think.

"I've taken the castle."

She couldn't help gasping, though she had guessed as much.

"As soon as my men finish locking up the servants, they'll carry one of your barrels of ale to the hall," Edmund said. "But I wanted to have a private celebration with you."

It did not reassure her that the noise below had died down. She prayed God Jacob had found somewhere to hide with Jamie.

"I thought you were on your way to see Thomas Beaufort."

"I paid a visit to Lord Grey instead," Edmund said, and winked at her. "That old fox has wanted a piece of these lands since the day he was born. He was happy to pay for the rabble downstairs."

She could well believe it of Grey. At dawn tomorrow, Grey would attempt to take as much of their lands as he dared.

"How did you take the castle?" She needed time, and she was counting on his vanity.

"Since the men know me as William's right-hand man, they opened the gate to me. I slit a throat or two, and in no time we had most of the guard chained in the gatehouse."

"You cannot think the king will let you keep Ross Castle," Catherine said.

"Nay, but neither will he give it back to William," Edmund said, his voice full of bitter anger. "You think he will be in the king's favor after losing his castle within six months? Ha!"

William would be lucky not to be drawn and quartered.

"Besides losing his castle, William will have lost his wife—not once, but twice!" Edmund gave a harsh laugh and slapped the table. "The king will have no respect for him after this. No one will."

"But why? Why would you do it?"

"After all I've done for him, he kicks me out! Sends me away like a dog with his tail between his legs. So I've taken his castle and ruined him."

Without taking his eyes off her, he backed up to the door and put his hand behind him. She heard the scrape of the bar sliding into place.

"And now I'm going to take his wife."

———

William cooled his heels Efor half a day at Monmouth while Prince Harry dealt with some unexpected business. Damn. He was anxious to get this appearance at the king's Christmas court over with and get back home. It was midafternoon before the prince was finally ready to start the journey to Eltham.

"What an hour to get started," William grumbled to

Stephen. "We'll have to stop for the night in a couple of hours."

As they mounted their horses, two score of men-at-arms bearing the Lancaster lion banner pounded through the main gate.

The prince watched them with narrowed eyes. "'Tis my uncle Beaufort."

William dismounted. They wouldn't be going to Eltham today. He scanned Beaufort's men but did not see Edmund.

After greetings were exchanged, William said to Beaufort, "I sent a man to you yesterday. If you came on the London road, you should have crossed paths."

"We traveled on it all the way from Eltham," Beaufort said. "We passed a few men but none stopped us."

An uneasy feeling settled in the pit of William's stomach.

"We are difficult to miss," Beaufort said. "Are you sure your man took the London road?"

It was the only road Edmund could take to Eltham Castle.

William tried to tell himself something could have happened to waylay Edmund. His horse took lame. Bandits attacked him. He got drunk and found a woman along the way.

William had fought beside Edmund for ten years. He'd trusted the man with his life more times than he could count. And yet, all he could hear were Catherine's words: *I do not trust him.*

He remembered the night he met her here at Monmouth Castle. She had told him her betrothed was not a man to be trusted. As an inexperienced girl of sixteen, Catherine had seen Rayburn for what he was. No one else had.

His heart thundered in his chest as he mounted his horse.

"Catherine may be in danger," he said to Prince Harry. "Make my excuses to the king."

He did not wait to hear the prince's reply.

He signaled to his men to follow and galloped out the gate.

Chapter Thirty-one

"Was it you who arranged my kidnapping?" Catherine asked in an attempt to divert Edmund.

"Aye, I did it to save him," he said. "William was a fool for you from the start. I could see you would be the ruin of him, bedding every man from prince to troubadour right under his nose."

Edmund sat in the chair on the other side of the small table and took another long drink from his flask.

"The Welsh wanted you as soon as I told them Prince Harry would pay any price for you," he said with a cold smile. "Then I made William believe you'd run off with a lover. Believe me, I just had to plant the seed."

She felt the smoldering anger beneath his taunting humor.

"I expected the ransom demand to the prince to remove any doubt about the sort of woman you are," he said, shaking his head. "After that, William should have been happy to leave you to rot in Wales.

"I meant to cure him of you. If the Welsh offered me money to sweeten the pot, why not?" Edmund slammed his fist on the table. "William got his land and wealth. By heaven, did I not deserve something as well?"

His shifting moods were frightening her as much as his words.

"But instead of paying me the rest of my money, that bastard Rhys Gethin had his men try to kill me!"

Rhys Gethin had the sense not to trust a man who betrayed his own.

"But how could you do that to William?" she asked. "You were his friend. His second in command. He trusted you."

He turned to gaze out the window at the dark sky. "I loved him like a brother," he said, nodding. "'Twas a time we had everything in common. We were the best of soldiers, but landless, with no bonds of family."

She heard the plaintive longing in his voice.

"There was freedom in the life we had. And always plenty of women. William drew them like flies." Edmund blew out a deep breath and shook his head. "But William was never content with it. Nay, he always wanted what he did not have."

He lifted his flask and, finding it empty, tossed it aside. He picked up her cup and took a deep drink. Though he showed little outward sign, she thought he must be drunk.

"Then the king hands him a castle, lands, and a title—and all for nothing more than refusing to follow his father into treason." Tiny drops of spittle hit the table as Edmund spoke. "Truly, his bounty was too much!"

"You understand him well enough to know what he truly desired was not wealth or lands," she said in a soft voice. "What he wanted was a family of his own, a home."

"I would not have begrudged William his good

fortune," he said, fixing her with a look that burned right through her. "But then, in addition to all else, he got you. And for you, he had to pay no price at all."

Edmund's words sent a wave of panic through her that threatened to swamp her.

"No matter what you were, what you looked like," Edmund said, "he would have married you because you needed saving. You see, William lacks his parents' pragmatism when it comes to honor. I could have forgiven him the rest of his good fortune if he had to take an ugly heiress into the bargain.

"Instead, the whore's son got a woman who puts all the others to shame," he said, his voice thick with bitterness. "It was more than one man deserved."

Her years with Rayburn gave her the sharp instincts of the hunted. She sensed Edmund was on the verge of attacking her.

"What about Tyler?" she asked, hoping to divert him again.

"Tyler knew some of the rebels. He served as my go-between with Rhys Gethin."

"What happened to him?" she asked, though she could guess.

"When William brought you back, I knew he would figure out someone here betrayed you. I gave him Tyler." He shrugged. "I suspect they'll find his body in the spring."

With an edge to her voice, she asked, "How is it you are not concerned William will come after you?"

"Well might you ask!" He laughed as he said it, but she heard unease in his laughter. "Believe me, I plan to be far, far away before William returns."

Praise God, he was going to take his rabble and leave

soon. She narrowed her eyes at him. "You might want to get started."

"I have three days, maybe more, before the news reaches him and he returns. All the same, we'll leave in the morning."

She just had to survive until morning.

"You do know I'm taking you with me?" he said.

She did not look down soon enough to hide the terror in her eyes, and he smiled with satisfaction.

"You bewitch men at every turn. One of them is sure to pay," he said. "I'll send ransom demands to them all and sell you to the highest bidder.

"Mind you, I'd make Gethin pay twice as much as the others, after what he did to me." He took another drink of wine and narrowed his eyes to slits. "But even if William could find the money after he loses Ross Castle, I'd never let him buy you back."

Catherine felt such a surge of rage it left her shaking. But then the child rolled in her belly, and her thoughts turned cold and clear. She would save herself and her baby.

"It would be a shame to give you to a man like Rhys Gethin. I suspect he has no refinement in bed," he said, leaving no doubt as to the direction of his thoughts. "He probably makes love the same as he fights—charges straight for the prize with all speed."

He leaned across the table and took her chin in his hand. She sat still, every muscle taut.

"Perhaps I'll give up the money and keep you for myself." His eyes were shining, and he was breathing hard. "Believe me, Catherine, I could make you call out my name and beg for more."

She was too late in wiping the revulsion from her face.
He released her chin and grabbed her wrist.

"Then you shall go to that vulgar Welshman, who will
use you as roughly as a whore and give away your child."

She felt his anger like the edge of a blade against her
skin. She tried to pull her hand out of his grasp, but he
held it in an iron grip.

"But I shall have you first," he said, jerking her to her
feet. "I want William to come home and smell another
man on your sheets."

Chapter Thirty-two

William and his men raced in silence through the increasingly gray afternoon light. All the while, he prayed he was wrong. Prayed she was safe. Prayed Edmund feared him enough not to do it. Edmund must know William would follow him across the earth and into hell to kill him if he...

The sun dipped below the horizon, and the air turned bitter cold. It was not the cold, however, but a sense of foreboding that sent a shiver up his spine.

At long last, the outline of Ross Castle was dimly visible in the early darkness of the winter evening. William pushed his tired horse harder over the last stretch and reached the gate ahead of his men. When he roared at the guards, nothing happened. They neither called back nor dropped the drawbridge. He looked at the gatehouse and the towers. No torchlight. All was dark, as if the castle were abandoned, empty of every living soul.

God help him. They took his castle. His wife and Jamie were inside. The protection of every member of the household was his responsibility. Somehow, he had to get inside. He thought of all his work, strengthening the castle's defenses. He could see the storage rooms filled with sacks of grain to withstand weeks, even months, of siege.

It would take him at least two days to get a siege tower here. Too much could happen in two days. He could not wait that long. He heard the trampling and snorting of the other horses as his men joined him.

"Ropes," he shouted at them, panic rising in his throat. "We need ropes to climb the walls."

The men were silent. One or two might carry a bit of rope, but it was unlikely to be long enough to scale the curtain wall.

"William."

He turned toward his brother's voice in the darkness.

"I know a way."

Catherine screamed as Edmund dragged her across the solar toward the threshold to the bedchamber.

"No one will come," he shouted over her screams.

As he carried her toward the high bed, memories of Rayburn came crashing down on her. She kicked and screamed and clawed at his face. She would not be taken against her will again without a fight.

He pushed her onto the bed and straddled her. Holding her wrists over her head, he leaned down close to her face. "We can do this rough or not," he rasped, breathing hard. "The choice is yours, but I will have you one way or the other."

She struggled against him, but he held her fast. Holding her with one hand, he reached inside his tunic and pulled out a length of rope.

God help her, he meant to tie her down!

He put his mouth against her ear and said, "Aye, Catherine, I will do it."

He pulled back to look at her, but he was still close enough for her to feel his breath on her face. It smelled of sour wine.

"You may as well cooperate and enjoy yourself," he said, his voice almost playful. "Then you can tell me if I am better than William."

He put his palm to her cheek and rubbed his thumb across her bottom lip. "What say you, Catherine? How shall it be?"

It was difficult to think with him holding her down, but she could not let him tie her. She must have her hands free to have any chance at all.

"Will you promise to be careful of my baby?" Her voice came out faint and high-pitched.

"Very, very careful," he purred.

She swallowed and nodded. "All right, I will do it willingly. But you frightened me badly. You must give me time to calm myself . . . if . . . if I am to enjoy myself."

"I've had enough of waiting. Waiting and watching while you carried on with William, the prince, even that troubadour."

His eyes fixed on her mouth. Oh God, she could not take it if he kissed her mouth. Without releasing her wrists, he leaned down and kissed her throat. She bit her lip to keep from screaming at him to stop.

"But I am an understanding man," he said with a thin smile. "I will give you as much time as it takes for me to remove my boots."

He lifted her to the floor with him.

"Light a candle while I take my boots off," he said. "It's getting dark, and I want to see you."

Her hands shook as she lit the candle stub. As she did it, she listened for sounds from below. She heard no sound of guards fighting their way into the keep to save her, only the soft rumble of male voices and hoots of laughter. If she was to be saved, she must do it herself.

Feeling his eyes on her back, she turned to find Edmund sitting on the bench holding his boots midair.

"You are beautiful," he said, raking his eyes over her. "I gave you your time. Now I want to see you naked."

She took two steps back but could go no farther. Her back was against the bed. Somehow, she had to slow him down and gain control of the situation.

"What about you?" She let a faint smile lift the corners of her mouth. "If you want me to enjoy myself, you will have to take your clothes off as well."

She fluttered her eyelashes and tilted her head to the side. "And you will most definitely have to take your time."

Praise God, he was even drunker than she thought! Judging from the way his mouth gaped like a fish out of water, he believed her act. Or he wanted badly to pretend he did.

"You did say we have until dawn, did you not?" she asked, drawing out each word. "That is a long, long time."

Edmund dropped his boots to the floor and stood up. Without a word, he methodically removed every article of his clothing. Apparently, he had not listened to the part about taking his time.

She tried to tell herself this was going well, but he was

standing naked before her, fully aroused. Fortunately, he was a vain man and misinterpreted the cause of her flushed cheeks.

As he came toward her, she dropped her gaze so he would not see her rising panic. When he ran his hands down her arms and kissed her neck, she thought for sure he would notice she was trembling and clammy with fear.

She need not have worried.

He turned her around and pressed himself against her. She felt the hardness of his erection through the layers of her clothing as he moved against her, groaning.

"I thought your growing belly would decrease my desire for you," he said, breathing hard against her ear. "But I want you more than ever."

This was going much too fast! She needed time, more time.

He kissed her neck as he undid the tiny buttons down the back of her gown.

"Please, I'm cold," she said, clutching her arms across her chest to keep the gown from falling.

"Then I shall keep you warm, for I am hot as fire."

In one quick movement, he pried her hands loose and jerked the gown down. It hung for a moment on her swollen belly and hips, then slid to her feet. She was left standing in only the thin tunic she wore underneath.

He lifted her in his arms and looked down at her.

"I promise you, Catherine, we shall make the most of our time together."

Chapter Thirty-three

εdmund laid Catherine down on the bed with unexpected gentleness. Taking care not to put his weight on her belly, he lay naked against her side. He threw one leg over hers, pinning her down. She felt trapped, surrounded by his smell, his heat, his male body.

No matter what he did, she told herself, she had suffered worse at Rayburn's hands when she was just a girl of sixteen. She was a more formidable opponent now.

Edmund brought a fistful of her hair to his face and breathed in deeply. "From the moment I saw you on the drawbridge that first day, I knew you were not like any other woman."

He rubbed his cheek against the hair he clutched and closed his eyes. Her muscles tensed in readiness. But she held back. It was too soon. She would have but one chance.

"I desired you from the start," he murmured as he kissed the side of her face. "But when I saw you on the castle wall that day with your hair blowing all about you, I knew I would take you under William's very nose if we both remained in the castle."

He rose up on one elbow and ran his finger down the side of her face and along her throat. As his eyes followed the line his finger traveled to the neck of her tunic, his breathing quickened, and she sensed his mood change. He leaned down and kissed her where his finger stopped, at the lowest point of the neckline of her tunic.

And still, she waited.

She drew in a sharp breath when he cupped her breast. Misunderstanding her reaction, he groaned with pleasure. He ran kisses along her collarbone, his breath hot and damp against her skin.

This was nothing like with Rayburn. It was a shock to realize Edmund wanted to make love to her, to give her pleasure. She felt violated nonetheless. Clenching her fists, she closed her eyes and counted.

The next thing she knew, Edmund was on his hands and knees above her, and his tongue was in her ear. Panic nearly overtook her reason; it took all her resolve not to scream and beat her fists against his chest.

He moved down her body, murmuring her name. When she felt the wet of his tongue touch her nipple through the thin fabric, she fought the urge to grab him by the hair and jerk his head away. That would not save her.

Slowly, she reached her arms up behind her head and under her pillow until she felt her dagger. The movement made her back arch slightly.

"Aye, aye," he moaned, and clamped his mouth painfully over her breast. He was moving against her now, pressing his erection against her hip and suckling her breast.

Holding the sheath of her knife with one hand, she pulled on the hilt with the other. She had the blade free. She was ready.

——

William and the other men followed Stephen through the brush and tall grass along the river side of the castle wall. The mud sucked at his boot as he stepped in a hole of icy water.

"Old Jacob told me about the tunnel," Stephen said in a low voice over his shoulder. "It's been here since the castle was built."

William would never criticize his brother for prying secrets from anyone again.

"No one knows about it but him and Catherine," Stephen said. "And Robert."

Of course.

"The tunnel comes up in a storeroom near the kitchen," Stephen said. "We're close to the opening now."

William felt along the wall. Behind a sprawling bush, he found the break low on the wall.

"Follow me," he called. "Silence in the tunnel and have your swords ready. Stephen, I want you last."

The tunnel was dank and pitch-black. The entrance was no more than two feet high, but once he crawled through it, the tunnel was large enough for him to walk upright. Animals scurried away as he felt his way along in the dark. After several yards, he came to the end of the tunnel and felt above his head. Wood, not stone. The trapdoor. He put his dagger between his teeth and pushed it up.

There was a crack of light coming from under the door to the room. He could see pots and sacks of grain. He climbed out and helped the next man, then went to listen at the door. When half a dozen of his men were crowded in the small room, he eased the door open. The thrush lamp in the sconce was lit, but no one was in sight.

He moved quickly down the corridor, sword in hand. As he passed the kitchen, he heard muffled sounds. Somehow he knew Edmund would not lock Catherine in the kitchen with the servants.

"Get the door open," he whispered to the man behind him. "But tell them to stay put and keep quiet until we come back for them."

He heard men's voices in the hall above as he took the stairs two at a time. He hit the room at a run, his sword in one hand and his dagger in the other. The drunken fools were falling over each other trying to get to their weapons. His men would make short work of these. He had no time to stop and help.

Catherine was not here. And neither was Edmund.

He ran for the stairs. He sliced through one man who tried to stop him and tossed another over his shoulder without breaking his stride.

—

Once, when they were children, Harry showed her where to slide a blade into a man to reach his heart. She hesitated, trying to remember. Perhaps it was enough to injure him.

Suddenly, Edmund was pulling feverishly at her tunic. She could wait no longer. Swinging her arm down with all her strength, she sank the sharp blade deep into his shoulder. Somehow she managed to wrench it free before he flung his arms out and arched back, howling in pain.

Seeing the murderous rage distorting his face, she knew she had made a grave mistake. She should have killed him.

He rose up on his knees and reached his arm across his chest to feel the stab wound in his shoulder. When he brought his hand back, it was covered with blood. He stared at his bloody hand and then at her with bulging eyes. Then he drew his arm back and slapped her so hard she saw stars.

Before her vision cleared, he grabbed the front of her tunic and wrenched it in two. The effort cost him, and he bent forward, clutching his arms high across his chest. She would never know whether he failed to see she still held the knife or whether he believed he had incapacitated her with the blow.

This time, she did not hesitate. Gripping the hilt with both hands, she plunged the blade straight up under his breastbone. The room reverberated with his single scream.

For one long and terrifying moment, he hung suspended above her, an expression of surprise on his face. Blood seeped in a thin line from between his lips. It gushed down her arms from where her knife was planted below his chest.

He fell forward on top of her, his chest on her face. The hilt of her blade pressed painfully into her shoulder, and she could not breathe. Frantically, she pushed against him with the strength of a madwoman to get his weight off her belly.

Grunting with the effort, she rolled him off her, only to find him lying face-to-face beside her. His cold dead eyes stared into hers. Screaming and weeping, she shoved at him with both her arms and legs until she sent his body over the edge of the bed. She heard the hard thud as it hit the floor.

Drawing her knees up, she curled her body into a protective circle around her baby. Only then did she let the darkness take her.

Chapter Thirty-four

*H*is heart racing with terror, William ran up the stairs to the family's private rooms. *Please, God, let me not be too late!* As he climbed, he heard the shouts and clatter of swords of the men fighting below. He hit the solar door running and slammed against it. It would not open. Howling with frustration, he rammed his shoulder against it again and again.

He was pounding it with his fists and calling her name when Stephen shouted, "William, move aside!"

He turned to see Stephen and three other men with a log from the hearth to use as a battering ram. He stepped back.

On their third run at the door, the hinges gave way and the heavy wooden door scraped against the floor. William was through the gap before they set the log down. He stood in the center of the solar, frantically looking back and forth in the near blackness. *Where is she? Where is she?*

Stephen pushed past him and lit the lamp on the table. William swept his eyes over the empty room, searching for clues. An empty flask on its side on the table. Catherine's embroidery frame on the floor. *Please, God, no.* His eyes went to the open door to her bedchamber.

She was in there; he knew it.

And he could smell blood.

He never felt fear in battle. When he fought, a cold determination settled over him, and his mind was sharp and clear. But he felt fear now. In every fiber of his body and deep in his bones. It took more courage than anything he'd ever done to walk toward the darkness beyond that open door.

He took the candle Stephen thrust into his hand and waved his brother back. Ignoring the signal, Stephen followed hard on his heels with the lamp. As soon as he entered Catherine's bedchamber, he saw Edmund's body sprawled across the floor in a dark pool of blood.

Stephen knelt beside the corpse, but Edmund was of no concern to William now. He couldn't kill a dead man.

His eyes traveled slowly from the inert body to the blood-smeared sheet that hung down the side of the bed. He followed the sheet up to the high bed, where the light from Stephen's lamp did not reach.

He caught the glint of a single strand of golden hair curling over the side of the bed. Unable to move, he strained to see into the shadows of the rumpled bed-clothes. There was a form on the bed. A form that was much, much too still.

Oh God, oh God, oh God. The candle fell from his hand as he cried out her name. In another moment, he was holding her lifeless body against his chest and keening over her.

She was dead. Catherine was dead.

At the sound of his brother's harrowing cry, Stephen jumped to his feet and ran to the bed. He sucked in his breath. At the sight of so much blood, he nearly dropped the lamp. It was everywhere. Dark swaths of it covered the bed—and the limp body cradled in William's arms.

Casting a look back toward the door, he saw the men who crowded into the room behind them were backing out. He turned back to the bed and saw what they saw: William hunched over Catherine, weeping; Catherine's head lolling over his arm; her blood-soaked tunic ripped asunder, gaping open.

Swiftly, Stephen swung his cape off and draped it over her exposed breasts and swollen belly.

"Thank you," William whispered.

The misery in his brother's eyes when he lifted his gaze for that brief moment would haunt Stephen always.

"Is she alive?" Stephen's voice came out as a croak.

When William did not answer, he asked the question again, more insistently. Still, his brother did not respond.

Stephen reached out and touched Catherine's cheek with the back of his fingers. A dead person should not feel so warm. Edmund did not. With growing hope, he found her hand under the cloak and felt for a pulse at her wrist.

"She is alive!" When William stared blankly at him, Stephen gripped his arm and said in a louder voice, "William, I tell you, Lady Catherine lives!"

Stephen turned to the men in the doorway. "Find Alys and bring her here. She will know what to do."

Several of the men rushed from the room.

Stephen was used to his older brother taking charge, but it was obvious William would be of no help. He'd seen his mother and Catherine deal with household illness and injury countless times. Biting his lip, he tried to recall what they did.

"Tell the servants to bring warm water and strips of clean cloth," he told the other men. "I'm not sure which we'll need, so have them bring both spirits and hot broth."

The men rushed out almost before he had the words out.

Relief washed over him when Alys burst into the room, raining curses on Edmund.

"That devil's spawn locked us all in the kitchen!"

She took command the moment she entered. Ignoring the body on the floor, she hurried to where William still held Catherine on the bed. She ran quick hands over Catherine.

"No wound!" she announced.

She left them to give direction to the servants setting up the washing tub in the solar. In no time, Stephen heard her shooing the servants, "Out with you now, out, out."

As she bustled back into the bedchamber, she called over her shoulder, "And shut that door behind you!"

"Lord FitzAlan, I need you to carry her to the solar," she said in her no-nonsense voice. "I must wash the blood off and get a better look at her."

William cradled Catherine in his arms, rocking her as though he had not heard.

Alys got up on the step to the bed and put her face in front of his. "M'lord, this is not your wife's blood. 'Tis only the blood of that bastard friend of yours."

When he only blinked at her, she raised her voice. "M'lord, you must get off your backside and help me. Now!"

Stephen could almost see the words penetrating William's skull as he looked from Alys to Stephen and back again. When William rose with Catherine from the bed, Stephen felt some of the tension go out of his shoulders.

The saints be praised, William was back with them.

In the solar, William sat on a bench next to the tub with Catherine on his lap. At Alys's direction, Stephen picked up the cup of broth from the table and knelt in front of Catherine. Holding the cup under her nose, he watched her draw in a deep breath of the steam. He wanted to shout for joy when she opened her eyes a crack and took a small sip.

The broth seemed to revive her, for she took another sip and another. He darted a look at Alys, who smiled and nodded.

Catherine lifted her hand to touch his wrist and whispered, "Thank you."

Stephen took her hand and kissed it, trying not to cry.

"Jamie?" Catherine asked.

"He is safe," Stephen said. "He and Jacob hid in the stable."

"Out with you now, Stephen," Alys said. When he turned, prepared to argue, she said, "We must get her in the bath."

Stephen leapt to his feet so quickly he nearly knocked over the bowl of broth. "I'll be just outside if you need me."

As soon as Stephen was gone, Alys directed William to put Catherine's feet into the tub. " 'Tis important we keep her warm."

She began a thorough inspection then, washing off blood as she worked her way up Catherine's legs. She nodded and murmured, "Good, good," as she went.

"The blood is not mine," Catherine said in a voice so

low William had to strain to hear it. "I do not think I am injured."

He pressed his cheek against hers and closed his eyes. *Praise God. Praise God.*

"Shhh, do not talk yet, dear," Alys crooned. "Now let us get this dirty gown off you and get you in this nice hot bath. That, and another cup of broth, and you'll feel much better."

He lifted Catherine from his lap so Alys could pull the torn gown off, then eased her into the steaming tub of water before she could get chilled. After tucking a folded linen cloth behind Catherine's head, Alys refilled the cup of broth. She held Catherine's hands around the cup until she was sure Catherine could hold it on her own.

Alys touched his arm and jerked her head to the side. Reluctantly, he stood and stepped away with her.

"I see no outward injuries except the bruises around her wrists and the one on her cheek," Alys said in a low voice. "Now I must find out if the man forced himself upon her."

"We find her in bed, covered in blood," he hissed through clenched teeth, "and you doubt he did it?"

"What we know is that he tried," Alys said in a calm voice. "Remember, it was him we found dead on the floor—and with her blade in his heart."

Alys cleared her throat and said, "Now, m'lord, 'tis best you leave for a bit. If the man did take her violently, she will have injuries I must treat. And I need to check the babe."

William rubbed his hands over his face, as if he could push the horrible thoughts away. "I am staying unless she wants me to go."

Alys did not look pleased, but she did not argue when he took his seat beside his wife. He held Catherine's hand under the water while Alys spoke to her in a low voice.

When he felt Catherine's fingers tighten on his hand, he said, "I will go if you wish."

She gripped the side of the tub with her free hand and leaned toward him. "Nay, do not leave me!"

Choked with emotion, he could not speak at first. That she wanted him with her, in spite of how badly he had failed her, was more than he had any right to hope. More than he deserved.

He lifted her hand from the water and kissed her wet fingers. "I will stay as long as you will have me."

His penance for his sins against his wife began in earnest then. He held her hand and stared out the window into the blackness of the night as Alys asked her terrible questions. Did Edmund strike her anywhere other than her face? Did he throw her to the ground? Was she sure she suffered no blow to her belly?

Eventually, in her straightforward way, Alys asked if Edmund raped her.

Catherine's answer, when she gave it, was indirect. "If I had been a virgin, I would yet have my maidenhood."

William let out the breath he had been holding, though her careful answer left him worried about what did happen. Alys, however, asked no more questions. Instead, she put her hands on Catherine's rounded belly. After a time, she looked at Catherine and then at William, a broad smile on her face.

"The babe is well!"

"God be praised!" William said, squeezing Catherine's hand.

All the way to Ross Castle, he had prayed God would protect his wife, never once sparing a prayer for their unborn child. But God, in his grace, had preserved the babe as well.

"Try to think of all you have to look forward to," Alys said, touching Catherine's cheek. "You have a fine husband and child, and soon you shall have another babe in your arms."

Catherine pressed her lips together and nodded.

"Active as this one is, I'll wager it's another boy," Alys said as she got stiffly to her feet. "Now, it is off to bed with you. Sleep is the best healer."

Before she left, Alys pulled William aside once more. "Your lady is stronger than you know. She's been through as bad as this and worse before." With a last pat on his arm, she said, "'Tis a blessing she has you to help her this time."

William was grateful to be left alone to care for his wife. As he helped her out of the tub, he dried her quickly and pulled a tunic over her head. He carried her to the bed in her chamber. After covering her, he shed his own clothes and crawled in beside her. He wrapped his arms around her and held her close.

He stayed awake most of the night, listening to her steady breathing. No matter how many years God gave them, he would be thankful for every night his wife fell asleep in his arms.

Chapter Thirty-five

Catherine awoke to the sound of voices outside the bed-chamber door. She heard the low rumble of William's voice, followed by Jamie's loud wail of complaint. Shivering as her bare feet hit the cold floor, she grabbed her robe and hurried to the door.

When she opened it, she found her four-year-old and her husband glaring at each other, hands on hips in identical poses. Stephen, who was standing on the other side of them, caught her eye, making no effort to hide his amusement.

"Jamie!"

The boy flew at her and threw his arms around her legs. Laughing, she sank to her knees to embrace him.

"Be easy with your mother," William said sharply, and took Catherine's arm to help her up. "I am sorry. I tried to make him wait until you were awake."

She smiled at Jamie to let him know it was all right.

"I will meet you all for breakfast as soon as I have dressed," she told them. "I had only broth for supper last night and am near starved."

The normalcy of sitting at table with her family soothed

her soul. Although the others had long since eaten, the cook sent out platters heaped high with bread and meats and bowls of stewed apricots and sugared nuts. While she ate, Jamie told her about hiding with Jacob and the new kittens in the straw. To her relief, Jamie had thought it all a game.

At William's signal, Jamie's nursemaid collected her charge. "The dogs are jealous of the kittens now," she told him. "They are so unhappy they've ceased to wag their tails."

"They have not!" Jamie protested, but he jumped up to go with her all the same.

"I thought it best not to tell the boy too much," William said when they had gone.

Catherine nodded. Jamie needed no reassurance beyond seeing her. From the dark circles under William's eyes and the pinched skin between his brows, it was apparent her husband would need more.

Waving down William's objections, she asked Stephen to recount their part of what happened the day before.

"You were clever to remember the tunnel," she said when he had finished.

Stephen blushed at the compliment.

She patted his arm. "And cleverer still to get the secret out of Jacob. I'm sure no one has before."

Still blushing, Stephen cast a sidelong glance at his brother. William jerked his head meaningfully toward the door. Taking the hint, Stephen got to his feet.

"It brings me joy to see you safe and well," Stephen said, sweeping her an elaborate bow. With that, he left the room.

Catherine shook her head, smiling. "That boy has enough gallantry and charm for two. Heaven help us."

William had no interest in discussing his brother.

"Time for you to rest." He stood and offered his hands to her. "Come, I'll help you back upstairs."

"But I have not been up an hour," she protested.

In the end, she gave in and let him take her upstairs, but she adamantly refused to get into bed. He settled her on the window seat with a stool propped under her feet and a blanket tucked tightly around her.

She tugged one arm free and patted the space beside her. "Sit with me a while."

She leaned into the comfort of his arms and rested her head on his shoulder. After a time, she said, "You must want to know the rest."

She looked at the hard planes of his face and watched the muscles of his jaw tighten and release.

"Only if you wish to speak of it," he said, his eyes fixed straight ahead. "And only when you are ready—not now."

"I cannot help but think of it now," she said. "Telling you may help me put it behind me."

He nodded and took her hand. "If it will help."

Once she began, she could not stop. She recounted the entire horror of it: every word, every look, every touch. The telling was cathartic for her—and torture for William. She understood that he had to hear it. Reliving the nightmare with her was a penance he needed to make before he could begin to forgive himself.

He kept his rage behind a careful mask. But when she told him what Edmund was doing to her when she stabbed him the first time and then how terrified she was when he backhanded her, William jumped to his feet. Clenching his fists, he paced the room, letting loose a rain of curses.

Then he collapsed beside her and covered his face in his hands. "I saw Edmund fight many, many times," he whispered. "I do not know another who gave him a second chance and survived."

He pulled her into his arms again. "I was arrogant and foolish to ignore your concerns about him."

Aye, he should have listened to her.

"Edmund was your friend," she said, leaning back to look at him. "You could not know he would do this."

"I pledged to protect you, and I failed—not once, but twice." He faltered for a moment, then said, "I do not know how you can ever forgive me."

"I am glad I saved myself."

"Please, Catherine. You don't need to lie to excuse my failings."

She bit her lip, trying to think how to explain it so he would understand. "The worst part with Rayburn was how helpless I felt. It was different with Edmund. Though I was frightened, I was never powerless. I believed I could get the better of him, and I was determined to do it.

"I am proud I was strong enough and clever enough to save myself," she continued. "That will make it easier to get over what happened and not be afraid."

She let her head fall against William's shoulder. Recounting the traumatic events of the day before had tired her. He kissed the top of her head and held her securely in his arms.

"I'm glad you are my husband, William," she murmured.

Only after her breathing became soft and regular against his chest did William give his reply.

"And yet, you had to save yourself."

—

After a couple days of rest, Catherine resumed her routine tasks. Edmund's attack would always be a bad memory, but she damn well was not going to let it rule her. She enjoyed managing the castle household. It was, however, a good deal of work. And now, every time she turned around, there was William, getting in the way and telling her to rest.

For the first day or two, it was reassuring to see him every time she looked up. But after several days, she was sure he would drive her mad with his hovering. He was unwilling to let her out of his sight for a moment.

She came upstairs this afternoon to do her sewing just to get away from him for an hour. At the sound of the door, she dropped her embroidery in her lap. It was William, of course.

"You do not need to keep watch over me from dawn till dusk," she said, not even trying to keep the edge from her voice. "Go out hunting or take the boys riding—or something!"

"I am happy to be here with you," he answered, the soul of patience.

"Well, I am tired of it, husband," she responded sharply, then sighed in exasperation at hearing herself sound like a shrew. "I know you mean well, but you act as though I will fall to pieces if you relax your guard for a moment. You will not even touch me at night."

There, she'd said it, and she would not be sorry for it.

"I was afraid it would remind you of—" He stopped himself, and she knew he could not bear to think of what that swine Edmund had done to her.

"I thought it too soon," he finished lamely.

"Too soon for whom, William?" she demanded. "Is it that you cannot touch me without thinking of Edmund's hands on me?"

She flung her embroidery on the table and stormed into her bedchamber, slamming the door behind her. He was still standing there staring at the door when she opened it again.

"It is not good for the babe to upset me like this!" she shouted at him and slammed the door again.

Mother of God, what had he done? William sank down onto the bench, which, thankfully, was just behind him. Propping his elbows on his knees, he ran his hands through his hair and over his face.

Should he go in to her now or leave her alone? Whichever he did was bound to be wrong.

A soft rapping at the solar door interrupted his thoughts.

"Blast it!" he said under his breath. He jerked the door open, ready to take his frustration out on whoever was there.

"Have you no sense at all?" he said, glaring down at Stephen. "Catherine could be resting!"

His tone would have put the fear of God into anyone else, but not this brother of his. He paused to take a better look at him. Stephen was fidgeting with his clothing and shifting his feet from side to side.

This was not like Stephen.

"What is it?" he asked.

Stephen fidgeted some more until William thought he might have to shake the answer out of him.

"We have a visitor," Stephen said at last.

"Catherine is not ready for visitors," he replied curtly. "Send them away." He started to shut the door but stopped when Stephen made no move to leave.

Pinning Stephen with a hard look, he said, "What is the problem, brother?"

"I cannot send her away."

"And why is that?" William asked through clenched teeth.

"Because the visitor is our mother."

Chapter Thirty-six

William grabbed Stephen's wrist and pulled him into the solar. "What did you say?"

"Our mother is here in the hall," Stephen said. "She says she's come to meet your bride."

William's head was pounding with a sudden headache that was so bad it made his eyes hurt. His mother had never troubled herself to visit him before. But he should have expected her. Aye, she would come now that he was a man of property and in the king's favor.

"I kept her waiting as long as I could," Stephen said, "but you really must come down and see her now."

Better to strike quickly, William told himself. He marched out the door, ready to do battle.

———

Because Catherine's ear was pressed firmly to the door, she learned as soon as William did of Lady Eleanor's arrival. The anger and irritation that plagued her since Edmund's attack were displaced, for the moment, by fervent curiosity. And a spark of excitement.

Her mother-in-law was an enigma to her. Both William

and Stephan painted Lady Eleanor as strong-willed, even manipulative. But while William professed to dislike and mistrust her, Stephen had strong affection for their mother.

Catherine was inclined to think well of the lady. No matter what her failings might be, she bore two fine sons whom Catherine loved with all her heart.

She could not wait to meet her! As soon as she heard the door close behind William, she called her maid to help her change. The challenge was to look her best—without looking as though she had taken any special care.

She decided on a new velvet gown of a silvery blue that brought out the color of her eyes. The gown, which had just been made to accommodate her growing size, fell over her protruding belly in soft folds from a tightly fitting bodice. Silver ribbon trimmed the neckline, sleeves, and high waist. The headdress was of the same silvery blue, with silver mesh encasing the braids on either side of her face.

After a last glance in her polished steel mirror, she hurried down the stairs. She paused to listen outside the entrance to the hall to gauge the tone of the conversation.

"Your visit comes at a most inopportune time." William's voice was politely formal but held a hard edge.

"Stephen told me of the recent misfortunes here." The woman's voice was rich and low. "I am most sorry to hear of them. How is your wife?"

Taking her cue, Catherine made her entrance.

"Lady Eleanor," she began, but stopped before she finished her words of welcome. Putting her hand to her chest, she said instead, "But... you are so beautiful!"

Catherine had never seen such a breathtaking woman.

Lady Eleanor's rich brown eyes, auburn hair, and creamy skin matched Stephen's coloring, but her features were more delicate, more feminine. The lady had to be in her midforties, but she looked ten—even fifteen—years younger. Her close-fitting gown showed off curves that must turn heads.

Catherine realized she had spoken the words aloud and flushed as she curtsied. "'Tis good to meet you at last," she said, giving Lady Eleanor a warm smile despite her embarrassment. "I am so glad you've come."

Lady Eleanor laughed and put her hands out to Catherine. "Thank you, my dear," she said, kissing Catherine's cheeks. "You do make me wonder how my sons describe me." Flicking her eyes toward William, she said, "Odious and overbearing?"

Catherine turned to look at William and Stephen. To her dismay, William stood with his arms folded, fairly seething with hostility. And Stephen might catch fire, backed up almost into the hearth.

"I wish you congratulations on your marriage," Lady Eleanor said. After sweeping her gaze over Catherine, she added, "And on your upcoming blessing! I am pleased to see such a bloom of health in your cheeks. You look lovely, dear."

"Thank you, I could not feel better."

"I was just telling Lady Eleanor that this is not a good time for us to receive visitors," William interrupted.

His rudeness shocked her. "I must disagree," she said, giving him a look meant to convey her disapproval. "It could not be a better time, with Advent here."

"It would be a burden on you to entertain guests when you are yet recovering from your ordeal." Dropping his gaze to her belly, he added, "You must take care of your health."

"Your mother will be no burden at all," she said with a tight smile. Turning to Eleanor, she said, "Your visit will divert me from my recent troubles. I shall enjoy having another woman for company."

William was outmaneuvered. From the look of resignation on his face, he knew it.

———

If William wanted to see his wife, he could not avoid his mother. Much to his surprise, the two women appeared to enjoy each other's company enormously. He had to admit Eleanor's presence had a soothing effect on Catherine. He often heard them sharing a laugh as he passed by.

Catherine's irritation with him, however, continued unabated. Knowing he deserved the sharp edge of her anger, he took it without complaint. And yet, he could not understand why she became more vexed with him with each passing day. He was doing everything he could to make her feel safe and protected.

He sent his men to remove Grey from his lands. He had not left the castle since finding Catherine limp on the bed, covered in blood. That image would never leave him. He lived in fear someone would snatch her away again if he relaxed his vigilance for a single moment.

Between his mother's presence and the tension with Catherine, he was in an unrelentingly sour mood. Lack of sleep did not help. And it was not just guilt and worry that kept him awake at night. Lord in heaven, he wanted his wife!

He wanted her with an aching need, a longing

past bearing. But he did bear it. He was afraid touching her would revive her memories of that night. Although Catherine gave broad hints she was ready to resume marital relations, he could not bring himself to risk it.

Late one evening, he found her alone in the hall after the rest of the household had gone to bed. He was pleased to catch her without Eleanor for once.

He approached cautiously. "You look a little tired," he said, trying to show his concern for her. "Perhaps you should retire?"

"I am not in the least bit tired," she snapped.

He sat down on the bench beside her and tried to think of something else to say.

"It has been too long since I visited the tenants," she announced. "I want you to take me for a ride around the estates tomorrow."

Her suggestion was so unexpected, he forgot his resolve to keep his patience and not rile her.

"I shall not permit it," he said flatly. "There are too many dangers outside the castle walls."

She slammed closed the prayer book she had been reading and banged it down on the table.

"Will you keep me under lock and key in my chamber, husband?" she demanded, her eyes burning holes into him. "You are a worse jailor than my Welsh captors!"

Her eyes flicked to the table. Before he knew it, she picked up a pitcher and threw it at him. She stormed out of the hall, so angry she did not appear to see Eleanor near the entrance.

He caught the pitcher, but cider splashed onto his clothes and was dripping from his hands. As he shook his hands, he looked up to see Eleanor watching him from across the room. She arched an eyebrow at him.

"How long have you been there?" he asked.

"Long enough to see you are going about this all wrong."

She walked over and handed him a cloth from the table. "Perhaps I did send you off to your father too soon," she said, shaking her head. "It is remarkable how little you know about women—at least about the woman who is your wife."

William wiped himself off as best he could and tossed the cloth on the table.

"Come, sit down," Eleanor said, gesturing to the chairs near the hearth. "Let me help you."

His mother had made colossal mistakes with her own life. So far, she'd caused nothing but pain and trouble in his. It was a sign of how desperate he was that he was willing to listen to her advice.

"You are forgetting whom you married," she said once they were settled by the fire. "A woman who would cross her husband to spy for the prince is not like other women."

"Of course she's not like other women," he grunted.

"You did not marry a demure child, so you should not expect your wife to like it when you treat her as one."

"I do not treat her like a child," he said through clenched teeth. "I merely wish to keep her safe."

"What you do not seem to understand is that Catherine takes pride in her strength," Eleanor said. "It is important to her that you value that in her as well."

"Are you suggesting I let her ride alone—pregnant as she is—all over the countryside at her whim?"

His mother sighed deeply to let him know he was trying her patience. "What I am saying is that you mustn't cosset her. If you do, she will find a way to defy you. Or worse, she will comply and become a different woman from the one you love. Either way, you will make her unhappy."

William thought back to when he arrived to take the castle. Catherine was magnificent that day, bold as brass, coming out alone on the drawbridge to meet them.

"I admired her courage from the start," he said.

"Then you must let her know that," his mother said. "A woman enjoys having her looks and charm appreciated, but she wants to be loved for what is best in her, for what she values in herself.

"Go to her now," she said, patting his knee. "She loves you, so it should not take much to set things aright."

For the first time since he was a very small boy, William kissed his mother's cheek. Long after he had gone, Eleanor gazed into the fire, her fingers stroking the place where her son's lips had touched her.

———

William searched their rooms, but Catherine was nowhere to be found. With his mother's warning that Catherine would defy him ringing in his ears, he looked about her bedchamber more carefully. There was no sign of hurried packing. No open chest with gowns hanging over the side, as when she had run off to the abbey. Praise God.

What a fool he was. She must be up in Jamie's chamber. He turned to go, then turned back. Everything was in its place....

Her riding boots were missing.

He grabbed his cloak and ran down the stairs two at a

time. As he raced across the bailey, his breath came out in white puffs in the cold night air. How long had it been since she left the hall? He prayed it was not time enough for her to escape.

As he slipped through the stable door, he saw the glow of a lamp in the far corner. He was not too late.

When he saw her hooded shadow, the memory of their first meeting at Monmouth swept over him. As he thought of the straightforward and determined girl he found in the stable that night, it struck him with sudden clarity that his mother was right.

He was a wiser man back then. Though he was young and she a stranger to him, he had understood her intuitively. That night, they managed to find a compromise between her determination to do what she felt she must and his equal resolve to keep her safe.

It gave him hope they could do so again.

Taking care not to make a sound, he crossed the stable. When he stood just behind her, he said, "I see you still have not learned to saddle a horse in the dark."

She let out a short scream and whirled around to face him.

After a long moment, she cocked an eyebrow and said, "I suppose I should be grateful you did not knock me to the ground this time."

"Just as I am grateful you do not have a blade aimed at my heart." Tilting his head, he added, "Though I suspect you wish you did."

"I pray you do not drive me to it." Her tone made William hope she had left her blade behind.

Without another word, she turned to take her horse's bridle from its hook.

He clasped his hand over hers. In a quiet voice, he said, "Let me do that for you."

She looked at him sharply. But as she examined him, her expression softened. "You will go with me?"

"I shall go with you, or you shall not go," he said. "Just as before."

His heart felt tight in his chest when she responded with the first genuine smile she had bestowed on him in much too long.

The men at the gate were not able to cover their surprise when he ordered them to open it. Telling himself it was safe enough, he stifled the impulse to grab her reins and turn around. God's beard, even rebels had more sense than to be out on a night as cold as this.

She led the way around the castle to the path by the river. He was relieved to see that, in deference to her pregnancy, she kept her horse at a walk. Despite the fact that she had him out riding at midnight on a December night, he must try to remember she was usually a sensible woman.

They dismounted and walked up the bank overlooking the dark river. The moon and stars were bright in the night sky. William wrapped his cloak around them both and held her close against him.

"Are you warm enough?" he asked.

"Mmm," she murmured, leaning back against him.

"I know why you came riding with me that night at Monmouth," she said. "You were afraid of what would happen if you carried me kicking and screaming to the keep."

"Aye, that was one reason." He chuckled, remembering, and rubbed his chin against the top of her head.

"But later, after just one kiss, I wanted to forget my honor and steal you away." He closed his eyes and tightened his arms around her. "That is what made it so hard for me to believe about Jamie's father. If I'd had you in bed even once, I could not have left you as he did. I would have killed Rayburn and defied the king if need be, but I could never have let another man have you after that."

After a time, she asked, "Why did you come with me this time? What made you change your mind about keeping me in the castle?"

He took a deep breath and let it out. "I wasn't hovering over you because I thought you were weak," he said, though it was hard to admit. "I did it because I knew I was."

She turned around to face him. "You don't have a weak bone in your body, William FitzAlan. What can you be talking about?"

"I never felt true fear until I knew Edmund had you behind that barred door. And then, when I saw you covered in blood and believed you were dead…" He swallowed hard against the memory. "I was lost in a darkness so deep I thought I would never come out of it. And I did not care if I did."

She took his hand and held it against her cheek. "I should have realized how it was for you to find me like that."

"I would not change you from the strong, bold woman I love, but you must help me find my way," he said, wanting to make her understand. "Twice I have nearly lost you. I live in fear another disaster will befall you—and that when it does, I shall fail you again."

"You are a good man, William. A man of honor." She

slipped her arms around his waist and rested her head against his chest. "I do not know why God chose to bless me by making you my husband, but I am very grateful."

Later, as they rode back to the castle, William felt light, as if a burden was lifted from him. A feeling of happiness welled up inside him. They pulled their horses up in a clearing to take a last look at the river. When Catherine suddenly threw her arms up to the heavens and laughed with the same joy he felt, he knew he had all he ever wanted.

—

They stopped in the hall to warm their hands before the hearth. As soon as Catherine could feel her fingers and toes again, she raised an eyebrow at William and cocked her head toward the stairs.

When they reached the solar, he removed her cloak and wrapped a blanket around her shoulders.

"'Tis late," he said, and kissed her forehead. "You must be tired."

She pulled away from him and went to the door to slide the bolt. Then she turned and gave him her best wicked smile.

"What is it?" William asked.

She nearly rolled her eyes, the man was so thick.

Keeping her eyes fixed on his, she dropped the blanket at her feet. She began undoing the buttons at the back of her gown. When he rushed over to help her, she grabbed the front of his tunic and pulled him against her.

"Kiss me." It was not a request.

He gave her a slow smile, then leaned down and brushed his lips against hers.

She was having none of that. Clasping her hands behind his neck, she gave him a kiss to remember. When they finally came up for air, she grabbed his belt before he could get away. She unfastened it and slipped her hands under his tunic and shirt. When her fingers touched warm skin and rough hair, she smiled.

Victory was within her grasp.

William grabbed her wrists to stop her. "What are you doing?"

"You did tell me I would have to help you find your way," she said, fighting a grin, "but I thought you would remember this part."

He released her wrists and took her face in his hands. "I do not think you are ready for this, love."

"Oh, but I am." She tilted her head back for another kiss, confident he was losing his will to fight her.

When she felt him melt into the kiss, she ran her hand along his erect shaft. He sucked in his breath and tried to pull back. She drew him deeper into the kiss and lifted his hand to her breast.

Thankfully, he did not need further direction.

She was breathless when he turned her and lifted her hair to finish unfastening her gown. He kissed her neck, sending thrills down her spine.

"Are you sure?" he whispered against her skin.

"Aye," she sighed as he worked on the buttons, "I have grown weary of waiting for you."

He chuckled and eased the gown down to kiss her shoulder. Impatient, she tugged the gown down to her waist.

No more hesitation, no more light humor. His passion exploded. He pulled her hard against him, his mouth hot and wet on her neck, his hands cupping her breasts. She closed her eyes and dropped her head back to rest against his shoulder. This is what she needed to wipe away the memory of Edmund's touch.

William scooped her up in his arms and carried her into the bedchamber. Again and again through the night he told her he loved her.

And now, Catherine believed him.

Epilogue

1417

William ran his finger up her arm. "We have the afternoon without the children underfoot. Do you wish to spend it *all* discussing them?"

Catherine laughed and squeezed his hand. After a dozen years, their love and their passion for each other remained strong.

"God has truly blessed us," she said.

"His blessing today is that the children are gone," he said as he pulled her to her feet.

Before they reached the stairs, Catherine heard male laughter behind them, and Stephen and Jamie burst into the hall.

"This is a happy surprise!" she said as she crossed the room to greet them. "We did not expect you for another fortnight."

"We missed you too much to wait," Stephen said as he leaned down to kiss her cheek.

"I suppose the ladies at court believe all your lies," she

chided. "You must tell me later what truly brought you home early."

She settled the men by the hearth and sent for wine.

"I am certain the king intends to return the Carleton family lands to you," William said, "so there is no reason to delay arranging a betrothal for you."

She sighed. Did William have to raise the subject even before the wine was poured? She and William were in perfect accord on the need for Stephen to be settled, but she would have waited for a quiet moment to speak with Stephen alone.

"There is no cause to hurry either," Stephen said. His tone was light, but she caught the obstinate look in his eyes.

"Still," she put in, "there can be no harm in discussing it."

"I have presents for the little ones," Stephen said in a blatant attempt to divert her. "Where have you hidden them?"

"They are visiting the abbess." She folded her arms. "Now Stephen—"

"Truly, Catherine, every young lady you've asked me to consider is exceedingly dull." To annoy her, he turned to Jamie and said in a loud whisper, "And pliant in all the wrong ways."

"You should have let us arrange this betrothal long ago," William said. "Now Mother and Abbess Talcott have put their minds to it."

"I thought Mother's new husband would keep her better occupied," Stephen grumbled. Lady Eleanor had married a man a dozen years her junior after the death of Stephen's father.

William's eyes gleamed with amusement. "I suggest you settle the matter soon, or those two are sure to trap you in some scheme of their own."

"I told you a long time ago," Stephen said, winking at Catherine, "if you can find me a woman like yours, I'll be wed as soon as the banns can be posted."

Catherine rolled her eyes and waved her hand in a dismissive gesture. "Save your false flattery for the foolish women I hear you spend your time with."

As the men continued talking, she bit her lip and stared into the fire. She should have known the young girls of marriageable age would bore him. Perhaps a foreign bride would pique Stephen's interest. Or a young widow...

When she looked back at Stephen, something in her expression caused his smile to falter. She was a more formidable opponent than his mother and the abbess combined, and he knew it.

"We have news," Jamie said. "Maredudd Tudor has come forward to be pardoned."

"Praise God!" Catherine said, putting a hand to her chest. Maredudd went into hiding eight years ago when Harlech fell and the rebellion was crushed. "Poor Marged. How difficult these years must have been for her."

"He waited long enough," Stephen said. "Harry offered Glyndwr and all the Welsh rebels pardons when he was crowned four years ago."

"If Maredudd wants to help that son of his, he should send him on campaign with us to Normandy," William said. "Fighting the French would go a long way toward demonstrating his loyalty to the Crown."

Catherine put her hand on William's arm. "Will that be

soon? I hoped Harry would wait another year before making a second expedition."

"The king has been preparing all winter," William said in a soft voice. "He'll not let another summer pass before returning to fight for the lands our prior kings lost to France."

"Everyone at court was talking of it," Jamie said, his eyes alight. "We came home to tell you the king has commanded all the men to gather in a few weeks."

Catherine closed her eyes. It had been so hard when they went on the first expedition two years ago.

"Jamie," Stephen said in a low voice, "let us go collect your brothers and sisters from the abbey."

Their footsteps echoed in the hall as they made their escape.

William pulled her onto his lap. "No harm will come to us," he said, lifting her chin with his finger. "You forget what a fearsome trio we make. The French will run like rabbits when they see us."

Please, God, let my men come home from this war.

She thought of how the course of her life had been changed, more than once, by the events of a single day. No matter how much William tried to protect her, it could all change again.

But for now, she would count her blessings and be grateful for the time she and William had together.

She would not waste a day of it.

"William, take me upstairs." She stood and held her hand out to her husband.

Much later, as she lay with her head on William's chest, she heard their children entering the hall below. She took comfort in their laughter and in the strong, steady beating of her husband's heart.

Historical Note

The more I read about the great Welsh rebellion of six hundred years ago, the more I came to admire both Prince Owain Glyndwr (rhymes with *endure*), the Welsh rebel leader, and young Prince Harry, who spent much of his youth putting down the rebellion.

Glyndwr took control of all of Wales, inspired a ten-year rebellion, won recognition from foreign countries, and pressed a forward-thinking reform agenda. My natural inclination would be to take the rebel side, but history was against them.

Henry V (Prince Harry in this book) was also a leader of stunning accomplishments. In writing about him as a young man, I could not see him as the frivolous youth Shakespeare depicted. At eighteen, he was already an experienced commander in charge of the English forces fighting the Welsh. As king, he appears to have devoted every waking moment to his duties. After the disastrous reigns of Richard II and Henry IV, he united England as both beloved warrior king and a skilled and tireless administrator. He reconciled the noble factions, fostered nationalism across the classes by making English the language of his court, and decisively turned the tide in the Hundred Years' War with France.

Another interesting historical character in this book is the child Owain (or Owen) Tudor, son of a Welsh rebel. After Henry V died in 1422, Owain held the lowly position of clerk of the queen's wardrobe. He had an affair with the king's young widow that sent the Lancasters into apoplexy—and resulted in five children. It is ironic that the grandson of this Welsh rebel and Henry V's French princess would usurp the throne in 1485 and begin the Tudor dynasty.

I drew personality traits for these and other historical figures from the information I had—and made up the rest. I apologize to descendants of the Welsh rebel Rhys Gethin, in particular, for giving him unappealing characteristics to serve my story.

Please turn this page for
a preview of the next passionate
book in Margaret Mallory's
All the King's Men series!

Knight of Pleasure

Available in mass market
in December 2009.

Caen, Normandy
November 1417

Stephen cursed Sir John Popham as he followed the path along the castle wall to the bailiff's residence. With mist hovering over the ground, the bailey yard was eerie at this hour. Did Popham set their appointments earlier each day just to spite him?

He tried to turn his thoughts to the business of the day, but they kept returning to the more interesting subject of Lady Isobel Hume. The more he saw of her, the more intrigued he became. And he saw her often; he made sure of that.

Flirtation seemed not a part of her social repertoire. Unusual, especially for such a pretty woman.

Her smiles rarely reached her eyes. He'd yet to hear her laugh. As with flirting, his efforts there came to naught. He tried to imagine what her laugh would sound like. A tinkling? A light trill?

Aye, he was intrigued. Almost as much as he was attracted. It was not just that she was beautiful, though she was that. He wanted to know her. And her secrets.

Curiosity had always been his weakness.

A peculiar sound interrupted his musings. Peculiar, at least, to be coming from one of the storerooms built against the wall. He went to the low wooden door and put his ear to it.

Whish! Whish! Whish! The sound was unmistakable. Drawing his sword, he eased the door open to take a look.

"Lady Hume!"

She looked as surprised as he was to catch her alone in a storeroom attacking a sack of grain with a sword.

"The poor thing is defenseless," he said, cocking his head toward the sack. Grain was seeping onto the dirt floor from several small tears.

"Close the door!" she hissed. "I cannot be seen here."

And what a sight she was, with her cheeks flushed and strands of dark hair sticking to her face and neck. *God preserve him.* He stepped inside and firmly closed the door behind him.

"I meant for you to remain outside when you closed it."

Though she took a step back as she spoke, she kept a firm hand on her sword. As she should.

With her glossy dark hair in a loose braid over her shoulder, she looked even more beautiful than he imagined. And he'd spent hours imagining it. No man saw a grown woman with her hair uncovered unless he was a close family member. Or a lover. The intimacy of it sent his pulse racing.

Aye, the lady had every reason to feel nervous at finding herself alone with a man in this secluded place.

"That sack cannot provide much of a challenge," he said, trying to put her at ease.

"You make fun of me." There was resentment in her tone, but he was pleased to see her shoulders relax.

"I believe I would serve as a better partner, though I must warn you"—he paused to glance meaningfully at the sack of grain—"I will not hold still while you poke at me."

Her sudden smile spilled over him like a burst of sunshine.

"But I wonder," she said, raising her sword in his direction, "will you squeal like a pig when I do stick you?"

He laughed out loud. "I am shamed to admit this is my first time matching swords with a woman, so please be kind."

She barely gave him time to take up position before she attacked.

"You have natural skill," he allowed after a few parries and thrusts. "All you need is more practice."

"But you, sir, are astonishing," she said, a little breathless. "Quite the best I've seen."

His chest swelled as if he were a youth of twelve.

"And I thought you excelled only at drinking games."

Ouch. "So you've been watching me. I am flattered."

The deep flush of her cheeks pleased him to no end. He deflected a determined jab to his heart.

He played with her as he did with the younger squires—hard enough to challenge, but not so hard as to discourage. When she pulled her skirt out of the way with her free hand, though, he missed his footing and very nearly dropped his sword.

She stepped back, her brows furrowed.

"Showing your ankles was a clever move," he said, giving her a low bow. "A trick I've not seen before."

"It was not my intention to rely on anything other than my skill." Her tone was as stiff as her spine. "I would not be so dishonorable as to stoop to tricks."

Good Lord. "If your opponent is both stronger and more skilled than you are," he said, keeping his voice even, "then you must use what advantages you do have."

Sword arm extended, he motioned with his other hand for her to come forward. He suppressed a smile when she took up her sword again and came toward him.

"Then, once you have an opening, you must use it," he said. "Never give up your moment, as you just did. Do not hesitate. Your opponent may not give you a second chance."

"You do not care how you win, sir, so long as you do?" Her tone was scathing.

He sighed inwardly. How naive could she be?

"Use whatever rules you like when you are playing, Isobel. But if a man less honorable should find you alone as I did today, you will wish you knew how to fight without the rules."

She narrowed her eyes at him but did not speak.

"It would be preferable, of course, if you did not wander about alone. You forget you are in dangerous country here."

" 'Tis not your place to lecture me."

Someone should. "Now, do you want to continue playing at sword fighting?" he asked, deliberately baiting her. "Or do you want to learn how to protect yourself from someone who intends you harm?"

Green eyes sparking with fire, she raised her sword and said, "Teach me."

Oh, what he would love to teach her! God help him, she was breathtaking like this.

"You should carry a short blade as well," he instructed as he fended off her attack.

"Why? You think you can knock my sword from my hand?"

"I can." He saw a half-empty sack on the floor behind her. "But I will not have to. You will drop it."

She fought better angry, a good quality in a fighter.

Still, he was better. Much better. He forced her to step back, and back, and back again. One more step and her heel caught on the sack. She threw her hands up, sending the sword clattering against the wall as she tumbled backward.

The next moment, she was lying back on her elbows, her hair loose about her shoulders, skirts askew, chest heaving.

He could not move, could not even breathe.

She looked like a goddess. A wanton Venus, sprawled on the dirt floor at his feet. Then she threw her head back and laughed. Not a light trill, but a full-throated, joyful laugh that made his heart soar.

What he would not do to hear her laugh again!

"I'm afraid you have the advantage of me," she said, her eyes dancing. She reached her hand up for him to help her to her feet.

He took it and sank to his knees beside her. "Not true, Isobel," he said in a harsh whisper. "'Tis I who am at your mercy."

His eyes fixed on her lips, full and parted. Well beyond thought now, he gave in to the inexorable pull toward them. The moment their lips touched, fire seared through him.

He tried to hang on to the thin thread of caution tugging at his conscience. But she was kissing him back, her mouth open, her tongue seeking his. His ears roared as she put her arms around his neck and pulled him down.

He cushioned the back of her head with his hand before it touched the dirt floor. Leaning over her, he gave himself wholly to kissing her. He splayed his hands into her hair and rained kisses along her jaw and down her throat, then returned to her mouth again.

The sweet taste of her, the smell of her, filled his senses. He was mindless of anything except her mouth, her face, her hair, and his burning need to touch her.

He ran his hand down her side to the swell of her hip. When she moaned, he knew he had to feel her beneath him. Beneath him, pressed against him. Skin to skin.

Slowly, he lowered his body until he felt the soft fullness of her breasts against his chest. Sweet heaven! Oh God, the little sounds she was making. He let himself sink down farther and groaned aloud as his swollen shaft pressed against her hip.

There was a reason he must not do what he wanted to do, but he could not recall it. And he did not want to try.

He buried his face in hair that smelled of summer flowers and honey. "Isobel, I want you so much."

The breath went out of him in a whoosh as he cupped the rounded softness of her breast in his hand. It fit perfectly. And felt so wondrously good he had to squeeze his eyes shut.

He froze the instant he felt the prick of cold steel against his neck. All the reasons they should not be rolling around on the floor of an empty storeroom came flooding back to him.

"You are right," she said so close to his ear that he could feel her breath, " 'tis wise to carry a short blade."

"Forgive me." He breathed in the smell of her skin one more time. Then he made himself get up.

As soon as he set her on her feet, she set to vigorously brushing off her clothes. She was quite obviously embarrassed, but did she regret the kisses? He wished she would speak.

"Isobel?" He stepped close and touched her arm, but she would not look at him. "I cannot say I am sorry for kissing you." Kissing seemed hardly to cover it, but he thought it best to leave it at that. "But I do apologize if I have upset you."

"The blame is not all yours," she said, her face flushed and eyes cast down, "though I might like to pretend otherwise."

Ah, an honest woman. And a fair one too.

"You know I am soon to become betrothed."

"I did forget it for a time," he said, hoping in vain to draw a smile from her.

"It was very wrong of me," she said, lifting her chin. "It shall not happen again."

"If it will never happen again," he said, "then let me have a last kiss before we part."

He thought his outrageous request would cause her to either laugh or shout at him. When she did neither, he put his hand against her soft cheek, then leaned down until his lips touched hers. This time, he kept the kiss soft and chaste. He would not upset her again.

But when she leaned into him, he was lost again in deep, mindless kisses. When they finally broke apart, they stared at each other, breathless.

"I must leave now," she said, backing away.

He caught her arm. "These things happen between

men and women," he told her, though it had never happened quite like this to him before. "Please, Isobel, you must not feel badly or blame yourself."

The huge eyes she turned on him told him his words had done nothing to reassure her.

"Come, you will want to put this on," he said, picking up the simple headdress he saw lying on the ground.

She snatched it from his hands, slammed it on her head, and began shoving hair into it.

"'Tis a shame to cover such lovely hair." Unable to keep his hands from her, he helped push loose strands under the headdress. He let his fingers graze her skin as he worked and tried not to sigh aloud.

"Let me go first to be sure no one is near," he told her. "Watch for my signal."

He felt her close behind him as he eased the door open. "I am happy to practice with you whenever you like," he said as he looked out into the yard. "Sword fighting or kissing."

He spun around and gave her a quick, hard kiss, looking straight into her open eyes.

THE DISH

Where authors give you the inside scoop!

♥ ♥ ♥ ♥ ♥ ♥ ♥ ♥ ♥ ♥ ♥ ♥ ♥ ♥ ♥

From the desk of Kate Brady

Dear Reader,

One of the first things people want to know when they find out the nature of the books I write is, "What's *wrong* with you?" I confess, for anyone acquainted with Chevy Bankes in ONE SCREAM AWAY (on sale now), it's a valid question. Here we have a villain with serious mother issues, bizarre sister issues, and a folk song driving him to kill. Forget the fact that he stockpiles screams and travels all the way across the country to obtain the final entry in his collection.

So please, folks, allow me to go on record: I am generally a nice person. I am not prone to violence. I don't have any deeply buried hatred toward my parents, nor do I have any deeply buried skeletons in my gardens. I have basically healthy relationships with my husband, children, sibling, in-laws, colleagues, friends, and neighbors. To be frank, my life is pretty darn dull.

I love it that way—heaven knows I wouldn't want to face the type of excitement my characters face on every page. But maybe my basic normalcy is the reason I spin tales about larger-than-life characters. In most cases, they are people I would never want to meet, doing things I would never want to do. (Except for those Sheridan men . . . I admit it would be nice to meet one of them but, alas, they're engaged with heroines far more beautiful and exciting than I.) When you write about people who don't exist, the possibilities for perilous physical exploits and heartrending emotional journeys are infinite, and far more exciting than shopping for groceries or weeding those gardens.

So when I started writing ONE SCREAM AWAY, I knew I wanted three things: (1) a smart villain who would hunt down a heroine in some really creepy way for some really twisted reason, (2) a smart heroine with a secret past too horrific to contemplate and chutzpah from here to the moon, and (3) a smart hero so drop-dead gorgeous and profoundly tortured that you couldn't help but cheer for him, even when he was being a jerk. Beyond that, I didn't know much of anything and decided simply to follow the hero, Neil Sheridan, step by step, as he tried to solve a murder. I didn't know so many innocent people would die before he succeeded, or that he'd unravel the truth about his own tragic past along the way. That's one of the many joys of writing: discovery!

I hope you'll enjoy the first of the Sheridan

stories as Neil tracks down Chevy Bankes in ONE SCREAM AWAY. And I hope you'll be inspired to come back for more when his brother Mitch makes his debut in the next book!

Please feel free to visit my Web site at www.kate brady.net.

Happy reading,

Kate Brady

♥ ♥ ♥ ♥ ♥ ♥ ♥ ♥ ♥ ♥ ♥ ♥ ♥ ♥ ♥

From the desk of Margaret Mallory

Dear Readers,

While writing KNIGHT OF DESIRE (on sale now), I discovered how much I enjoy writing part of my story from the hero's perspective. After years of guessing what men are thinking, I found it profoundly satisfying to *know* what was in my hero's head and heart. I loved being able to show the reader why William does the things he does. (Men do have their reasons.)

The more surprising thing I learned about myself as a writer is that I like tortured love scenes. The hero and heroine's misunderstandings and conflicts can be revealed with such high drama in the bedroom. (My parents and children will miss these scenes of wrenching emotion, since I am razor-blading them out of their copies.) Of course, the hero and heroine eventually are rewarded for their suffering!

Speaking of heroes and tortured love . . . Stephen, the younger brother in KNIGHT OF DESIRE, is the hero of my second book, KNIGHT OF PLEASURE (December 2009). Stephen is in Normandy fighting with King Henry (Prince Harry in book one), when he crosses swords (literally) with Isobel, a woman he wants but cannot have. Although we know Stephen has a hero's heart beneath all that charm, our serious-minded heroine dismisses him as a knight of pleasure.

KNIGHT OF DESIRE is my first published book, so I would dearly love to hear from readers. I hope you will visit me at my Web site, www.Margaret-Mallory.com. Readers may be interested in photos I've posted there of Alnwick Castle, the Percy stronghold where my hero William grew up, and a wonderful statue of Hotspur, William's famous half-brother. Hotspur, in full armor on a rearing warhorse, looks exactly as I imagined him.

Margaret Mallory

♥ ♥ ♥ ♥ ♥ ♥ ♥ ♥ ♥ ♥ ♥ ♥ ♥ ♥ ♥

From the desk of Amanda Scott

Dear Reader,

Bonnie Jenny—or, more properly, Janet, Baroness Easdale of Easdale—the heroine of TAMED BY A LAIRD (on sale now), sprang to life because I wanted to introduce the main characters of my new trilogy and its setting, Dumfriesshire and Galloway, without using the central story. That one will be the second book, SEDUCED BY A ROGUE, which comes out next.

Having based the new trilogy on fourteenth-century events described in an unpublished sixteenth-century manuscript in Broad Scot (a language somewhat like Robert Burns poetry only more indecipherable), I quickly saw that the research would take longer than usual and decided that some issues would be clearer to readers if introduced from more than one perspective. For example, in Scotland, unlike England, if a man had no sons, his eldest daughter became his heir. So a baron's daughter, even with countless male cousins, could become a baroness in her own right, or an earl's daughter a countess, with all the powers and privileges of the rank . . . as Bonnie Jenny does.

Thanks to incessant fourteenth-through-sixteenth-century warfare and raids causing the deaths of thousands of men in the Scottish Borders, women inherited with unnatural frequency. One might think such a lass would be in high demand as a wife, but that generally became true only *after* she had inherited. You see, until her father had actually died, folks assumed he might still produce a son.

However, Jenny's father, having refused to remarry after the death of his beloved wife, raised Jenny to understand, as well as he understood them himself, the position and duties she would one day assume. So imagine her shock when he dies while she is still unwed and underage. Then imagine her even greater shock when her guardian (an uncle) and his wife decide to marry her to the wife's younger brother in order to provide that obnoxious creature with a tidy income and—as they suppose— a fine, ancient title.

Because they have moved Jenny miles from her home in Easdale to their own home in Annandale, she believes she has no choice but to obey them. That attitude, however, lasts only until her betrothal feast. Repulsed by the man to whom they have betrothed her, Jenny escapes with the minstrel troupe hired to entertain their guests.

Her uncle, finding her intended groom incapacitated from far too much whisky at the feast, asks Sir Hugh Douglas, the lad's older brother, to retrieve Jenny.

Sir Hugh, a knight, experienced warrior, and member in high standing of the all-powerful Douglas clan—and rudely awakened from well-earned sleep—curtly refuses. Because he is also a widower with a large estate of his own to manage, he takes little interest in his brother's affairs and even less in Jenny's problems. But, Dunwythie persuades him by appealing to his sense of honor and family duty.

Naturally, being a strong-minded male with considerable ingenuity who rarely changes tack once he has made a decision, Hugh has made up his mind without giving a single thought to Jenny's feelings. So when she politely but firmly declines his "invitation" to return with him to her uncle's household, explaining that before she can do so she has a mystery to solve . . .

Well, let's just say that TAMED BY A LAIRD pits a powerful, rebellious young baroness against an equally powerful, determined baron and lets the sparks fly wherever they will.

Happy reading and *suas Alba!*

Amanda Scott

http://home.att.net/~amandascott/

Want to know more about romances at Grand Central Publishing and Forever? Get the scoop online!

GRAND CENTRAL PUBLISHING'S ROMANCE HOMEPAGE

Visit us at www.hachettebookgroup.com/romance for all the latest news, reviews, and chapter excerpts!

NEW AND UPCOMING TITLES

Each month we feature our new titles and reader favorites.

CONTESTS AND GIVEAWAYS

We give away galleys, autographed copies, and all kinds of fun stuff.

AUTHOR INFO

You'll find bios, articles, and links to personal websites for all your favorite authors—and so much more!

THE BUZZ

Sign up for our monthly romance newsletter, and be the first to read all about it!